Tante Minnie

MARILYN PARKER

ISBN: 978-1-4834-7686-5 (sc)
ISBN: 978-1-4834-7685-8 (e)

Library of Congress Control Number: 2017917761

Lulu Publishing Services rev. date: 01/09/2018

To Barry, April, Matthew, Josephine, and to the memory of the real Tante Minnie.

Remember the ones who descended here
Into the mire of bedrock
To bore a hole through this granite,

To clear a passage for you
Where there was only darkness and stone.

Billy Collins

Preface

This novel, *Tante Minnie*, evolved from a short story I wrote approximately twelve years ago in an upstate New York creative writing class. Minnie was my great-aunt and something of a mystery to me. I remember her as an old, frail lady with sparse white hair, lying in bed, in a cramped room in Brooklyn. As a child I had little or no curiosity about her, but as I became an adult and listened to family lore, my interest in the why, how, and what of her life grew. I learned the bare bones of her story: She came to America as a young woman; worked as a laborer on a potato farm in Suffolk County, New York; was childless; and may (or may not) have been married. It was whispered that she had a secret, which forced her to leave her family and flee to America.

Tante Minnie was the pioneer and reason why the rest of our family was able to come to the United States from the Pale of Russia around the turn of the twentieth century. In the immigrant tradition, she sponsored my grandfather's journey to America so he could escape being conscripted into the czar's army. A year later, she helped bring her sister and her three children, one of whom was my mother, to the United States.

Although much of my novel is fictionalized, the characters are inspired by real members of my family: Frima/Fannie, my grandmother, Gelde/Anne, my mother; Chaje/Ida, my maternal aunt; Szol/Irving and Yussel/Joey, my maternal uncles; and the character of Yaakov (based on my maternal grandfather). I took poetic license with details, but my family's characteristics ring true. Most of the family folklore came from my mother and my Aunt Ida, but they often disagreed. For example, my cousin (Ida's daughter) said that Tante Minnie never married. My mother was convinced that Minnie married a man named Zelig. The conflict was resolved when I came across a photo of Minnie, as a young woman, with a man by her side. It was a formal portrait taken by a photographer, which must have been an engagement or marriage photo. So . . . Zelig existed after all.

My great regret is that I wasn't more interested in our family heritage until I was past middle age. By then my mother was unable to recall names, dates, and events with any clarity. Rumors about why Minnie left Russia for the United States as a young woman always involved a ruinous relationship with the son of her employer. This story has been repeated many times in many cultures: a destitute young woman from a small village has an affair with a man above her social status. The man blithely goes on with his life while the young woman is blamed and left to deal with the consequences of the unfortunate affair. I remember asking my mother whether the young man in question dallied with a willing Minnie or if she was raped. Nobody knew.

Anne, my mother, was a perfect example of a person who straddled two generations and cultures. She arrived at Ellis Island with my grandmother, Frima/Fannie, and her siblings Ida and Irving (Joey was later born in the States), only to be rejected by the health authorities because her head was riddled with sores and probably lice. The authorities were finally persuaded to accept the little girl, and within a few days she was enrolled in school, knowing no English, with a shaven head.

From the time she was a small child, my mother had always been interested in education and becoming Americanized. Interestingly enough, she did not become an American citizen until she was in her mid-forties. I never asked her why she waited so long.

The family was very poor and lived in a two-bedroom apartment. The second bedroom was rented out to a boarder and my mother and Ida had to sleep on two hard-backed chairs in the kitchen while the younger boys slept in their parents' room. The only advantage was that the kitchen was the warmest place in the apartment since they had a wood-burning stove nearby.

The principal of Anne's elementary school pleaded with my

grandmother and grandfather to allow her to attend Hebrew Tech, an accelerated program that was open only to the top students. She completed all the high school requirements in one and a half years. Throughout her life, she was extremely proud of her accomplishment, which in those days was probably tantamount to earning a PhD. Most Jewish immigrant children were pulled out of school in the early grades in order to help support the family. Education for a girl was considered superfluous since she would marry, have children, and remain a housewife.

After Hebrew Tech, Anne obtained a good job as a secretary in a firm that made dolls. However, she had to promise the boss she would never reveal that she was Jewish—those were the days of "Jews, Catholics, Negroes, and any other form of 'riff-raff' need not apply." In her mid-twenties, she met and nearly married a lawyer from California, with whom she planned to live out West. This must have caused a considerable stir; young Jewish women were supposed to marry boys from the neighborhood and live near their families.

Traveling in steerage was the worst way to come to The New World. My grandmother must have been a very strong, intrepid woman to have made that journey with two young girls and an infant son in tow. I learned this from the ship's manifest, which I obtained from Ellis Island. I was surprised that the entire family did not make the journey together, but I later learned that my grandfather had come to the United States a year earlier, having fled from the czarist draft. My maternal grandmother died when I was a young child, and my memories of her are derived from pictures and stories told by my mother. According to Anne, she was a devoted mother, a very hard worker, and an excellent cook and baker who helped with the family finances by becoming a janitor in the building in which the family lived. Like most women from Eastern Europe at that time, she was illiterate, and my mother recounted reading the Yiddish paper and the funnies to her. She never learned English, which was not unusual, since there was no need to do so in her neighborhood.

The character of Yaakov in the story resembles my maternal grandfather, who was a scamp, somewhat of a lecher with dubious morals, and an embarrassment to my mother when she was a young woman. If she was with school friends and saw her father, she would cross the street in order to avoid him. He would be filthy, covered in coal dust, and he looked like a vagrant. To her great chagrin, when she contracted pneumonia and was out of work for several weeks, her employer came to see her. My grandmother, who kept the apartment spotless, was ready for the visit with fresh-baked mandelbrot and coffee cake. My grandfather walked in, caked with coal dust from head to foot. Despite this, Anne's employer walked over, shook my grandfather's hand, and told him that he was honored to shake the hand of an honest, hardworking man.

My grandfather lived with us for six months a year and then took the train to Florida, where he stayed with Aunt Ida. On one of his trips, he latched onto an older man and began to regale him with stories of the old country, one of which included a horse thief. The man said to my grandfather, "Maybe you were the horse thief?" and my grandfather pummeled him to the ground. The older gentleman took out a warrant for his arrest, and Aunt Ida had to sneak him back to Brooklyn. Sensitivity and honor were not his strong suit. He did do a stretch in a Siberian prison when he was a young man for being the lookout in a horse-thieving scheme. My mother was mortified by this and insisted that he didn't know the true intention of the thieves. Aunt Ida, however, who was more direct and blunt, said my grandfather knew the thieves' real motive.

When my grandfather lived in Russia, the czar needed fodder for his army. What better place to look than a small, Jewish village in the Pale of Russia? My grandfather punctured his eardrums so that he would not be eligible for the draft. It didn't help him a bit since keen hearing was not needed on the front lines. My Aunt Minnie helped him get to America by sponsoring him and probably paying for his passage.

Grandpa, or "Pop," as we called him, liked the ladies, particularly the plump ones. If a skinny woman sat next to him in the theater, it would spoil the whole show for him. When my sister was a teenager, she had two rather obese friends who were twins. They would come to our house each week to play cards. Pop usually went to bed about eight o'clock, but on the nights the twins visited, he would stay up, park himself near one of them, and caress her upper arm. My mother lost several cleaning people because they were afraid to hang clothes in the basement when Pop was in the house. It turned out that he was propositioning them down there, but only the zaftik ones.

In his later years he became religious and went to synagogue each morning to be part of a minyan, which makes up the required number—ten—of men needed for prayer. However, he was mugged one morning, and that was the end of his religious period. Pop lived until he was in his eighties, succumbing to a heart attack and passing quickly.

Many years went by without my giving much thought to my great-aunt. I remember when I was a child, being unwillingly dragged along to visit her. I thought she was in a nursing home, but my sister insisted that she was in a board-and-care facility in Coney Island. I also recall seeing Tante Minnie at a cousin's wedding in New Jersey. There was a picture taken of a sweet-faced little old lady, apparently riddled with arthritis, being held up between the bride and groom.

I don't know why I became curious about Tante Minnie in later years. Perhaps it was the realization that if she hadn't been forced to flee Europe as a young woman, my grandparents might have remained in Russia. Despite the need for immigrant labor, destitute people coming from all parts of Europe had to be sponsored by a relative or friend so they would not become a burden to the United States. The same situation exists to this day.

Both my mother and aunt were deceased by the time I became interested in writing Tante Minnie's story, and there was nobody to corroborate information about Minnie, even secondhand. My cousin remembers Tante Minnie visiting her house on weekends, and she said she absolutely hated those visits. Minnie was religious, and she "got up with the chickens," which meant my cousins couldn't make noise or play the radio after dinner. She would come to visit with just a paper bag, presumably containing a change of clothing or underwear, in her hand. My mother told me that at one point Minnie had owned a framing shop either in East

New York or Brownsville, Brooklyn. This was a remarkable achievement for a woman who came to America as an indentured servant. It also corroborated the fact that she had been married. There would have been no other way she could have made the leap from laborer on a potato farm to owner of a shop without a man to sign contracts and take out loans, since those were the policies of the day.

So while I have information, which I've amplified, for some of the characters in the novel, others are completely fictional. I do know that Minnie worked as a laborer on a potato farm in Suffolk County when she first came here, but nothing about the other people who worked there. Thus the characters at the farm, such as Monaghan, the owner; the Irish girls who worked with Minnie; and even Zelig, who was to become her life partner, are completely fictitious. Much of the fun in writing this novel was in being able to use my imagination to create flamboyant characters. I particularly liked inventing Monaghan, a somewhat complex individual, venal yet occasionally generous. Maya, the socialist freethinker who briefly becomes Zelig's lover, was well ahead of her time and a joy to invent. Dina, also fictitious, evolved from whispers that two cousins accompanied Minnie when she gave birth in the woods. The "real characters," my grandmother Fannie, my mother, Anne, and her three siblings, Ida, Irving, and Joey, are based on stories told to me by various members of my family. My grandfather, Yaakov (Jacob), is fictionalized, but many of the episodes told about him actually happened. Tante Minnie's story, while a work of fiction, has pockets of facts as well.

My first attempt at depicting Minnie began in a short story class called "Critics' Corner" in upstate New York; the story, "Tante Minnie in Russia," was published in a local journal. The story ended before Minnie unwillingly made her voyage to the United States. I always intended to write a fictionalized, short continuation of that story, portraying the arc of Minnie's life after her arrival in the New World.

Tante Minnie was put on hold for a couple of years until a friend invited me to join a small writing group consisting of three women and a teacher. Somehow the tale of Minnie morphed from a companion short story to a novel. My work on *Tante Minnie* straggled along for over six years with a number of fallow periods, but I always came back to the story.

The narrative is told in three parts: Minnie and her husband Zelig's experiences on a Suffolk County farm; their life in Brownsville, Brooklyn; and the remaining decades of Minnie's life.

My original intent in writing this story was to share an unknown part of our family history with my children and other members of the family. As the story grew exponentially and increasingly became a work of fiction, I began to think of a larger audience and the possibility of publication.

Although it's my family history, I believe it carries elements that are universal, or at least common to the descendants of the many immigrants who came to build the United States. It's an old tale of the immigrant struggle that many families can identify with. In a larger sense, it shows how an experience that feels disastrous at the time can have positive consequences for an entire family, such as my grandparents' move to this country. It's a story full of contradictions, which is how I think many assess their family histories and their own lives.

Acknowledgments

As any writer can attest, no book is an island and always benefits from the input of many readers and individuals who offer help along the way. I'm extremely grateful to the "group of three": Andrew Craft taught me to be a better writer, and Marsha Beyda and Naomi Meyers listened to the emerging story, critiquing each chapter. The Roxbury Arts Group "Critic's Corner" class was the springboard for the original short story, and I thank them for their encouragement and advice. Many thanks to my reader, Tina Kahn, who was my "Yiddish" consultant and advised me on the authenticity of Jewish culture in the early to mid-twentieth century. Luba Ostashevsky, a literary editor, did me a great service by reading my first draft, editing later versions, and advising me how to make the story and characters more cohesive and meaningful. Donna Cherry copy edited the story and offered invaluable advice that went far beyond improving the grammar, syntax, and style of the novel. Lois Lovett, a dear friend, offered to cast her professional eye on my finished manuscript. Barbara Apoian's careful reading of the story encouraged me to soften Minnie's sharp edges. David Lewis, grammarian *extraordinaire*, guided me through the thickets of English verb usage. I give thanks to my sister, Sheila Poutsiaka, who is recently deceased, and cousin, Roz Eisner, who gave me their remembrances and interpretations of our family's story. My daughter, April Spicer, helped her analog Mom get this project off the ground when it was gathering dust in a computer file. I'd like to thank my husband Barry, who read each portion thoughtfully and was my greatest cheerleader. Most of all, I want to thank the real Tante Minnie for being the catalyst of my novel and the reason why I was born in this country.

Suffolk County

1

Zelig's Voyage

O n the ship over to America, Zelig Frumkin got little sleep. Dreams of his wife Leeba screaming in pain and spurting blood all over the bed sheets kept him awake. Mama and Papa were calling to him, but he couldn't reach them. Worst of all were the nightmares of being pursued by mobs of Cossacks carrying knives, axes, and torches.

It wasn't just the pogrom that chased him out of Russia. He remembered when he first thought about leaving his home. Zelig's father, a talented furniture maker, taught Zelig how to construct well-made bedroom and dining room pieces from the time he was a boy. Mama wanted Zelig to become a rabbinic scholar. Although Zelig excelled in Jewish scholarship, he found it too constraining and was often rapped on the knuckles by the rabbi when his attention flagged. How many times had he been caught drawing sketches when he should have been assiduously studying Torah!

Zelig's Papa had been given a large commission to make an expensive bedroom suite for a rich gentile from St. Petersburg. He and Zelig worked together for months, and Papa had praised Zelig's work on the project. When they presented the furniture to the buyer, he offered to pay a pittance of what they had agreed upon, stating that the work was inferior. Zelig was furious when his Papa meekly accepted the reduced amount, but what were they to do? If Papa had gone to the authorities, he would probably have received nothing for all their hard work. Zelig knew that if he had remained in Russia, his future would be defined by his religion. Hatred of Jews was an epidemic in Russia.

Soon after the furniture debacle, his friend Moishe approached him, bubbling with enthusiasm. "Zelig, I decided to go. Come with me. I met someone who can make arrangements for the two of us. I know how attached you are to your family, but in the end you'll be doing them a favor. You'll be helping them financially."

"What are you talking about?"

"We discussed this before. There are large farms in a place called Long Island, New York. The owners are recruiting refugees. They pay for boat passage and all the extras for coming to America."

"What kind of extras?"

"You know, like getting the documents you need to leave Russia and to bribe the officials. You have to promise to work on the farm for five years. Workers get a stipend, but that goes for room and board. You can do some work on the side to send money home."

"I don't want to be an indentured servant, slaving away in the fields. It's worse than working for goyim."

"But Zelig, you can start off in the fields and work your way up. You're smart and good at numbers. Maybe you could work your way into an office job, especially if you learned some English."

It sounded appealing, but Zelig was in turmoil. He had been thinking about going to St. Petersburg to start a new life. At least there he'd be within a short distance from family and could go home to visit. How could he leave Mama and Papa? Now that his sisters were married and starting their own households, his parents would be alone. Mama and Papa would never leave the girls, especially if there were grandchildren. They were too old to start in a new land, even if by some miracle he could send for them.

The dilemma was paralyzing him. But Moishe kept at it, urging Zelig to make up his mind. "I have to tell my contact by next week. You're going to be sorry; this may be your only chance to get the hell out of this shithole country. Look what happened to you and your father. Do you want to have to accept any scrap that goyim decide to throw at you? You have the intelligence and talent to make something of yourself in the New World, not here!"

The decision was made, and Zelig gathered his family together to tell them the news. Mama, distraught and furious, refused to speak to Zelig. However, Papa understood and became his ally. Papa had been demoralized and humiliated after being cheated. There was nothing he could do, but at least his son would have a chance to hold up his head in America.

Moishe made arrangements for the necessary papers. The two young men traveled overland from their small village to the large port of St. Petersburg, a distance of approximately sixty miles. During the journey, they were aware of the possibility of encountering highway robbers or government agents who trolled the dusty roads, scooping up men to be hijacked for service in the czar's army. They were fortunate to reach the port without incident.

When they saw the *Finlandia* for the first time, Zelig felt a surge of excitement. The vessel was enormous, and its flags were billowing in the late spring breeze. Moishe was beside himself with joy. He glanced lecherously at the beautiful ladies in their fine silk dresses and parasols, his eyes fixed on their bustles and bosoms. Zelig had to poke him to stop staring.

The elite passengers strolled near the ship while dozens of porters transported their trunks and suitcases up the gangplank. Handsomely suited men with stiff, white collars and elegant leather shoes covered with spats joined the ladies. What a contrast the two disheveled young men made, traveling in their rough and rumpled clothing, full of dust and grime from the overland journey from their small village outside of St. Petersburg. Moishe discarded his yarmulke and tzitzit as soon as they left. With his homespun clothing and shoddy work boots, he resembled a huge serf. Zelig, on the other hand, maintained his Jewish appearance in spite of Moishe's attempts to convince him otherwise. They made an unlikely pair. Zelig, with *peyes*, or earlocks, pushed behind his ears, was a slight man with regular features, accentuated by a sparse brown beard and mustache. He wore his Shabbat suit, which was stained, wrinkled, and sooty. His black yarmulke was perched atop his lank, slightly thinning hair. Despite his dusty attire, he resembled a Talmudic scholar standing next to a burly bear.

As the ladies and gentlemen were escorted to their cabins, Zelig and Moishe soon found their accommodations less luxurious. Moishe and Zelig were herded below deck to the steerage compartments along with the other unfortunates traveling third class. The air below was rank, smelling of oil and coal, and was hot as blazes. Rows of iron cots were jammed next to each other and everyone's belongings were thrown together. Zelig feared that what little they possessed would be lost or stolen in the mishmash of trunks, boxes, and battered suitcases. There was a thin curtain separating the steerage area into two parts, with women and children on the other side. Once the ship's engines began operating, the noise was deafening and they had to shout to hear one another. Even Moishe, usually so optimistic and ebullient, blanched at the stench and noise below deck, but it hadn't taken him long to figure out a scheme to improve their conditions. He bribed one of the crew to assign them cots away from the disgusting, reeking toilet area.

Their first meal was wretched. The food was vile and definitely not kosher. Even the herring and potatoes were rank. Zelig knew he couldn't subsist on stale bread and murky water for three weeks, so he had tried to eat the meat of suspicious origin and immediately ran to the toilet area to vomit. Moishe's stomach, made of sterner stuff, retained the miserable fare, even though Zelig saw he was having a hard time chewing the malodorous, tough meat.

Zelig was awake most of that first night, nauseated by the stench of the engines and stale bodies. Even worse were the sounds of scurrying rats beneath his cot, and he lay there, terrified, until he was so exhausted he nodded off. Moishe, as usual, had slept like the dead. His loud snoring diminished even the sound of the engines. When Zelig dragged himself from the cot the next morning, he heard distressed buzzing from the passengers. Rats had bitten three children behind the curtain. One baby was bitten so badly that he wasn't expected to live.

Yet in a few days Zelig adapted to the abysmal conditions in steerage. Then the *Finlandia* was caught in an unseasonable storm. It felt like an earthquake, with cots sliding, belongings flying around, and passengers being thrown into one another. Then the vomiting started. The stench of regurgitated food permeated steerage, but it was hardly noticed as all the passengers tried to find something stable to hold onto—a door handle, a pole, anything. Zelig prayed to the Lord out loud. "Dear God, please make it stop—I can't survive this voyage without Your help." Maybe the passengers' joint prayers were heard, because after several hours the ship emerged from the maelstrom into calm waters. How had Zelig ever been stupid enough to join Moishe on this ill-fated voyage? Was he so softheaded that he hadn't foreseen any of the obstacles and had allowed himself to be persuaded by a meshugena like Moishe?

They were at sea about a week, and then the drinking and gambling started in earnest. There also were night visits behind the curtain, and Zelig heard the laughter and carousing above the sound of the engines. Clusters of men gathered in groups, swilling vodka and playing either dice or cards. Moishe got the bright idea to get into the games.

Zelig refused to join in, but he watched the ongoing games to make sure Moishe didn't do anything stupid. Then Zelig saw a Russian mountain of a man slipping cards into his hand from under his sleeve. Zelig whispered to Moishe, and the Mountain tossed down the cards and attacked Zelig.

"You miserable little Yid; who told you to interfere with the game?"

He jumped on Zelig and began to pummel him. Zelig tried to protect his face and genitals, but the Mountain was too strong to stave off. Moishe came to his rescue, piling on top of the Russian and beating him with his mammoth fists. The gambling group dragged them apart, but Zelig heard the Mountain say to Moishe, "I won't forget this. No Jew bastard gets away with putting his filthy hands on me."

7

Moishe had taken it philosophically. "Don't worry Zelig, he's all hot air. We have to show these bullies they can't scare us."

When Zelig awoke the next morning and turned to his left, he expected to hear Moishe's reassuring snores from the next cot. But in the dim light he made out that Moishe's cot was empty. Zelig looked for him all around the steerage compartment, even venturing into the dreaded toilet area, but he did not find him. He remembered that Moishe had bribed one of the seamen to allow him on deck during the night when the first- and second-class passengers were asleep. Zelig became frantic. Moishe wouldn't be allowed to remain on deck past daybreak, when some of the early risers might want to get fresh air. He ran up on deck, only to be restrained by the crew.

"You don't understand," Zelig told them, "my friend is missing. You have to help me find him!"

To their credit, they searched the ship thoroughly, but there was no sign of Moishe. The purser said, "Sometimes a troubled man will sneak up on deck and either fall or jump over the side. We've had a number of third-class passengers disappear without a trace. He might have gotten drunk and leaned over too far."

Zelig took to his bunk, staring at the cot next to him, which was quickly commandeered by a massive Polack. Moishe was Zelig's friend and protector, the closest thing to a brother he ever had. Anxiety and depression overwhelmed him. At least when Leeba died, he had the family around to help him grieve and give her a decent, Jewish burial. He would have to write Moishe's family to tell them that he disappeared on the ship. Zelig said Kaddish for him and some of the Jewish men formed a minyan to pray for his soul. Zelig continued to say prayers for him during the whole year of mourning. He felt crushing guilt. If he hadn't protected Zelig from the Russian, Moishe might be alive today. Zelig was sure that evil Russian bastard was responsible. It ate at him that he couldn't do anything about it except pray for his dearest friend. Now he was really alone.

One of the seamen, a Finn, was sympathetic toward him and allowed him up on deck when the more privileged passengers had retired for the night. It was warm enough to spread his thin blanket on the wooden planks, and on clear nights he could look up at the constellations and inhale the briny ocean air. His losses weighed on him—first Leeba, then his family, and now Moishe. He'd been carrying the loss of his wife for three years.

On those nights, staring up at the myriad pinpoints of light in the sky, Zelig began to question.

I'm an insignificant, tiny speck in the universe. Was it ordained that I would be tested like this? First Leeba and then Moishe. Why was I the one to survive?

He looked up at the enormity of the night sky, scanning the constellations.

Who am I to question all of this?

Zelig recited the *Shma,* the prayer said by all observant Jews that reaffirms the oneness of the Lord. He hadn't known what else to do.

A few days later, all passengers were allowed on deck. He stood with the other immigrants, watching the Statue of Liberty come into view. Zelig was transfixed by this symbol of freedom and possibility. He felt a modicum of energy and optimism returning. Maybe some of Moishe's indomitable spirit was entering his heart and giving him strength.

He would try his best to put grief behind him.

2

Escape

Michla looked out the window, watching the sunrise on what promised to be a lovely spring day. It was nearly Purim, and the warming sun was beginning to thaw the packed snow surrounding her relatives' cottage in Nolopina. She shuddered, thinking how drastically her life had changed in little more than a year.

Mama and Papa had urged her to leave Chalupanich for a while, just to hush the clacking tongues and rumors going around since her return from Minsk. The neighbors had never believed her story about contracting diphtheria. Oh, they were courteous enough when the family went to the village square, making small talk with Mama and Papa, but Minnie could feel their eyes boring into her back when they passed by.

Of course Madame Ostrovsky would have told Mendel why Michla was dismissed from her household. Madame Ostrovsky was his cousin, and Mendel had arranged for Michla to work there. *Lashon Hara*, or evil tongue, was considered a dreadful sin, but that wouldn't stop Ruchel, Mendel's wife, from spreading such a juicy story. If it went no further than the Jewish neighbors, the family would be socially isolated. If the rumors spread to the ears of the Russian villagers, or even worse, the authorities, Michla didn't want to imagine what would happen to her and the family.

Michla's paternal aunt and uncle, Malka and Yosef Shteynberger, together with her cousins Raisa and Dina, had moved to Nolopina. Yosef got a job as a blacksmith, and the girls hoped they would have improved marriage opportunities in a larger village—more *chasans* to choose from. Raisa and Dina weren't pretty, but they were both strong, strapping girls, equally good as farmhands and at running a household.

Michla had been staying with her relatives for over a month, but she felt useless, just an extra mouth to feed. She helped Aunt Malka with the household chores, volunteering for every unpleasant task, but she still felt like a burden to the family.

One day, she was cleaning out the stable where Uncle Yosef shoed horses. Dina came running in, babbling excitedly about a wonderful opportunity. She was the adventurous one in the family. Her marriage prospects were diminishing rapidly in spite of the move; Nolopina didn't have as many eligible single Jewish men as she'd hoped, and she didn't have a sufficient dowry or good looks to attract the few available ones. Dina was already twenty-five years old, considered on the cusp of un-marriageable. Of course, there was the dour old widower with a mess of half-grown children who would have been willing.

"Ugh, he's repulsive!" Dina would shudder at the mention of his name. "I'd rather be an old maid than settle for that one."

Michla asked Dina to wait until the workday was over before telling her news. Later that afternoon, the three young women went for a walk from the barn back to the house. Both Michla and Raisa were very curious to find out what Dina might be planning. Raisa was used to Dina's flights of fancy, but this time Dina seemed determined to make a move. Michla said, "Tell us about your new opportunity."

"There were signs in the town square. I heard people saying 'America' and 'work.' I asked someone to read me the notice, and it says there are jobs in a place called Suffolk County in New York, even for women."

"What kind of jobs?"

"I'd be working in the potato fields. I was hoping things would be different in Nolopina, but they're not. Even if I worked in Minsk . . .," Dina broke off and looked at Michla uneasily before she continued, "I'll talk to my parents. I'll need to get documents, like a visa to leave Russia.

11

I understand the farm in America pays for your passage and even gives you money for work."

"Dina, suppose it's a trick?" Michla said. "How can you leave your home? Aren't you scared to go alone? Anything can happen to a woman traveling by herself!" There was another uncomfortable silence.

Finally, Dina replied, "Look, Michla, I'm twenty-five years old. The only thing I have to look forward to is that awful old man or being an old maid in my parents' home. Maybe Raisa can come with me. Besides, it's *America!* Everything is possible there!"

Over the next week Dina pleaded with her parents to help her leave. Michla heard them arguing day and night until she finally wore them down. They grudgingly agreed to help Dina, but would not allow Raisa to go with her. "We can't lose two daughters at once."

They made inquiries and soon found out that only one person per family would be allowed a visa, unless the husband, wife, and children left together. The law extended to first cousins, nieces, and nephews, all considered part of the same family unit.

* * *

Magistrate Poltinkov was almost asleep at his desk. It had been a long, miserable winter with nothing much happening in the villages under his jurisdiction. Of course there were the usual drunken brawls and petty thefts to deal with, but nothing to really investigate. Poltinkov desperately wanted to be promoted out of this backwoods, tedious assignment to a decent job in Minsk. You'd think that after three years in this hellhole, his boss would give him another chance. Chief Magistrate Blavatnik had never liked him anyhow and was looking for a chance to send him into obscurity. When Poltinkov had arrested that drunken lout in Minsk, how was he to know that the little turd was the nephew of one of the top police authorities? Of course, he'd beaten the little bastard roundly; he'd deserved it. For that mistake he had been lucky not to be sent to Siberia, but this jurisdiction wasn't much better.

At that moment his assistant Aleksandr rushed into his office without even knocking.

"What the hell is wrong with you, Aleksandr? How about showing a little respect?"

"Magistrate, there's a farm boy out here. He just discovered a baby's body in the woods near Chalupanich."

Magistrate Poltinkov jumped up. "Get that kid in here!"

A boy, about eleven years old, was brought into the magistrate's office. He looked terrified. Sweat was pouring down his face in spite of the frigid temperature.

"Don't be afraid, boy. What's your name?"

"Vladimir, sir."

"Where do you live, Vladimir?"

"My family has a farm outside the village."

"What were you doing in the woods, Vladimir?"

The boy shifted uncomfortably from one foot to the other.

"Don't be frightened, son; we need your help."

"Papa sent me to collect firewood, and I stumbled over this . . . this . . ."

"Can you show us where you found the body?"

"As soon as I saw it, I started running as fast as my legs would carry me. I don't remember, sir."

Vladimir's coat and pants were torn from his flight in the woods, and brambles clung to his clothes. His sweating face was scratched and bloody.

"How would you like to be a big inspector and be my assistant? We can work together to find out who did this."

"Oh sir, I can't go back in the woods again. I can't look at that . . ." Poltinkov put a reassuring arm around the boy's shoulders. "We wouldn't ask you to do that, Vladimir. You can help us in another way. Do you know the people in the village?"

"Oh yes, sir, everyone comes to the village square every Sunday."

"Can I call on you to come along when we question the villagers? It would be a great help to us, having an assistant who knows all the people who live in Chalupanich."

Poltinkov reached up toward the wall peg behind him, took down a police cap, and placed it on Vladimir's head. "Now you look like a real inspector. No, keep it; you'll need to wear it when we do our investigation." The boy beamed with delight through the scratches and dried blood on his face. "Now," Poltinkov continued, "tell me where you live, and we'll come for you after we find the baby . . . er, I mean, body."

Poltinkov put on his official coat and hat, and ordered Aleksandr to get the bloodhounds. He felt more alive than he had in months; this "find" was his ticket back to Minsk.

The hounds bayed furiously. Even though they didn't have a scent to follow, Poltinkov knew that combing the woods would bring results. After searching several hours, they came upon the gruesome remains. The baby couldn't have been more than several hours old, and it had been partially devoured by wild beasts, probably a pack of wolves. Poltinkov searched for evidence of knife slashes on the cadaver, but it was hard to do since the baby's body was so badly damaged. Apparently someone had dug a shallow grave, but it wasn't deep enough to protect the body from the keen noses of the rapacious wolves.

"I'll bet it was those damn Jews! Everyone knows they use the blood of Christian children to make their disgusting flatbread. It's the right time of year too. Isn't this the time they celebrate that holiday where they only eat those funny crackers? I'm sure it's in the spring. Those Christ killers, wait until I catch them! Aleksandr! I want you to go to every house in that godforsaken village to see if any infants are missing."

"But wouldn't it have been reported as soon as it happened?"

"Aleksandr, you're an ass. Suppose a baby was born that wasn't . . . you know, quite right."

Poltinkov felt a surge of righteous anger. What could you expect of scum that cut their baby boys' *hooys* and then celebrated with a big party? You could smell them coming, that Jew smell of garlic and cabbage coming out of their pores and mouths.

"After we wrap up the evidence, we'll start questioning everyone in the village. If nothing turns up there, we'll go to the villages in the surrounding area. This time the Jews won't get away with it!"

That night Magistrate Poltinkov called a special meeting with his sergeant, Aleksandr, and several police officers. "Boys, this is a big case. I'm willing to bet my last ruble it was the Yids that did this. Remember the case in Bialystok last year?"

"Was that when they caught the bastards kidnapping a baby and slitting its throat right on the altar inside their stinking synagogue?" asked Sergeant Smolinskay as his face reddened at the memory.

Officer Petrovsky interjected. "I hear the Jews collected the blood, and right then and there mixed it into cracker batter. They were just about to bake it when they got caught."

"What do you call that Jew cracker stuff anyhow?"

"Matzo, Magistrate. I heard the Cossacks castrated the Jew priest along with three of his cronies, and then all the houses in the Yid section of town were burned down with the bastards inside. That must have spoiled their holiday." Sergeant Smolinskay smiled broadly, trying to remember who told him the Bialystok story.

"Okay, boys, back to business," Poltinkov said. "I have a village kid who knows the families in Chalupanich. Smolinskay, I expect you to go to the town hall first thing tomorrow morning and get the village census. I especially want every family and farm record in the area. Aleksandr and I will get the kid and start the interrogations. We have lots of work to do!"

The next day police officers descended on Chalupanich. They banged on every door, questioning Jew and gentile alike in the houses and on the farms. They dragged some of the Jews to jail for interrogation just to throw the fear of Christ into them. The magistrate's office examined every birth and baptism record, although they knew it was really an exercise in futility. This infant hadn't been registered. Not only were the village records notoriously inaccurate, but Poltinkov was sure the baby had been sold to the Jews for its blood. However, he couldn't leave a stone unturned if he wanted to better his future.

* * *

Magistrate Poltinkov and Sergeant Smolinskay stopped by Vladimir's house on their way to Chalupanich. The boy was already dressed and wearing his police cap.

"Smolinskay, stay outside and make sure nobody leaves the houses. Vladimir," Poltinkov said, "first you must tell us if the families are Christian or Jew and who lives in the house. Do you think you can do that?" The boy nodded expectantly. Poltinkov knocked courteously on the door of the first Christian home, that of an elderly couple.

"We're investigating a terrible crime that happened near your village," Poltinkov told them. "We need to ask you some questions." When the pair heard about the baby found in the woods, they crossed themselves quickly three times. After a cursory interrogation, Poltinkov was ready to take his leave, admonishing them, "You must let us know if you hear anything at all, even if it's a rumor."

"If we hear of anything, Magistrate, we'll let you know immediately. What kind of animals would do that to a baby?"

The next house belonged to a Jewish family. Vladimir was aghast at the change in the magistrate's tactics. Poltinkov banged fiercely on the wooden door and stormed in, shouting in a shrill voice at the cowering family.

"Please, Magistrate, we didn't do anything wrong!" The man was dressed in his work clothes, ready to leave for the barn. "I need to milk the cows. May I please talk to you in a few minutes?"

"Don't you open a mouth to me, you piece of filth. I don't give a damn about your miserable cows." Poltinkov saw Vladimir shivering in the corner, all color drained from his face. "You wait here, Jew bastard!" he said to the man, then took Vladimir out of the house and sat him down on a rock in the meadow.

"Listen, boy, we're sure it was the Jews who did it. You're lucky it didn't happen to you when you were little." Vladimir got up and backed away from Poltinkov. "Vladimir, the Jews use the blood of Christian babies to make matzo for their holiday. We're sure it was one of them. Do you have a little brother or sister?" Vladimir nodded at Poltinkov. "Then tell your Mama to keep that little one close by. This is the time of year the Jews look for little children to kidnap and kill. Don't you want to be my assistant?" Again the boy nodded. "Then you'll have to trust me. If I get a little rough, just think of that baby you found in the woods. Can you be a strong inspector? This is the way we catch murderers."

"I want to help you find whoever did it!" Vladimir was now strong and assured. They went back to the farmhouse, and Poltinkov continued terrifying the Jewish family with shouts and abusive language.

The Bromoffs had heard the commotion in the village all day and tried to prepare themselves for the onslaught. At least it wasn't the drunken Cossacks—they would have rounded up every Jew by now, stuck them in some barn, and set fire to it. It was fortunate that they had sent Michla to Aunt Malka and Uncle Yosef's house in Nolopina, *Baruch Hashem*. The Jewish community wouldn't say a word about Michla to the authorities despite their suspicions, but who knew if the rumors had leaked beyond the Jews of Chalupanich?

They waited anxiously all day—Frima, Michla's younger sister, vomited from the tension; Papa prayed, invoking Hashem to save them; Mama tried to allay her terror by going about her daily chores briskly. It was almost dark in the little parlor when they heard the pounding on their door. Mama was preparing dinner, and the aroma of onions and cabbage permeated the kitchen. The magistrate, the sergeant, and Aleksandr stormed into the house, followed by Vladimir. Mama, stirring a pot of soup, dropped the large, wooden spoon on the floor. Papa, reading the Holy Book, jumped up from his chair, and Frima ran to hide behind the skirts of her mother. "How many people live in this house?" the magistrate bellowed at them. Vladimir whispered into Poltinkov's ear. "There's someone missing; *where is your daughter?!*" Poltinkov grabbed the front of

Papa's shirt, dragging him up to his height until they were nose-to-nose. "God, you Jews always stink! I asked you where your other daughter was, and don't you lie to me." Papa was paralyzed with fear. He opened his mouth to speak, but nothing came out. Poltinkov grabbed Frima by the arm from behind her mother's skirt, pulling her roughly. "Tell me where your sister is!" Papa found his voice and leaped over to Frima, who was wailing in terror.

"Please, sir, she's just a child, let her go."

Poltinkov spun around, letting go of Frima, and punched Papa in the mouth with all his force. Papa fell backward, blood spouting from his cracked lips, and spat out two teeth. Mama shouted, "I'll tell you, please don't hit him again! My daughter went back to work in Minsk. She was very sick for a while with diphtheria. When she recovered, she went back to the city to work."

"You'd better not be lying to me; we can check any story you miserable Yids tell us." With that, Poltinkov, with Smolinskay trailing behind, left the Bromoff household, bent on terrorizing the next Jewish farmhouse.

"Do you think they're hiding anything?" Smolinskay ran to keep pace with Poltinkov.

"You're a dummy. Those Jews are too scared to be involved in anything." Even so, Poltinkov wished he still had his contacts in Minsk so he could check on the missing daughter. All those bastards who had pretended to be his friends turned their backs on him when he got in trouble with the chief magistrate.

After the police left their home, little Frima cowered in the corner, weeping piteously as Mama attended to Papa's bruised, swollen mouth with trembling hands. "*Bubbala*, please stop crying. They won't come back again. Papa and I won't let anything happen to you."

The Bromoffs tried to make a rational plan. "I think Nolopina is just outside the magistrate's jurisdiction, but I'm not sure. We certainly can't go to the Town Hall and ask." Mama twisted her apron nervously.

"If it is in the magistrate's jurisdiction, they'll eventually get around to questioning all the residents. How can Yosef and my sister Malka explain Michla? The records will show she isn't one of their children. We can't endanger them along with our own family." Papa paced the floor nervously, trying to think clearly. He was still badly shaken from the blow he'd received from Poltinkov; his head was pounding relentlessly.

Mama and Papa decided to go to Nolopina and speak to their relatives as soon as they could. They would have to take Frima as well. The child clung to them, refusing even to go to the privy alone. The Bromoffs made swift arrangements with an impoverished family to tend to their livestock and left hurriedly in their creaky wagon with the rusted wheels, dragged by their saggy old horse.

"We can't tell Michla that her baby was discovered," Mama told Papa. "She'll fall into melancholy again. Remember how she wouldn't eat for weeks, and how I had to force tea and soup into her mouth? She's just coming back to herself."

When it came to family decisions, Papa always left those matters up to Mama. His job was to provide for the family, and he felt ashamed that he hadn't been able to during the terrible harvest last year. If it hadn't been for that, Michla and the family wouldn't be in such dire straits.

"Whatever you think, Mama. We have to protect her."

* * *

When the Bromoffs arrived, Michla knew this wasn't a casual visit; they'd had to make arrangements for someone to tend to the farm in their absence. This couldn't have been easy since they were no longer on solid terms within the Jewish community.

After greeting each other warmly, the families got down to business. Mama and Papa spoke to Malka and Yosef in private. Michla later learned that they had begged for her to remain in Nolopina for a longer period of time. It wasn't safe, but right now it was safer than going back to Chalupanich. The magistrates were still interrogating the village, and it would take a little time for them to expand to the surrounding village before reaching Nolopina. "Maybe we're not even in the Jew-hating magistrate's precinct," Yosef said.

"Yosef, we can't take that chance for the sake of our own family. Something must be done."

Malka told Mama and Papa about Dina's intention to emigrate. She was the one to think of it first. "Let Michla take Dina's place and go to America."

"Why can't they go together?"

"It's an impossible amount of rubles for our families to scrape together. Besides, only one person in an extended family can get an exit visa."

"Even with bribes?"

"We would have to bribe every official in Nolopina and Chalupanich to get papers for both girls . . . Michla needs to leave; Dina only wants to."

"Can it be done in time? I understand that getting a visa quickly is harder than making friends with the Cossacks."

"Don't worry. With the right amount of rubles to grease those thieving officials' palms, wonders can be done. We can replace Dina's name with Michla's. I'm sure the Americans won't care which girl is sent over as long as she's a good worker. It'll be easier to get a girl out of the country. It's harder with boys since the czar started the army conscriptions. We'll get Michla out; visas are forged all the time."

Mama, Papa, and Yosef agreed to Malka's plan and told the children later that day. Dina cried in anger and frustration while Michla hung her head in guilt. She had taken away all of Dina's hopes, and she didn't even want to go.

Michla tried apologizing to Dina. "Don't think I don't appreciate everything that you've done for me. I'll never forget the debt I owe to you and Raisa. Please don't be furious with me; if it were within my power to change things, you would be on your way to America."

"You get yourself in trouble, and I'm the one that has to pay the price. You've always gotten your own way, and now you've taken any chance I have to make a new life. I'll never forgive you."

"Dina, if this chance came, surely it won't be the last. If it is, I promise to save everything I can to help you come to America. I'm not adventurous like you, but I have no choice. I'm a danger to the whole family."

No amount of apologies from Michla mollified Dina. She refused to speak to Michla.

Michla didn't feel the full emotional impact of the decision until her trunk was packed and she was ready to start her journey. She pleaded with Mama.

"Please let me stay. I can't leave knowing I'll never see anybody again. Mama, I'm scared to travel alone. How could you tell me to go after all I went through? You and Papa sent me away to Minsk, and look what happened." By now, she was sobbing and hiccoughing uncontrollably.

Mama pulled Michla into her lap and held her for a long time. She stroked Michla's hair, and Michla could hear her sniffling.

"Why can't I stay in Nolopina?"

"It's too dangerous, Michla. We can't inflict our troubles on our relatives. You know how gossip travels. It isn't such a far trip from Chalupanich to here." Mama sat up resolutely. "We'll find you a travel companion, at least until you get to New York. You'll be safe once you get to the farm."

Michla wailed like a small child. "I'll never see you and Papa again. I'll never see Frima." At the thought of her little sister, she felt a crushing weight in the middle of her chest.

"Nothing is forever, Michla. We must do what is needed for now. You're in danger."

"I won't go, Mama. I just can't!"

"Michla, they found the baby in the woods." Mama's voice was faint but audible.

Michla shot up from her mother's lap, all color drained from her face and her eyes glassy with terror.

The two women sat together, clutching hands for a long time. There was nothing more to be said.

* * *

Poltinkov and his staff worked relentlessly, digging up records, questioning every villager in Chalupanich, and creating havoc for the Jewish population of the tiny village. He was very disappointed in the lack of results achieved in Chalupanich, but knew he had left no stone unturned. It was time to widen the search to the neighboring village of Polotnik.

He mused about what he would do when he finally caught the vile baby-killers. He and the boys would beat them soundly before turning them over to the Cossacks for their real punishment. "It's just too damn bad that we have rules and regulations to follow," he confided in Aleksandr. "I'd love our office to complete the job, but we'd have the court system to contend with. It's okay, the army will do a very thorough job, and we'll come off as the responsible arm of justice. You can be sure the chief magistrate will hear about my triumph." Poltinkov imagined himself ensconced in a large, sunny office in Minsk, after having received the substantial promotion he deserved. But there was no time to daydream. They had to finish their investigation in Polotnik quickly before going on to the larger district of Nolopina.

* * *

The four adult Bromoffs and Shteynbergers haunted the small office that was responsible for processing exit visas. They had to deal with a particularly nasty and venal character named Shepletsky, always toadying to him in an effort to expedite the processing of Michla's exit visa.

"I thought the girl's name was Dina Shteynberger?"

"No, sir, she's changed her mind, and her cousin, Michla Bromoff, will be taking her place."

"Well, that will cost an additional fifty rubles, and if I have to make more changes, there'll be an extra surcharge."

The two families were frantic and willing to agree to anything to speed up the exit visa for Michla. There were rumors that Magistrate Poltinkov had finished his investigation in Polotnik and would be advancing on Nolopina in a few short days. The Bromoffs and Shteynbergers had pooled all of their resources and resorted to borrowing money from relatives. Shepletsky sensed their desperation and upped the ante. After haggling over the cost—and when Shepletsky assessed that he couldn't squeeze the Jews any more—they finally came to an agreement, and Michla's name miraculously appeared on the exit visa. It wasn't a moment too soon, as the magisterial staff appeared in Nolopina on the day that Michla finally received her visa and fled the village.

Mama, always resourceful and practical, found a traveling companion for Michla. She was a young woman from Nolopina, joining her husband in New York after being separated for over a year. Her name was Shifra, and she chattered excitedly on the long train ride they shared to Bremen, Germany, where they would board the boat that would take them to America, the Golden Medina.

Feeling depressed, angry, and distraught, Michla felt like strangling Shifra just to shut her up. How could she listen to her happy chatter all the way to New York? She would have been better off going alone.

* * *

After Michla left for America, the family tried to resume their lives, but a pall hung over the house. Frima, usually pleasant and compliant, became moody and obstinate, refusing to do her chores. Ordinarily Frima's behavior would have resulted in a hard smack and extra chores, but Mama knew that Frima was grieving and tried to be understanding. But one day, when Frima refused to help with the weekly washing, Mama had had enough. She gave the child a resounding smack and sent her to bed. Mama heard muffled sobs and sniffling coming from the bedroom and went to comfort her.

"Mama, will Michla ever come home?"

"I don't know, Bubbala. It's in Hashem's hands."

"I pray to Him every night, but He's not listening."

"Hashem has His own ways. Maybe it's just not the right time."

Two weeks after their return from Nolopina, Mama was cleaning out dresser drawers and found Michla's hairbrush with strands of long, light brown tresses clinging to the bristles. She took the brush outside to see it in the light. The hair glistened golden in the sunlight. She clutched the brush to her breast, took it inside, and gently began to extract each strand, taking care not to break the hair. When Mama had a handful of Michla's hair, she put her hand up to her nose, inhaling deeply. Then she took her best handkerchief and carefully arranged Michla's hair on the flat surface. She knotted the handkerchief and placed it in the cupboard, next to their Shabbos candles and Hanukkah lights.

3

Minnie and Zelig Meet

M urphy, the head foreman, noticed that there was a discrepancy in
the amount of potato bushels tallied and the produce that was
actually available for market. Profits were down despite a bumper crop
that year. He spoke to the owner, and they decided to keep a closer watch
on the employees, from the farm laborers to the office staff.

Zelig knew what was happening but said nothing. He was always
scrupulous in his own count, even when Murphy's assistant urged him
to cheat by including blackened, insect-ridden potatoes in his tally. Some
of the laborers, the assistant foreman, and the bookkeeper colluded by
overestimating the bushel count to their benefit. When Murphy found
the discrepancy, he immediately reported it to the owner, Mr. Monaghan.

Monaghan fired the bookkeeper and assistant foreman on the spot
and made sure that they'd never be hired by any of the local farms in
Suffolk County. The hapless laborers were punished by having their time
of servitude extended by one year, and Murphy made their lives miserable
in any way he could.

Zelig approached Murphy. By now he had learned enough English
from the Irish farmhands and the overseers in the field to express himself
reasonably well, although the native speakers laughed at his speech. It was
riddled with Yiddish syntax and intonation, with a hint of Irish brogue.

"Mistah, I could voik de office? I'm goot mit de numbers. Maybe can

I stay dere 'til dey get ah new counting mahn—vat you call it—ah bookey mahn?" Murphy laughed uproariously, but he did present the idea to Mr. Monaghan. The owner was a self-made Irishman who started with nothing, so he appreciated Zelig's boldness and decided to give him a chance. Of course, he'd have to hire a main bookkeeper, but maybe this little shrimp with the fractured English could fill in for a time. What did they have to lose? They were stuck. At least they knew the little Yid was honest.

Zelig reveled in his new, albeit temporary, position. The first break he'd had in this *fahkokta* country, and he made it himself. Zelig felt the spirit of Moishe smiling on him.

In light of his new position, Zelig planned to shave his beard, cut his earlocks, and remove his yarmulke. These were vestiges of the old country, and he'd do anything to remain in the office. However, this proved harder than he had ever anticipated; he visualized his parents' shock if they were ever to see him like this. Zelig procrastinated for three days before finally cutting off his peyes without using a looking glass. Once that was done, he enlisted the aid of one of the Irish workers who served as the unofficial barber of the farm.

"Sean, I vant you should cut off and shave mein beard and mustache. Also, you should teach me vot should I do mit de razor. I pay vatever you vant." Sean was amused and sat Zelig down, snipping away at the long beard. When it finally came to the actual shave, he instructed Zelig in the art of sharpening and handling the straight razor.

"Sure, and yah rub it back and forth on yer belt first. Make sure the edge is very sharp, den yah shave down, never up. These things can give a nasty cut if yer not careful." Zelig couldn't look and asked Sean not to place the looking glass in front of him. When it was done, Sean beamed at his handiwork. "You're a right fine-looking lad; all the girls they'll be comin' after yah." Sean placed the mirror in front of Zelig, who recoiled at what he saw. Who was this stranger, this goy peering back at him? Zelig felt a churning in the pit of his stomach and wished that he could undo what was just done. He had to admit he looked younger and would make a better appearance in the office. *I'll get used to it; I'm in America now.*

With that said, he removed his yarmulke. But when he sent back a sketch of himself to the village, all the Jewish accoutrements were present. He felt the wind blowing on his face and unconsciously reached to stroke his now-absent beard. How long would it take for him to gaze in a looking glass and recognize himself?

Zelig was transferred to the office, and he was even given a small room in which to sleep and store his belongings. He took it upon himself to inspect the tally sheets in the fields, making sure that every potato counted was actually saleable. Once he saw how the books were kept, he devised his own system of keeping scrupulous records. Nobody would be cheated; not management, and certainly not the workers who drove themselves to earn a little extra by delivering above the quota. He was never strong or swift enough in the fields. He killed himself just to make quota, but maybe here he could show his true worth.

For the first time in his life, gentiles had treated him fairly. No, that wasn't true. The Finnish seaman on the *Finlandia* had allowed him up on deck after Moishe's death. They had no common language, but Zelig felt the seaman's compassion in his gestures and facial expressions. Maybe he'd lost a close friend at sea just like Zelig had.

Zelig settled into the job, and it became his responsibility to pay the field workers their salaries and anything extra they managed to eke out. He also kept accounts for the company store and earned extra money by penning letters for illiterate Jewish workers.

Except for absolute necessities, Eastern European Jews rarely bought in the company store; they sent every extra penny back to their relatives in Europe. But the buxom, rosy-cheeked colleens bought ribbons for their hair and fake lace to embellish their coarse muslin blouses. Broad Irish and Scandinavian men spent it all on rotgut liquor, swilled down on Saturday nights. It was a sorry, hungover bunch of men who attended church service in the small chapel on Sunday mornings with an itinerant priest and minister. The same chapel was used for Friday night Jewish services, but there was no official rabbi, so the Jewish men formed a minyan and cobbled together a service with a few worn prayer books and a bottle of wine. At first Zelig attended services, just to hear Yiddish spoken. But once he was transferred to the office job, he noticed a change in attitude among the men. He overheard two of them talking about him in loud voices.

"He thinks he's such a big shot; too good for the rest of us. You see how he looks now? Just like a goy, with no peyes or beard. Why does he even come? He used to be a mensh; now he must think he's Irish."

They began to laugh. After that Zelig chose to say prayers for Moishe in private.

* * *

Minnie arrived at the farm in late September, just in time for one of the most labor-intensive jobs, harvesting potatoes. She gazed in astonishment at the rows and rows of mounds where the potatoes were planted, as far as the eye could see. Sheltered by hills, generally at the side of the dirt roads, were clapboard structures that resembled the upper part of a farmhouse. She later found out that potatoes were stored in these potato barns for up to a year, when they would be sold at market. On her father's small farm, a diversity of crops was planted, such as barley, corn, wheat, alfalfa, and vegetables. She had never seen crops that were all the same; vertical lines as far as the horizon. There were other fields to plant food for the horses and mules that supplied the animal labor.

Minnie was immediately placed in the fields. She followed behind a pair of horses, attached to a machine that dug up the hillocks and loosened the potatoes. It was the job of the laborers to pick the potatoes, put them in gunnysacks, and place them on carts drawn by horses or mules. Minnie was used to hard work in the fields, but toiling from early morning to dusk, constantly bending to retrieve the oval treasures while hauling the gunnysack with her, depleted her entirely. In those early days in the fields, she could barely eat supper and wash the dirt and grime from her hands and face before tumbling like one of the sacks onto her cot in the dormitory. In a way she was glad to be so exhausted. It enabled her to fall into a deep sleep rather than weep for the loss of her family and country.

* * *

New workers kept appearing at the farm, mostly from Russia like Zelig. They were fleeing pogroms and conscription into the czar's army. Zelig was surprised to see a group of single young women in the latest batch of transplanted migrants.

One day one of the new women appeared in the office. The first thing he noticed as she passed her payment chit across the makeshift desk was her hand. It was almost like a child's, with small, tapered fingers, roughened skin, and dirt under the broken nails and cuticles. His gaze swept her small frame, visible above the waist, and finally rested on her face. She had deep-set, hooded eyes and a painfully thin face with a pointed chin. High, Slavic cheekbones were emphasized by the lack of spare flesh. A tuft of nondescript, lank hair escaped from under her faded babushka.

Zelig spoke to her first in English. "You come de last boat?" No response. He followed up in Yiddish, and the eyes flew open to meet his. She had lovely, large hazel eyes, fringed by almost imperceptible lashes.

"Du bist a Yid?" She gazed at him in wonder. Where were his facial hair, peyes, and yarmulke? What was it about these transplanted Jews who shed their identity as soon as they could get their hands on a razor?

Minnie handed Zelig her chit, taking care that their fingers not touch in the paper transaction. As she turned to leave, Zelig noted the set of her shoulders, straight spine, and determined gait. There was something tough and unyielding in that waif-like body that distinguished her from the rest of the girls. A vision of Leeba flashed through his mind. How different this girl was from soft, mischievous, laughing Leeba, with round cheeks and an ample body.

Several of the field girls resembled Leeba in stature and complexion. He occasionally felt a sexual surge around them, which he willed away.

Minnie was different. Her childlike stature belied her determined stance. She wasn't pretty, although her large eyes were arresting.

Daytime in the office was very busy. When the office closed, Zelig would spend his time studying English or sketching scenes from memory. He'd had artistic talent since he was a child. He would draw peasants digging in the fields with the sun poised above the furrowed earth, and he had a special affinity for capturing interesting faces.

The next time Minnie approached his desk with averted eyes, he gave her a portrait he'd drawn of her. Of course, he enhanced her image somewhat, plumping out her cheeks a bit and softening her pointed chin. It was the Minnie she could be with adequate nutrition and an easier life. The one thing he rendered faithfully were her deep-set hazel eyes, the thing that had attracted him in the first place. Minnie favored him with a shy glance but seemed unsure about what to do next. Finally she took the sketch and whispered, *"Shaynem dank."*

Zelig began attending the makeshift synagogue again each Friday in hopes of seeing Minnie and having a conversation with her in Yiddish. The men continued to ignore him unless they needed an extra body to fill in for a minyan. Of course there was a high partition between the men and women's section, but it was dismantled after the service and everyone mixed freely during the meager *Oneg Shabbat*, the snacks served after services.

Imagine men and women fraternizing in synagogue in the old country; Zelig's and Minnie's parents would be scandalized if they knew.

At first Minnie would leave immediately after services, but one Friday night Zelig saw her in the corner, standing apart from the rest of the congregants. He approached her tentatively, unsure of his reception. They talked briefly about the new, itinerant rabbi, and one evening, after a few more of these Shabbat meetings, he asked her to take a walk with him. To his great surprise, she accepted. They talked about how life on the farm was so hard.

They also talked about how difficult it was to toil in the fields with hardly a break, scooping up potato after potato. The harvest was in, and it had been an abundant one, but it seemed Monaghan and his minions were never satisfied. Each worker had a quota to fill, or they were docked the little bit of money they earned. The women's quota was a bit less than the men's, but it was much harder for pregnant and menstruating women to fill those sacks.

"The worst is the food," Minnie said. "Sometimes I get nauseated just smelling the meat, and I'm afraid even the vegetables are cooked in *treyf,* probably lard. Mostly I eat bread and whatever vegetables and fruits are raw. Otherwise I'd probably starve to death or just eat potatoes, corn and hay from the fields!"

Zelig responded by nodding. He rather liked the food, but of course he wouldn't say it to Minnie. He told Minnie about how Murphy's assistant tried to swindle Monaghan, but didn't mention that work in the office was heaven compared to work in the fields.

How on earth does a little thing like Minnie manage to dig potatoes all day? I could barely get out of bed each morning; every bone in my body ached.

Minnie and Zelig continued to meet after the Oneg Shabbat, taking walks and chatting. After a few weeks, Minnie asked Zelig if he would write a letter home for her.

"I'll pay you, of course."

"I don't take money from friends. We are friends, aren't we?" Minnie didn't reply but gave him a sidelong glance.

The following Sunday, they met in the office. He sat behind the desk and she sat opposite him.

"What do you want me to write?"

"Can you say 'Dear Mama—no, put 'Dearest Mama, Papa, and Frima.'"

After several false starts and many revisions, Minnie seemed to be satisfied. Zelig read the letter back to her.

31 December 1891
Dearest Mama, Papa, and Frima,

I'm sorry it took me so long to write, but life here has been very hectic. I know you must be worried, but I want to assure you that I'm safe on the farm. The work is hard, but you know I'm used to hard work and I'm managing.

I live in a dormitory with about ten other girls. One of them is Jewish, and I'm becoming friendly with her, which makes me feel less lonely. We have more than enough to eat, although I don't eat meat since it's treyf. Sometimes they serve fish from the bay, and there are plenty of vegetables, fruits, and bread. Mr. Monaghan, the boss, makes sure that his workers stay healthy. If someone gets sick, he even has a real doctor examine the worker.

Don't worry Papa, on Friday nights I always go to services. There are more Jewish men than girls, enough for a minyan, but there is a mekhitza *to separate the men and women.*

Frima, it will be your birthday soon. Don't think I forgot. I'd like you to have the locket that Mama and Papa gave me for my twelfth birthday. Every time you wear it, think of your big sister and how I hold you close to my heart.

Mama, as soon as I can save some money, I'll send it to you. It won't be much because I have to pay off my passage, but at least it will be a little extra. Maybe you can send Frima to the village girls' school to learn the aleph, bais *with what I send.*

I think of you every day. I pray for your good health and a prosperous year. Please send me word through the village scribe so I know that you're all well.

I love you all so much.
Michla

When Zelig finished reading the letter, he looked up to find Minnie's eyes swollen with tears. She buried her face in her hands, trying to stop the sobs welling up inside of her.

Zelig fumbled for his handkerchief but found it dirty and shoved it back in his pocket. He pulled over a chair and sat next to her.

"I know how you feel; I would give two years of my life to catch a glimpse of my family in happier days."

Minnie wiped her face on her blouse sleeve. Zelig patted her shoulder, with tears in his eyes as well. She patted the back of his hand consolingly. He turned his hand and clasped her palm in his. They sat silently for a moment, and then Minnie got up. Zelig folded the letter, placed it in an envelope and turned to Minnie.

"So, 'Michla' is your original name."

"They changed it when I got to Ellis Island. I told them my right name, but the clerk marked it down as 'Minnie.' Now it's my legal name. I decided since I was starting a new life in America, I might as well have a new name. I'm getting used to it."

Minnie took the envelope, opened the door and they stepped out into the late afternoon glare of the Suffolk sun.

* * *

Minnie was never overtly friendly to Zelig when she collected her pay in the office, but she waited for him after services. She felt better seeing him with a prayer shawl and yarmulke; then he didn't look so goyische. The girls were beginning to tease her, saying Zelig was her beau, but she didn't care. He was kind to her and made her feel safe in his presence.

Minnie thought back to the nightmare voyage in steerage when she was tormented by horrific remembrances of the last months at home and the ensuing panic to get her out of the country quickly. She cried bitterly every night, overwhelmed by loss and loneliness until she fell into a dreamless sleep. Zelig was her first real friend in the new world. He was always correct in his behavior toward her. When he tried to take her hand, she recoiled, and Zelig was sensitive enough to back off.

Minnie never mentioned Zelig in her letters. He was her teacher and mentor. She could never imagine herself flirting and simpering over a man like the other girls in the dormitory. Minnie heard those ridiculous girls giggling and whispering together. Even though there was a strict curfew, and romances between laborers were strongly discouraged, Minnie witnessed plenty of stolen kisses and caresses behind the wooden dormitories.

How could they be so bold and stupid? Don't they know what is going to happen?

Several of the Irish girls became pregnant, but at least their beaus married them. There was finger counting after the rush weddings, but the shame and stigma of becoming pregnant before marriage wasn't like in the old country. Not that people turned a blind eye, but at least a girl wouldn't be killed if she had a baby out of wedlock.

Minnie swore she would never marry. The idea of physical intimacy nauseated her. Zelig would have to accept her on her own terms, or the friendship could not continue.

4

A Change of Heart

Monaghan was livid. "What kind of a stupid bastard did I hire to run my office? The only thing he can do well is kiss my arse and get under the skirts of the field girls. I was an idiot for hiring that dumb squarehead. He can't keep the books straight—the son-of-a-bitch already cost me hundreds of dollars. Without Zelig to clean up his mess, it would have been in the thousands."

His beefy face turned bright red and his blood pressure was about to go through the ceiling. He knew he'd have to calm down; Doc said he'd give himself a stroke if he wasn't careful. He plopped himself in the rickety wooden chair facing the scarred mahogany desk and put up his feet. Calming down a bit, he contemplated his next move. The little kike still owed him two more years. He checked a ledger with the service records of the farm immigrants. Yup, it was just over two years. He had hired Lars, thinking that Zelig might not be up to the responsibility, being right off the boat. Now he thought, *Where was my head, thinking Lars would do a better job?* Dumb move. If he played his cards right, Monaghan could get Zelig to stay when the indenture contract was over. Even if he doubled Zelig's pay Monaghan would still be way ahead—and Zelig was sparkin' with that skinny gal from the fields. Monaghan checked the ledger again. Her name was Minnie Something-or-Other, and she had nearly four years to go. Zelig wasn't going to leave her, especially if Monaghan let them

35

have that little house in the back of the dormitories. The lad was going to think he died and went to heaven.

He shifted in his chair and sat up. "Lars, get your arse in here." The bookkeeper pretended to be working on bills of lading, even though he could barely hold his head up after last night's drinking binge.

"You callin' me, boss? I was just getting all the end-of-month bills together."

"How many times did you screw up since you been here? You're a one-man bankruptcy disaster. I'm givin' you two days to clear out, and that's because I'm in a good mood. I should kick your drunken arse to kingdom come. Jaysus, Mary, and Joseph, what I have to put up with."

Monaghan bellowed for Zelig, who'd heard the commotion from the inner office. Zelig was sure he'd done something wrong and would be sent back to the potato fields. He was literally quaking when he walked into the outer office and faced the boss.

"Zelig, I fired Lars and I want you to take over. Can you handle the job? I'll raise your salary five dollars a week and after you pay me back for your passage, we'll talk again."

"Mistah Boss, I promise you von't be sorry. I didn't vant to say, but Lars vas no gut for business."

Zelig couldn't wait to tell Minnie the extraordinary news and ran out in the fields to look for her. He asked Murphy to give her a ten-minute break, grabbed her by the hand, and pulled her to a secluded place away from prying ears.

"Minnie, the boss fired Lars. I got the job. Me, a Jew, running the whole office!" She took his hand and gave him a surreptitious peck on the cheek. Zelig lifted her high in the air and twirled her around. "Zelig, stop that! If somebody sees, we'll get in trouble," she said tersely.

With Lars gone, Zelig could do more than mind the books. Monaghan didn't care as long as he kept on top of the office work, and he overlooked it when Zelig took out his artist's pad and drew with charcoal and pencils. One Sunday, he got to the office about an hour before he was to meet Minnie. Zelig sat in Monaghan's chair and looked out the window. He saw Maureen carrying her newest baby in a sling made of multicolored material. She was jiggling the baby up and down and seemed to be laughing. Zelig tore a sheet of paper from his pad and began sketching, at first tentatively with pencil and then with more fervor in charcoal. The result was a detailed sketch of Leeba's face. In the drawing, her round face was sunken and her eyes projected terror. Zelig was so engrossed in the sketch that he didn't hear Minnie open the door and peer over his shoulder.

"Zelig, tell me about her. You never speak about your wife."

He pushed the picture to the far end of the desk, got up, and looked out the window. Zelig started to speak in a hoarse, strained voice.

"I could only afford the village midwife when she started labor too soon. The doctor, that miserable *mamser*, wouldn't cross a Jewish threshold unless he was paid triple his usual fee. Minnie, she labored in agony for hours, shrieking in pain. I couldn't stay in the room—I clapped my hands over my ears and stood outside, praying for God to intervene. She died a horrible death, and the baby died with her. The midwife asked if I wanted to close Leeba's eyes or hold the baby. I couldn't."

Minnie stood silently. Zelig expected her to comfort him; instead she muttered, "Zelig, I'm so sorry," and bolted out of the office. Zelig was astonished.

Why is Minnie acting this way?

* * *

Zelig continued writing faithfully to Mama and Papa, but received no letters back from them for a period of several months. He kept checking the mailbox every day, but there was no news, even though he had written them about Minnie. He stopped by the mailbox again and saw a letter addressed to him in a strange hand. It was from Gittel, his oldest sister, written by the town scribe. Panic gripped him as he ripped open the envelope.

21 March 1892
Dear Zelig,

> *I just don't know how to tell you. I put this letter off as long as I could, but you have to know. In January a terrible flu epidemic swept the village. Most of our family left—we had to protect the children—but Papa refused to go. We all pleaded with him, but you know how stubborn Papa could be. He was afraid to leave his home, thinking that Cossacks would storm the village or it would be vandalized. Mama wouldn't leave him though she tried to persuade him to go to Petersburg with us.*
>
> *We came back after the illness passed. Half the villagers who stayed were struck down. I never expected that Mama and Papa would survive—after all, they were frail, already in their fifties.*
>
> *This is the worst part. When we came back we found out that Mama and Papa were buried in a mass grave with all the dead jumbled together. We don't know where they are. How can we put up a gravestone?*

> *Gittel*

Zelig was devastated. When he left Russia, he knew he'd probably never see them again. At least he could feel his Papa's presence while looking at his handwriting and words. Mama always sent little handmade gifts, even though she never truly forgave him for leaving. Now he'd never be able to make it up to her. *Gut in Himmel*, they weren't even buried with their own kind—just thrown in a pit like dead animal carcasses with lime poured over them.

Zelig lamented for months, and Minnie was a tremendous source of comfort to him. She sat silently, holding his hands when grief overcame him. She gave him water and tea in those first days when he wouldn't eat. They spent every Sunday together, talking about their lives.

A year later, when the period of mourning was officially over, Zelig glanced in the looking glass and saw that his hairline was receding. By then, Minnie had gained some weight and now had a noticeable bosom and curving hips under the folds of her dress. Zelig felt a twinge of sexual desire when he saw her at the Oneg Shabbat that Friday night. He thought, *Maybe . . . I'm thirty-two already.*

One Sunday morning when he was teaching her to write, he leaned toward her and smelled the fresh aroma of her hair and skin. Zelig became aroused and quickly placed his jacket over his lap. He took Minnie's face in his hands and tried to kiss her. Minnie became panicked and pushed him away with all of her strength.

She avoided him all week.

The next Friday, Zelig skipped synagogue and spent the evening with Sean, the barber, and his Irish compatriots, swigging away at bottles of bad whisky. A few Irish girls, who were well known for loose morals and a desire to earn some extra money, joined them. Sean and the other men goaded Zelig on. Reeling from whiskey, Zelig followed one of the girls behind the pitch-black dormitory. She raised her dress, unbuttoned his pants and he immediately felt an explosion from the base of his penis. He spilled semen all over his pants and her petticoats.

"What kind uh man are yah? Yah can't hold it 'til you're inside a girl? You should be ashamed, wettin' your pants like a kid takin' a piss. Now look what you done to me clothes. Get on wit yah!"

Zelig was humiliated and felt filthy as he lurched back to his room above the office. Suppose Minnie heard about this? She was such a proper girl. She would think he was a disgusting lecher and wouldn't want anything to do with him.

His fears were unfounded, however, when Minnie approached him in the office.

"Zelig, I'm sorry I pushed you away from me. I was brought up very strictly. I become frightened when a man comes too close, and I felt—well, you know what I felt. That kind of thing isn't right unless two people are married."

Zelig blurted out, "So marry me, Minnie. I'll be good to you and take care of you. You're the only one here that means anything to me. I love you."

Minnie took Zelig's hand and searched his face for a long moment, with tears welling up in her eyes.

"Please give me some more time. I care for you very much, but I'm just not ready."

* * *

Zelig began to think of the future, when his indentured service would be over. He had heard from some of the Jewish workers about opportunities in a place called Coney Island in Brooklyn, New York. It was a famous beach resort, packed with multitudes of bathers and fun-seekers, enjoying carriage rides on the long boardwalk that paralleled the beach and ocean. Bathhouses and amusement parks were springing up to accommodate the bloomer girls with their parasols and young men in sporty, striped bathing suits covering their torsos and thighs. It was even said that the famous screen star, Eleanor Boardman, was building a huge beach house, like a mansion, in an exclusive community near Coney Island called Sea Gate.

An enterprising and astute man could do well here. Zelig was itching to leave Suffolk County, but there remained the problem of Minnie. He couldn't just leave her behind, and she still owed the farm nearly three more years for her passage.

Zelig mentioned his desire to pursue new paths to the boss, and Monaghan became alarmed. He promised Zelig the title of Chief Bookkeeper with a substantial pay raise and a small, rent-free house suitable for newlyweds. He even offered to take Minnie out of the fields and give her an apprentice job in the office now that she knew some English.

Zelig presented the boss's offer to Minnie, hoping that she would accept him. "I'll wipe out your debt to the farm. Then we'll be free to go.

Minnie, don't keep putting me off; I care for you, but I can't keep putting my life on hold, waiting for you to change your mind."

After Friday services, they took a long walk. "Minnie, write your family and ask their permission to marry me. I know how much you miss them, and we'll do everything possible to bring them here if they want to come. My sisters will never leave the old country, so your family will be mine."

Minnie couldn't sleep, riddled with anxiety and doubt. She longed to see her family, especially Mama and Frima, but how could she be sure they wouldn't slip and let Zelig know what had happened to her in Minsk? Suppose they brought Cousins Dina and Raisa over—could they be trusted not to tell? If she didn't accept Zelig's proposal now, would he leave without her? She imagined him finding a more amenable, loving woman in Coney Island among those bathing beauties and felt anger at Zelig and jealousy toward those phantom girls who would lure him away from her.

During one of those sleepless nights, she came to a decision. She had to take a chance—she would have no future without Zelig. She would toil in the fields like a peasant until she died of overwork. He was kind and gentle, and she did care for him deeply. The past was in the old country; she couldn't be afraid all her life.

Minnie felt a surge of relief and optimism when she finally accepted Zelig's proposal of marriage. She was bombarded with advice from her co-workers about how to make the marriage a success.

"Minnie darlin', even if yah don't like it at first," they told her, "pretend you're havin' a good time. It'll hurt the first time, but you'll get used to it real fast." The girls were very kind to her, helping her put together a trousseau. Zelig, with his extra income, bought her lovely dresses, night-clothes, bed linens, and quilts. Minnie protested, feeling embarrassed by the luxurious items, which she hid in her trunk.

"Zelig, please don't buy me so much!"

"But you're my queen. I love to see you in beautiful dresses and hats. I can't wait for us to stroll on the boardwalk, looking like the upstanding couple we were meant to be."

Minnie received letters from Chalupanich, congratulating her on her good fortune. Zelig drew pictures of the two of them, with Zelig sitting in a plush chair and Minnie, in her finest attire, standing next to him with one hand on his shoulder, looking like a prosperous American couple. They even sent a photograph, taken by a man hunched under a black cloth attached to an enormous black box. When he pressed a bulb, Minnie heard a loud *puff*. It was like magic to see their image in black and white, although Minnie preferred Zelig's lovely, hand-drawn sketches.

Despite her reservations and fears, Minnie was caught up in the excitement of being a prospective bride.

5

The Wedding

There was no mikva in all of Suffolk County. Minnie wanted to begin her life with Zelig in a state of purification and needed the ritual bath as a spiritual cleansing in preparation for her marriage.

After Friday night services, Minnie approached the itinerant rabbi who would marry them, explaining her predicament.

"You must be over your bleeding for seven days before you go under the chupah. Let's plan the wedding for that time. Since there's no mikva, you'll have to ask one of the Jewish girls to help you." Minnie could see that he was as uncomfortable as she was in discussing the ritual bath. After all, it was women who took care of these details. Minnie longed for her mother. Mama would be able to lead her through all the intricacies of when, what, and how that was incumbent on becoming a Jewish bride.

She tried to think of who could help her. There were very few Jewish women at the farm, and they were rather coarse. Minnie was a shy, reticent young woman who'd never developed a deep friendship with any of the girls. They always seemed so silly and boisterous. She thought about Rivka, a new girl in the dormitory who was always reading her prayer book, ignoring the tumult and gossip around her. Minnie approached her and spoke in rapid, furtive Yiddish.

"Rivka, I must ask you a favor. I'll be forever indebted to you if you'll be my bath attendant the night before I marry Zelig. You know there's no real mikva, and I'll have to improvise. We can use the old tub outside of the bath area, and I'll supply all the things we need."

Rivka was even younger than Minnie and knew nothing about wedding rituals. She thought for a moment and finally said, "I'd be honored. Would you like the other girls to help?"

"I'd feel more comfortable with just one bath attendant." Minnie hated the idea of a group of young women seeing her naked.

The night before the wedding, a group of girls went into the bathing area, dragging the heavy zinc tub inside. One girl filled it with pails of heated water while the others brought in towels, brushes, cloths, and soap. Of course it would have been much easier to bathe in the wooden tub in the kitchen of her tiny new residence, but Minnie wasn't sure of the rules of purification and believed that it had to be done outside of her new home. Again, she longed for her mother to show her how to do things correctly.

When the two girls were alone, Rivka looked away while Minnie disrobed and stepped into the tub. Rivka began rubbing a soft rag with soap over her very tentatively. "No, Rivka, use the brush. I want you to rub as hard as you can, even harder than that."

"But Minnie, I'm going to hurt you, the bristles are sharp."

"I don't care. Just do it, please."

A confused Rivka vigorously scrubbed Minnie's body with the rough bristles.

"I need more water. We have to fill the tub again."

"Minnie, the water will be too cold by now. I can't call the girls to reheat more."

"Pour more water in, I don't mind if it's cold."

A shivering Minnie emerged from the tub, and Rivka reached for the extra pails of cooled water. She kept pouring until the tub was nearly overflowing. Minnie stepped in again; her teeth were chattering uncontrollably.

"Minnie, get out—you'll catch a terrible cold! You'll be sick for the wedding."

"Do it again. I need to be clean."

Rivka gave up trying to reason with Minnie. She scrubbed her again briskly, studiously examined and cleansed the nails of each digit, and as a finale dunked Minnie's head under the murky water. Minnie came up sputtering. Her usually pale skin was blotched and ruddy, mottled with goose bumps.

"Rivka, you've given me the best gift I could ask for."

Rivka took Minnie's hand to help her out of the cold water, averted her eyes, and wrapped a large sheet around Minnie's immaculate body.

* * *

The wedding day had arrived. Minnie was swept up in the festivities despite her earlier fears. Mr. Monaghan paid for a chupah, the wedding canopy, festooned with fragrant flowers and a white bolt of silken cloth for the bride and groom to walk on. He even arranged for the itinerant rabbi to perform the ceremony and paid for a kosher-style meal catered for the guests.

Minnie wore a modest white gown and a long veil to cover her face. She held back her tears when surrogates stood under the chupah with her instead of her beloved family. She circled Zelig seven times, according to Jewish tradition, and when Zelig stepped on the glass, to commemorate the destruction of the Temple in Jerusalem, even the Irish and Swedes yelled, "Mazel tov!"

She promised herself that she would be a good wife to Zelig. If sex was something she'd have to endure, Minnie now had the maturity and strength to cope with it.

Minnie and Zelig left the nuptial feast very late and walked side by side to their new home. Not a word passed between them; they were absorbed in their own intense discomfort about what was to happen next. Minnie knew that according to Jewish tradition, they were expected to consummate the marriage that night. In the dark, she remembered how Zelig looked at the wedding. He was slight, not very tall, and with his yarmulke slightly askew and his best suit on, he resembled a Talmudic scholar. What would he be like, stripped of his clothes and touching her under the bed sheets?

Zelig broke the silence. "The simkhe was beautiful, wasn't it?"

"Yes, Mr. Monaghan was very generous to us. I only wish our families could have been there."

They stepped into the tiny frame house in back of the dormitories.

"Shall I light the oil lamp?"

Minnie nodded while Zelig fumbled with the matches and wick. They entered the bedroom and saw that her friends had made up the bed with new linens from her trousseau trunk. The girls even placed fresh flowers on the pillows and scented the air with cologne. Minnie felt deeply grateful for their kindness and could even overlook the coarse jokes they'd made about the wedding night.

"I'll leave the lamp here and get ready for bed in the kitchen."

Zelig undressed in the dark, putting on a fresh nightshirt. He waited a few minutes and knocked on the door. When Minnie opened it, Zelig felt an electric surge through his body. She was dressed in one of the satin gowns he bought for her, and her long brown hair, usually tied up in a knot, was illuminated by the light and draped sumptuously down her shoulders and back.

"Which side would you prefer?"

"Near the bed stand would be best."

They delayed the moment of climbing into bed until the chilly night air forced them under the quilt. They lay silently for a few moments. Finally Zelig said, "If you're too tired, we can just rest tonight. We have the whole day off tomorrow."

Minnie relaxed a bit. How like Zelig to be thoughtful and give her time to become accustomed to sharing his bed. She rewarded him by reaching for his hand and moving closer to him.

Zelig began to caress her gently, with soft, lingering kisses on her cheeks and lips. He ran his tongue slowly along her neck. His hands stroked her shoulders and back, moving downward to rest lightly on her buttocks and thighs. Minnie began to return his kisses, and felt an unfamiliar, pulsating sensation between her legs as his hands caressed her breasts and stomach through the thin material of her gown. Her body began tingling with sensations she'd never experienced before.

His breathing deepened and became ragged. Zelig's fingers grew more insistent as they reached under her gown, and she felt his penis, hot and hard, as it aggressively poked her inner thigh. They were facing one another when, in a sudden movement, he mounted her. She was overcome with terror, stiffening and trying to push him away. His weight felt immense upon her, bile rose up in her throat, and there was buzzing in her head. She was suffocating under his weight, unable to struggle any longer. Minnie fainted beneath him, her body becoming limp and inert.

Zelig was in a panic. He leaped out of bed, all passion drained from him, and rushed to the washstand. He dampened a rag and placed it on Minnie's forehead as he felt for a pulse.

Merciful God, don't let her die!

Her breathing returned to normal as she regained consciousness. She turned her back to him and began to sob. He lay down next to her, stroking her hair and murmuring comforting words.

"Don't cry, Mamala; it will be alright."

He lay silently for a while, listening to her labored breathing.

How easy it had been with Leeba. She was so responsive to his touch, even on their first night. He remembered how lubricated she was, her nipples erect and her voluptuous body trembling with desire, even when he penetrated her hymen.

"Minnie, darling, what's wrong? What did I do? I thought you wanted to . . ."

By then her sobs had subsided, but she wouldn't look at him.

Zelig knew that Minnie'd had trouble in her young life. Why else would a girl leave home and come alone to this godforsaken place? Still, he didn't know what was going on with her.

She soon fell asleep, and he listened to her breathing deepen and become regular.

Zelig spent the rest of his wedding night lying awake, fretting and wondering.

6

A Confession

Minnie woke up just after dawn, alone in bed and beside herself with anxiety. She dreaded facing Zelig. What could she tell him? She finally whispered to herself, "I'll have to tell him about Chaim."

. . .

"Don't make a sound," Chaim said. "If you scream, I'll tell my parents that you tempted me and asked me to come to your bed." She was to endure five more terrifying attacks before he went back to yeshiva. Each night she waited in dreaded anticipation of whether this would be the night he'd creep silently into her room.

. . .

Minnie watched daybreak arrive through the dirty windows of the bedroom. *I'll have to clean the windows first thing*, she thought, but remembered that she probably wouldn't be living here with Zelig. How could she face going back to the dormitory? If they didn't consummate the marriage, was she actually Zelig's wife?

She'd tell Zelig that she would accept a get if that's what he wanted. Minnie had a very rudimentary knowledge of how Jewish divorces worked, since nobody in Chalupanich had ever gotten one. There were some terrible marriages in her village, but none of the families had the luxury of divorce, especially after having children. Where would a woman go without the protection of a man? She knew that the man offered the divorce, and it was the woman's role to accept the get. Somehow the *Bais Din*, the religious court, was involved, but she wasn't sure of the details. Was there a Bais Din on Long Island? Maybe the rabbi would know. She heard of women whose husbands left without offering them a get and those poor souls were *aguna*, never allowed to marry again. Minnie was sure Zelig would never do that to her; he was too honorable.

She could hear Zelig in the kitchen and imagined him attempting to light the stove for some extra warmth. Minnie reluctantly got out of bed, threw on a shawl, and pattered with bare feet into the kitchen to face Zelig.

She sat down in the hard, wooden chair across from Zelig. At first they didn't speak, but she took in his haggard face with deep circles under his eyes. At last she said, "I'll get the quilt for you—you must be freezing."

"Don't bother. I'll be getting dressed and going out soon." More silence.

"Zelig, I beg you not to tell anyone what happened last night."

Zelig looked into her large, hazel eyes, searching them for answers.

"Minnie, tell me what's wrong."

"Please don't look at me. I have to tell you, but I can't look at your face right now."

Turning away from him, she struggled to speak. "You always asked me why I left the family to work like a slave in the potato fields when I could have married a local boy and remained in Russia. It tore me apart to leave, but I was forced to go."

She fell silent for another moment, and then continued.

"When I was seventeen, there was a drought in my village; all the crops died. Mendel, one of the villagers, got me a job with his cousins in Minsk. I worked as a maid for a rich Jewish family there. They had a son."

There was a long pause before Minnie was able to go on, speaking

49

in a low, cracked voice. "I never encouraged the son, but he thought he could do what he liked to a poor servant girl. One night during *Peysekh* he came into my room and forced me."

Minnie began to weep soundlessly.

"Right after it happened, he was sent back to yeshiva. His parents suspected, but I don't think they really knew. I learned it wasn't the first time he'd taken advantage of a maid from the country. As soon as he left, they sent me back to Chalupanich. We made up lies about why I was dismissed, saying that I had diphtheria and came home to recover. But Madame Ostrovsky told Mendel that I made advances to her son. His wife was the village gossip and told every Jew in the village the story. You know what these *shtetls* are like. We were afraid the Cossacks would hear and burn down the farm with us on it. The family thought of sending me to a neighboring village—we have family there—but decided the best thing would be for me to leave the country. If I stayed, my sister Frima would have no chance of making a suitable marriage, and I could never find a husband. My cousin Dina managed to get a work visa with the help of the farm. I'll always be grateful to her—she gave up her chance to leave Russia for me. I took her place."

There was a long silence again. Finally Zelig got up, put on his coat, and prepared to leave the house.

"Zelig, please say something to me. I'll do whatever you want."

At first Zelig was stunned, and then became agitated and furious with Minnie. She had lied throughout their courtship. While he unburdened himself to her, she was harboring this terrible secret and never would have told him if she hadn't been forced to. It wasn't just her lies that made him feel wretched. Zelig couldn't stand the idea of someone else invading Minnie's body. She always passed herself off as a proper girl, not like those loose women in the dormitories. She was soiled and had presented herself to him during those months of courtship as the innocent virgin. Maybe he *should* get out of the marriage. After all, who knows how many more lies she had told him or what else she'd withheld from him?

"I need to be alone to think, Minnie. I'll be back later."

Zelig ran into Sean on his aimless walk around the grounds of the farm. "So, sonny boy, you look like yah have a twinkle in yer eye. Now here's a happy bridegroom. Is she jumpin' all over yah dat you had to git out for a breath uh fresh air?"

Zelig managed a wan smile and dissembled, "I need to voik duh office."

"Now isn't that just like a boss to drag yah in the day after yer weddin'. He should be ashamed of hisself."

Sean gave Zelig a wink and said, "Hurry back to the pretty missus. You don't have much time; we have work tomorrow."

Zelig walked some more, trying to clear his head. The gray drizzle turned into a drenching rain, and he ran back to the shabby little house with soaked feet and shoes encrusted with mud.

When he opened the door, he found Minnie cleaning furiously.

"What on earth are you doing, Minnie?"

"I couldn't sit still; I had to do something."

Zelig strode purposefully into the bedroom, opening and banging shut the flimsy dresser drawers. He finally found dry socks, and his fingers touched the letters sent by Gittel right after his parents' death.

Zelig sat on the bed and reread the letters, remembering how important Minnie had been in keeping him from going crazy. How could he be so mean to her? A beast attacked her without any provocation, and he was sulking like a child because she was "spoiled." Who was he to think badly of her after that incident with the Irish whore behind the dormitories? Minnie had been forced, and he'd chosen to *shtup* the shiksa. He recalled how good Minnie had been to him when his parents died and all those wonderful Sunday mornings, talking about their lives before coming to America. He was teaching her to read and write. How smart she was, efficient and quick to pick up anything she needed to learn. Zelig remembered how beautiful and hopeful she looked under the chupah. In some ways she was still a child, trying to overcome her dreadful past. He would overlook the lies. Minnie was always quiet and reticent, but he certainly could understand why she didn't tell him the truth. Would he have acted differently in her place?

Zelig walked into the kitchen where Minnie was scrubbing the cabinets.

"Sit down, Minnie darling, we have to talk."

When Minnie heard him call her "darling," she collapsed with relief in the wooden chair.

"We'll just go very slowly. I'll be as gentle as possible with you, and we'll find ways to show love toward each other. What law says we have to make love immediately? I'm willing to give you all the time you need to be comfortable with me. After all, we're best friends as well as husband and wife. Minnie, I don't want to dissolve the marriage—I really need you. We can make a good life together; it'll just take a little more time."

She began to cry.

"I'm so ashamed, Zelig. I just couldn't tell you what happened. What if you lost all respect for me? I promise to be a good wife to you if you'll be patient with me."

"Minnie, you must promise that from now on you won't lie to me. We're one now, and we have to trust each other."

Minnie lowered her eyes and whispered, "I'll try."

"No, Minnie, I need to know that you won't lie to me again. I can't bear it. Look at me and tell me you'll always be truthful with me."

Minnie looked into Zelig's eyes and said, "I promise."

* * *

They held hands across the kitchen table for a while. Finally Minnie got up from the chair.

"I'll make supper for us. Just think, this will be the first meal I'm making as your wife in our own kitchen. I hope you like my cooking."

This was one area that Minnie was confident about. Mama taught her all the domestic skills, and as the eldest daughter, she had taken over much of the cooking and baking. Everybody in the family loved her challahs and *rugelach*, and nobody could make a kugel the way she could, not even Mama.

After dinner, Zelig helped Minnie wash the dishes and they began putting away the pots, pans, dishes, and utensils into the cupboards. The specter of last night slipped away as they busily tended to setting up the kitchen of their new home.

They delayed going to bed until they could no longer keep their eyes open.

"Minnie, we have a long work day ahead of us. Let's retire early."

When they got under the quilt, Zelig held Minnie in his arms, stroked her hair, and sang a lullaby to her from the old country.

Ofen pripenchik se brent ah fieral en duh schteebahs heis, und de Rebbele und kleiner kindelah dem aleph bais . . .

7

Marital Problems

I'*ve been tired and irritable all day. The cramps and headache just began and I know the bleeding will follow very soon. I'm relieved. It will give me over a two-week reprieve until my ritual bath when we have to start again.*

I'm trying to be a good wife to Zelig, and he's gentle and kind with me. It's just not working. When we go to bed, things start out fine. I enjoy the hugs, and when he fondles and kisses my breasts, it arouses me. I even like when he caresses my stomach and thighs, but then he places his hand there, *and I can feel all my muscles stiffen. I hate when he lies on top of me, as if I were a horse and he the rider. Zelig tries to be considerate. He doesn't pin me down, resting on his elbows, but I feel his heat and weight below, trying to push inside of me. I squeeze my eyes shut, willing myself not to faint, commanding my muscles to relax, but it's no good.*

He smells like Zelig, always washing up before and using a store-bought soap . . . Heaven knows how much he paid for it . . . not to remind me . . . but when he starts to sweat and pant, his knee forcing my legs apart and his thing starting to push inside of me, I panic. My heart starts racing and it takes every bit of will not to cry out.

I know I'm a terrible disappointment to him and wonder if he compares me to Leeba. Not that he ever said a word about that part of their lives together. How pathetic to feel jealous of a dead girl.

Last week something strange happened. When Zelig felt me tense up, he rolled over and pulled me on top of him, holding me against him and spilling his seed on my stomach. It was sticky white stuff that smells like bleach. Since then he's been doing the same thing; relieving himself against my stomach or thigh. I think it's a sin. Doesn't the Bible say that a man's seed is God's precious gift to make babies?

I admit I don't feel frightened when he holds me on top of him, but this isn't right either. He's never fully entered me or spilled himself inside of me, and we've been together over two months.

I wish I had someone to talk to. Dina or Raisa would be able to advise me, even if they aren't married. They're both wiser in the ways of men and women than I am. I certainly can't talk to those brazen girls in the dormitory, and Rivka has even less experience than I do. She's been so sweet to me, helping me with bathing to cleanse myself for Zelig after my bleeding stops. I invite her for a Shabbat meal every Friday, and I know it helps her overcome her homesickness, but I can't really say anything to her about the men-and-women business.

I want my Mama. She'd know what to do.

Zelig is the kindest, most considerate husband possible, and I'm afraid I'll lose him. We'll have to speak about this before my next ritual bath. I hope I can get up the nerve.

We never talk of children, except when he told me about the stillborn child. Does he even want children with me? Maybe he's so dissatisfied that he really is thinking about a divorce. That's why he won't spill his seed inside of me. I want Zelig's child. I long to cradle a baby in my arms and feed it from my breasts.

* * *

She doesn't wear her pretty nightgowns anymore or let her hair hang loose. When she gets into bed with the shapeless flannel gown and hair in a tight bun, she reminds me of an old spinster. The gown even smells musty, as if it's been lying at the bottom of her trunk without ever being washed. When I ask her, "Minnie, why don't you wear the silk gowns I bought you?" she tells me it's too cold for silk nightclothes. This week she started wearing heavy hose to bed. Minnie's so young, but I feel like I'm climbing into bed with my great-aunt. When the summer comes, I'm going to burn those rags!

If only Moishe were alive. I need a good friend to confide in. I can imagine what Sean would say if I ever confided my problems to him. "What's the matter, Sonny Boy, over thirty years old, married two times already, and you don't know how to make a woman happy? What's that you say? Your thing won't stay up? Maybe you should swallow an iron rod; it might land in the right place." How long would it take for that news to travel all over Suffolk County?

I've been thinking about approaching the rebbe, but he's all ritual and mealy-mouthed sanctimonious talk. "It's better to spill your seed in the body of a whore than cast it on the ground. Trust Hashem, my son; he'll guide you." What does he know about sex? He was never married, and he acts like a prissy old lady.

Once I get through the flannel suit of armor and wool hose, her skin is so white and delicate, like the finest French porcelain. I know she enjoys my touch as long as I caress her gently. Minnie has pink rosebud nipples that harden into tiny red mounds when I lick and kiss them. I feel her body heat and listen as her breathing deepens, and I'm encouraged. It's all fine above the waist, but as soon as I become erect, the thin porcelain teacup develops cracks and threatens to shatter into pieces.

I try to remain the gentleman, propping my full weight off her body with my elbows, but then the pleasure is gone and I go limp. I've taken to closing my eyes and pretending that I'm with one of those buxom colleens with their rounded behinds straining against their skirts when they're bending in the fields. Sometimes images of Leeba flash across my closed eyelids, but I push them away. Thoughts of the colleens are enough to restore my hardness until I try to penetrate Minnie. It feels more like trying to drive a nail into hard, resistant wood than making love to a wife.

I know she was terrorized by that beast; may he die young and rot in hell. Heaven knows I try not to remind her of him, but I don't know what else I can do. Last week, when I felt her tensing up, I rolled her on top of me. She seemed less frightened, but I couldn't maintain the hardness that way. She was so small and dry at the opening. I finally stopped trying and released myself by rubbing against her stomach.

She's been nervous and irritable all evening. It's her time of the month, so I won't say anything to her when she's so uncomfortable. We'll talk before she has her next ritual bath. Anyway, it's a relief not to have to keep trying for a while. It's only been two months. Maybe with more time . . .

8

Marital Advice

Zelig was hacking furiously in the office when Monaghan walked in. "I don't like the sound of that cough, Sonny Boy."

"It's just uh cold, Mr. Monaghan, I be better soon."

"Jaysus, I don't want you gettin' sick on me. On Friday, the doctor's comin' to check me blood pressure. I want him to have a look at yah."

"By Friday, I be all better, Mr. Monaghan."

"Now, if you get pneumonia, what good are yah to me? Don't argue, Zelig, I want Zablonsky to look at you. I only use Jew doctors; they're supposed to be the best."

By Friday, Zelig had developed a fever and the cough persisted. Monaghan insisted that the doctor take a look at him. "Don't be a fool, Zelig; the doc's comin' anyhow. He won't bite yah."

Dr. Zablonsky finished with Monaghan and called Zelig into the boss's office for a checkup. He did the usual things, checking his heart, thumping his back, carefully listening to the sounds in his chest. He took out a large apparatus with a disc on the end and listened intently with a device that went in his ear.

"Your chest is clear, but you'll need bed rest for a few days. What concerns me more is that your heart rate is irregular and too fast. Do your parents have heart trouble?"

Zelig asked him to repeat what he said in Yiddish, and Dr. Zablonsky complied.

"I don't know about my heart. Sometimes I feel it racing, especially at night. The only time it was ever checked was at Ellis Island, and it was probably okay, otherwise they wouldn't have let me into the country. I don't know about my parents; they died from the flu."

Dr. Zablonsky listened to Zelig's heart and felt his pulse again. "It's still too fast, but it sounds more regular than before." The doctor had compassionate eyes, and he wasn't much older than Zelig.

"Let's sit and talk for a few minutes. It's good to speak to a landsman. I don't have much chance to speak Yiddish these days."

They settled themselves in two chairs facing one another.

"Tell me, how are things going at the job?"

"Good. Mr. Monaghan is very kind to me and my wife. He even lets us live separate from the others."

"How long are you married?"

"A little over two months."

"Was the marriage arranged, or did you meet at the farm?"

"Minnie and I met here."

The doctor kept questioning him about the new marriage, and as he did, Zelig began to shift uncomfortably in the chair, becoming noticeably agitated.

"Is something wrong between you and your wife?" Zelig hesitated. "Don't worry, anything you say to me will never leave this room. We're two Jews in a foreign land. Goyim don't need to know anything we talk about."

The words began to rush out. How after two months they still hadn't consummated the marriage and how frightened Minnie was of sex. "I don't have that much experience in the bedroom, but I was married before and nothing like this ever happened."

He told Dr. Zablonsky how he couldn't penetrate Minnie because of her dryness, and how she resisted when he tried to get on top of her. "When she becomes so frightened, I lose all my desire and go limp." Zelig explained that Minnie was responsive to gentle caresses above her waist, but no more. However, he was too embarrassed to tell the doctor about ejaculating on her stomach.

"Was your wife ever frightened or attacked by another man?"

How on earth did he know?

Zelig couldn't bring himself to divulge Minnie's shameful secret.

"I don't know anything about that."

Dr. Zablonsky asked him if he knew what a clitoris was, but Zelig was completely at a loss. The doctor drew a diagram of a woman's genitalia, and where this tiny pleasure organ was in relation to the rest of the vagina.

"What is that?"

"It's to give a woman pleasure and excite her. If you use firm, continuous, and gentle pressure with one finger, it becomes like a hard button. You'll know when you find it by your wife's response. Stroke her gently with the other hand, and whisper love words to her. I'm willing to bet she'll be ready to take you inside of her."

The doctor reached inside his bag and pulled out a tube of ointment. "This is for you to use on your penis to make entry easier, or you can put some around your wife's opening if she's still not wet enough."

"What is it?"

"Petroleum jelly. It's very safe. You'll have it even if you don't need it."

Zelig couldn't believe how relieved he was to talk to another man about his intimate problems. He didn't feel that he was betraying Minnie because, after all, this man was a doctor—better than the rabbi, who had all the religious answers but no practical advice. Not even Moishe could have given him such information, and he blessed his cough, which brought Dr. Zablonsky into his life.

When the doctor was packing up his medical bag, Zelig finally confessed his fear of impregnating Minnie. He told Dr. Zablonsky about Leeba and his dread of Minnie dying while trying to deliver his child.

"Is she sick or very frail?"

"No, but she's small, and her hips don't look wide enough for childbearing."

"Small women can have healthy babies easily without any harm to themselves. Was your first wife a tiny woman?"

"No, Leeba was rounded and robust."

"But she died in childbirth. In Russia, poor Jews could never afford good medical care. You're in America now. If you and your wife want children, the boss will make sure she's in good hands. Monaghan wants to keep you happy. I'm more concerned with getting down your fever and heart rate. I'll check you again next week when I visit your boss."

At this point, Monaghan walked into the office without knocking. "How's the boy, Doc? What magic potion yah givin' him to make him better?"

Dr. Zablonsky's face had a serious, concerned demeanor. "I gave Zelig some cough medicine and something for the fever. He'll need at least five days to rest and someone to take care of him. Is it possible for his wife to take some time from work to make sure he's properly cared for?"

"Doc, I need Zelig in the office. How can I let him have a lie-about when there's so much work tah do? And Minnie too?"

"Would you rather that he got pneumonia? Then he won't be able to work for weeks."

Monaghan weighed the options and grudgingly conceded. "All right, he and Minnie can take three days."

* * *

Zelig went home elated after work, feeling more energized than he had in a long time. He entered the little house whistling, in spite of his illness and the long, arduous day trying to make sure nothing went wrong at the office.

Now was the time for their promised talk. Her monthly bleeding was over, and she had gone to the makeshift mikva.

Minnie was ritually clean and ready to resume lovemaking.

"You're in a good mood today. I never heard you whistle before. Was it something good that happened at work?"

"In a way yes; in a way no."

"How was the office today?"

"It becomes like a madhouse around the payment periods. At least that's over. I should be exhausted, but I'm not." He smiled at Minnie. "Do we have anything for dinner? I really don't want much; I'd like us to retire early."

"I have leftover soup, or I could make you some eggs."

"Soup and some bread will be fine."

"What happened with the doctor? Did he give you any medicine?"

"That doctor is an angel. He actually persuaded Monaghan to give both of us a few days off now that the busy period is over. It comes at a wonderful time, doesn't it? Can you imagine Minnie, we'll have three days together with nothing to do but please each other."

Minnie blushed, and Zelig could see the worry lines etched on her forehead. He didn't tell Minnie about the other conversation with the good doctor, but he couldn't wait to try out Zablonsky's advice.

Being sick, Zelig had a good pretext to get to bed early, but it seemed forever for Minnie to get ready. She put on one of her silk nightgowns like Zelig had asked, but her hair was still tied up in a bun at the back of her neck. He began by kissing her there and then traveled down to her breasts and stomach. As he became passionate, Zelig reminded himself to go slowly with her. After at least half an hour of kissing and stroking, he rested his hand gently on her vagina, all the while stroking her thigh with his other hand. When she became responsive, he dared to slip one finger in the triangle with its soft, curly hair and found his mark. At first Minnie tried to pull away. Zelig gently persisted, all the while stroking her thigh and whispering in her ear. "Mamala, don't be afraid; I love you." She began to enjoy his touch, and as he circled her clitoris, the pleasure became more and more intense until Minnie experienced electric sensations like she never felt in her life. It was as if bolts of lightning were expanding to all her limbs, radiating from her sex. It lasted only a few seconds, but the feeling was so strong that it seemed to be jolting through her body interminably, pulsating rhythmically in her vagina and anus. She was sighing and clinging to Zelig when she felt him turn and push her on top. The quilt toppled to the floor.

Zelig was very excited by Minnie's response. He quickly coated his penis with the ointment, clutched her buttocks and entered her, thrusting his fully erect penis until he felt an enormous explosion. It happened so quickly, but the intense release of all his stored juices made time stop. He lay there, spent and gasping, murmuring unintelligible love words in the curve of her neck.

"Zelig, what did you talk about with Dr. Zablonsky?"

"I told him we were having some trouble with the husband/wife business. He gave me some suggestions about how to please you."

"You didn't tell him about Minsk, did you? I would die of shame!"

"Of course not. I would never do anything to shame you."

He suddenly felt an unpleasant change of pressure and temperature. A cold breeze chilled his coated penis, and Minnie was gone. She rolled off him quickly, placed a pillow under her buttocks, and propped her feet up on the wall.

"What in God's name are you doing? Come next to me and let me hold you for awhile."

Minnie shook her head. "I don't want to let anything come out."

"What are you talking about?"

"Don't you want a child, Zelig?"

"Of course I want children, but why are you in that ridiculous position?"

"To hold in your seed. Imagine if I became pregnant tonight? Wouldn't that be wonderful?"

"Don't worry, darling; we have three whole days to try."

* * *

Minnie woke with a start the next morning, worried she'd be late for work but then remembered that she and Zelig actually had the next few days off. She reached across the bed for him but heard him whistling in the kitchen and called to him.

"Stay in bed awhile. I'll make us some tea."

"Zelig, you're the one with the cough. I should be making you breakfast."

"Rest awhile, Mamala. I'm wide awake."

Minnie sank back on the pillows and began to think about last night. She could still feel wetness on the sheets and smell Zelig's soap and lotion scent along with a faint sperm odor. When she thought about those acute sensations, Minnie began to blush and grow warm under the heavy quilt. Was it normal to feel such a thing? Where did Zelig learn that? Although it was wonderful, Minnie felt out of control of her body, as if the sensations were overwhelming her. She still didn't like Zelig penetrating her, but at least she wasn't afraid any longer, as long as he didn't press down into her.

Minnie put on a robe and slippers and pattered into the kitchen. Zelig's back was to her as he tried to work the stove. She slipped her arms around his waist and rested her head on his shoulder.

"Zelig, how did you know to do that?"

"What, Minnie?"

"You know, touching me there. I never felt anything like it. Did you ever do that before?"

Then she mumbled something into his shoulder. "What did you say?"

"Did you ever do that with Leeba?"

Zelig extricated himself from her and turned to look at Minnie.

"What happened in my first marriage is done, Minnie. Let Leeba rest in peace; there's no reason for you to be jealous. Actually, it was Monaghan's doctor who told me."

Minnie imagined Zelig and a strange doctor talking about her as if she were a clinical specimen. "Zelig, I'm so embarrassed. If I ever meet him, how can I ever look that man in the eye? It's as if he was looking up my skirts with you."

"Wouldn't he be doing that if he delivered our baby? Minnie, he's a *doctor*, not some shlemiel on the farm. You're too sensitive, darling. I could tell you liked it." He gave her a coy smile.

The next night Minnie wore Zelig's favorite silk nightgown and opened the bottle of cologne that he had bought for her months before. Best of all, she released the tightly coiled bun and her hair cascaded down her back in waves.

"Zelig, would you like to brush my hair?"

Minnie Is Pregnant

Over the next several weeks, Minnie and Zelig settled into a pattern of lovemaking. Zelig was a considerate lover, making sure that Minnie got satisfaction as well. It was enjoyable enough, but Zelig would have preferred more variety, particularly the pleasure of moving freely as he had done with Leeba and not worrying about Minnie turning into a resistant block of ice beneath him. But he was willing to be patient.

She didn't say anything about her first missed bleeding to Zelig, although she was sure he knew. The rags she scrupulously washed for that purpose didn't appear on the makeshift clothesline. By her second missed period, Minnie was certain. She recalled the sensation of fullness and sensitivity in her breasts, her pink nipples began to darken and enlarge, and her almost concave belly swelled ever so slightly. Food smells began to nauseate her, particularly strong ones like herring and mutton. She began to gag and vomit at the most inopportune times. The smells wafting in from the fields would set her off, particularly the manure used as fertilizer. After she emptied her stomach, however, Minnie became ravenous, stuffing herself with bland pieces of bread. She searched the company store for any kind of soda crackers, which seemed to settle her stomach. Minnie was exhausted most of the time, dragging herself out of bed in the morning and falling asleep over supper.

Her nights were the most difficult, with snatches of dark dreams from which she awoke with a start. Minnie found herself wandering about in the kitchen during the night, not wanting to disturb Zelig with her restless tossing and turning. He told her she often moaned and talked in her sleep.

"What do I say?"

"I don't know, mostly just words I can't make out. You've done that ever since we're married but a lot more lately. Minnie, don't get out of bed at night. I'm usually a sound sleeper, and you won't disturb me."

She had been praying to God for a child from the first time they'd been together, but now that it was a reality, why wasn't she happier? Hashem was giving her another chance; why couldn't she rejoice?

She sat down with Zelig in the kitchen after dinner.

"Zelig, it's happened. I know we're being blessed with a child. Two times I missed already."

"Mamala, I know. I was waiting for you to tell me. Why did you wait so long?"

Minnie turned pale and stammered, "I just wanted to make sure it was true. I was afraid to raise both our hopes. Sometimes I've missed a month of bleeding in the past."

"Next time Dr. Zablonsky comes to see Monaghan, he has to examine you. We'll make sure you get the best medical care in Suffolk; no midwives for this baby!"

"Zelig, I don't have to see the doctor. I know I'm expecting. What else is he going to tell me?"

"Please, Minnie, let him examine you. I worry that you're very narrow and we want to make sure things are right with you and the baby. Don't argue with me about this. I promise to be right by your side when he examines you. It's a first baby; anything can happen. Besides, he can tell you the right foods to eat to make the baby strong."

"I can hardly hold any food down. Please stop worrying; I really don't think it's necessary to see the doctor now. Why can't we wait until I feel life? By then I'll start showing and it'll be time to tell everyone that I'm expecting. I'll wait to write home to the family until then."

"Minnie, he's coming this Friday. Please don't be stubborn; I want him to look at you. Besides, I don't want you to work as hard as you do. I'll ask Monaghan to shorten your hours, even if it takes longer to fulfill the contract. And you can't work in the fields anymore."

"If it's a good pregnancy, I can work at anything. You know the boss only calls me into the fields when they're shorthanded. Look at Bridget and Tessie. They dug potatoes to the day they gave birth, and they both had big, healthy babies. There wasn't even a midwife to help them. Those babies popped out in a few hours, and the girls in the fields cut the cords."

But Zelig was adamant, so he spoke to Monaghan. After the doctor set a worker's broken hand and took care of routine examinations, it was Minnie's turn.

She and Zelig entered the makeshift examining room in the office. Minnie's eyes remained downcast, and Zelig did all the talking.

"Minnie's missed two periods, and we're positive she is pregnant. We want to make sure everything is going right. Is it okay if I stay here during the examination, Dr. Zablonsky? This is very embarrassing for her."

The doctor spoke kindly to Minnie. "I know this isn't the way it was done in the old country, but I've delivered over a hundred babies and haven't lost one yet. I'll be very gentle, and we can talk after the examination."

The doctor asked Minnie to step into Monaghan's office and remove her undergarments. Then he asked Zelig to help Minnie up to the table covered by paper sheeting. After she hoisted up her skirt and petticoats, Dr. Zablonsky placed a large blanket over her legs and stomach. Minnie squeezed Zelig's hand, pressing her fingernails into his flesh until the examination was complete.

"Well, everything looks like it's progressing normally. Minnie, put on your underclothes and we can talk. Zelig, can you step out for a moment? Your wife needs a little privacy, and I want to advise her about what to expect."

After Minnie dressed behind a small screen, she reluctantly faced Dr. Zablonsky.

Dr. Zablonsky coughed and rustled some papers.

"You know, Minnie, a doctor and patient's words are confidential unless it's a matter of life and death. I want you to know that everything I talk to you or Zelig about will never go further. Just listen for a moment and look at me."

Minnie eyed him distrustfully.

"Is there anything you'd like to tell me?"

Minnie shook her head. She sat there with lowered eyes and a stony look on her face. She knew she shouldn't have let Zelig convince her to see this doctor. At home she would see a midwife only when she was about to deliver the baby, surrounded by her close female relatives.

She whispered, "There's nothing to say."

"Alright, Minnie, we'll take it from here and keep you and this baby in good health. You should be eating lots of meat and vegetables, now that you're eating for two. I'd like to check you whenever I come to the farm."

How strangely things were done in America. Minnie felt so out of place.

* * *

Minnie reached her third month when it happened. She felt terrible pains in her back and gripping cramps in her stomach, much more severe than the pain and discomfort she felt on the first day of her bleeding. She woke in the middle of the night, frantic when she felt terrible drawing sensations in her abdomen and pelvis. Minnie shook Zelig and screamed, "The baby!" Then the bleeding began. Gushing blood and huge liver-colored clots emerged from her, along with rhythmic pushing sensations. The baby was being expelled from her body, and she foolishly tried to hold back the blood and clots by lying in a prone position, cramming rags into her vagina.

Zelig was frantic, not knowing what to do. Finally he said, "Minnie, you have to let it go. Let's go to the privy and let everything out." He half-dragged her out of the bed and placed her in a seated position on the rickety toilet. When she finally expelled everything, Zelig carried her back to bed, both of them sobbing.

"We'll ask Monaghan to call in the doctor tomorrow. He has to make sure you don't get any infections." Zelig didn't know much about women's problems, that always being the domain of the female family members and the midwife. He only knew he wanted the doctor to heal her.

Minnie screamed at him. "I don't want to see that *farshtunkena* doctor! For all I know he caused this by poking around in me. I told you I didn't need that examination—it's probably his fault."

"It can't be, Minnie, he examined you weeks ago."

The next day, when Minnie's bleeding finally stopped, she reluctantly consented to be examined by Dr. Zablonsky again.

"You had an early miscarriage. It's not unusual, and it doesn't mean that you won't have other healthy children. Sometimes it's God's way of telling us that there was something wrong with the baby. It could have been damaged or wouldn't have survived to delivery. Better early than late."

The women at the farm had suspected that Minnie was pregnant—they knew all the symptoms. After the miscarriage, she confided in Rivka, who was her closest friend in Suffolk, almost like a sister. She told Maureen as well, and word spread quickly. The other girls tried to comfort her as best they could. Bridget confessed that she lost her first: "But now look at this little man—healthy as they come and the apple of his father's eye." Minnie heard consolation stories from all sides, but it didn't lessen her grief. She knew this was her punishment; things had been too good for her.

She sank into a depression, refusing to eat, and had very little energy to do anything. Zelig was beside himself with worry, but thankful Minnie had survived even if the child hadn't.

"Darling, we'll have others. Remember what the doctor and all the girls told you? It sometimes happens with the first. We'll wait until you feel better, and we can try again—of course, not until you feel ready."

* * *

After the miscarriage it took more than six months for Minnie and Zelig to resume marital intimacy.

Minnie barely managed to drag herself to work, and when she returned to the little house behind the workers' quarters, she would flop on the bed and remain immobile for hours.

Zelig took it upon himself to do the housework and prepare the nightly suppers, but Minnie would hardly eat anything.

"Please, Mamala, just a little soup. You're falling away to skin and bones. You can't live without nourishment."

He insisted that she see Dr. Zablonsky, pulling him aside on his next visit to the farm to examine Monaghan.

"Can I speak to you in private, doctor?"

Zablonsky ushered Zelig into the boss's office.

"I'm worried about Minnie," Zelig began. "She isn't eating and hardly talks to anyone, even me. She was never much of a talker, but now she acts like a ghost. She only goes to work and Friday night services. In the middle of the night she's in the kitchen with the oil lamp lit, reciting from the prayer book—you know, I taught her how to read the prayers. It seems to be her only comfort. What's wrong with her, Doctor? Is she losing her mind?"

"Be patient, Zelig. Women react differently to the loss of a child. Give her some time. In the meantime, I'll give her a tonic to help restore her appetite. Have Minnie take a spoonful twice a day; hopefully we'll see a change in a few weeks."

Minnie didn't protest when Dr. Zablonsky examined her, but she didn't seem to want to hear his assurances that she would start feeling like her old self very soon.

She sat up on the table and stared at him.

"Tell me the truth. Can I carry a baby or will this happen again?" Her voice was surprisingly strong and direct.

"If you don't start eating, your monthly bleeding will never come regularly. You won't have the strength to hold a pregnancy. Don't ruin your health, Minnie; you can have lots of babies if you keep yourself strong."

71

From that day Minnie began to recover. She dutifully swallowed the tonic and resumed her household chores. Her appetite improved, and she had renewed energy.

The first time she initiated a conversation, Zelig was startled and delighted.

"So how was the office today? Is Mr. Monaghan driving you crazy with the end-of-the-month billing? I'm having a hard time just keeping up with all the filing. I need to make up a better filing system. If you have time, can you help me?"

Zelig didn't answer, but he wrapped his arms around her waist and rocked her gently. Minnie allowed him to hold her but didn't return his embrace.

That night Zelig bridged the invisible divide in the middle of their bed and began stroking her lank hair. He sang songs to her from the old country, just as he had done from the very first night of their marriage. She nestled her head in the crook of his arm and began to hum along.

It was the first night that she remained in bed without lighting the kitchen oil lamp and opening her prayer book.

Her monthly bleeding began to come regularly. After three months, she asked Rivka to help her with a ritual bath.

10

Trying Again

Gone were the lace nightgowns and Minnie's soft, loose hair brushing Zelig's bare chest. Gone were the nights of lying together, limbs entwined, whispering and caressing. Their lovemaking became urgent and purposeful, with the single intention of impregnating her.

At first Zelig was surprised and delighted when Minnie suggested that he mount her.

"Minnala, I thought it made you afraid. I'm happy to go on the way we were before . . ."

"No, I want to make sure we're doing it right. I heard that if any seed comes out, the baby might not be right."

"Who told you that *bubbe meiser*? One of the Irish girls, I'll bet. Was it Bridget or Maureen? They don't even know how to read, and they're giving you scientific advice!"

When Zelig took the superior position, he could feel the old tension emanating from Minnie's body even as she clutched his hips and buttocks against her. They went through the motions, with Minnie passionless below him. Zelig's thoughts strayed once again to the rounded, buxom colleens, allowing him to ejaculate quickly.

Minnie immediately pushed him off and propped her feet against the wall, pillows elevating her buttocks.

"Stop being ridiculous! Soon you'll be standing on your head. Come next to me and let me hold you."

"Zelig, now is the right time. I don't want anything to go wrong."

"Didn't you get pregnant the way we were doing it, and in just a couple of months?"

"Yes, and you see what happened."

Zelig stormed out of bed, put on his nightshirt, and stood over Minnie. "You know, you make me feel like a coal delivery system. Just open the chute and pour it in. Why are you making it so hard for us? It says in the scriptures that making love joyfully is a mitzvah. It's a husband's duty to satisfy his wife."

Minnie didn't change her position, and she gave an exasperated sigh.

"Let's not fight over this, Zelig. This is my fertile time. Don't you want a son?"

"Of course I do, but it doesn't mean that our lovemaking has to be so . . . grim. It's like taking medicine for a bad cold."

Minnie didn't respond. Zelig put on his slippers and paced in the kitchen, reflecting on the irony of their changed sex life. He had finally gotten his wish, but now he longed to return to their old lovemaking patterns.

After several months Minnie hadn't yet conceived.

"Maybe it's too soon after the miscarriage."

"Minnie, it's been well over six months. I think it's not working because we're trying too hard."

* * *

The next month after Minnie's ritual bath, Zelig had a plan. He surprised her with flowers and delicacies from the company store. He lit candles, even though it wasn't Shabbat, and strategically placed a bottle of schnapps on the table next to the extravagant crystal goblets he had purchased.

"Zelig, what is this? You know I don't drink schnapps."

"This one is sweet; you'll like it. Dr. Zablonsky says it's good for the digestion and relaxing. Just take a little."

Minnie munched on the fancy cheese and crackers, sniffed the flowers, and took a sip of the schnapps. "It is good. I thought it would burn going down, but it's sweet and smooth." As Zelig kept refilling her glass, she became giggly and coquettish.

"Mamala, let's not waste the evening. Put on the blue silk gown I like."

Minnie was staggering by then, so Zelig carried her into the bedroom, foregoing the silk nightgown. He helped her undress, stripped off his clothing, and maneuvered her under the quilt.

Minnie giggled. "We left the dirty dishes. We'll get mice."

"Let the mice enjoy themselves. We have more important things to do."

That night there was no propping of feet on the wall. Zelig fulfilled his biblical obligation to please his wife with renewed passion and intensity. Minnie's inhibitions were obliterated by the schnapps. It was by far the best sex they'd ever had in their short married life.

Minnie woke with a pounding headache the next morning. She hardly remembered the night before, but Zelig kept teasing her about the schnapps.

"Minnie, I'm going to turn you into a *shikker*. You were wonderful last night! I'm going to keep a bottle of schnapps on our bed stand from now on!"

"Zelig, be serious. We have to get to work, and look at that kitchen. Oh, I need a bromide for my headache. How am I going to concentrate?"

He gave her a pinch on the cheek, a pat on the rear end, and he went off to the office whistling.

* * *

After what became known as "the night of the schnapps," Minnie missed her next two periods. They told no one but rejoiced together in secret and prayed to the Lord.

Hashem, we beg you. Let this one live. Let it be healthy. We don't care if it's a boy or girl; just let it live.

Minnie began experiencing the symptoms of pregnancy—the nausea and fatigue, but not as pronounced as the previous time. They waited until after the third month to ask Monaghan for an appointment with Dr. Zablonsky under the guise of "women's problems."

Dr. Zablonsky examined Minnie in Monaghan's office the following week.

"When was the last time you had a period?"

"This is the third time I skipped my bleeding."

"Have you had any staining or unusual cramps?"

"Nothing."

Zablonsky beamed at her. "Well, you're definitely pregnant, and everything seems very normal. You're past the time it happened." The doctor couldn't bring himself to say the word "miscarriage" to Minnie.

He called Zelig in from the outer office.

"Mazel tov! Everything is fine with Minnie. I would just recommend a little more caution with this pregnancy."

"What do you mean, Doctor?"

"Well, I wouldn't want her doing any heavy lifting, just in case. Do you work in the fields, Minnie?"

"I mostly work in the office, Baruch Hashem. Sometimes Mr. Monaghan calls me into the fields if they're shorthanded."

"I don't expect any problems—it looks like a very good pregnancy—but after your last experience, I hope that Monaghan will excuse you from heavy field work. Do you want me to talk to him?"

"Zelig will do it, Doctor. He's always been very good to us, treating us very special."

While Minnie dressed, Zelig caught Dr. Zablonsky in the outer office.

"I suppose this means that Minnie and I can't . . ." he said, stammering and blushing, "you know."

"You can have relations with your wife safely until two months before delivery without problems."

Zelig looked doubtfully at Zablonsky. "You said we have to be extra careful."

"I can assure you nothing will happen from having sex. Have fun, Zelig, you won't have so many chances after the baby is born!"

When Minnie and Zelig spoke that night, he told her what the doctor said about sexual relations.

"I can't believe you asked him such a question, Zelig! Am I a plaything? What's the purpose when I'm already *shvanger*? Would you jeopardize this baby for the sake of having fun?"

"Of course we won't do anything, Minnie. I'd never forgive myself if anything happened to this baby because of me. I'll have to tell Monaghan in the morning, and you can be sure it will be all over the farm by lunchtime."

Minnie laughed. "Oh, I'm sure the girls know already. I'm always running to the outhouse to throw up, and they're already teasing me about eating plain crackers."

Then she looked wistfully at Zelig. "I wish my family were here to share in this blessing. Mama and Papa's grandchild, and they're not a part of it. Do you think it's still too early to write them?"

"Let's wait until you feel the baby move. You should be showing by then, and I'll draw pictures of you and your belly to send to your parents. Imagine them seeing their little girl pregnant! Would you like that?"

Minnie turned away and scrubbed the kitchen sink.

"If it's a boy," Zelig continued excitedly, "we'll name him after my Tati, and a girl we'll name her after my Mama—Minnie, stop fussing and look at me—is that alright with you?"

Minnie gripped the sink tightly and half turned to Zelig.

"Of course, whatever you say."

11

It's A Boy

M innie had never looked better. Her small, angular body softened into rounded curves and her usually sallow complexion glowed, as if lit by starlight from within. No longer plagued by the nausea and fatigue of early pregnancy, she felt a sense of calm and well-being that had always seemed to elude her, even in her early years on the farm in Chalupanich.

By her fourth month, she felt life. One day, as she filed away papers in the office, Minnie became aware of a fluttering sensation in her stomach, as if a swarm of monarch butterflies inhabited her body. She sat down and closed her eyes, visualizing a meadow in the summer, strewn with glorious wildflowers, spotted butterflies opening and closing their wings on each bloom. Minnie couldn't wait to go home to Zelig and describe the wonderful sensation. Now she felt confident enough to write to Mama and Papa with the news. She imagined Mama's weathered, chapped face lighting up with joy as the town scribe read her Minnie's letter. It would be bittersweet, knowing that they could never see this precious bough of the family tree, but Minnie would write to them often, describing the baby's changes and development. Perhaps they could save for one of those new camera contraptions or splurge and have a photographer make films of their new family.

"What's for dinner, Minnie?" Zelig asked when she walked in.

"I have something very important to tell you!" Minnie's face radiated joy. "I couldn't wait for work to be over so I could tell you that I felt the baby move today." She described the fluttering sensation while Zelig immediately reached for her stomach. "No, it's too small yet, you won't feel anything. I wish for one moment I could trade places with you so you would have the joy of feeling our baby moving."

Zelig grabbed Minnie, sat her on his lap, and buried his face in her hair bun and babushka. Then he straightened up with a resolved look on his face.

"I'd better start making the cradle for this little one."

"Bridget offered to lend us hers for as long as we need it."

"No, Minnie, I want our baby to have the best. I'll look for a fine piece of mahogany, and I can borrow the tools from the carpenter. This cradle will be a piece of art that I make with my own hands."

"Shouldn't you ask the carpenter?"

Zelig laughed. "In the old country I built furniture and kitchens. I think I can fashion a cradle for our new baby."

Zelig bought a magnificent piece of mahogany and applied his artistic energy to making the cradle each night after work. At first Minnie objected, but she felt so good that she gave in to Zelig's reasonable arguments that the baby shouldn't have to sleep in a cramped dresser drawer or a rough pine cradle.

Rivka started to knit tiny garments for the baby; she considered this child her niece or nephew since she had no relatives in the New World.

"Please, Rivka," Minnie told her, "the wool and needles are so much money for you. I wish you would let me pay for it. Also, I'd really prefer if you wait until the child is born. I don't want anything to happen."

"What do you mean, Minnie?"

"I don't want to encourage the Evil Eye. My Mama always said you shouldn't bring any baby clothes and furniture into the house until after the birth."

Even though she felt uneasy about bringing baby things into her house, a few of the girls in the dormitory gave her clothing for the expected arrival. Despite her trepidations, Minnie placed the knitted kimonos, hats, and tiny slippers into a special drawer. Each night, while Zelig worked on the cradle, she would take them out, feel their soft texture against her cheek, and lovingly refold and replace them in the drawer.

Zelig pooh-poohed Minnie's concerns. "No more bubbe meisers and superstitions. We're modern people, Minnie. Look how well the baby is growing inside of you."

As the months passed, the fetus became very active. By the seventh month, Minnie could see the imprint of a tiny foot or hand pushing against the taut flesh of her burgeoning belly. As it grew and competed with her internal organs for more space, she could feel the child pressing up on her ribcage and down on her bladder.

"Oy, Zelig, this baby won't let me sleep. It keeps pressing down on me, and I feel like I have to *pish* all the time." Despite her complaints, no matter how exhausted she was, Minnie rejoiced in the tumultuous feeling of new life in her belly.

It was especially active at night, and Zelig loved to feel the baby's movement. He would kiss her stomach, and he never tired of placing his hands on a protruding baby hand or foot.

Dr. Zablonsky was pleased with the progress of the pregnancy. On his weekly visits to Monaghan's office, he would monitor the size and position of the baby. He allowed Zelig to listen to the baby's heartbeat with a trumpet-shaped device inserted in one ear. The wide end was placed on Minnie's abdomen. Dr. Zablonsky told Zelig that the device was called a monaural stethoscope. Zelig was amazed and thrilled to hear the rhythmic *thump-thump* of the baby's tiny heart.

The eighth month passed without incident. All the farm girls insisted that Minnie was having a boy. "Yup, it's a wee lad. It never fails when a woman carries the child all in front. If it was a lassie, you'd be thicker in the waist and behind."

Zelig took the news of the baby's alleged sex with derision and amusement.

* * *

At the beginning of the ninth month Minnie woke before dawn with pressure on her bladder. After relieving herself, she lay in bed and waited for the tumultuous movement of the baby, but there was nothing. She closed her eyes, trying to sense even the slightest motion, but felt an eerie sense of quiet in her womb. She tried without success to tamp down the panic she was beginning to feel.

When Zelig awoke, Minnie went into the kitchen to prepare their breakfast.

"You look tired, Mamala; weren't you able to rest last night?"

"I kept getting up to go to the outhouse. There's so much pressure down there."

"Are you sure you're alright?"

"I'll be fine, Zelig. Just go to work and don't worry."

Minnie went to work but nervously paced the floor. She looked out the window and spied Maureen in the fields with her new baby tied to her back. Minnie waddled outside and called to her. "Maureen, please ken I talk mit you uh minute?"

Maureen was behind in her work and looked annoyed at the intrusion until she saw Minnie's white, drawn face.

"Minnie, what's wrong, darlin'? You look like you seen a ghost."

"I'm scared, Maureen. I don't feel de baby moving inside like it should."

Maureen laughed. "I didn't feel this little devil move fer two weeks before I birthed him. He was so big; he had no place to go. And look at him now—startin' to get into trouble already. Your little one is just restin' for the big journey it's about to make."

When Zelig came home that night, Minnie told him about the lack of movement and her conversation with Maureen. They kept trying to reassure each other that nothing was wrong.

"Just to be safe, you'll see Dr. Zablonsky tomorrow when he comes for his weekly rounds. He'll tell us nothing is wrong."

The next morning, Minnie and Zelig were the first ones waiting outside Monaghan's office when the doctor came for his early morning rounds. He looked at their worried faces and ushered them inside the office.

"What's wrong, Minnie?"

"I can't feel the baby moving."

"For how long?"

"A day and a night."

"Get up on the table and we'll have a look."

Minnie struggled onto the table, fumbled to pull down her drawers, and lay perfectly still as Dr. Zablonsky listened to every area of her stomach with the trumpet-shaped stethoscope. He placed the wide end on her belly and crouched over to listen on the small end. He gave her an internal exam, all the while pressing on her distended abdomen as he tried to ascertain the baby's position. Then he carefully listened again with both the trumpet-shaped device and another object that hung from his ears that he called a binaural, or two-eared, stethoscope.

When he finally finished the examination, Minnie tried to read his facial expression, which remained neutral.

Finally, Minnie said to him in an unnaturally calm voice, "Is the baby dead? Tell me the truth."

Zelig burst into tears and turned away. Minnie stared at Dr. Zablonsky, trying to see beyond the lights glinting from his spectacles.

"I must know the truth."

The doctor helped sit her up, took her hand and said softly, "I don't hear a heartbeat, but that doesn't mean anything. The baby is probably turned in a position where I can't hear it. It will be alright; I'll come see you again tomorrow."

"What happens now, Doctor?" Minnie struggled to keep her voice calm.

"You'll deliver the child. The baby's dropped and it won't be long."

* * *

Early the next morning Minnie went into labor. Her water broke, and the contractions were about ten minutes apart. Zelig dressed hurriedly and ran into the office. He begged Monaghan to send out one of the workers on horseback to find Zablonsky before he started early morning rounds. He could see Monaghan was annoyed.

"Yah know, all the other girls help each other. I'm gettin' complaints from the rest of dah work crew that I treat you so special."

Zelig planted himself in front of Monaghan's desk.

"Please, Mr. Boss, already Minnie lost uh baby, and she ain't so strong."

Monaghan grudgingly called in one of the field hands and sent him to saddle up a horse in search of Zablonsky. He was just about to start rounds from his house, which was adjacent to the farm, when the hand caught up with him. He grabbed his medical bag and jumped in the waiting buggy.

Minnie was lying on the bed, moaning each time a new contraction squeezed her stomach into a tight ball.

"Zelig, get one of the mothers to help me, and for God sakes, tell her to wash up thoroughly. We don't need any infections."

Zelig ran to get Maureen, pleading with the overseer to release her from work that day. He supervised her washing up with heated well water and lye soap before letting her into the house.

It seemed like the labor went on for days instead of hours. The contractions weren't regular, sometimes coming with relentless ferocity and other times stopping.

Monaghan ordered a frenzied Zelig out of the room and said softly to Maureen, "This baby seems to be in the breech position; I may need your help to get it the right way." Hours later the infant was no closer to birth than when labor first started, and Zablonsky used every device in his obstetrics kit, trying to ease the child into a head-down position. Maureen held onto Minnie's hands when she screamed and dug her nails into Maureen's palms.

Between contractions the doctor went to the kitchen to speak to Zelig.

"I'm afraid we can't turn the baby—I'll have to do a caesarian birth or the baby won't be able to get enough oxygen."

"Doctor, what does that mean?"

"It means I'll have to cut Minnie's belly open to take the child from her womb. Don't worry, I've done this before, and I'll give Minnie ether so that she'll be asleep."

Zelig looked at Zablonsky's haggard face and said, "Do what you have to, Doctor; please save Minnie."

Zablonsky went back into the room to prepare for the cutting. He put on new rubber gloves and a mask and boiled his surgical instruments in a large kitchen kettle. Zablonsky insisted that Maureen also put on a mask and gloves and cover her hair although he could hear her muttering that she never heard such nonsense.

"Minnie, I need to open your belly if we're to save the baby. Do I have your permission? You won't feel anything; I'm putting you to sleep."

An exhausted Minnie whispered, "Do whatever you have to, Doctor; please save my baby."

He doused a clean white cloth in ether and placed it over Minnie's nose and mouth. "Breathe in and out; count to ten."

When the surgery was over and the child plucked from Minnie's womb, Zablonsky's worst fears were confirmed. The baby was strangled by the umbilical cord. It was a beautiful, perfectly formed infant except for its blue color. Zablonsky sutured Minnie's stomach after cutting the cord and delivering the afterbirth. Maureen, tears streaming down her face, gently washed the dead baby and wrapped it in one of the blankets so lovingly made for the child.

Zablonsky found Zelig pacing back and forth from the kitchen to the little porch.

"Zelig, I'm so sorry. The baby was strangled by the cord."

Zelig gripped Zablonsky by the shoulders. "What about Minnie? Is Minnie alive?"

"She's still under the ether, but she'll be okay. She doesn't know yet."

Zelig collapsed in the kitchen chair, his hands hiding his grief.

"Zelig, do you want to hold the baby? Sometimes it's comforting for the parent."

When Leeba died, I was too cowardly to look at her or the baby. I just ran away. I'll never forgive myself.

"Bring the baby to me," Zelig said finally. "I want to hold it."

First he rocked the dead infant in his arms, sobbing all the while. When he quieted down, he removed the blanket. It was a little boy.

12

Moishe

The next afternoon, Zelig met with Rabbi Berkowitz, an itinerant rabbi who was never able to hold onto his congregation. He floated around, ministering to local farms and isolated communities without their own shul.

He approached Zelig about Jewish rituals for burial of an infant less than thirty-one days old.

"A bris must be performed before the burial."

"Why?"

"Hashem intended that the baby be perfect in his eyes when the child is reunited with The Holy One. If the child has a foreskin, he's blemished in the eyes of the Lord."

Zelig couldn't have given two figs about circumcising his lost child, but out of respect for Minnie, he knew he would carry out the funeral in the *halakhik*, legal manner.

"There are no eulogies or shiva period. A marker for the grave is optional, but you can't go to visit the grave."

"If my child has to be circumcised to be considered worthy in God's eyes, why isn't he treated like a real person, worthy of mourning?"

But the rabbi was adamant.

"That's the way it's been done for generations. Learned rebbes much smarter and more scholarly than I am have interpreted G-d's commandments correctly."

"Can my son be buried in the Jewish section of the cemetery?"

"He won't have visitors to place stones on his grave. It is better that the baby is buried outside of the cemetery."

Zelig was becoming increasingly furious with this smug, pompous interpreter of Judaic law, but knew he'd have to hold his tongue if Minnie's wishes were to be carried out.

"We were going to name the baby after my father if it was a boy."

"You can't do that!"

"Why not?"

"We name stillborn boys after Shase, son of Noah."

"Why?"

The rabbi fumbled for a response, but couldn't come up with a good reason for the obscure edict. Finally he responded, "Suppose you and Minnie have another boy? You'd use up the name on a stillborn when your father's name could roll off the tongue for a lifetime?"

"I doubt that we'll have other children. Already Minnie and I have gone through enough."

The rabbi looked at him sternly. "You would ignore Hashem's commandment to be fruitful and multiply?"

Zelig knew he had pushed the rabbi far enough and changed the subject.

"Who'll circumcise the child?"

"Dr. Zablonsky can do it. We don't need a *mohl* since there won't be any rituals involved." Zelig looked stricken.

The rabbi attempted to ease the pain etched on Zelig's face.

"Rebbe Feinstein, of blessed memory, wrote about the special souls of children who die too early. He said that they're angels, pure from sin and will have an exceptional share in the afterlife."

Zelig repressed an angry retort and said quietly, "Then why can't my pure and angelic child have a decent burial?"

The following morning, Dr. Zablonsky performed the circumcision in Monaghan's office and handed the bundled child to Zelig. He placed the baby in a tiny pine box that had been hurriedly knocked together by the carpenter. Zelig, Zablonsky, and the rabbi carried the box to a small clearing that was adjacent to the Jewish section of the cemetery.

Zelig didn't feel the cold on his ungloved red hands as they trudged to the clearing surrounded by white-flecked pine trees and bare elms weighed down by the snow. Sean and another Irishman dug a small hole, just deep enough to protect the tiny infant from being desecrated by wild woodland animals.

Nothing was said as the tiny box was lowered into the grave.

Beautiful Boy, I name you Moishe after my dearest friend. Your name may not be on everyone's lips, but it will always be with me.

Zelig began to shovel the nearly frozen dirt over the tiny coffin. Tears streamed down his face and his lips moved inaudibly. Dr. Zablonsky took the shovel from his hands and continued pouring dirt on the small gravesite until the hole was completely covered.

Just then, Monaghan showed up with a large bottle of hooch in his hand.

"Yah know, it's the Catholic tradition tah celebrate when someone is buried. I don't know how you Jews do it, but let's toast the tiny lad on his way upstairs."

Even though it was Monaghan's belief that an unbaptized baby could never make it into the pearly gates and was forever doomed to purgatory, he had the good sense not to articulate his thoughts.

"Come on now, this is damn good bourbon. Let's all have a drink and salute the wee lad."

The rabbi stomped away in disgust. Zelig, Zablonsky, and Monaghan each took a long swig from the bottle with frozen fingers as it was passed around.

Monaghan brandished the bottle. "Here's to yah, little one. Let's hope you get a better deal upstairs than yah did down here."

Zelig and Zablonsky looked at each other and began reciting Kaddish, the Jewish prayer for the dead.

Yisgadal v'ee visgadah shmay rebor . . .

When they were through with the prayer, Zelig was shaking with cold and anguish. Zablonsky put his hand on Zelig's shoulder, and they proceeded back toward the farm. They saw that Rivka had prepared a pail of water and some clean rags to cleanse their hands before once again entering the land of the living. They each poured the freezing water over their hands and dried them. The two men spontaneously and clumsily gave each other a bear hug, and Dr. Zablonsky left wordlessly to collect his medical satchel.

Zelig heard Rivka and Maureen attending to Minnie, who was prostrate with grief and pain. He did not enter the cottage. Instead, he went onto the tiny porch that housed the intricately carved cradle. Zelig carried it out to a deserted clearing and set it on fire.

The baby clothes would go to expectant young mothers but not the cradle.

No other child will inhabit your place, Moishe, my beautiful son.

For the rest of his life, although he was not in the least observant, Zelig would light yahrzeit memorial candles for his two dead children.

13

Rivka

Minnie turned toward Rivka and let out an agonized gasp. She clutched Rivka's hand, squeezing with all her might.

Rivka winced from the pressure. "Are you still in so much pain, Minnie? I thought that the stitches would be almost healed."

"Every time I make a move, it's like hot knives in my belly. Zablonsky said it could take a few more weeks until the pain goes away."

Rivka was bending over the bed, shifting nervously from one foot to the other. After an awkward moment, she began to speak.

"Minnie, I need your advice. Maybe this isn't the right time with you in so much pain, but I have nobody else to talk to. I'm thinking of getting married."

All the color drained from Minnie's face.

"What do you mean? What are you talking about?"

"Our old rebbe came to visit the other day. He still goes from place to place, but now there are more Jews at Slattery's farm, and he's there almost every Shabbos. There's a boy who just came from Poland. His family was killed in a pogrom—he's an orphan like me—and the rebbe said he's looking for a Jewish wife."

"Would he come to our farm to work?"

"No. If I do decide to accept the match, I'd have to go there."

"How could you even think of such a thing? You have no idea who this man is. How could you go under the chupah with a stranger? There are some Jewish men here—how about Asher? He's always looking at you at the Oneg Shabbat after Friday night services. If you gave him the least encouragement he'd be courting you."

"Asher? He's disgusting! He's so smelly and dirty—always picking his nose and his ears. I think the only reason he comes on Friday night is to drink the schnapps. He's on his way to becoming a shikker just like the Irishers he pals around with during the week."

"What about Schmuel? He's available."

"Oh, Minnie, he's so much older than I am. Already he looks like a grandfather."

"In the spring there'll be another ship coming. I bet there'll be some nice young Jewish men coming over. You'll have the pick of the lot, and you can get to know them before you decide on a chasan."

"Minnie, please. How many decent Jews have shown up on Monaghan's farm, men or women? You got the only decent Jewish man here. The others are dirty and coarse, and they're *old*. I'd rather take my chances on the rebbe's choice than wait for some *greena* just off the boat. That is, if the shlemiel ever shows up in the first place!"

"You're so young! How old are you now, Rivka? Twenty? You can't wait a while? No, you want to rush into a marriage with a complete stranger. How do you know what kind of background this boy came from? Nobody knows his family—he might be a thief or worse—maybe that's why he took the boat out of Poland in such a hurry!"

"He was a yeshiva student. There was a pogrom in his village; that's why he had to come to America. He lost his whole family and barely escaped with his life. I trust our old rebbe to look out for me. Look, Minnie, I have a picture of him."

Minnie barely glanced at the picture.

"He seems nice, no? Don't you want to know his name? It's Yehuda Rosenstock. If I do marry him and I'm lucky, he could turn out to be just as fine a man as Zelig."

"You still don't know. He could be the biggest goniff, telling lies to you and the rebbe."

Rivka sighed and shook her head.

"I'm just considering the match—I thought you would give me some encouragement. I'll have no life here. You have a husband, and you'll make other babies. I'll either be a bitter old spinster or end up by marrying some beer-swilling goy."

Minnie began to sob.

"Minnie, what's the matter?"

"Please wait awhile. I can't bear the thought of not having you here. You're my only real friend. If you leave, I don't know what I'll do."

"You have Zelig."

"It's not the same. There are things I can only talk about to another woman. Who am I going to tell? The Irish shiksas?"

"You never tell me anything personal—you're a very private woman."

"I know I could if I needed to. I'm begging you not to go. You'll be very lonely if you go to Slattery's."

Rivka had a rigid look on her face that Minnie had never seen before. She pulled her hand from Minnie's grasp and started toward the door.

"I have to go now. I have things to do. Tell Zelig if you need anything, and I'll drop it off at the office."

* * *

After Rivka left, Minnie fell into an exhausted sleep. Fragments of the old country careened by—Mama standing in the doorway; Papa's rough hands, encrusted with soil, clutching a glass of tea. She woke with a start of pain. The bromide had worn off, and red-hot needles were plaguing her.

The look on her face! She'll never speak to me again. Even if she did, what good would it do? She'll be at Slattery's, and we'll be stuck here. If only I could think of something to make her stay—no, that's not right . . .

Minnie felt a jolt of remorse intermingled with the pain in her stomach.

I'm being so selfish, trying to cling to her. How could I try to push those shmendriks *on her? They're not worth her little finger! She'll end up with an Irisher or with nobody if she stays here.*

Minnie's face reddened with shame.

When Zelig came home, it was already dark.

"I'm in so much trouble!" she told him.

He laughed. "How much trouble can you get into lying in bed?"

"Rivka will never talk to me again."

"What do you mean?"

Minnie recounted the gist of her confrontation with Rivka.

"Zelig, sit on the bed for a few minutes." She grabbed his hand. He lifted up her clenched fist and kissed it.

"Mamala, stop worrying. How do you know she'll accept the match? She said she's just thinking about it."

"Even if she stays, it will never be the same between us. I've been such a rotten friend, only thinking about me!"

"So tell her you're sorry. She'll understand."

"I can't face her, Zelig. What should I do?" She began to hiccough through her sobs, unable to catch her breath.

"Mamala, calm down. You'll break the stitches." He stroked her hair and waited for the outburst to subside.

"Write her a letter," he suggested. "It's easier than apologizing face-to-face."

"She can't read Yiddish. Rivka can only read the prayers in her psalm book in Hebrew. You think girls like us were ever taught to read and write in the old country?"

"Then I'll read it to her. If you don't write an apology to her, you'll be up aggravating yourself all night. Let's do it now."

He brought one of his art pencils and paper to the bed.

"You dictate, and I'll write what you say."

The next day, Zelig found the overseer and asked to speak to Rivka for a few minutes. She followed him into the office, and he began to read the letter to her.

My dearest friend Rivka,

I call you that even though I haven't acted like a good friend to you. I only thought of myself. Ever since we met, you've been like a real sister to me, always doing things for me without asking anything in return. Who else could I have asked in this place to be my bath attendant when we don't even have a proper mikva? You never needed to be asked, you always did for me. Instead of treasuring you like a best friend, I tried to make you into another Frima, my baby sister. I never thought of your needs, that you're a young woman now, and how you must feel living in that dormitory with all those Irish girls. I remember how they used to make snide remarks about our clothes and you reading the prayer book. All the time they pretended to be nice to our faces, they were really making fun of our Yiddishkeit. Of course you want your own home, with a husband and children. How could I begrudge you what every woman wants because I don't want you to go?

Forgive my stupidity. I could blame it on losing the baby, but I won't take the easy way. I can only ask your forgiveness and promise that I'll be different. He looks like a nice man—please forgive those foolish things I said about Yehuda. You said you hope your chasan will be as good a man as my Zelig. I pray it's true—Zelig is a very kind, considerate husband.

Zelig shrugged his shoulders and gave Rivka a bashful smile before continuing,

I would come to you if I could, but the doctor said not to get out of bed just yet. Please come—I promise to be a better friend from now on.

Regretfully, Minnie

* * *

The next day, after work, Rivka knocked on Minnie's bedroom door. She sat on the bed and gave Minnie a kiss on her forehead.

"I'm so ashamed," Minnie began.

"Please Minnie, don't upset yourself. We'll always be best friends even if I'm living somewhere else. Everything I did for you was as much for my benefit as yours. You say you never did anything for me? I was here for every Shabbos meal. Do you know what it meant to me, coming from that smelly dormitory and stepping into your home? It was heaven, inhaling the aroma of your delicious challah and pot roast. You and Zelig are my only family here. Any time I needed help, I came to the two of you. Never say you were a bad friend."

When Zelig came home later that evening, he found Minnie and Rivka lying on the bed together, holding hands.

14

Monaghan's Business Deal

Ian Slattery, the owner of the neighboring farm about five miles from Monaghan's, arrived at ten in the morning. The two men hadn't seen each other in quite a while, but both hailed from County Kerry, Ireland.

"Been a long time, Ian," Monaghan greeted him. "How yah been doin'? We need to get together more often, not just fer business."

"This is the first slow time I had in this crazy business. Now that it's winter with no plantin' or harvestin', we kin knock down a few together."

"Speakin' of the sauce, I got the best Irish whisky sittin' right here. Is it too early for yah now?"

"It's never too early for a wee dram."

Monaghan poured big shots of whisky in two tumblers.

"Cheers to yah now. Tell me, how's the missus and the kids?"

"Oh, yah know, they're all healthy as horses, but the missus has her nose in everythin'—the books, all me business matters, and everythin' else. She thinks I'm foolin' around with the field girls. I should've listened to me mum and married a colleen from the old country, instead of one of them high falutin' American gals. Not that she's a bad wife, mind yah! I ain't complainin'. Gave me three nice kids and there'll be more tah come. How about you, Michael? Any little gal catch your fancy?"

"Oh, I'm not a priest, mind yah, but I'm married to the farm. It's tough when you're the boss."

They finished their drinks in a few gulps and got down to business.

"Well, I got this Jew girl here—very good worker—still has nearly three years left on her contract," Monaghan said. "I'm willin' to make a swap for one of the Irish gals, if she's good in the fields."

"Aileen's a good worker, never sick. Quite a tasty dish, if you git what I mean—oh, not that I'm interested; after all, I'm a married man. You're a single fellah; you could git more than just a field hand, if yah catch me drift."

Slattery winked broadly at Monaghan.

"It's bad business foolin' around with the help. When I want a good time, I go far away where nobody knows me. I wouldn't give up Rivka— quiet gal, no trouble, and a damn good worker—but the Jew priest wants her to marry one of your new Yids. It's a damn good deal. How many years left for the colleen?"

"This one just got off the boat a few months ago. She got plenty of time left on the contract."

"So why yah want to trade her if she's a good worker and has practically five years left?"

Slattery's face, already flushed from the whiskey, reddened even more.

"I'll tell yah the truth, Michael. The missus thinks there's somethin' goin' on between us. Not that there is, mind yah! Just because she seen me in the office alone with the gal a couple of times. Aileen come to me for some help with her papers, but you know what these farms are like. Gossip mills!"

Monaghan burst into a loud yelp, exploding with laughter.

"Fuckin' hell! Yah been bangin' that little bitch, ain't cha? Yah sneaky bastard, where yah been doin' it? On the floor in the office? On the desk? I bet yer old lady walked in on yah! That must have been a sight fer sore eyes. Your big bum pumpin' up and down—did yah at least clear the papers off your desk?"

Slattery's beefy face deepened a dark crimson.

"I ain't sayin' yes; I ain't sayin' no." He gave Monaghan a sheepish grin.

"You bastard—I kin just hear the little missus—'I'm going home to me Ma and Da. You'll never see the kids again and you'll never get another cent out of me Pa, yah rotten bastard!'"

"Come on, Michael, that ain't the way it happened."

"Tell me, how was she? Does she take it up the bum? If that's the case, I may relax me rule about foolin' about with the help."

Monaghan slapped Slattery on the back and burst into new peals of laughter. After he calmed down, he gave Slattery an appraising look.

"We County Kerry mates stick together. I'm willin' to get the little bitch out uh your hair—an even switch—but you'll have tah give me some seed money fer next year's plantin'—say, a hundred dollars, and I'm lettin' yah off easy."

"Yah ain't bein' fair, Michael. Aileen's got nearly five years on her contract and yah said the Jew gal got only three? Plus seed money? Now where the hell do I get the money from?"

"The way I see it, lad, the switch is even. Where's Rivka goin' when her contract runs out? She'll marry the Jew boy and be on your farm another two years until the little Yid pays off his passage. Yah may have tuh pay her a little for the extra two years, but that ain't a big deal. Ain't it worth a hundred to save yer marriage and keep the father-in-law dolin' out the bucks if yah have a bad harvest?"

"Yah drive too hard a bargain, Michael."

Monaghan gave Slattery a steely look.

"Everything's costin' more these days. I may need an extra two hundred dollars to cover feed costs."

"Now yer really puttin' the screws to me."

"Business is business, lad. I'm givin' up a gal who's no trouble fer one that could be like a fuckin' firecracker. What do yah say? An extra hundred. Do we drink on it?"

Slattery signaled his surrender by holding out his empty glass for another shot.

"Yer a dumb mick! Next time yah feel the need for some fresh stuff, send me a message. There's a pub down in Nassau County with gals like yah never seen. Tits a man can bury his face between and never come up fer air. Yah tell the little missus yer goin' away on a business trip or somethin'. We'll have the biggest piss-up ever!"

Slattery reluctantly clinked glasses with Monaghan.

"And next time don't be a fuckin' eejit."

15

The Christmas Party

Christmas arrived on a gray, snowy Sunday. Zelig was looking forward to the party Monaghan was throwing for the whole farm. At least it would relieve the boredom of day after day—scratching out numbers at the office, followed by coming home to a cold, cramped house and sick wife. Minnie was still very depressed and ill from having a stillborn wrenched from her stomach. Zelig was tired of working all day and then coming home to prepare a sparse, unappetizing dinner for Minnie and himself. And Minnie wasn't even willing to accompany him to the party. As the office accountant, he felt obligated to show his face. Convincing her was something else.

"Minnie, we have to. How would it look if the head of the office doesn't show up? Besides, I'm the one who hands out the holiday bonuses."

"So you go. I don't feel well enough even if I wanted to. A Christmas party? All that goyische stuff I don't have to look at!"

"Mamala, you haven't been out of the house in three weeks. How would it look if I went by myself, like I don't have a wife? Be a little broadminded. We have to work with these people, and it doesn't look nice if we don't go. Besides, it's a holiday party—they know we don't eat treyf—they'll have things there we can eat."

"I wouldn't touch a thing. It's bad enough we can't be kosher the way

100

I would like, but we don't have to eat what the goyim make. Who knows what's in it and how they cook it?"

"So you'll come."

Minnie lifted her eyes to the ceiling, sighed, and shrugged.

"Thanks, Mamala. We might even have a good time. You know, some of the Irishers have been very nice to us. Maureen and the other girls made all those stews and puddings when you were sick, even if they did end up in the garbage. They mean well."

"I'll go for a little while, but please, don't make me stay longer than I can stand it."

* * *

That Christmas would come on a Sunday was very convenient for Monaghan—he wouldn't have to give the workers another day off. He was in such a good mood because of the bountiful harvest and the higher prices of potatoes at market this year. Maybe he would be able to buy a couple of the new Aspinwall potato planters and an Avery Self-Lift Plow. He might even be able to replace some of workers with these new labor-saving machines when their indentures were over. Less people to feed and fewer headaches with the help! His good deal with Slattery and the felicitous timing of Christmas made him feel particularly generous, and he went all out in planning the Christmas party. There would be the best Irish food—roast suckling pig, a gigantic cooked ham, sausages and blood pudding—and all the vegetables that went with it—roasted potatoes, carrots, parsnips, turnips, and lots of cabbage. He'd even have roasted chicken for any of the Yids that turned up. He knew for sure that Zelig would be there and maybe that plain scarecrow of a wife. For dessert there would be figgy duff and his favorite—spotted dick. He could almost taste the sponge pudding and custard on his lips. Monaghan planned to give some of the Irish girls the day off before Christmas so they could prepare for the feast and maybe decorate the offices and the tree.

Most important would be the drinks—big cases of stout and, of course, Irish whiskey. Some of the lads would probably bring in their best homemade poteen, but of course he would have some handy just in case. Maybe some sherry for the women would be in order, although some of those colleens could drink any paddy under the table.

And what would a party be without music? One of the lads could play a mean fiddle. Sean was good on the *boweron*—nothing like that Celtic drum to remind everyone of the old sod. He might even be able to find a bagpipe player. They had that old pianola for the Christmas carols—it didn't work so well, but by that time, everyone would be so pissed, they'd think the Christmas songs were being sung by a heavenly choir. What a ceili that would be! A good piss-up would buck up the worker's spirits and keep them from raising holy hell the rest of the winter.

Monaghan reflected on the past year. It had been a good one at the farm—a fine crop, not too many roustabouts he couldn't keep in line, and the office running very smoothly. Maybe it was time for his quarterly visit to the pubs in Nassau. This time he might include that dumb mick Slattery—a little payback for the good deal Monaghan negotiated with him last week.

* * *

"Minnie, are you dressed yet?"

"In a moment, Zelig." She came out dressed in an oversized *shmate* with a babushka on her head. Her normally pale skin looked ghostly and sunken, and he could see lines forming around her mouth and forehead, even in the dim light of the kitchen.

"Mamala, can't you wear that pretty blue dress with the lace collar I bought for you—and you have such beautiful hair. Why hide it under the babushka?"

"I can't fit into the blue dress even if I wanted to, and I won't look like a goya with my hair uncovered. I'm a married woman!"

"Does that mean you have to dress like an old *bubbe*? You're a pretty young woman—I like to show you off."

"It's enough that I'm going—and remember what you said about leaving when I've had enough."

* * *

The suite of offices where the party was being held wasn't far, but it was hard to negotiate in the snow and ice. Zelig held a shivering Minnie up by the forearm as she clutched her thin wool coat to her chest. They were greeted by a blast of heat from the wood-burning stove and an overpowering odor of cabbage and turnips, with an underlying sweetish scent from the platters of meat arranged on a long wooden table that was overladen with strange foods. The rooms were decorated with green and red crepe paper, tacked rakishly to the ceilings, and jars filled with scented pine cones attached to sticks surrounded by small pine needle branches, which intermingled with the food odors.

In the most prominent corner of the room was the Christmas tree. It reached almost to the ceiling and was festooned with all sorts of colored balls, angel ornaments, Irish icons, colored candles, and strips of silver tinsel. At the top of the tree was a huge red star and under the tree was a plethora of gaily wrapped gifts.

Monaghan and his foreman stepped forward to greet Minnie and Zelig.

"Let me take your coats now. Come in near the fire and I'll get yah a drink to warm yah up. How about a spot of sherry fer the little missus? A glass of stout or whisky fer you, Zelig?"

Zelig quickly responded after Minnie shot him a black look.

"Ve'll just varm up by duh stove, boss. The doctor says dat Minnie can't drink no alcohol yet, and I just vait avile."

"Make yourselves comfortable. There's plenty of food on the table, and I got chicken 'specially for yah, knowin' that yah don't touch nothin' from a pig. Try our blood puddin' though; ain't nothin' like it."

Minnie and Zelig looked at the groaning table. The chicken was surrounded by unidentifiable meats, and steam permeated the glistening skin of the chickens.

"Ve'll just sit for ah little bit boss, before ve eat. Minnie don't have much an appetite."

"Come on now, it's a party—the girls been cookin' fer days."

Monaghan filled two heaping plates for Zelig and Minnie, being careful to exclude the pork but piling the blood pudding high. He thrust the plates in their hands. Minnie blanched, nodded a curt thanks to Monaghan, and looked for the least offensive place to sit. She had to get away from the table, with its overwhelming, nauseating smells, but hesitated to sit near the tree. They finally settled on a spot near the pianola. Minnie poked at the chicken and vegetables, pushing them around the plate. She wondered how she could get rid of the food without offending Monaghan and the Irish girls. Zelig offhandedly bolted down the food on his overladen plate with gusto. She discreetly placed the untouched food under her chair.

"Zelig, I hope they don't intend to give us presents. I didn't bring anything. I should have made a potato kugel—at least I'd have *something* to eat."

"Stop worrying so much, Minnie. Nobody expects you to bring anything when you're just out of a sickbed. Just get yourself comfortable, and I'll go over and talk to the men. You know some of the girls—say hello to them."

He strode over to a small group of men who were slugging down pints of black beer.

"Top off de mornin' to yah!"

They all laughed good-naturedly. "It's nearly evenin', Zelig. You have to catch up wit us. How about a nice glass of poteen?"

"I'm mit duh missus. Is it very strong?"

Sean muttered under his breath, "Fuckin' deadly!"

"Try just one, Zelig, it won't hurt cha. Callahan brewed it hisself— he'd be insulted if yah didn't give it a try."

"Vell, maybe just uh little—I shouldn't give no insults."

Zelig choked on the acrid firewater they poured into his glass, but gamely downed it. His head started spinning, and he could barely feel his feet encased in the heavy boots.

"Never drink poteen on an empty stomach, lad! Did yah eat now? Go get somethin' from the table before yah have another."

"Already I ate." The greasy food Zelig had just eaten did nothing to lessen the effect of the poteen.

Zelig glanced across the room at Minnie, sitting quietly by herself.

"I'll just check on duh missus. See you lads later." He started walking unsteadily across the room to join Minnie.

Just then the band, headed up by Patty Murphy on the fiddle, came to play. Sean played the boweron, and Johnny O'Neil, resplendent in his plaid kilt, took up the bagpipes. What a cacophony as they warmed up to play an Irish jig. Minnie, barely able to keep from covering her ears, leaped up and escaped to the next room.

The band started playing an Irish tune that hardly sounded different from their warm-up attempts. The shrill, whining sounds filtered into the next room, and this time Minnie did put her hands over her ears.

"What's wrong, dear? Yah don't like the music?" Maureen, wearing a ruffled dress with her bosom pushed up and cleavage accentuated, bent over a seated Minnie. She smelled of cheap cologne, whisky, and onions.

She looks like a tart. In fact, all the women do with their fancy boots and gowns cut down to their pupiks. *Look at her face! She's wearing rouge and lip color, just like a brazen hussy—and this one is a mother? It's a* shande!

"Just ah little headache," Minnie said aloud. "The music is . . . interesting—I never hoid dose instruments before, except duh fiddle."

"Let's go back inside. They're about to start the Christmas carols. You'll like 'em."

Maureen led Minnie back inside next to the pianola. Mercifully the band had stopped, but a large, drunken group was singing raucously. *Away in a manger, no crib for a bed, the little Lord Jesus lay down his sweet head . . .*

Minnie closed her eyes and tried to ignore the carols by reciting the *Shma* in her head.

Then Maureen left the room for a moment and came back holding her latest baby. Placing a napkin over her breast, she fumbled with her bodice for a moment and began to suckle the child. Minnie felt an emptiness in her chest that turned to contempt as she watched the tiny head bobbing up and down.

How could she, in front of all these people? Doesn't she at least have the decency to go into the next room? How could Hashem bless her with these healthy children? They just fall out of her every year, each one more robust than the one before!

"Minnie, be a dear and hold the little one fer me. I have to go fer a pee."

Maureen unceremoniously dumped the wriggling bundle into Minnie's arms and raced for the outhouse.

Minnie peered at the tiny face, scrunched up and about to wail. Her arms were stiff and awkward as she lifted the baby to her shoulder, rubbed his back and heard him give a resounding belch. She lowered the baby back to her lap. He caught her index finger and clutched it in his tiny fist, giving her a toothless smile. For a brief moment the noise and smells of the party drifted away. She lifted the child up to her shoulder again, inhaling his aroma of baby sweat, powder, and partly digested milk. He molded into her body as she rocked him and hummed softly.

"Now that wasn't long, was it? Thanks for mindin' him. He looks so comfy—do you want to hold him a bit longer?"

Minnie felt a knot in her chest as she relinquished the baby to the mother.

"He vas a good boy, Maureen—he just vent to sleep."

* * *

Minnie tried to signal Zelig with a discreet wave, but he turned his back as he conversed with some of the Irishers. Was he ignoring her on purpose?

The band started up again, and several couples were dancing in the center of the room. Minnie was appalled to see the girls pressing up against the Irishers, wiggling their bottoms in time to the caterwauling music, their hands interlocked around the necks of the drunken louts. She had never seen men and women dancing together before—and in such a lascivious way.

One of the new girls approached Zelig and pulled him by the arm.

"Come on, Zelig, give a girl a dance. Let's have a little fun."

Minnie watched incredulously as Zelig, unsteady on his feet, slipped his arm around her waist and was practically smothered by the girl's large breasts spilling out from her bodice. That was the final straw! Minnie stalked up to the dancing couple and said, "Now, Zelig! I want to leave right now!"

She went into the inner office to find their coats as he made his apologies.

"Boss, the missus ain't feeling so good yet. I promised to take her home."

He took the coats from Minnie, helping her put on her own. As her back was turned, Monaghan said with a broad wink, "Take the little missus home, but be sure to come back. You have to give out the Christmas bonuses. Before yah go, remember to take yer gifts from under duh tree."

"I'll get dem later boss, after I take de missus home."

Minnie said a stiff goodbye to Monaghan, thanking him for his hospitality. She gripped Zelig's arm and propelled him to the door.

They walked home without saying a word to one another. Minnie opened the door and immediately disappeared into the bedroom, slamming the door. Zelig knocked tentatively and stepped into the room. By now the cold air had cleared his head, and he apologized contritely for the dancing episode. Minnie just turned her head away from him.

"Minnala, I have to go back to the party. The boss expects me to give out the bonuses. I'll be back as soon as I can. Have a rest now—I should be home in an hour or two. Minnie? Minnie?"

No response.

16

The Last Straw

Zelig was helped home by two of the Irishmen, although it was difficult to figure out who was helping whom. It was 3 a.m. and Zelig, in his foggy state, was trying to shush the men as they got closer to the little house. Sean was bellowing a song:

> *Yah may think by me line of discussion,*
> *Dat I once kissed de ol' Blarney Stone.*
> *Well I haven't but I'll tell you a story,*
> *I often kissed Mother Malone.*

"Shush, Minnie's probably sleeping. Oy, vill I get a klop on duh head if she hears me."

"Who wears the pants, Zelig? Don't let the little lady scare yah none. A man got a right to a good piss-up now and den!" At that point, Sean staggered, fell into a snow bank, and continued his song:

> *Some lads when they go out a'courtin'*
> *Dey haven't duh spunk of a mouse,*
> *Dey sit by duh fire and whistle,*
> *Dey're afraid to go into de house.*

Dear God, prayed Zelig, *I hope she's sleeping.*

Aiden approached Sean with an unsteady gait and tried to help him up from the snow pile. They both landed in a heap, laughing uproariously.

"Lads, I can make it by myself from here," Zelig admonished them. "Just qviet down ah little!"

Zelig tiptoed into the house, taking off his snowy, muddy boots and sneaking into the kitchen. He tripped over one of his boots and felt a pang of alarm. Did he wake up Minnie? Zelig craned his head toward the bedroom door—silence. In a stupor, he tried to take off his trousers next, but collapsed on the kitchen floor with his pants stuck around his knees. He passed out on the cold, rough planks and remained there, snoring loudly.

* * *

The sun shone insistently through Zelig's pasty eyelids. His head pounding, he attempted to get off the kitchen floor, holding onto the legs of the table. He smelled himself, rank with the odors of poteen, sweat, and pipe smoke. His mouth tasted like someone had shoved hay and manure into it. When Zelig finally struggled to his feet, he saw Minnie watching him, her arms folded.

At this point, he ran to the outhouse and began to retch into the stinking hole in the ground. Zelig came back about ten minutes later, looking white and shaken.

"You see, I'm paying for how foolish I acted last night. I didn't realize how strong that poteen stuff was—not like schnapps, where at least you know when to stop . . ."

"Enough. Look in the glass, you stupid shmuck!" She stormed into the bedroom, slamming the door behind her, leaving an astonished Zelig shivering in the middle of the kitchen. He'd never heard Minnie use such language.

Minnie came back into the kitchen with lye soap, a scrub brush, and a cracked mirror.

"Take off those farshtunkena clothes!"

Zelig complied, and Minnie snatched his suit, shirt, and underwear and stormed out to the small porch. She disdainfully hung his suit over the wooden railing. Maybe the subzero weather would freeze the accumulated stench from the black fibers. She'd deal with the filthy shirt and *gotkes* later.

Minnie boiled water in the large iron kettle and began pumping water into a pail that she transferred to the zinc tub. She gave him the lye soap and stiff brush.

"Wash everywhere, and don't forget your hair!"

Then she stamped out of the house, leaving a naked Zelig looking in the cracked mirror.

My God, how did that red lipstick get all over my cheek and neck?

He quickly checked the rest of his body for red stains—thank God, no more. Zelig got in the tub, scrubbing everywhere. The acrid soap irritated his dry, bloodshot eyes, and he emerged from the bath sputtering and choking. As soon as he dried off, Zelig dressed quickly and left for the office.

Zelig dreaded coming home to Minnie. He thought of a million excuses for his behavior and vacillated between guilt and anger all day. After all, he was the man of the house. If he had a good time and got a little shikker, so what? It wasn't like he was running around with other women. But those lipstick marks on his cheek and neck—how did they get there? He remembered dancing with some of the colleens, but he'd never kissed any of them; he was a married man. He hoped nothing else had happened that he didn't remember.

When he got home, he found Minnie waiting for him with a meal on the table. They ate in silence, and when he tried to clear the dishes off the table, she pushed past him, piling them in the sink and pumping water over them. She didn't say a word, and he would have felt better if she'd started screaming at him. When the last dish was dried, she finally spoke to Zelig.

"Sit down now and let's talk."

They faced each other across the table. Again, he tried to apologize, but she stopped him with an upraised palm.

"Zelig, we have to leave here."

"Of course, Mamala. We only have a little over two years to go."

"Now."

"How can we do that? We have over two years on your contract. If we left now, I'd have to pay Monaghan every cent we have. We'd be paupers with no jobs and no place to live. Is this what we came to America for?"

"Zelig, I have to live with landsmen. You're becoming more like the Irishers every day, even talking like them. If I can't have a child or my family, I at least want to live with my own kind."

"Minnie, we've both had a bad time, especially you. It broke both our hearts to bury Moishe . . ."

"Don't speak of him. The only way I can get through each day is to push away the memories, as if he never existed. You named him, you ask me to grieve for him, and you ask me to light candles . . . Hashem gave us a sign; he doesn't want me to bear a healthy child. If I don't leave the farm, I'll go crazy. Do you want that?"

Zelig was angry. He knew she was using the party and his foibles to get her own way. Still, he wasn't so sure that Minnie was all wrong.

"Do you know how we'll have to live? In a stinking, dirty little room. That's if we're lucky! Do you want to be in somebody's rooming house, sharing a tiny room and a filthy outhouse with rats? You won't even be able to cook our food. We'll have to eat whatever disgusting dreck they put on our plates. It will make the farm look like a palace. How am I going to get a job if we just quit and leave? Do you expect to live on air?"

"I don't care if I have to live in a hole in the ground as long as it's around other Jews. I need to know that a *shokhet* slaughtered my chickens; that my beef is kosher. I have to be able to know kosher salt kashered our meat. I can't eat this treyf anymore! I need to hear Yiddish spoken around me and never see another Christmas tree. And never see another tart with her breasts pushed up to her chin. If I don't leave here, I swear I'll go crazy."

"Monaghan will charge us for the time we took off from work and every other thing he can think of."

"He was always nice to us."

"Grow up, Minnie. You only see one side of him. He's ruthless in business dealings, especially if he feels like he doesn't have the upper hand. The boss is going to be furious with me. The office is running well, and we got rid of the goniffs who were trying to cheat him. You think he'll let us go before the end of the contract without a lot of nastiness?"

"If we pay off my passage, he can't hold us here. Maybe the rebbe or the doctor knows someone who could help you find a job in a Jewish neighborhood."

"Minnie, this just doesn't make sense. Two years isn't such a long time, and then we can start fresh with a little nest egg, maybe even start our own business if we can save enough . . ."

"It will be two years in hell. Rivka's leaving, our old rebbe is going to that other farm; we have nobody."

"We have each other."

She glared at him and pointed outside to the crumpled clothing. He turned and looked at the suit, white with frost, hanging over the porch railing.

"Last night you came home stinking drunk, with lipstick all over you—and you're telling me that we have each other? You made a stupid fool of yourself and shamed me in front of all those goyim."

Minnie ran into the bedroom and slammed the door, which reverberated on its hinges. Zelig sat down, cradled his head in his hands, and rocked back and forth.

17

New Opportunities

Zelig's opportunity came from an unexpected source. During slow periods in the office, he had been making discreet inquiries about a job in a Jewish neighborhood, and the new rabbi, Rabbi Berkowitz, of all people, came up with a possibility. His cousin, Napthali Greenberg, was looking to hire someone to work in his new furniture and framing shop in East New York. The Lower East Side was burgeoning and over-populated with Jewish immigrants, and lots of younger Jewish families were looking for more space and opportunity in Brooklyn. To meet the demand, Napthali had recently expanded his business, opening a second shop in East New York, but he was finding it difficult to run two stores without help. Napthali would remain in the more lucrative shop, but he wanted an assistant with an artistic eye and carpenter's hands to build up the new one. Zelig would be perfect. Of course, he couldn't be paid much since the neighborhood and business were just being developed, but it would be a good situation for an enterprising man.

Napthali came to the farm on the pretext of visiting his cousin, and he and Zelig were able to meet and discuss the new job. He offered Zelig less than required to start a new life without a nest egg, but under the circumstances he and Minnie would have to make do. Of course, Napthali promised Zelig a substantial raise if and when the business flourished.

Minnie was thrilled that they got a stroke of luck in such a short span of time. Despite her proclamations that she couldn't stand the farm another day, she was sensible enough to know that this was a touchy issue and might take a while to resolve.

Now it was time to give the boss notice of his intention to leave before Minnie's contract was fulfilled, and allow adequate time for Monaghan to hire and train a replacement for Zelig. Knowing Monaghan's temper and Zelig's dislike of confrontation, he had put it off for as long as he could.

"Boss, I need to speak mit you."

Monaghan was planning his well-deserved excursion to Nassau County, and he wasn't in the mood to listen to office problems.

"Let's wait 'til I get back next week—can't it wait?"

"No, boss, it can't."

They went into Monaghan's private office and sat facing each other.

"Boss, I don't know how to tell you dis, so I just say vat I have to say. I vant to buy out Minnie's contract and leave de farm as soon as ve can."

Monaghan's face turned a bright shade of red as he gripped the sides of the scarred desk.

"Are you daft, man? Do you know what dis means? You owe me a fortune, considering all the time you and de missus took off from work. Over two years on the contract, and the times you and Minnie didn't work when she was sick. Why would yah even consider doin' such a stupid thing? Haven't I been good to yah both—to the point dat everyone thinks I coddle yah too much? I thought yah liked the job here, and yah can't say I ain't been generous to yah, can yah now?" His face was turning a deeper shade of crimson as his voice escalated to a roar.

"Boss, please, remember duh blood pressure. It's not dat I don't appreciate, but Minnie vas in a bad vay after ve lost duh last baby, and she needs to be mit her own people."

"What's wrong wit yah, boy? Lettin' the little lady run dah whole show? I seen yah jump every time she gives you a look. Fer Christ sake, be a man and show 'er who wears de pants. It don't hurt none to give her a what-for every once in a while. Let 'er know who's boss in de house."

"It ain't like dat, boss. She goin' to get more sick and von't be able to voik no more. Den how she going to fulfill duh contract?"

"If it's more money yah want, we can work somethin' out, although I don't like feelin' like I'm bein' blackmailed. I been nicer to yah den I been to anyone else here, including me foreman, and dis is how you pay me back?"

"Mr. Monaghan, I ain't doin' dis to get no raise. I'm doin' it to save my marriage. I stay a extra month to train somevun tuh take my place. Dere plenty good managers—I ain't so special."

"How much money yah got saved, boy? It's goin' to take everything yah own and then some to get out of de contract—and you tell dat to de missus. I was plannin' big things for yah, Zelig. You could have a good position wit' me if yah want to stay. I might even cut you in on some of duh profits. You could be a part owner, not just a little Yid shlemiel off dah boat witout two cents to rub together. Do you have a job lined up? Have yah been lookin' for a job on company time? Pretty damn sneaky, I say. Now yah gone and ruined me whole vacation. I have to start lookin' around fer a replacement dat won't steal me blind! Yah think it's easy to be de boss when everyone cheats or disappoints yah? I thought I could rely on yah, but it looks like every time I put meself out fer someone, I get a kick in the arse!"

"I don't vant to disappoint. Duh missus and I appreciate vat you done for us—you vere always generous and kind. I did voik very hard to pay you back and got the office in tip-top shape."

Monaghan turned from him, taking out the office records in his desk. He riffled through them, finding Zelig and Minnie's time records.

"Let's see now, it was two weeks off when Minnie lost de first . . . a month off after de last one . . . not to mention time yah took off to take care uh her. You goin' to owe me a bit of change, boy, and I ain't lettin' yah off the hook so easy. Yah still owe me some for the fancy weddin' clothes, not tah mention all the money I put out fer your weddin'—all that kosher stuff, dah rabbi, givin' the girls time off to decorate. Jaysus,

Mary, and Joseph, I treated yah like a son—I should know better by now not to trust a little kike."

This time Zelig became tense and angry.

"No need to use mein religion against me. I have to save mein marriage more den I need to kiss your *tokhes*. I saved you plenty money ven I vent over duh books and see how you vas bein' cheated. I vas always honest and voik hard for yuh. No need to insult me!"

"I'll let yah know how much yah owe, boy. Don't get cheeky wit' me—I'm still dah boss."

Brownsville

18

Brownsville Beginnings

M innie stood on the frigid platform, waiting for the next train to New York City. It was Sunday, and the trains were on a reduced schedule. Even so, Minnie stood on tiptoe in her heavy work boots and leaned over the platform to see if a train was approaching. She clutched her thin coat and scarf as the cold, gusty air invaded her bones.

Zelig joined her on the platform after purchasing tickets. Although they started out at sunup, it would be nightfall before they could expect to reach Mrs. Epstein's rooming house in Brownsville.

They stood on the platform in silence, with Zelig's large steamer trunk between them. He silently pondered whether it would be better to take trolleys from the tip of Manhattan, and then hire a horse and carriage for the rest of the trip. He felt inside his pocket. Two tickets—second class— some paper money, and the jingle of change. He knew they couldn't afford the transportation by horse and carriage all the way to Brownsville, but certainly they couldn't walk, schlepping the steamer trunk. He hoped they would have enough money to pay for two weeks' room and board when they finally got there. Mrs. Epstein had first insisted on a month's rent in advance, but relented when the rabbi interceded on their behalf.

"Let's go inside the waiting room, Minnie," Zelig said. "It's freezing out here. The schedule says the train won't be here for another hour, at least."

They went inside the waiting room, but Minnie was too nervous to sit. She circled the small room a few times, then went outside and walked the length of the platform back and forth before the gusty wind drove her back inside. Minnie finally took a seat at the edge of the hard bench next to Zelig. He looked up briefly, and then went back to ruminating about his confrontation with the boss.

Minnie squirmed on the bench and huffed impatiently. Zelig didn't look up; he kept staring at his bills and papers. He couldn't believe the charges that Monaghan had included in his final accounting of what Zelig and Minnie owed him:

1. *One week of lost service for Minnie.* —After the miscarriage.
2. *Days taken off to recover (ten).* —That was when Minnie was so melancholy, she couldn't even get out of bed.
3. *Four weeks of lost service for Minnie.* —After the lost baby.
4. *Hours taken off by Zelig.* —These were to care for Minnie—they were itemized to the minute, and anything after twenty minutes was counted as a whole hour.
5. *Time taken by the carpenter to construct a casket for the baby.*
6. *Money for the materials used in constructing the coffin—pine wood, nails and use of saw, axe and hammer.*
7. *Charges for their wedding—the rabbi's fee to perform the ceremony, kosher-type food imported from New York City, decorations.* —All neatly itemized.
8. *Charges for sundries from the company store.* —Which Zelig didn't even remember buying. He was sure Monaghan had padded the bill just to aggravate him. Certainly Minnie wouldn't have bought ribbons, combs, and perfume. He decided not to dwell on it. At least they were getting out.
9. *Charges for Minnie's original indenture, with a forfeit charge.* — Tacked on for loss of services and the time needed to replace her.

The ones that disturbed Zelig most were the charges for Moishe's funeral—that was the final rub.

Vindictive Irish bastard! How could I ever have believed he had our welfare in mind? When I think back to all those hours I stayed at night when the payrolls were due, and all the times I was called in off hours to fix some mess in the office. I was never paid for that time; I never even got a thank-you.

* * *

Minnie was thrilled at the prospect of moving to Brownsville. The rabbi had once told her that it was by and large an upright, religious Jewish community with kosher food, cheders, synagogues, and mikvas. Best of all, Yiddish was the official language of the neighborhood; she could hardly wait to listen to the babble of Yiddish all around her.

Before they left Suffolk, they sold everything of value to the other workers. Minnie didn't mind giving up her finery—the beautiful night-clothes that Zelig bought for her trousseau, the dresses and hats he chose for her to parade around with on the Coney Island boardwalk. The only things she would not give up were Mama's treasured brass Shabbat candlesticks and the hand-embroidered quilt Mama had made for her before she left Russia.

Zelig took his art supplies, but he sold his best landscapes and sketches for whatever he could get. There would be time to draw and paint others during slow times in the furniture and framing shop.

The last thing Zelig did before they left was to visit Moishe's little grave, that insignificant-looking mound of dirt outside the chain-link fence of the cemetery. He sat on the ground, stared at the spot, and sobbed miserably. When Zelig knew they were leaving, he scoured the farm, searched for an outcrop of rock, and carved Moishe's name on the flat surface. He placed the rock at the head of the mound and looked for a small stone to place on top of the rough-hewn rock.

When I have the money, I'll come back and put up a proper headstone, my beautiful boy. I'll never forget you.

* * *

The train finally arrived, and Zelig and Minnie dragged the steamer trunk up the steps. They placed the large trunk on the overhead rack and settled comfortably in the upholstered seats. When the conductor came to their compartment, he disdainfully examined their tickets, gave them an impatient look, and said, "You're in the wrong car. This is first class; second class is at the end of the train." They scrambled up to get their trunk.

"You'd better hurry; the train is leaving in a couple of minutes."

Zelig and Minnie attempted to move the trunk between the train cars but were stopped by the conductor.

"No! You can't go through the cars. Get back on the platform . . . second class is on the other side of the train."

Sweating from exertion in the frigid air, Zelig dragged the steamer trunk across the platform, followed by an anxious Minnie. They barely made it to second class in time, once more struggling up the steps and seating themselves on a hard wooden bench with the trunk between them. Just then the train whistle blew, and the train began to move along the tracks. Minnie was delighted to be on her way to Brownsville, but Zelig worried about how they would get the trunk to the rooming house. Paying for a hired horse and carriage from Manhattan would put them into a deeper financial hole; they would have to take the trolleys. Once in Manhattan, they dragged the steamer trunk on and off three crowded trolleys, much to the chagrin of the drivers and other passengers. When they reached Brownsville, they had to carry the trunk uphill for several blocks before finally arriving at the rooming house.

Minnie's first days in Brownsville were spent getting acquainted with city life. After helping Zelig clean and set up the furniture shop to his liking, she wandered the streets of Brownsville, peering into store windows with slanted awnings on Pitkin Avenue. She dodged pushcarts laden with fruit and vegetables and marveled at the multistoried buildings that obscured the light. She passed imposing synagogues, small garment factories, kosher butchers, and storefront businesses of every ilk. The ever-present, noisy crowds on the main thoroughfares of Pitkin and Sutter Avenues were a difficult adjustment for a farm girl, but she never regretted leaving Monaghan's potato farm.

* * *

Zelig looked at himself in the glass, always a bit astonished by what peered back at him. He remembered how he'd felt when he first shaved his beard and cut his peyes; now it was just the reverse. Who was this stranger staring back at him with facial hair, gray intermingling with the coarse brown hairs of his beard and mustache, and wearing a yarmulke? And where did those lines in his face come from? He stared at the deeply etched vertical slashes from his nose to his chin and the worry lines in his forehead. Well, no point in dwelling on the change in his appearance. Minnie was right. If he wanted to make a success of the business, he'd have to look the part—a Jew in a Jewish neighborhood. He just didn't remember getting old so soon.

And old he felt. Zelig was laboring long hours in the furniture store without a break, except for a hurried midday snack. Managing the store for Mr. Greenberg included constructing tables and chairs, beds and night tables. Since he was in the back room cutting, sanding, staining, assembling, and polishing new furniture, Minnie stayed in the front of the store in case customers ventured in. There was very little merchandise to sell, and the unsold furniture he'd inherited from Greenberg's more lucrative store was shoddy and unattractive. The furniture would have to be refurbished to make it saleable. Zelig hardly ever got back to the rooming house for dinner, relying on a covered dish brought by Minnie, who usually left the shop early due to lack of business. When he would get back to their room, everything ached, and he could barely undress and wash before caving in on the bed. Every day was the same, except for

Shabbos. On those days Minnie insisted that he close early, bathe, and dress in his suit before the meal. He would watch her bless the candles, eyes closed as she gestured for the spirit of the light to enter her being.

Minnie had recently joined a *shteble,* the tiny synagogue on Hopkinson Avenue, rushing out after Saturday breakfast so as not to miss any of the service. She had tried to get Zelig to go to Friday night prayers, saying that if he became friendly with the other congregants, it would be good for business. But that was his time to rest, and he had no intention of gobbling down the Shabbat meal and racing to shul.

Minnie attended services, came home before lunch, and tiptoed around the bedroom to avoid disturbing Zelig. But he woke up and, feeling rejuvenated, watched her as she changed from her Shabbos clothing. He came up behind her and kissed her on the neck.

"Zelig, it's been a difficult week. I'm really tired, and I have to make us lunch."

"Mamala, it's been such a long time since I held you. I really miss you."

"That's silly! We spend hours together at the shop . . ."

"You know what I mean."

"Between the shop and all the preparation for Shabbos, I'm really tired. At least you took a nap."

Zelig turned Minnie around and gave her a peck on the forehead. "All right, Minnie—another time." He got back into bed and began reading.

"I'll let you know when lunch is ready."

* * *

"We need to advertise," Minnie suggested. "The shop looks better, but people are still just walking by. At least on Sunday when they window shop, more people should be coming in, if only to look."

"You know Greenberg won't give us a cent to put an ad in the paper. How do we advertise without money?"

"We could make up little cards or papers before the holidays, saying we're having a sale. Look, Purim is coming soon. More people will be on the street. You're such a good artist, Zelig; you could draw or print one paper, and I would try to copy it."

"How many could we make? I don't have the time. And how do we get the papers and cards to neighborhood people?"

"You're the one who's so busy. I have plenty of time, sitting in the store, waiting for customers that don't come. I could copy the papers and go around the neighborhood handing them out. Maybe even attach them to the poles under the lamplights."

Zelig couldn't imagine Minnie going up to strange people and talking to them. Not that he was so brazen, but Minnie had always hung back whenever they met new acquaintances. He had to admit that she was less shy now that she could communicate in Yiddish. And she did join the shul on her own.

He made a template and Minnie spent hours in the shop trying to copy it.

GREENBERG'S FURNITURE STORE

THE BEST QUALITY FURNITURE FOR LESS MONEY

TABLES, CHAIRS, DRESSERS, SIDEBOARDS, BEDS!

PURIM SALE GOING ON NOW!

ASK FOR ZELIG OR MINNIE

129 AMBOY STREET

The first few days Minnie was able to make only twenty acceptable copies of the advertisement. Oy, the paper she had wasted trying to get it right, but after the first week she was able to practically knock them out in her sleep.

With her stack of papers, she went up and down Amboy Street, Hegeman Street, Lott Avenue, Hopkinson, and Bristol, leaving them in stores and asking the owners if they would hang them up on the walls for their customers to see. She would return the favor in Greenberg's Furniture Store. Zelig constructed a huge bulletin board to house the advertisements. After all, one hand washed the other. Minnie placed flyers on lamplight poles and even stood at the busy intersection of Hertzl and Hegeman Streets, handing them out to passersby.

It began to pay off. They had more traffic one Sunday than they had seen in two weeks. There were newlyweds coming in to look at Zelig's finely crafted furniture, and they told their friends. Lots of haggling went on. It turned out that Minnie was quite persuasive in getting the store a better deal, pointing out the craftsmanship and care taken in making each piece.

"This dresser will last you a lifetime. It's an investment in your future."

Zelig and Minnie were becoming known and accepted in the neighborhood, and the store, little by little, began to pay for itself. Greenberg was delighted, knowing how long it took for a new business to succeed, but of course he didn't show any outward signs. He worried that they might ask for a raise if he did. At Minnie's urging, he did put a small ad in the local Yiddish paper. He also began to give Zelig better quality wood and some newer tools.

"I have extra maple from the last shipment. See what you can do with it—but don't give it away. It's expensive wood."

One Sunday Mrs. Greenberg visited the store with her husband. Minnie and Mr. Greenberg were inspecting Zelig's improvement of the original furniture. Mrs. Greenberg walked around the shop and stopped at the bulletin board when she noticed a charcoal sketch of Minnie between ads for Morris' Knishes and Grunfeld's Butcher Shop.

"Zelig, this is just lovely. Did you do the sketch?"

He nodded.

"Do you have a portfolio I could see?"

"I don't understand, Mrs. Greenberg. What's a portfolio?"

"It's a folder of your other work. Do you just sketch, or do you paint as well?"

"I've done lots of paintings of the old country and of the potato farm where we used to work. Unfortunately, I had to leave most of them behind."

"Bring whatever you have to the store. I'd love to see them. Maybe next Sunday I can come back with Mr. Greenberg, and you can show me your drawings and paintings."

The following Sunday, he brought into the shop his remaining pictures from the farm, each separated by brown wrapping paper, piled together in a cheap folder and tied with string. Mrs. Greenberg appeared impressed, perusing each picture carefully. Then she separated and gazed at the sketches he had done of Leeba from memory.

"They're all extremely good, but these pictures are exceptional. I love the feeling you portray in these sketches, as if you were able to capture this girl's soul. Would you consider doing a portrait of me?"

"It would be an honor, but I have so little time. The shop is a full-time job."

"Surely you can find some time. I can sit for you on Saturdays if you don't mind working then."

"You would sit on Shabbos?"

"Zelig, I'm not a religious woman. I don't wear a *sheytl*, I don't go to synagogue, and I don't even fast on Yom Kippur. I only keep a kosher home because of Mr. Greenberg, and frankly, I don't think he would care that much if I didn't. Does that make me a bad person?"

He looked at Mrs. Greenberg with awe and new respect.

"No, that makes you your own person. I'd be very pleased to do a portrait of you. Would you prefer an oil painting?"

"Let's do some preliminary sketches and decide then. I know I'm taking up the little bit of free time that you have. I'll certainly make it worth your while."

Zelig felt excitement and enthusiasm, things he hadn't experienced in a long time.

"You've already made it worth my while."

19

A Brick Wall

It was months before Minnie's cycle returned to normal after losing the baby. She could feel the unspoken whispers from the women in the shul and the boarding house.

Why wasn't a young woman like Minnie going to the mikva? How come they don't have children? They've been married a while. Was there something wrong with the marriage?

Not that it was their business, mind you, and not that it was said aloud. It certainly wasn't their concern. Even so, she didn't want people talking about her and Zelig. She was finally making some friends in the community and at the shul. Would they shun her or whisper behind her back? It would be terrible for business if they didn't fit in.

Minnie missed Rivka. She remembered her first quasi-ritual bath at the farm with Rivka as her attendant. Her need to feel spiritually and physically cleansed for the wedding had been overwhelming. There were the occasional letters between them, and Minnie knew that Rivka was pregnant. She was happy for her friend, but it was very hard to write a genuine mazel tov! Besides, since she and Zelig had resettled in Brownsville, there was very little time for anything except trying to get the business going and establishing a new life. When things calmed down, she would write to Rivka again.

One late afternoon, before Minnie left the shop for home, she approached Zelig.

"I can't bring you supper tonight," she told Zelig. "I'll be home late."

"Do you have something doing at the shul?"

"No, I'm going to the mikva with Elisheva."

Zelig took her hand and squeezed it.

"Don't worry about supper. Maybe you can ask Mrs. Epstein to put aside a cold plate for me."

They'd shared the same narrow bed for months but hadn't been intimate since before the baby. Zelig had made a few feeble attempts, but Minnie would always come up with some halfhearted excuse, and most of the time he was too exhausted to press the matter.

This time he would be ready.

When Minnie returned from the mikva, she eyed the two glasses of wine sitting on a tray atop their dresser suspiciously.

"What's this?"

"It's to celebrate being man and wife again."

Zelig was in bed with the coverlet exposing his bare torso. His thinning brown hair was still wet from his bath.

Minnie sighed and sat down on the hard chair next to the dresser.

"Zelig, I can't face it again. What's going to happen if I get pregnant? It's my most fertile time."

"That's why I bought this at the pharmacy." He held up a tubelike piece of soft rubber between his thumb and index finger.

"What on earth is that?"

"It's to catch my flow so you won't get pregnant."

Minnie's body stiffened as she grasped the edge of the dresser.

"You mean you're supposed to put it on your . . ."

"That's the idea. We can be man and wife again, and not have to worry about . . ."

"How could you? You bought it at the pharmacy? We know Mr. and Mrs. Birnbaum. She's a member of the ladies' sisterhood at the shul—how can I face either one of them?"

"No, I bought it out of the neighborhood. The Birnbaums don't sell them. Why are you always so panicky about what the neighborhood yentas think? What we do in the bedroom is our own business. Why did you go to the mikva in the first place?"

Minnie sat twisting her hands in silence.

Zelig continued, "Oh, I see. You're more concerned with the appearance of a marriage than actually having one. Again with the yentas. Did they have the chutzpa to ask why you haven't been going?"

"Zelig, we live in a community. We make our living in this community. You think that this *shande* won't get around? Why didn't you talk to me first before buying that . . . that *thing*? You can't use it! Hashem doesn't allow a man's flow to be stopped that way. How could you ever think that I would agree to that?"

Zelig was momentarily stunned. *How could I be stupid enough to think she'd agree, always with her nose in the prayer book, following every rule to the letter?*

His voice rose as he jumped off the bed and stood in front of her.

"What you're saying is that we'll never be man and wife again. What does Hashem say about that? Isn't it written that a real marriage includes love and passion? Why do you deny me, Minnie? Why do you get my hopes up, only to shatter them because of craziness you interpret as God's will? All right, it was foolish of me to buy the rubber without talking to you first—I wouldn't make that mistake again—but can't you see this is a solution? You worry about the neighbors? What about us? We both know you shouldn't get pregnant again. We can prevent it and still be man and wife . . . don't you see?"

Minnie was silent for a moment.

"I can't go against what it says in the scriptures. Why can't we go back to what we did when we were first married?"

"You think we can go backwards in time? I don't understand you. You won't let me use a condom but you'd allow me to spill my sperm on your stomach? Isn't that the same so-called sin? Is this what we're going to have—a loveless marriage? If I wanted a business partner, I'd get another man."

Dear Lord, I can't do it again. I can't let him put his penis inside me—I don't want it anywhere near me! What can I say to him? I don't want to hurt him.

"Zelig, please don't . . . we don't see things the same way. I understand that men have needs that maybe women don't have . . . I just can't be the wife you want . . . I do love you . . . maybe not in the way you want, but you've always been my best friend, the one I rely on most in the world."

There was a tense silence. Minnie placed her hands over her eyes and rubbed them, then finally looked up at Zelig.

"Listen, Zelig, we can stay together, and I'll never ask you what you do or where you go."

"What? You give me permission to be with other women? Because of some stupid rules in a book? Isn't that more shameful in Hashem's eyes than making love with protection?"

"Please, Zelig, don't make fun of me. We come from the same tradition. You were a yeshiva *bucha*. I don't know what happened to your faith. Those years with all the goyim changed you, made you so cynical. I thought living with our own kind would make you a real Jew again."

"You think I've changed? Look at you, Minnie; a pretty young woman who's becoming old and dried up before her time. Do you think praying and going to shul all the time is going to make you a better wife? What about us?"

"We're going in circles, Zelig. It's like we speak different languages. I'm really tired. We have to get up for work tomorrow."

Zelig fumbled for his nightshirt on the bed, and lay down on his side facing away from Minnie. She went down the hall with her nightclothes over her arm. When she came back, the gaslight was out. She slipped under the covers, avoiding the touch of his back. They lay awake for hours, not saying a word.

* * *

A week later Zelig lay in bed, staring at the makeshift curtain Minnie had put up to section off his part of the room. There was another narrow bed, more like a cot, in the room, along with a small dresser and a night table dominated by a kerosene lamp. His art books were piled on the floor to prevent a fire. He picked up one of his favorites and began to thumb through the pages of brilliant gardens, Paris boulevards, and voluptuous can-can dancers. He stopped to study a replica of Degas' outstanding nude emerging from her bath. Zelig closed his eyes for a moment, and imagined entering that private moment, toweling off the luminous flesh of her back and buttocks, entwining his fingers in her damp hair and kissing the nape of her neck.

He turned toward the white, hanging sheet, which was illuminated by the faint glow of Minnie's lamp. Zelig heard rustling sounds and caught a glimpse of Minnie's small, shapely breast in profile through the muslin fabric as she struggled to get out of her corset. When they were still intimate, Zelig would loosen the stays on the corset, enclose her in his arms and fondle her breasts. But those days were over. The light abruptly went out.

"Minnala, are you still awake? I'd like to talk to you."

"I'm really tired. Can't it wait until tomorrow?"

Zelig lifted the curtain and gingerly sat on the side of Minnie's bed.

"Do you still care for me?"

"What a silly question. Of course I do. You're my best friend . . . don't we get along well together?"

"Minnie, stop it! You know what I'm talking about. Except for a peck on the cheek or the forehead for Shabbos, we never touch. Don't you miss being held by me? Remember when we used to lie in bed after we made love, stroking each other and cuddling? I want to be man and wife again."

"Zelig, we've been through this before. I can't get pregnant again . . . it would kill me."

"If we can't make complete love, I'll agree to do what we did when we were first married. I'd accept that just to be near you again."

Minnie sighed and was silent for a minute.

"That was before I knew how sinful it is to do those things without the chance of having a child. I was little more than a child myself . . . it's G-d's commandment that lovemaking is for making babies, not just for lust."

"Minnie, we're married! What kind of an arrangement is this? It's killing me. That sheet is like a brick wall."

"I'm sorry I'm such a disappointment to you, but marriage is a partnership, and we have a good one."

"I know what a good marriage is. I had one with Leeba, of blessed memory."

Tears flooded his eyes.

"It's me, isn't it? I repulse you."

"No, it's not you, Zelig."

"Then what is it?"

"I don't know, but I do know this. Hashem doesn't want me to do those things."

"You're completely meshuge. You make absolutely no sense!"

Zelig stalked back to his side of the curtain, shut off his lamp, and tried to compose himself for sleep. It was impossible. He could hear the rapid, irregular beat of his heart, pounding in his ears. How was he going to get up early the next morning to do more sketches for Mrs. Greenberg's portrait? Without rest he'd do a terrible job, and that would be the end of his budding career as a portrait painter for all her rich society friends. How could he sleep with this pounding in his head and a stone lying in his chest? Was he getting a heart attack? No, he always got that feeling when he was upset. Maybe he should get up and take a bromide.

From the other side of the muslin sheet he heard muffled sobs and sniffling. Good! He was happy he'd made her cry! At least he wasn't the only one awake, mourning for a dead marriage.

20

News from the Old Country

M innie would stop at the post office several times a week, hoping for news of the family. They received an occasional letter from Gittel, Zelig's sister, but very little from Chalupanich. It was a big expense for Mama to write, so when a letter did arrive, it usually contained important news. Minnie went through the mail and saw the letter. She waited to get home before anxiously tearing the envelope with ice-cold hands.

Something bad has happened to Mama or Papa. Maybe there was another pogrom . . . the farm was destroyed. Did they have another crop failure? They were just tenant farmers; maybe the landlord wanted to get rid of them. Papa is sick or worse—even before I left I could see the change in him—he was getting old and tired.

21 March 1902
Dearest Michla and Zelig,

> *We hope you're well and enjoying your new neighbor-hood. We also have news. Frima got married just after Chanukah and is already expecting. The chasan is Yaakov Scholich. He was a mischievous boy but has settled down and is now apprentice to the village blacksmith. A good job, no? I'm sending a picture of Frima and Yaakov. We all*

send our love. Write back soon. Love, Mama, Papa, Frima and Yaakov

Minnie was very proud that she learned to read and write Yiddish quickly, thanks to Zelig. He was a patient teacher and they still spent many hours poring over papers and books when the shop was empty. As she mastered the written language, she saw that Zelig was happy to share in her accomplishment. Minnie's English was improving as well. She and Zelig spoke English at dinnertime (except for Shabbos) and he was pleased with her progress. It helped to heal part of their marital rift.

She counted the lines in the letter. Minnie knew that Mama had to pay the scribe by the line, if not by the word, and was being very careful with her kopeks. Besides, Mama was very private and would want to put a good face on things. It's true that scribes were generally very discreet; their living depended on their ability to keep their mouths shut. Still . . .

Minnie should have been pleased, but she felt a knot in her stomach. Most of the village boys had dissolved from her memory but not this one. Yaakov was always in trouble. He was dismissed from the yeshiva after he put a tree crab on the rabbi's seat. Always with a sneer on his face and trying to pinch the girls' behinds when he thought nobody was looking. He always chose the worst friends despite the pleadings of his parents. They could never control him. This is what Fannie ended up with?

It's my fault. If it weren't for me, she would have had a chance at a better marriage. Someone more educated, more settled and respectful. Good grief, not even seventeen and already she's married and expecting.

The stomach knot migrated upward to a whopping headache. Was she imagining something in the tone of the letter that reeked disapproval? Maybe it was the way the scribe translated Mama's thoughts. Had Yaakov fleeced Papa for a large dowry? Was he unkind to Fannie? Was he disrespectful to his new in-laws? Where did the wedding take place? Maybe in Nolopina—she couldn't imagine a photographer showing up in a little shtetl like Chalupanich.

There was so much unsaid. She wished fervently to be able to have five minutes alone with Mama, to truly know what was going on.

Minnie placed the picture in Zelig's hands after reading the letter to him.

"Well, he's handsome. Look how buxom your sister is. I remember you telling me she was a thin little thing. Would you recognize her?"

"Maybe by her face, but if I saw her in the street, I don't think I would recognize her. Zelig, you don't think she had to get married?"

An image of Yaakov luring Frima into the barn while Mama and Papa were working in the fields flashed through her mind.

Frima looked squat and Slavic in the photo—high cheekbones, a downturned mouth, little definition between chin and neck. What happened to her dancing hazel eyes, the slender arms that wrapped around Minnie in her worst moments? The arms beneath the gauzy long sleeves of her wedding dress were plump and solid, and her hand, resting on Yaakov's shoulder, was almost as large as his own. Where was the little Frima she remembered?

"Minnie, it may be a perfectly fine match. Everyone changes, especially young boys after they sow their wild oats. No, I don't think she had to get married. You can be sure your parents were strict with her."

"I'd feel better if there was a smile on her face. Look how she frowns. I don't like the sounds of Mama's letter. You'd think she would be thrilled with Frima expecting her first child. I don't get a good feeling."

"Why are you so upset? You're always expecting a tragedy. Feel happy for your sister; she's not the child you remember anymore. What can you tell from a smeary picture and a letter that your mother didn't even write herself?"

* * *

For weeks Minnie ruminated about the letter from Mama, trying to read between the sparse lines. That morning, she cornered Zelig at breakfast, just as they were ready to leave for work.

"Look, we finally have enough money saved to move to our own apartment. I've been looking around the neighborhood. You know those old tenements they fixed up off Pitkin Avenue? Some of them have two bedrooms. When Mama and Papa come, they could have their own room. In the meantime, we could rent out the extra bedroom to a boarder until we are able to send for them. Maybe by next year we'd have enough saved for their passage."

"Minnie, you never listen. What makes you think your Mama and Papa would want to come? They would have to give up everything they're familiar with—their daughter, their grandchild, relatives, friends; their whole way of life!"

"And I'm not their family? Believe me, Mama isn't so fragile. She was the one that ran everything on the farm, except for the heavy work. Mama made all the decisions, and Papa always listened to her. She could help in the shop—everyone here speaks Yiddish. You'd be surprised at how adaptable she can be. Papa is very quiet and he could help you make the frames. I know they would be happier with us than on that rubble patch they call a farm!"

"And the trip over?"

"Mama was the one who found a young woman to accompany me over here. I'm telling you, Zelig, she's resourceful and strong, and they're not so old. I know you would like them. They mind their own business and know how to get along. I miss them so much, especially my Mama."

Tears started pouring out of her doleful, hazel eyes.

Zelig went to the shop and stewed the whole day. Against his better judgment, he gave in and began looking at apartments with Minnie the next Sunday after work.

"We'll put two beds in the room we share, and rent out the other room for awhile. It could pay for almost a quarter of our rent."

"No, Minnie."

She looked at Zelig quizzically.

"I want my own room. That's the deal. When your Mama and Papa come, we can put up a screen and they can share the bedroom with you."

"Zelig, if you want a studio for your artwork, you can use the back of the shop. There's enough light when you open the door."

"I don't want it for a studio. I want my own room."

Minnie lowered her eyes and was still for a moment. Then she gave Zelig an oblique glance.

"Is it so terrible sharing the bedroom with me? I understand that it's awkward being in the same room. I can section off the room, just like we do now. We'll have our own beds."

"I want my own room."

"What will I tell Mama when they come?"

"Tell her I snore, tell her I fart, tell her I keep you up all night. Tell her whatever you like. I don't give a damn. I have to get something out of this too."

"Are you so angry with me?"

"If we were in different circumstances, I would offer you a get. We're locked in together—we can't survive financially without each other, especially you."

"I do love you, Zelig. I'd be lost without you."

"You want a father or a brother, not a husband."

* * *

Minnie and Zelig rented a modest, four-room apartment in one of the refurbished tenements off Belmont Avenue near the new open-air market. They took the top-floor apartment—it was cheaper than the one closer to the parlor floor, but at least they had light coming through the two windows of the kitchen, which faced the street. Zelig settled himself in the smaller of the bedrooms.

Minnie was overjoyed to have her own kitchen after enduring the boarding house for over three years. There was a cast-iron stove in the kitchen and a sink with running water. When they left the boarding house, Mrs. Epstein cried, hugging Minnie to her ample breast.

"Just like a daughter you are. How am I going to find someone who makes challah and babkes like an angel? I'll miss you so much!"

Minnie promised to bake extra for Shabbos and bring it over to the boarding house. In exchange, Mrs. Epstein gave Minnie some pots, pans, dishes, and cutlery to get started in her new kitchen. Minnie was delighted to find all the kosher foods she wanted at fair prices in the open-air market. Since coming to Brownsville, Minnie had gone from being a shy, reticent girl to a confident woman. She also developed quite a flair for haggling with the pushcart vendors.

"You call this a fish? It's all bones! Show me a bigger one with some meat on it. How much did you say? Too much for a codfish—you think you're selling caviar, maybe? That one over there—not that one, it looks like it's been dead a year already. The bigger one, and throw in some heads and tails so I can make broth. How much? I'll pay you a quarter, take it or leave it!" Grown men cowered when they saw Minnie's slight figure approaching their stall.

Flush toilets were mandatory after New York City enacted a law in 1901, requiring one on each floor. This should have made chamber pots a thing of the past, except that the flushing device didn't always work well, and the modern toilet got clogged up by the other tenants on the floor. There was usually a foul odor of poorly flushed sewage seeping out below the closed door of the shared lavatory. The dark, narrow hallways always smelled.

They still had to use the bathhouses. Minnie insisted that they go at least once a week before Shabbos, even though Bravitsky's Bath House just raised its price to four cents a bath, which included a tiny bar of soap and a worn towel of indecipherable color. He used to offer a discount to patrons who brought their own soap and towel, but he discontinued the policy when he raised the bathhouse fees.

Zelig began keeping a jar of coins on top of the wardrobe when they moved to Brownsville. These were the coins he'd been saving toward Moishe's tombstone, and he regularly added to the jar. He hesitated to tell Minnie what it was for, instead saying that the money was to buy art materials.

He did need to buy new art supplies as an investment in his venture with Mrs. Greenberg and her rich friends. But he never touched the jar; he used money from their weekly salary.

Minnie held her tongue when Zelig bought over three dollars' worth of new paper, charcoal pencils, oil, and watercolor paints. That money could have gone toward Mama and Papa's passage, and he had so many art materials stashed in the back room of the furniture shop. It was true that he was getting clients interested in portraits and landscapes of the old country. In fact, he'd sold a couple of paintings that Minnie had previously displayed in the shop.

The boss grudgingly gave them a small raise when business started picking up, no doubt at the urging of Mrs. Greenberg. Thanks to Zelig's fine craftsmanship at reasonable prices and Minnie's advertising efforts in the neighborhood, the business began to flourish. Minnie learned how to keep the sales records and was becoming adept at closing a sale with unsure customers. The raise was just enough to augment the rent in the new apartment without having to take in a boarder.

Minnie's competency in running the business end of the furniture store allowed Zelig to devote more time to his artwork. He began to visit the Greenberg home on Saturdays in order to make preparatory sketches for Mrs. Greenberg's portrait.

Minnie was still furious.

How could a man so learned in Torah desert his faith by working on the Sabbath?

"Zelig, must you work on Shabbos? What about Sundays?"

"Stop nagging! I told you already. I can't ask Mrs. Greenberg to change her schedule for me."

Minnie was getting lots of pointed questions from the yentas at the shul.

"*Nu*, Minnie, you're such a *frum* young woman. We never see Zelig in shul davening with the men. You'd think your husband, the spiritual leader of your household, would be praying in shul every Shabbos."

"Zelig prefers to daven at home. That's the way he's always done it."

Minnie and Zelig were under enough suspicion. Why didn't they have children after so many years of marriage?

* * *

15 October 1903
Dearest Michla and Zelig,

There's been some trouble. Yaakov was sent to Siberia for eighteen months. It really wasn't his fault. He thought that a couple of friends just wanted to borrow two horses to take for a ride. He promised to watch out for the owner. The goniffs stole the horses and got away. Yaakov, who didn't do anything, was caught and thrown in jail. He was always too trusting. I'm taking care of the baby while Frima is working in Minsk. Don't worry, she's looking after an old couple that can't manage by themselves. Pray G-d that Yaakov will be released soon and our Frima can come home. Sorry to have to write bad news.

Love, Mama and Papa

Leave it to Yaakov to befriend the dregs of the earth, Minnie thought. *I can't believe that he didn't know the true motives of those thieves! He was lucky the Cossacks hadn't skinned him alive and left him for dead!*

"You think I'm always looking on the bad side, Zelig?" Minnie said. "A rotten child turns into a worse man. My poor sister, stuck for life with such a no-goodnik. I can imagine how ashamed they are, how they can't hold up their heads in the village."

At least it wasn't their child by blood who shamed them, she thought. *Not like what they went through before I came to America.*

Suppose the old couple has a son? How safe would Frima be then?

In the next few letters, Minnie found out that Yaakov had been released early, returned to the village, and even managed to sweet-talk the blacksmith into giving him back his old job. He swore on the lives of his wife and child that he didn't know what his "friends" had planned. He thought they just wanted to ride the beautiful chestnuts and would return them before anyone knew they were missing.

A likely story!

Zelig glared at the blurred wedding picture of Frima and Yaakov, which was displayed on a round mahogany table with a doily under the frame. What kind of a family had he gotten himself into? He could accept living with Minnie's parents (not that he was crazy about the idea), but he had an uneasy feeling that they would end up supporting that bum's family as well. No sense in dwelling on that possibility. At least Frima and Yaakov would remain in the old country and, as far as her parents were concerned, Zelig believed Minnie's wish that her parents would come to America was only a pipe dream. At least he hoped so.

* * *

15 January 1904
Darling Michla,

> *We lost Papa. He was complaining about pains in the chest and stomach, but he went to work in the fields anyway. He came home early, saying the pains were worse and he was throwing up. You remember that Papa always had stomachaches. I gave him a tonic and some tea. Papa said he felt a little better and fell asleep in his work clothes. In the morning when I tried to wake him, he was gone. We buried him in a double plot where he'll be at peace. Baruch Hashem, when it is my time, I will join him. I'm sorry to*

write such terrible news. Papa was a very good man. With
love and great sorrow,

Mama and Frima

Minnie was shocked and saddened by her father's death, but she realized that time and distance had dulled her feelings for Papa. He had always been at shul or working the farm. When he was home, Papa was a silent presence, reading his prayer book and deferring all household decisions to Mama. Minnie also harbored a subconscious anger because he hadn't protected her from having to go to Minsk. As the family provider, he had failed her.

She sat shiva for him and sent money for his burial and future expenses for the unveiling of his tombstone.

Minnie reflected on how much worse it would have been if Mama had died.

21

The Socialist

Zelig made a couple of friends at the *shvits*, the local bathhouse, who belonged to the Brownsville Labor Union, a community house with a Socialist bent. They began to play chess together, and Zelig listened as they talked about the philosophers Karl Marx and Friedrich Engels, encouraging him to read their books. He didn't agree with their philosophy about everyone sharing according to their needs. He was breaking his back to make a living; why shouldn't he reap the profits instead of sharing them with lazy louts? However, Marx's writing about religion being "the opiate of the masses" definitely struck a chord in Zelig's consciousness.

Could you still be a Jew but not believe in God? He would feel bereft without the delectable smell of challah and roast chicken at the Shabbos table and watching Minnie light the Sabbath candles, gesturing for the light to enter their kitchen. He enjoyed the ritual of cutting the challah and saying a blessing over the bread. Even though belief had left him, he still fasted on Yom Kippur and lit candles for Leeba and his dead children. Was he being a hypocrite?

Leeba, my love, I miss you more than ever. If there's a God above, he took away everything that was dear to me . . . the love of my life, my children, and the chance of making a new life with Minnie. If there's a just God, how could he rob me of everything that matters? Minnie is always trying to get me to go to shul with her. Why should I bother? I have to make an appearance once in awhile for the sake of the business, but any comfort or faith that I once had in prayers is gone.

He began going to the community house on the nights that Minnie was busy at shul. As he met more people and made friends, he felt less lonely. He began to enjoy the give-and-take about politics and literature, and he even liked the lectures on Socialist thought. The main thrust of their discussions was protecting the worker, but the community house also did good works in the neighborhood. There were committees for local improvements such as roads, more lamplights, and better police protection. Other committees focused on helping the poor and recently arrived immigrants in the Brownsville community.

When Zelig told Minnie that he was joining the community house, she was outraged.

"It's a place of godlessness! How can you spend your time and energy with those atheists when you could be doing good works at the shul? If anyone in the neighborhood finds out you're a member, they'll stop buying from us."

He brought her pamphlets and leaflets to read, explaining the function of the community house, but she wouldn't touch them.

"Don't be so closed-minded, Minnie. I'm not asking you to join, but I want you to know that it isn't a house of evil demons. The members really are very intelligent and community-minded. There's more than one path to doing good deeds, you know."

Zelig didn't invite her to any of the community house events. She would have been horrified by the lectures denouncing Hashem as a fiction made up by man. Minnie had her shul; he needed something besides his work. He still got a lot of satisfaction from his paintings and drawings, but it was a solitary pursuit; often less creative than he would like since the main purpose was to make money. He had to defer to Mrs. Greenberg and her society friends when he did their portraits, enhancing their pictures with jewelry and finery they didn't possess. The Crown Heights ladies wanted decorations over their mantelpieces, not authentic works of art.

Mrs. Greenberg's enthusiasm for Zelig's artwork also seemed to be fading. Yes, she introduced him to two or three of her friends, and he had done some small portraits for them. However, she wanted to be a patroness at the forefront of the art world. She viewed Zelig's work as old-fashioned now that post-impressionism was becoming all the rage. Her new artistic pet was a young man who had studied in Paris and been influenced by a group, led by Matisse, that was starting a new movement called Fauvism. In French, "Fauvist" meant "wild beast," and judging from pictures Zelig had seen in a current art publication, it was an apt title.

Mrs. Greenberg began collecting outrageous canvases that looked more like big blobs of color than true art. Zelig wasn't such a traditionalist; he loved the paintings of Monet, Degas, and Van Gogh but couldn't understand the allure of these distorted, garish canvases.

In the past, when he'd had difficulty with the irascible Mr. Greenberg, he only had to ask Mrs. Greenberg for help and whatever he needed—new tools, materials, even a raise—magically became a reality. These days, when he played courtier to her queen, she would put him off with a disclaimer.

"Oh, Mr. Greenberg takes care of those things. I'm sure he's prepared to give you what you need."

When Zelig was still in Mrs. Greenberg's good graces, she had been very enthusiastic about setting up an individual show of his work. They had even talked about possible galleries, dates, and tentative pieces to be displayed. Recently he'd tried to broach the subject of a show, but she quickly changed the subject.

"I really don't have time to talk about that now. By the way, did you hear from Mrs. Cohen? She mentioned something about having a small portrait of her niece painted."

Minnie listened sympathetically to him when he told her about his disappointment with Mrs. Greenberg.

"You create the most beautiful pictures, Zelig. How could that woman prefer such atrocious paintings to yours? To her anything that's new is good, even if it's dreck. And believe me, that's what it is; it will never last. All she wants to do is show off to her rich friends how modern she is."

Minnie encouraged him to make a separate portfolio of artwork showing religious themes. Zelig half-heartedly threw together some sketches of prominent rabbis and families celebrating Shabbat together. Whenever she had any time, she would show them in shul and around the neighborhood to her devout friends. Oddly enough, it brought him extra work, even though it wasn't the type of art he enjoyed doing. He even began to illustrate *ketubas*, the wedding contracts that young Jewish couples hung up in their homes.

"Why don't you make frames for the ketubas?" Minnie suggested. "We have the wood right here, and if you make them fancy, we could charge double the price. There's no sense in throwing out Greenberg's wood scraps when we could make good use of them . . . I know that this isn't the type of art you like doing, but it's better than no artwork at all."

Thanks to Minnie's idea and crafty salesmanship, they sold three elaborate, framed ketubas and made more from those sales than working a month for Greenberg. Zelig hated doing it, but he was amazed at how much money they could make. Besides, he was developing a reputation as a talented artist in the neighborhood.

Minnie was delighted about the side business that might double their income.

"Who knows, if things continue to go well, maybe we can get out from under the thumb of that cheap *mamser* Greenberg and start our own shop. That is, after we bring over Mama."

* * *

Zelig was always careful when he went to the Brownsville Labor Union, making sure that prying eyes weren't following him. Fortunately, the community house was situated in an out-of-the-way place, and the meetings were usually held quite late to accommodate the working members.

The first time he noticed her, she was sitting in the front, listening intently to a speaker railing against capitalism. Her upswept hair was unencumbered by a covering. He lost track of the speaker's gist as he gazed at the light glinting in her auburn hair. After the speech, she stood up to clap. She wasn't tall, but she appeared to be because of her confident bearing and high-heeled shoes. The woman was full-figured. She wore a green dress with a v-shaped neckline that showed off her long, elegant neck and creamy skin with just a hint of her bosom peeking from the audacious neckline. As she turned to step away from the row of chairs, she glanced at Zelig before starting to speak to someone she knew. A jolt of jealousy went through him. He wished he were the man she was smiling at. As she walked away, giving a throaty laugh and coquettish backward glance at the man she had been speaking with, she noticed Zelig staring at her. She gave him an appraising look, went to get her wrap, and left the center.

He turned to Reuven, his bathhouse acquaintance, who attended meetings regularly.

"Who is she?"

"Who?"

"The woman with the green dress and auburn hair."

"Quite a looker, isn't she? She's also a real firebrand and very dedicated to the Socialist cause. She's speaking next week on the role of women in Socialism."

"What time?"

"It's posted on the board. Her name is Maya Teitelman."

"Is she married?"

"Are you kidding? Maya doesn't believe in tying herself down to any man. She's a real freethinker. You should come and hear her speak. She's radical, but it's worth sitting through a lecture just to look at her."

Zelig went home whistling that night.

"You're home late, Zelig," said Minnie. "You seem to be in a good mood. I saved you some food in a dish on the stove if you want."

"No, thanks, I ate something at the center. By the way, don't cook dinner for me next Wednesday. There's a meeting I have to attend."

"I hope the food is kosher there," she muttered.

Minnie had given up on getting Zelig back into the religious fold, and she didn't dare say anything about his weekly meetings at the center. They had been through many "discussions" about his involvement there. Well, he needed something in his life to make him happier. Evidently, it wasn't going to be a righteous life.

* * *

The following Wednesday, Zelig arrived promptly at the center and was the first one seated to hear Maya's lecture, "Women's Role in Socialism and the Modern World." She ascended the platform and stood behind the speaker's lectern, carefully placing down her notes. Although she was half hidden by the lectern, he could see that she was wearing a figure-hugging, mutton-sleeved black dress and jangling jewelry. A few strands of hair escaped from her auburn sweep, framing her face. To an admiring Zelig, she looked radiant.

As the chairs began to fill, Zelig turned and noticed that most of the listeners were men, although it was a topic that would definitely appeal to modern women. As she began to speak, Zelig's attention was focused on the rich, expressive tone of her voice, deep and throaty in pitch. He was so enthralled he missed the content of her speech. She spoke for about twenty minutes, at first glancing at her notes, but she cast them aside as she became more impassioned about the subject. She spoke about how women were still cast into a subservient role, despite the fact that Socialism promoted egalitarianism for all. Maya cited how few women were in leadership positions, quoting facts and figures about prominent people in the movement. She expanded her topic to how women did not get equal opportunities in the workplace, being relegated to positions of handmaidens.

Zelig, in his front-row seat, took out a notebook and pencil and began to draw, looking up from time to time at the speaker.

After Maya's speech, the audience crowded around to congratulate her and talk about different aspects of her major points. Zelig, too shy to approach Maya, especially with the bevy of men surrounding her, was rooted to his chair. After the crowd thinned, Maya walked over to Zelig and sat in the vacant seat next to him.

"I see you were taking notes. Are you a reporter? What did you think of the speech?"

"I was just doodling. You did a wonderful job. I'm amazed that you could speak so well without notes."

"I'm talking about the topic, not the presentation. What do you think about universal suffrage for women?"

"Well, I, um, think it's a good idea."

"What about equality for women in the workplace? Tell me what you thought about that?"

The corners of Maya's lips began to turn up, but her look was serious and direct.

"Well, I, I . . ."

"You didn't hear a thing I said; you were too busy staring at me. Why? I don't think you're taking my topic seriously. Let me see what you were doing!"

Maya grabbed the notebook from an unsuspecting Zelig's hand and gazed at a detailed sketch of her at the podium.

"So that's how you listen to a serious topic!"

Zelig blurted out, "You're a very captivating woman. I wasn't listening as well as I should have . . . I'm sorry if I offended you."

"You don't have to apologize. I guess I'll have to give you a private reading of my address."

Zelig blushed like an adolescent.

"I . . . I'd like that." he stammered.

"Good! You can take me to a café and I'll explain what my speech was about. Shall we go now? I'm really starving. There's a place just down the street that serves strong European coffee and delicious pastries. Then you can walk me home. By the way, I'd like to keep the picture."

She didn't wait for an answer, instead instructing him to retrieve her wrap from the wardrobe. Zelig hastened to comply.

He came out of the cloakroom, holding his coat and her wrap. Zelig couldn't believe his good fortune. Out of all the men in the room, she chose him to take her to a café and walk her home.

They sat in the café, drinking strong coffee and nibbling on apple strudel. She had three pastries, professing that she couldn't eat a thing before her talk. Maya proceeded to touch on the major aspects of her speech.

"You know, this is my passion. I thought when I left Europe, women would have more freedom here, but attitudes are just the same. By the way, are you married?"

Zelig didn't reply for a few seconds. He finally found his voice and said,

"Yes, but my wife and I don't have a real marriage . . ."

He was interrupted by her throaty laugh.

"Don't explain. It's perfectly all right. As a matter of fact, I'd prefer it this way . . . less complications."

"I was told by one of the men that you're a single woman."

"Believe me, I've had my taste of marriage and it's definitely not for me. I was married for five years when I was a girl. They were the worst years of my life, catering to that man day and night. I was young and stupid; I didn't know a woman could lead an independent life. When he gave me the children ultimatum, I left the next day. I'm just not the motherly type."

"How do you make a living?"

"I write independent articles for leftist newspapers, and I do some editing for a new journal that concentrates on women's issues. I also get a stipend from my first husband. He wanted to marry again, and I wouldn't accept the get without something for those years of slave labor. It was only fair. And you?"

"I run a furniture store for a living, but I'm also an artist."

"What kind of art? That is, when you're not drawing unsuspecting women."

"Mostly figurative drawings and paintings; you know, people and landscapes. I'm also doing wood carvings now." He didn't mention that the carvings were for ketuba frames.

"Are you politically active? You know, there's going to be a lot of changes in the next few years."

"Unfortunately, I haven't had the time, I've been so busy working, but I have become much more interested in Socialist thought . . . I just joined the labor union and maybe I'll serve on one of the committees."

Maya smiled broadly at him from across the small, round table. She reached for his hand and said, "I think I'm going to have to recruit you to our cause. You could do with an education. I'll have to teach you a thing or two."

Zelig was speechless and began to sweat, but he managed to squeeze her hand in return.

"Well, I'm full now. It's time for you to walk me home."

"Where do you live?" He was praying that it wouldn't be near his street.

"Oh, I live just a couple of blocks away. I'll show you where."

He helped her with her wrap, and they stepped out into the brisk night air. The lamplights exuded a misty glow, and each time he looked at her, she seemed more beautiful in the combination of night shadow and gaslight.

They got to the door of a rather old and dilapidated tenement house.

"This is it. Not exactly a palace, is it?"

"It's a palace when an elegant queen resides there."

"Zelig, you're positively poetic. I must give you a kiss for that lovely compliment."

She entwined her fingers in the thin, soft hair surrounding his neck and pulled him toward her. Then she placed a lingering kiss on his mouth with her plump, red lips. He was engulfed in the lilac scent of her perfume and the rose taste of her lipstick. He had never kissed a woman who wore lipstick before. His heart was pounding wildly.

"Now be a good boy and go home. Will you be at the center next Wednesday? I can't make it earlier in the week; I have a writing deadline. Get home safely, dear boy. Don't stop off in any of those disreputable dives with gut-rotting liquor and loose women."

She gestured toward his notepad, and Zelig fumbled to get it open. He tore out the sketch and placed it in her hand.

Again a smile played on her lips, and she had a mischievous look in her eyes.

"What time next Wednesday?" Zelig asked.

"I'm not sure; I'm not so good with following time schedules. But don't worry; I'll come by. Go now."

She stared at his retreating back, musing to herself.

He's not bad. Perhaps he's a little shorter and slimmer than I usually like, but at least he's not unattractive. He's starting to get bald, but there's something sweet and appealing about him. I like his eyes, and he has a nice face; he's a real gentleman. He'd be a welcome change from Max. That man absolutely wore me out. I was glad when he left for Paris. So demanding and argumentative; he didn't give me a moment's peace. If he weren't so good in bed, I would have thrown him out long ago. He never supported me about women's rights in Socialism—always had to have things his way. I'm glad he's gone to Paris. Zelig and I can have a good time together for a while.

Zelig looked back and waved to Maya. Then he walked the long way home with the lightest heart he'd had in a long time. He just couldn't believe his good fortune.

22

Lovers

He'd waited all week for Wednesday night, going through his work and home life like an automaton. Finally!

Zelig was at the center before 7:00 p.m. and sat through a lengthy diatribe about how property is really theft. He took his pocket watch out of his vest every few minutes to check the time. Zelig waited over an hour and was beginning to lose hope that she would appear. Suddenly he felt a tap on his shoulder. When he turned around, he recognized one of the men who always clustered around Maya.

"Here's a note for you."

He knew she was canceling their appointment, and with shaking hands, he opened the note scribbled hastily on the back of a shopping list.

> *Meet me at my apartment. Third floor, second door on the left.*
>
> *—M*

Zelig dashed for his coat and ran the few blocks to her house. He'd never been with a woman other than his wives, not counting the unfortunate encounter with the Irish tart.

He knocked tentatively at the door. Maya opened it and let him into the vestibule. She smiled, ushered him into the parlor, and flung his coat over a broken wooden chair. Zelig looked around and noticed unwashed dishes in the kitchen sink. Papers and books were strewn around the parlor.

She was wearing the same jade dress he'd admired when he first saw her.

Maya went into the kitchen and came back with an open pastry box, several plates and glasses.

"I brought some cakes from the café. Mmm . . . these pastries look delicious. Sit down on the divan; make yourself comfortable."

Maya handed him a chipped plate and wine glass.

"Well, I hope I didn't keep you waiting too long."

"It was about an hour. I was beginning to worry that you wouldn't remember."

"I told you, I'm not a good timekeeper, but if I make a promise, I keep it."

Zelig sat uncomfortably on one end of the divan. *Imagine how Minnie would carry on if I dared eat on our divan!* He quickly put the thought out of his mind.

After they ate the pastries and drank the sweet wine, Maya lay down with her head in his lap and kicked off her shoes. She reached up and tilted Zelig's face down toward her own.

"You have crumbs on your lips. Let me help you get them off."

Her tongue darted out of her red mouth, and she licked the remaining pastry residue from his lips.

"Let's go to the bedroom," she murmured between passionate kisses.

Maya got to her feet, tugging at Zelig's hand. She led him to her bedroom, which was dark and smelled of musk and lilac. An ornately carved bed, strewn with her dresses, blouses, and underwear, was in the center of the room. As they entered, she unbuttoned his jacket and shirt, removing his tie with a practiced hand. Her left hand tugged at his belt. She knelt, deftly undoing the buttons on his trousers. His underwear fell to the floor.

Maya stood up and placed his hand on her breast.

"Well?"

With that invitation he helped Maya undress, fumbling with buttons, hooks, and the strings holding her corset. As they made their way to the bed, kissing and embracing, Maya pushed away the clothing, flung back the covers, and lay down. Against the sheet Zelig could make out the outline of her naked body, her generous hips and long legs belying her small frame.

"Wait, I'll light a candle," Maya said, "I want to see your body."

She leaned over and lit a taper on the small table beside the bed. Zelig could now see her rounded breasts with rosy nipples and the dark triangle of her sex. His penis had never been so hard, not even when he was a very young man making love to his first wife.

He leaped on top of Maya, poking her thigh with his aroused member.

"No, let's not rush. It's so much nicer when we play a bit."

She nibbled his ear, licked his neck, and bit gently on his nipples. He could barely hold himself back. Maya maneuvered him on his back, and with darting tongue licked his skin down to the hair above his penis. She cupped his balls in her hand and slid his penis into her round, puckered mouth. It was more than he could bear, and he exploded in her mouth.

"Maya, I'm so sorry. Forgive me; it never happened so fast. Nothing like that ever happened to me before."

"It's all right, Zelig, don't worry. I just want you to reciprocate."

His hand reached down between the lips of her sex.

"Use your tongue," she whispered, and positioned herself on her back with open thighs. Zelig had never done anything so intimate, not even with Leeba, but seeking to redeem himself, he put his head between Maya's legs.

Her breath quickened as she grabbed his hair and gave a cry of release. Zelig slid up her body and they began kissing deeply.

"You're a quick learner. Did you ever do that before?"

"No, but now that I know how pleasurable it is, I'll do it all the time."

Zelig became aroused again. Maya placed a condom on his engorged member and straddled him. She rocked back and forth and then circled his penis artfully. After a few moments, he ejaculated once more, this time into the rubber sheath.

Panting, Zelig held her on top of him, caressing her back and nuzzling the crook of her neck when she rolled onto the other side of the bed. He tried to kiss her again, but she patted his cheek gently.

"It's getting late, Zelig. You have to go home to the little wife, and I need my beauty sleep."

They agreed to meet the following Wednesday, but this time he would go straight to her apartment and let himself in. Maya would leave the key hanging in the alcove next to her door.

"I'll probably be late, so why waste time meeting at the center? After all, I have my good reputation to preserve." She laughed at her own joke.

After dressing and giving Maya a final kiss at the door, Zelig floated home, not even aware of his feet touching the pavement. Somehow the stars and street lamps glowed much brighter, and the slick, wet sidewalk seemed to dazzle with reflected light. When he got home, he took off his shoes at the door and tiptoed into his room.

Zelig lay on the bed with his clothes on, trying to reclaim the magic of his night with Maya. He felt as if someone else had inhabited his body; someone vital, vigorous, and powerful. He was stunned. Had this exquisite woman actually been in his arms, doing things with him that he never imagined before?

How could he wait until next Wednesday? On the other hand, he would savor each moment of their lovemaking until next week. It would make the anticipation all the sweeter.

23

Turning The Tables

Minnie had not seen Zelig in such a good mood in years. He was bursting with energy at work and filling all the new orders for ketubas and frames without once complaining about what boring work it was. She could hear him whistling and singing in the back room as he cut wood for furniture or crafted another table that resembled all the others. Something was going on.

Zelig was coming home very late from his meetings on Wednesdays at the Socialist Meeting Hall and began to come back later and later on Saturdays when he was supposed to be sketching and painting for Mrs. Greenberg's high-society friends.

"You seem awfully happy, Zelig." Minnie gave him a suspicious look.

"Why shouldn't I be happy? We're making more money than we ever did. I'm getting some new art commissions through Mrs. Greenberg. Also, I'm enjoying the company and work at the center. They're talking about having me chair one of the committees."

I hate lying to Minnie, but what can I do?

Zelig salved his conscience when he remembered that Minnie had given him permission, not in so many words, mind you, but more than tacit consent to satisfy his physical needs.

He left the shop early on Tuesday and told Minnie he needed to look for some new clothes.

"What do you need a new suit for? It's not as if you need it for work or for going to shul on Shabbos. What's wrong with your good black one?"

"The suit is years old, and I'll need to make a better impression if I become chairman of the Neighborhood Planning Committee. Listen, Minnie, I've been urging you to buy some new clothes instead of the same old shmates you've been wearing since Suffolk. At least get a new wig; you're still wearing the secondhand one Mrs. Epstein gave you. It makes you look like a *greena bubbe* just off the boat."

"I don't have to be a fancy fashion plate like Mrs. Greenberg's friends, always pretending to be a high society shiksa. I know who I am. Besides, we need the money for the relatives."

"No, *you* need the money for the relatives, not me. I agreed to help you, but not at the expense of living like a poor *shlub*. Do we have to deny ourselves everything? I want to get to the shops before they close. I'll see you for dinner."

* * *

When Zelig walked in that evening, Minnie was surprised to see him holding a large bag with fancy lettering on it.

"Didn't you go to the secondhand shop for a suit?"

"I went to the Lower East Side to a men's shop. I don't want somebody else's leftovers."

Actually, he had gone uptown with Maya to R. H. Macy & Co., a large department store on Broadway. Maya helped him select the suit, two matching shirts and ties, a very spiffy hat, and shoes with spats. On the way home they stopped at a flower kiosk where she bought him a white carnation and put it in his lapel.

When he arrived at his apartment, he'd hidden the wilting carnation in the inside pocket of his suit jacket.

When he told Minnie the cost, she nearly *plotzed*.

"How could you spend so much? It would practically pay for half of Mama's ticket! When did you become so vain?"

"Look, Minnie, I'm really tired. Can't we have supper and not argue about this? We're in America now, not the shtetl. Why is it vain to want to look nice?"

Minnie deeply resented Zelig taking money out of the box in her drawer. She was the one who handled all the finances and knew just how much was needed for their living expenses and what she could put away for her mother's passage. Her face reddened, but she couldn't say a word to Zelig. Without him, she'd still be a slave on the potato farm.

They didn't say much at dinner, except for sparse conversation about any new orders and materials he might need. After Minnie cleared the table and washed the dishes, she sat silently for a while, drumming her fingers on the table.

"Nu, at least show me the suit so I should know what they're showing in the fancy men's magazines."

"I'm taking it to the center after work. I don't want to get it creased by refolding it."

"I can refold it just like it is now."

As she reached toward the smartly lettered, bulging bag, he snatched it away.

"Minnie, this is my business. Do I ask you to show me everything you buy?"

Zelig scooped up the bag, mumbled goodnight, and went into his room.

Minnie watched him walk away, clutching the clothing bag to his chest. His retreat told her everything she needed to know.

He has another woman.

* * *

The next night was Wednesday, Zelig's center night. Minnie crept into his room and went through his wardrobe. It smelled faintly of a perfume. Could it be that he was now putting cologne on his handkerchiefs? She took out his black suit and sniffed it; that's where the odor was coming from—a lilac scent. She brought his shirts and suit to the gas lamp on the wall and went through his pockets. Minnie found a crushed white carnation with wilted brown edges in the inside pocket of his black suit jacket.

Next she went across the room to where he stored the leather portfolio she had bought for him as a peace offering. Instead of the two ribbons that normally closed the case, it was wound around at least ten times with a strong, tightly knotted cord. When Minnie finally opened the knot and unraveled the cord, she was sweating with effort and fear. Several sketches and paintings fell to the floor.

She placed the artwork on the bed and brought over the gas lamp. Minnie gasped when she saw the first three sketches. A woman, totally naked, posed in lewd positions with her head thrown back in abandon. Minnie stood, frozen to the spot, in front of his narrow bed for several minutes before looking at the other pictures. All were of the same woman, but in some she was dressed in a scanty gown, leaning forward to accentuate voluminous breasts barely contained by her bodice. Some of the sketches were done in colored chalk, and she could see the woman's reddish hair, unpinned and tumbling around her face. Her mouth looked like a smiling red gash in her face, as she held up the folds of a jade green gown to display her entire leg.

Minnie felt faint as she glared at the pictures and steadied herself against the large bureau. When her head stopped spinning, she collected the pictures, returned them to the portfolio and rewound the rope around the leather case as near to the way she found it.

She turned off the gas lamp and fled to her bedroom, flinging herself on the bed and weeping inconsolably.

Half an hour later, Minnie was starting to calm down. What could she say to him? Who could she tell? She certainly couldn't say a word to the yentas at shul. Maybe Mrs. Epstein? She'd always been kind to Minnie, and Minnie had done her many favors. No, Minnie would be too ashamed. Maybe the rabbi could give her advice; she was one of his favorite congregants. She could hear the conversation in her head.

Rebbe, my husband has another woman. What should I do? I'm afraid he's going to leave me.

Minnie dear, a man usually strays for a reason. Are you a good wife to him? Do you keep him happy in the bedroom? A woman who has no children gives her husband a legitimate excuse to look elsewhere. Why is it you have no *kinder?*

What could she say? That they slept in separate bedrooms? Her visits to the mikva were a sham? She refused Zelig in her bed because she was afraid to have another child?

Minnie, many women lose three or four babies before they have a good birth. Where's your courage? It's Hashem's will that you keep trying.

Minnie heard herself speaking in the quiet room. "No, Rebbe, you're wrong. It's Hashem's will that I don't have babies."

If only her Mama was there, she'd understand. If only she could fly across the ocean, just for an hour, to speak to her. It was terrible having nobody to confide in. What was she going to do?

Minnie wouldn't have felt so badly if it were just some prostitute that he could visit once in awhile to relieve himself, especially if she didn't know about it.

Could she confront him? No. The woman was obviously a whore. Only a *kurve* would act like that, posing like she was a Jezebel without a stitch of clothing on. Only a prostitute would wear clothes and paint her face like that. Minnie couldn't believe that Zelig, always so sensible and reserved, would want a tart like that. It was obvious that he was besotted with this woman.

Maybe he would come to his senses and stop seeing her. In the meantime, Minnie knew what she had to do to safeguard their savings before he spent it all on the whore or on expensive, frivolous things like that new suit.

Minnie finally heard Zelig's key in the door around three o'clock in the morning. At breakfast, Zelig looked bleary-eyed at the table but had a ridiculously contented look on his face. She tried to be pleasant to him but was only able to answer him in monosyllables. She found it easier just to keep out of his way when they got to the shop.

* * *

The next day, with a pile of bills and change in her handbag, Minnie opened an account in her own name. She wanted to make sure that the money would go toward Mama's passage. She would work doubly hard to get her sister and family over as soon as possible, but it had to be Mama first.

She said nothing to Zelig about the money until the following week when he opened their cash box and found it empty. Even the jar that contained change toward Moishe's headstone was missing. He stormed into the kitchen where Minnie was preparing supper.

"Minnie, the money is gone! Did some thief get into our apartment? How could this happen?"

"It wasn't a thief, it was me."

Zelig's face turned white with astonishment, then purple with fury.

"How dare you! How could you take the money that *I* earned without telling me? What did you do with it? You even took the money that I was saving for Moishe's stone. Do you think I'm some kind of shmuck to take everything from and give nothing in return?"

He could barely restrain himself from smacking her face.

"You say I give nothing in return? Who cooks for you, cleans for you, washes your dirty gotkes, runs the store, gets you customers, takes care of the books, and comes up with ways to make decent money instead of just that farshtunkena salary you get from Greenberg? I deserve at least half the money, and I'm going to use it for getting my family over instead of pishing it away on stupid things. It's not something you didn't know and agree to. So don't tell me what I can or can't do!"

Zelig slammed the door as he ran out of the apartment. His fury abated a little when he realized that what Minnie said was at least partially true.

Does she know about Maya?

He nodded sheepishly.

She knows about Maya.

24

Breakup

They had been meeting on Wednesday nights and Saturdays for three months. They were wonderful months with adventurous lovemaking on her creaky bed, on her divan, and even the parlor floor. Maya taught him how to reach the point of climax, then to allow the urgency to ebb and rise again. Their lovemaking went on for hours; in every conceivable posture . . . it was exquisite. Zelig had never felt happier or more fulfilled.

This Saturday Zelig bounded up the stairs, lightly knocked on the door, and stood in front of a fully dressed Maya. Usually when he arrived, she was in her silk housecoat, naked underneath. He attempted to kiss her plump red lips and caress her breast, but she turned away.

"Is something wrong, darling?"

She sighed.

"Just a headache. I've been cooped up for days, trying to finish my article for *The Women's Advance*. It's such a lovely day, Zelig. Let's walk in the park and get a little sunshine."

This is the first time she ever refused me, thought Zelig.

She put on her wrap and waited for Zelig to follow. Instead of placing the key in its usual spot on the hook, she slipped it into her purse. Zelig followed, listening to her high heels clattering down the steep stairway.

They headed toward the small park several blocks away. Usually she would slip her hand into the crook of his elbow or hold his hand, but this time they walked side by side. They strolled for half an hour, chatting about the foliage and flowers in the park and what was happening at the Socialist center.

"My feet hurt. Let's stop here and get some ices."

Zelig went over to the ices cart and bought two cones of shaved ice with lemon and strawberry syrup poured on top. He gave Maya the strawberry one and they sat on a bench, eating the snow cones in silence. When they finished, Maya got up and stretched, placing her hands on her lower back.

"I should really get back now. The air did me good; my headache is almost gone."

Zelig walked her back to the tenement.

"Can I come up for awhile?"

"Just for a bit. I'm too tired to do anything but take a nap before I finish the *Women's Advance* article. I have a deadline to meet."

Zelig followed the staccato click of her heels up the stairs. His face and ears were burning, and his stomach was in a free fall.

Maya opened the door. They took off their outer garments and sat on the divan. She kicked off her shoes, wiggled her toes, and sank back on the sofa with an exhausted sigh. Zelig turned toward her and grasped her hands.

"Get some rest now. I'll see you next Wednesday night."

"I'm meeting somebody."

"About your article?"

"No, just a friend."

"What about next Saturday?"

"I'm not sure . . . my friend Max is in town."

"Who is Max?"

"A dear friend."

"What kind of a friend?"

"Like you, Zelig. You're my dear friend too."

"Maya, what do you mean we're 'dear friends'? These last three months have been the most wonderful time of my life. I love you so much; I think about you day and night. I just want us to be together all the time."

"Why haven't you listened to a word I've said? Zelig, love is a bourgeois concept, like that sentimental drivel on penny valentines. What is 'love' anyhow?"

"It's what I feel for you. I want to be with you, provide for you, be a comfort to you, and hold you in my arms every night. I'll leave Minnie, and we can live together."

"No, Zelig, you want to own me like a well-carved piece of furniture. Remember, property is theft! Do you want to divorce Minnie so we can petrify together into decrepit old age? I told you from the start I'd never be with one man. Did you expect that we'd marry and I'd be the dutiful wife waiting by the hearth for you to come home every night? What you want is a Minnie who gives you sex. I'm not that woman."

"Are you sleeping with that man?"

Maya gave a sigh of exasperation.

"Please don't get jealous and possessive. I never promised to be exclusively with you. Why shouldn't I sleep with Max?"

"Does this mean it's over between us? I'll never see you again?"

"I never said that. I just want to spend some time with Max. When he leaves for Paris, who knows? You need to make up your mind that you can accept it."

"Are there others?"

"What if there were?"

"How would you feel if I showed up at the Socialist center with a 'dear friend' on my arm? Wouldn't you feel angry and humiliated?"

"Not at all. I believe in the principles of free love. I won't be tied to any man and of course the same applies to any lover I take. He's free to be with another woman if he chooses. You know Zelig, you should think about going to Paris. That's where all the new literary and political thought comes from. It would expose you to new ways of thinking. It's where everything in the art world is happening."

"I can't just run off to Paris. I have responsibilities."

"So did Gauguin. He had a wife, children, and a dull job. That didn't stop him from following his dream."

"I'm not like you or Gauguin, Maya. I'm not a rolling stone who crushes people along the way."

Maya leaned over and reached for the bottle of liqueur and a cordial glass on the small table next to the divan. She held the amber fluid up to the light, then turned to Zelig.

"How have I crushed you? Did I ever ask you for anything or promise you anything? I never asked for those dresses and hats you bought. I never asked you to paint my portraits or fix my furniture. That was your idea."

Zelig staggered up from the divan, found his coat and turned for a last look at Maya. She stretched out on the sofa and placed a pillow under her head.

"Think about what I said, Zelig. We can still be part of each other's lives."

Zelig managed to get to the door, closing it quietly. He sank down on the top step, unable to move. Zelig's face turned gray, his hands shook in his lap, his heart beat erratically in his tightened chest, and he had a strange, metallic taste in his mouth. He was unaware of dragging himself down the stairs, walking to the shop with his coat open, and taking the long way in spite of the autumn chill.

It was only when he got into the dark, cavernous workshop that he burst into racking sobs. After he got control of himself, he dried his eyes, blew his nose, and began walking aimlessly back to his and Minnie's apartment.

* * *

Zelig took to his bed for nearly a week.

"Zelig, what's wrong? You look terrible! Let me see if you have a fever."

Minnie placed her hand on his forehead. It felt cool and clammy.

"I must have the grippe. All my bones ache."

"Let me get Dr. Shapiro."

"No, I just need some rest and quiet."

For the next few days, she tiptoed around the darkened bedroom, placing trays of hot soup, tea, and crackers on the bed stand. She left an empty glass bottle so he wouldn't have to go down the narrow hallway to the small, malodorous toilet. Each time Minnie returned from work, the trays were untouched.

"At least drink something, Zelig. You have to flush the grippe out of your system."

Why is he being so stubborn?

Zelig began to eat and drink just enough to keep Minnie from calling for Dr. Shapiro. When she lit the gas lamp by his bed and placed his art and philosophy books on the table, he pretended to read, even though the letters were jumbled and incomprehensible to him.

Finally, on the fifth day, he got up from bed and dressed, not even bothering to shave or wash. Minnie cajoled him to eat breakfast. To placate her, Zelig took a bite of toast and washed it down with strong tea.

At the shop, he was terribly behind in fulfilling orders for pieces of furniture, ketubas, and frames. Zelig threw himself into the work. With each nail he hammered, he imagined smashing Max's *beytsem*.

He returned late from work and found a plate of food Minnie had prepared for his supper. He poked at it with his fork but found the strong odor of stuffed cabbage nauseating.

"Zelig, you never took your lunch. Now you're not eating supper? Are you still sick? Maybe an egg would go down better?"

"Enough! Stop fussing."

Almost overnight Minnie watched Zelig change from a vigorous, confident, fastidious man to an old man, stooped over, with gray hair overtaking the brown in his unkempt beard. Each day, he seemed to collapse within himself a little more.

The next Shabbos, after lighting the candles, Minnie sat down across from Zelig.

"It's over, isn't it?"

He looked up, startled, finally making contact with her hazel eyes. His breathing was shallow, and he cleared his throat.

"Yes."

They looked at each other until Minnie got up and served Zelig chicken soup with noodles. Minnie and Zelig ate the entire meal in silence.

The next time Zelig went out, Minnie went straight to his bedroom, struggling once again with the cord and knots surrounding his bound art portfolio. When she finally opened it, most of the paintings and sketches were gone. There were a few landscapes, but the whore's lascivious pictures had vanished.

Thank you, Hashem, for answering my prayers.

* * *

Zelig hid Maya's paintings and sketches in his workshop behind large pieces of plywood. Each evening when Minnie left the shop, Zelig would lay them out on a large sheet of oilcloth, studying the erotic, nude poses and close-ups of her face. He would pour a drink from his bottle of schnapps, trying to hold on to his memories of Maya's laughter, her throaty voice, and her facial expressions in their moments of passion. After another schnapps, he'd carefully wrap the canvases and sketches in protective cloth and return them to their hiding place.

Zelig closed the workshop early on Fridays so he could go to the baths before Shabbos. One Friday he saw Reuven from the Socialist center being doused with water on the stone steps. Zelig turned his back, but Reuven called to him.

"Zelig, I haven't seen you for ages. You're not coming to the center anymore?"

"No, I needed a break. I have so much work at the shop, I couldn't get away."

Reuven stared at Zelig's diminished, nearly naked body.

"You know, you're looking a little *shlekht*. Why are you so skinny; aren't you eating?"

"I was sick, but I'm much better now."

Reuven kept staring at the scarecrow in front of him, his hips barely holding up the towel wrapped twice around his waist.

What the hell did Maya ever see in this stick? When I tried to talk to her, she'd walk away, never giving me the time of day. I look a hundred percent better than him.

"So what's doing at the center since I've been gone?"

Reuven rattled off a list of proposals coming from committees he was involved in. He told Zelig what was happening in the Neighborhood Advancement Committee, of which Zelig had been a nominal member.

"By the way, our center enchantress Maya went off to Paris with Max, but I guess you knew that."

"No, I didn't," Zelig mumbled.

"I thought you two were . . . umm . . . friends."

"Not anymore."

Reuven laughed. "She's done this before. Whenever Max became too nasty or left the country, she'd take up with someone else. She was with Mordechai for a while, then that *shmuck* Yankel. She was even shtupping the head of the finance committee right in front of his wife. Boy, oh boy, did that cause a scene! But as soon as Max came home or left his latest *bubbala*, she would run right back to him. I always wondered why he has such a hold on her—he must be some stallion."

Zelig bit his bottom lip and flushed.

"I'll try to come this Wednesday if I can catch up on my orders."

Zelig began attending the Socialist center sporadically, now that he knew he wouldn't run into Maya and Max. Mostly he went to play chess with a few of the regulars, avoiding the bombastic, tedious lectures on Socialist thought.

If I hear one more word about "property is theft," he thought, *I'll throw up. What horseshit!*

He did learn from Reuven that Maya would be abroad for at least a year, writing for a French women's periodical.

"I didn't know she spoke French."

Reuven looked at Zelig quizzically. "Everyone knows she was born in Paris. She spent most of her early years there."

"There are lots of things I didn't know about Maya."

The next evening, Zelig extracted all of Maya's portraits and sketches from behind the plywood, took them out to the refuse barrel, and burned them.

25

Yaakov's Escape

Minnie took over additional responsibilities in the shop, which allowed Zelig to spend more time painting and sketching when he didn't have a furniture order. His Saturday painting sessions were paying off. Even though Mrs. Greenberg had found a new avant-garde pet artist, her friends preferred more traditional paintings and were impressed with Zelig's work. He was getting small commissions from the rich Crown Heights ladies, which augmented his salary.

It had taken several months for Zelig to start recovering from his affair with Maya. He repaired physically, but never fully regained his confidence and vigor. However, he enjoyed the freedom of going to bed whenever he pleased without having to tiptoe around Minnie. He'd sometimes take a bottle of schnapps into the room and have a couple of drinks while he read in bed, feet propped on Minnie's immaculate coverlet. He liked having an entire wardrobe to himself without stiff, high-necked blouses, skirts with bustles, corsets with stays, and shawls crowding out his clothing. There were no knickknacks, starched curtains, and feminine smells obstructing the little air he got from the open window.

Things were beginning to return to "normal."

One afternoon, after a visit to the post office, Minnie ran into the back of the shop, holding up an envelope.

"Zelig, I just got very disturbing news from home."

"Is somebody sick?"

"No, just read the letter."

8 March 1905
Dearest Children,

I hope you're both well. Unfortunately, I have bad news to report. First, the Cossacks came through the town, taking names of all the men under the age of forty-five. We heard there's been fighting at the border. Then Yaakov got a letter from the enlistment office in Minsk. Yaakov thought if he made himself deaf, they wouldn't take him into the army. He punctured his eardrums, but it didn't matter. When he went to the enlistment office with a note from the village doctor, the officer just laughed at him and said he'd go deaf from the noise of the guns and cannons anyhow.

If he doesn't get out of the country, they said he'd be drafted before the summer for six years at the front. What will we do without Yaakov? Frima is worried to death. Can you help us get Yaakov to America? You're the only ones who can save him.

I'm sorry for sending you bad news.
Love, Mama

"We have to bring Yaakov to America."

Zelig's heart sank. Not only would they have to bring over that lout to live with them, but they'd have to spend all of their hard-earned money to get him over. There would be documents to purchase, officials to bribe, money for ship's passage, and heaven knows what else. They also would have to send money to Russia so that Mama, Frima, and the children would have bread on the table. He hadn't minded bringing over Minnie's Mama so much, but now they'd be responsible for the whole family.

"You'll have to go to the Immigration Office and find out how we go about it. We don't have much time."

"Minnie, it may be too late. You know how it is in Russia. Who says they'll wait until the summer to draft him? He's probably in the army already. Heaven forbid, maybe he's been killed or wounded."

"We don't know that. We have to try."

* * *

When Yaakov got the money from America, he was able to bribe a drunken official at the Immigration Office to quickly issue the papers he would need to leave Russia. In fact, the bribe was less than expected, and Yaakov pocketed the rest of the money, to be used for his entertainment on the ship to America. Rumor had it that there were excellent gambling opportunities on board, and Yaakov prided himself on his ability to win at cards.

At their end, Minnie and Zelig went to the Immigration Service and signed documents saying that they would sponsor Yaakov. They had to put up a bond, showing they were financially responsible for him. It was very clear that America didn't accept the "diseased, depraved, or dependent immigrant" on its soil.

Well, at least he's not diseased, thought Zelig.

Between what they sent to the old country and the outlay of sponsorship money, they exhausted all their savings. Zelig had to ask Mr. Greenberg for an advance on their salaries.

"You can be sure Greenberg will charge us plenty of interest on the loan," he told Minnie. "For that irresponsible shmendrik we have to go into debt again."

"It's not Yaakov's fault that he got drafted. Remember how scared you were before you came that the Cossacks would catch you before you got to the ship? They're my family, Zelig. If your sisters asked for help, we'd give with a generous heart."

Zelig knew what Minnie said was true. He thought of his sister Gittel. If her husband were in the same circumstances, Minnie would be the first one to offer help, but at least Dovid was an upstanding, responsible person, worthy of respect.

Zelig began to silently tally the costs of bringing over the family's black sheep.

1. *Yaakov's passage in steerage—$50.00.* Forty-five extra hours of work in the shop or four custom tables.
2. *Bribes to officials—$25.00.* More than twenty hours lost from working on pictures for the Crown Heights ladies.
3. *Sponsorship fees—$15.00.* Relaxing for ten Saturday nights in his room, drinking some schnapps, napping, and reading *The Daily Forward.*
4. *Transportation and food for the journey.* That would depend on whether Yaakov had any money for his own expenses, which was highly unlikely. Probably $20 to $30—at least twenty hours of refinishing tables, chairs, and wardrobes.
5. *Money to care for Mama, Frima, and the children.* That would depend on Frima's ability to find a job while Mama took care of the children. Approximately $40 to $50. At least several weeks' salary, providing Frima was able to find work.
6. *Overtime in the store.* Going in an hour earlier and staying at least an hour later to get the jobs done quickly. His craftsmanship would go out the window; he'd be making the same dreck for the special orders to save time.
7. *Loan from Greenberg with interest.* Knowing Greenberg, the interest would be usury.

The worst: giving up his room to that shmendrik and moving back to Minnie's bedroom. How could he give that up? God only knows how long it would take for Yaakov to get a job and his own place to live. It would take at least a year for Yaakov to move into a boardinghouse, if he was lucky enough to get work. Then he'd have to start saving to bring over his own family. It could take years!

He turned to Minnie in a rage.

"When that deadbeat gets here, he'd better find a job right away and work his tokhes off. I won't support that mamser for a minute longer than I have to!"

* * *

Luck was on Yaakov's side for a while. The Minsk recruiting office was in total disarray, and all the papers from Chalupanich and Nolopina were lost. The czar's Supreme General sent all the officials responsible for the mess to a remote outpost somewhere in the Ural Mountains, never to be heard from again. New bureaucrats began quickly collecting information about eligible men in the district.

Within days, Yaakov got himself on a train to Bremen, Germany. Once there, he was able to arrange for passage on the next ship to America, bribing the ship's petty officer for a bunk in steerage.

When they heard the news, Minnie rejoiced for her family, but Zelig was miserable. There was no way out of this mess.

Yaakov was coming to live with them in Brownsville.

26

Mishpokhe

The ship arrived from Bremen on a Tuesday, docking at Ellis Island, and Minnie and Zelig waited for six hours on hard benches only to find out that Yaakov had been detained on "legal grounds." At the Information Department, they found out that the official copy of the ship's manifest didn't agree with the records of sponsorship. They would have to appear on Friday for an appeal to the Board of Special Inquiry, proving that they were Yaakov's official sponsors. This could have been avoided if Yaakov had carried $25.00, showing that he wouldn't become a public charge even without a sponsor. However, Yaakov came off the ship without a kopek in his pocket.

"We sent him enough money," Zelig fumed. "We wrote him that he had to have $25 when he got off the ship in case there was a problem with his records! What happened to that money? I bet that goniff spent it on kurves or gambled it away! I wouldn't put anything past him!"

"Maybe he had to pay out more for bribes than we thought. Maybe the money was stolen. Don't be so quick to blame him, Zelig."

Minnie was also angry and suspicious, but she wanted to give Yaakov the benefit of the doubt and not rile up an already furious Zelig. The truth was that Yaakov had gambled away practically every cent, believing that he could outsmart the card sharks. He also gave two dollars to one of the comely women on the ship, who allowed him to fondle her breasts and tokhes while rubbing against her. Nothing more than that. After all, he was a married man, and there wasn't an inch of space where you had the privacy to do anything else.

When Minnie and Zelig came back to Ellis Island on Friday, they were barely speaking to each other; last night's argument still echoed in their ears.

"What! Take another day off from work to meet the shmendrik? I have all these orders, Minnie. I can't afford to fall behind—if the customers have to wait too long, they'll cancel. You go! Take the sponsorship papers and meet him yourself!"

"I'm going to get lost. I can't read all those signs. Besides, my English isn't so good. They'll ask questions."

"If you learned to read English instead of burying your head in the prayer books, maybe you'd be able to find your way around. There are lots of translators at Ellis Island. You're acting like a child. Get started earlier and ask someone for help if you get lost. You have a mouth—you certainly use it on me!"

"How does it look, Zelig? He's our *mishpokhe* and only I go to greet him? Suppose I get mistaken for one of those 'picture brides'? I'll never be able to get off the island. It's no place for a single woman. Even if it were safe for me to go alone, it's not welcoming."

"For him I have to be welcoming? Isn't it enough we're supporting that shmuck and the whole family? Just show them the sponsorship papers; you're making a whole *megile* out of nothing."

Then there was the bedroom problem. Zelig wanted to stay in the spare room until Yaakov arrived.

"I'll need to change the linens again and make the room nice. You still haven't taken down your pictures. I want to make sure they're taken down properly."

"Don't touch my sketches! I'll take them down myself!"

"Now who's being a child? What's the difference if you spend a night or two less in the spare room? I'll give you as much space as you need."

In the end, Zelig agreed to stay with Minnie in her bedroom and accompany her to Ellis Island. He took down his sketches carefully and stored them in the secondhand portfolio on his side of the room. At least he had his own cot, and Minnie placed a night table, found at a rummage sale, next to his bed. She placed his art and English books on the table neatly, even the art books with the naked women. In a way, it was comforting to be back in the room with Minnie. Although they didn't share a bed, they talked about the events of their day and joked about the more outrageous expectations of some of the customers. He felt less lonely.

* * *

They had been sitting on the same hard bench at the Arrival Hall at Ellis Island for several hours, waiting for the ship from Bremen. Minnie had packed a large basket of food for Yaakov's arrival, anticipating that he would have to be inspected by the medical officers, interviewed by various officials to prove his worthiness to stay in America, and, most of all, show his sponsorship papers.

Minnie was so engrossed in her prayer book that she almost didn't respond when their name was called by an official in front of the Office of Special Inquiry.

"FRUMKIN, SPONSORS OF YAAKOV SCHOLICH!"

They scurried around, trying to follow the signs, and finally found the small office labeled BOARD OF SPECIAL INQUIRY, LEGAL DEPARTMENT. The sign was almost obscured by a flock of immigrants, laden with bundles and steamer trunks, and speaking a multitude of tongues. Minnie felt faint from the accumulated odors of unwashed bodies and strange food smells. Zelig took her arm and steered her around a puddle of vomit. He approached a dark-uniformed official peering out the door.

"Our names were called."

"Frumkin?"

Zelig nodded and the official accompanied them into the office. There they caught their first glimpse of Yaakov, who was shifting uneasily from one foot to the other in front of the official's desk.

He was filthy and smelled to high heaven. The official went over to the window and opened it to capacity even though the cold ocean wind made the room unbearably uncomfortable. Minnie shivered, wrapped her shawl closer to her body, and stared at Yaakov. She remembered the scrawny, snot-nosed, obnoxious child from twenty years ago. He was now a muscular, squat man in unspeakably filthy clothing. His unkempt beard and mustache were flecked with food particles and tangles of long, oily black hair escaped from his greasy sailor cap. Yaakov reached toward the desk with a dirt-encrusted hand to steady himself.

"Don't touch my desk! Stay behind the white line!" The official barked at him in Yiddish. Then he turned to Zelig and Minnie.

"What relationship do you have to this immigrant?"

Zelig responded in his best English.

"He's our brother-in-law. I have his papers here. Please check and make sure everything is in order."

The security official extended his hand without a word. He took the envelope from Zelig and rummaged through the contents. He finally took out the last three pages, stamped them, and checked off what looked like a name on his own roster sheet.

"Show the stamped papers at the Registry Desk on the second floor. You also have to show his medical clearance in order for him to get his Landing Card." He stamped another page and shoved it into the bulging envelope.

"Make sure he takes all that junk with him." The security official pointed to an assortment of packages and a steamer trunk in the corner. Then he turned to Yaakov.

"Why didn't you leave your baggage in the disinfectant chamber? Do you want to bring lice to your relatives?"

"I was afraid it would get stolen. When I got off the barge, I was pushed by a bunch of goniffs who stole all my money. Just my luck; it was the only time I took it out of my shoe—I put the money in my inside . . ."

The official impatiently cut Yaakov off.

"Enough, Greena; you're a lucky man. Don't get into any more trouble. Good luck! NEXT!"

As they left the office, Minnie approached Yaakov tentatively.

"Yaakov, welcome. I hope your voyage wasn't too tiring. Meet my husband, Zelig." Zelig nodded but did not extend his hand.

"I can't tell you how much we all appreciate what you've done. I would have died in the army. A six-year conscription, and for fourteen years they could call me back anytime. Knowing how they treat Jews, I wouldn't have lasted a year. You saved my life."

Minnie smiled and lowered her eyes shyly. Zelig acknowledged Yaakov's gratitude silently but nodded curtly and stared straight ahead.

As they headed toward the Registry Office, Minnie noticed a group of single women and some women with children sitting on the floor, since all the benches were taken. The children were unusually quiet, huddled up against their mothers.

"Why do you suppose those women are waiting there?"

"Some are the 'picture brides,' " Zelig told Minnie. "They're waiting for their chasans to come and get them. The women with children won't be allowed off Ellis Island unless a husband or relative comes to pick them up."

"What will happen if nobody comes?"

"It's the steamship's responsibility to take them back to where they came from. Most of the women are met by someone, but not always."

As they climbed the stairs, they noticed a number of officials looking intently at the flood of immigrants streaming up the stairs. Every once in awhile, they would pull an unfortunate wretch out of line and chalk his or her lapel with a letter. The immigrant would be sent to another office, despite the protests and cries of the family.

"What's going on?"

"Those are medical officers," replied Zelig. "If they see someone who looks lame, hunched over, or seems to have an eye or back problem, they have to be reexamined. If it isn't serious, they can rejoin their family. If it's serious, they're either sent to Wards Island or they're deported. A couple of the men at the farm were detained like that."

"Well, I hope they don't decide to stop us. That's all we need on top of everything else."

"If we get stopped, let me do the talking. We have valid visas and the sponsorship papers. Let's just get Yaakov out of this place."

After taking care of the registration and medical release, they stood on the landing and waited for a barge to take them back to the mainland.

They missed three barges, since there was limited space on each ferry. They finally squeezed into the fourth barge, dragging Yaakov's trunk and packages. Fortunately Minnie had packed lunch for them, knowing full well that even if they could afford the food sold at Ellis Island, she would never eat the unappetizing, non-kosher *chazarai*.

* * *

At the first opportunity, Minnie plucked on Yaakov's sleeve.

"Please tell me how my Mama is. Is she well? What about Fannie and the girls? Will they be able to get along on their own? Have there been . . ."

"Everybody is all right. The trip wasn't as bad as I expected. With the steamships, it doesn't take as long—only eight to ten days. Not like it used to be, but with all those thieving goniffs, I had to sleep with my money under the pillow . . ."

Zelig interjected, "When you got off the boat, why didn't you put the money in your shoe, instead of your pocket? Didn't we warn you there were plenty of thieves at Ellis Island, not just on the boats? For this we had to spend two whole days . . ."

The screech of the whistle, sound of the motor, and babble in strange languages drowned out their disjointed attempts at conversation. When the noise died down, Zelig changed the subject.

"We have a very long trip to Brownsville on three trolley cars. Why don't we talk when Yaakov has a chance to get settled? By the way, Yaakov, we may have a job for you."

Minnie shot him a warning look.

"You're right, Zelig. I'm sure Yaakov needs a chance to rest. We can talk later."

* * *

The trolley ride up Broadway astonished Yaakov. He ran from one side of the trolley to the other to stare at the enormous buildings, stores, carriages with beautiful horses, and, most important, the elegant ladies strolling along the streets and gazing in the shop windows. He had never seen so much activity and commotion in his life. He stared at a woman ascending the steps of a carriage, catching a glimpse of her shapely ankle and undergarments as she struggled with her parasol and packages. Yaakov's avid interest was not lost on Minnie and Zelig.

"What's that big store called? What kind of business is that? Is everyone rich here? How do they make all their money?" Yaakov barraged Zelig with questions as the trolley creaked up Lower Manhattan on its busiest commercial street. Even though the streets weren't paved with gold (the mud and horse dung belied that bubbe meiser), it seemed as if the walls and floors of the majestic buildings might be. As they left the financial and commercial district, they entered a different world.

Mott Street was crowded with strange-looking men who spoke a language that was at once harsh and melodic. They screamed to each other while squatting down on the muddy street, holding round bowls under their chins with one hand and two sticks in the other, shoveling what looked like rice into their mouths. What a sight! Men dressed in long robes that dragged in the mud, wearing strange, cone-shaped hats with a lone pigtail trailing down their backs. Their features were oddly flat; some looked like Mongols. And the smells that came from those streets. Sweet, pungent, exotic flavors mixed with the pervasive smell of garbage, which overflowed from barrels next to the stores.

"Who are they? I never saw anything like this. Don't they have any women? What are those sticks they're eating with? What kind of language is that?"

Zelig answered. "They're Chinese workmen—I don't know what the sticks are called, but that's what they eat with. You never see women on the streets; they're not allowed to bring their women to America. Sometimes you can see the men gambling right here in the streets. I've even seen them pee in the street! I guess there are no outhouses for them."

Yaakov looked at the strange signs, a bunch of zigzag lines slanting downward instead of from right to left, like Hebrew. What crazy writing these strangers had!

Crossing over Mulberry Street, they were assailed with pushcarts, people hawking their wares, and the strange aromas of garlic, cooked tomatoes, and unidentifiable spices. Yaakov was again befuddled by a language he had never heard before.

"What kind of place is this? Where do these people come from? They look poor, like us."

"They're *Italyanas*, not good people. There are lots of thieves and gangs down here. If one of them stops you in the street, keep going. He'll try to pick your pocket, or worse."

As the trolley creaked up Broadway, they approached the elevated tracks that crossed the Williamsburg Bridge. Yaakov had never seen such an imposing structure, all concrete and steel, with massive cables running up toward the monstrous steel trusses of the bridge. Maybe those cables would break and they would be thrust down into the murky water, on top of the boats and barges, which looked like children's toys. He finally sat down and was silent, clutching the seat back in front of him with a white-fingered grip.

Once off the bridge, they proceeded down Broadway on the Brooklyn side, where they again made a trolley change toward Brownsville. It took hours until they arrived at their final destination. Yaakov, exhausted from his voyage, perked up when he began to hear Yiddish spoken. To hear his language spoken again was wonderful; even the Galitziana accents mixed with the familiar Litvak cadences were music for his soul.

"Thanks to Hashem, they speak regular here. I can understand even when it's a little mixed up with English."

Minnie replied, "You won't have to worry. You can get by without a word of English in Brownsville. Everyone here is from a shtetl. Just look at the signs."

It was true. Except for the undecipherable street signs, all the stores had their writing in Yiddish. Yaakov was able to read Yiddish, but was kicked out of yeshiva before he could learn to write.

They walked several blocks to a tall building, at least four stories high. "Here's where we live, Yaakov. Our apartment is on the third floor."

They started climbing upstairs, Minnie and Zelig helping Yaakov schlep his bundles. Minnie went first, then Yaakov, and finally Zelig. Yaakov lifted his steamer trunk, slung it over his back, and effortlessly walked up the three flights of stairs. Zelig looked at him in amazement. When he'd tried to drag the trunk onto the ferry, he couldn't budge it. What on earth could he have in there? How could he lift it so effortlessly?

Yaakov let out a gasp of amazement as they entered through the kitchen. It had a large cast-iron stove, a sink with metal inside, and a strange-looking spigot pointing toward the basin. Minnie turned the spigot, and water came out! She washed her hands and asked Yaakov if he needed to use the toilet. Where was the outhouse? Was it behind the building? Zelig pointed to the hallway and escorted him to the tiny toilet near the stairway.

"After you go, you have to pull this chain. It makes the waste go down to the sewer." He demonstrated the overhead flushing device to a thoroughly mystified Yaakov. How could shit and piss go from the third floor all the way down to the sewers? What a country!

When he returned to the apartment, Minnie showed him the second bedroom, with Zelig following close behind. A real bed with a beautiful coverlet, in all different colors and edged with lace. A wooden bureau to store his belongings and a gas lamp, its slender brass handle jutting from the wall. Minnie turned a valve, lit a match, and a steady flame appeared. Wooden planks were anchored to the floor, and a small, circular rug was next to the bed. Yaakov was overcome. He flung himself on top of the coverlet with his filthy clothes, malodorous body, muddy shoes, and closed his eyes.

Zelig mumbled something and rushed out of the room. This was too much for even hospitable Minnie.

"Yaakov, you can't lay on top of the coverlet. That's for show! And you never go on the bed with your muddy shoes. You need a bath and clean clothing! Zelig will take you to the shvits before we have supper. Zelig, where are you?"

She was about to open his trunk to look for some cleaner clothes but remembered what the Ellis Island official had said about lice. Minnie would have to go to the rooming house and boil all of his garments. G-d only knew what vermin he was carrying with him. Even better, they'd go to the secondhand shop and buy him some new underwear; maybe even a Shabbos suit. It was obvious that Zelig's clothing would never fit Yaakov's stocky physique, but for at least this evening's supper, he would have to wear them whether they fit or not.

"Zelig, where are you? You both have to go to the bathhouse before supper. Take some clean clothing for Yaakov, and while you're gone, I'll prepare something for us to eat."

Zelig, who was sulking at the entrance of the apartment, heard Minnie and complied. He knew he couldn't eat at the same table with that farshtunkena mess. Unless he got him cleaned up, they would never eat. Hunger pangs mingled with an anxious churning in his stomach. Grabbing several towels and a large bar of soap to augment the ones at the bathhouse, he scrambled through his dresser drawers to find something that might half-fit the shmendrik.

"Let's go, Yaakov, or we'll never get to eat."

Minnie called out to them.

"Be back in an hour! Just get him cleaned up and come home. Supper will be late enough as it is!"

* * *

They walked to the shvits just down their street. As they entered, Yaakov was enveloped in steam and couldn't see past Zelig's back. Zelig headed toward a room with pegs on the wall and wooden cubbies stuffed with clothing. Boots and heavy shoes lay helter-skelter around the room.

"Hurry up and get undressed. Put your clothing and shoes in the corner." Zelig tried to put his belongings as far away from Yaakov's as the room would allow.

They reentered the steamy room with a huge, coal-fired oven covered in what looked like concrete. The walls and floors were black-and-white tiles, all wet and sweating with hot moisture. There were steps going up and spigots of dripping water. Next to the spigots were large iron pails. Every few minutes one of the men would throw a pail of cold water on the oven, creating an avalanche of steam. Zelig pointed to a large bundle of oak twigs, fastened together with rope.

"Hand me that *besom*."

At that moment, a short man with an enormous stomach that seemed to emanate from his neck collected bars of soap from a few other naked men. He threw them into an enormous pail of hot water, and stirred a besom vigorously in the pail. Huge soap bubbles and suds sloshed over the pail. Then he took the besom out, splashed a man lying on a step with soapy suds, and proceeded to twirl it around the man's prone body.

"Ah, a *mekhia*! That feels wonderful," sighed the man, lying on his back, his penis nearly obscured by pubic hair and soapy water. Then his short, pregnant-looking friend twirled the broomlike stick all around his body and ended by scrubbing the prone man with the leaves of the besom.

"Now you do it to me!" The man with the enormous belly lumbered up a step, spread his towel, and waited for his comrade to return the favor.

"Let's get going, Yaakov. Minnie will kill us if we don't hurry up!"

He gestured toward a step away from the circle of friends. Zelig stood on a wretched-looking towel they picked up when they paid their shvits fee and proceeded to twirl and scrub Yaakov violently with the besom. It would take a lot of soap, water, and scrubbing to remove the accumulated filth from Yaakov's body.

"Take that scrub brush! Scrub your hands and nails—your toenails too. Minnie won't let you near her table with those hands." He took one of the smaller pails of hot water and instructed Yaakov to scrub all his hair from the top of his head to his crotch. Who knew what he was harboring in those follicles, especially around his groin?

When Yaakov was cleaned up to Zelig's satisfaction, they entered another room with a large pool of cold water. Men jumped into the pool directly from the steam room, shrieking as they hit the surface.

Zelig pushed a resistant Yaakov into the cold-water pool, held his nose, and jumped in after him. As they got used to the extreme temperature change, Yaakov began to float around, as if in a fog, bumping into other men.

"Let's go, Yaakov! We have to dry off and get dressed. I have other clothes for you. Dump yours into the trash bin. Just keep your shoes."

They entered yet another room, where men sat around wrapped in towels, schmoozing, playing cards, eating, drinking, and arguing.

"What, are you crazy? Pinkus on Mulberry is the only place to go for a good suit. Two pairs of pants and a vest. Very good prices."

"What do you know! I got a place near Canal that makes Pinkus look like a shmate factory. The best material, good tailors, their clothes wear like iron!"

After they argued for a few minutes more, having resolved nothing, the men sat down for a cup of tea laced with a shot of schnapps. Yaakov joined the group when it turned out they were landsmen from a nearby village. They offered him a shot of whiskey, some herring, and a roll.

Zelig poked his head out of the room and inquired about the time from one of the attendants.

"Hurry up, Yaakov. We're here over two hours already. You can schmooze another time; we're late!"

On the way home, Yaakov kept touching his mustache and beard while rubbing his cheek. His facial hair was soft and springy instead of the usual coagulated mess, stiffened with food, drink, and mucus. His cheek was also soft to the touch, plumped by moisture and heat. He felt positively euphoric and couldn't wait to go back to the bathhouse again.

More than two hours later, a thoroughly scrubbed Yaakov appeared at Minnie's table.

"What on earth kept you so long? I said an hour; not the whole night!"

Zelig muttered, "There was a lot to clean up. You think it was easy?"

Yaakov couldn't button Zelig's pants and shirt, so Minnie gave him an apron to cover his hairy chest and stomach. She set the table with her good dishes and a fancy tablecloth.

They waited as Zelig said a blessing over the bread and wine. Yaakov mumbled a prayer and tore off a large chunk of dark bread, dunking it into his filled soup bowl. He slurped the soup, holding the tablespoon like a shovel, and picked up the soup bowl to drain the last drops. Cabbage and soup liquid dripped from his mustache and beard as he held out his bowl for Minnie to fill again.

Minnie and Zelig exchanged glances across the table. Obviously there would be a lot for them to get used to.

27

Unwelcome Guest

Yaakov's snoring thundered throughout the apartment. Zelig had left for the shop hours before, and Minnie had already borrowed a huge kettle from the boarding house to boil Yaakov's clothes. She was in the midst of sorting through a pile of crumpled-up, damp rags that she found in the top layer of his trunk. Under the clothing were heavy tools, starting to rust from the water that seeped into the trunk. Thank G-d, no lice, but everything smelled of mildew from the soggy clothing. She breathed through her mouth as she drew out the stinking clothing with a huge pair of tongs, placing them in the kettle of lye soap and boiling water. Fortunately he didn't have much, but where on earth would she be able to dry the faded rags once she got them clean? Even his wedding suit, rolled up in a sheet, was a mess. Besides, only a real greenhorn would wear the embroidered vest and shirt with the voluminous sleeves to shul. He didn't even have an extra pair of shoes or boots, just the worn-out muddy boots he came in.

She would have to take him to Markowitz's secondhand clothing store first thing, but how could he be seen on the street in Zelig's skimpy outfit covered by her apron? Minnie went to the apartment next door and knocked.

"Mrs. Pinchek, can I ask a big favor? My brother-in-law just got off the boat. We have no clothes to fit him. Can I borrow a pair of trousers and a shirt from your mister until the next wash? Yes, a coat would be a big help too . . . thank you."

"Whatever you need, Bubbala, you just ask. So how long is he staying with you? What about your mama and sister? Are they coming too? By the way, my mister loved the babke you baked—maybe you'll tell me how to make it."

"I'll make him one for this Shabbos. I'll let you know when I'm baking so you can come in and watch."

She's a kind person, Minnie thought. *I just don't want our business all over the shul.*

When she got back to the apartment, Yaakov was sitting in the kitchen, looking like a bear in cub's clothing.

"I slept like the dead last night. Between the shvits and your cooking, it was like being rocked in my mama's arms again! Zelig's gone already?"

"It's nearly noon. You needed a good night's sleep, but we have lots to do today. Have some bread and cheese—I left some for you on the table. Would you like a glass of tea?"

After Yaakov had eaten and was sipping tea through a sugar cube held between his teeth, Minnie sat down at the table across from him.

"Yaakov, how is my Mama really feeling? Is she still mourning for Papa? Does she miss living on the farm? It's so hard to know what's really going on from the letters I get. I know she pinches pennies with the scribe, and she was never such a talker anyhow."

He extracted the half-melted sugar cube and placed it on a saucer.

"You know your Mama. She doesn't complain much, always making herself busy with the girls and the cooking and cleaning. When I say to her, 'Mama, enough already, sit down!' she picks up some knitting or sewing."

"How about those terrible headaches she used to get on one side of her head? Does she still get them? She used to have to lie in bed for hours in the dark before they went away. How about her hip? Does it still hurt her when the weather is damp and cold? Sometimes she could barely stand on her two feet . . ."

"I don't know about that. I was always out of the house from early to late shoeing the horses. Now that I think about it, sometimes she'd rub her hip and sit down."

"We send as much as we can, but I know money is scarce. Has Mama gotten any work in the village? Does she do any knitting or sewing for the rebbe or yeshiva teacher?"

"She sometimes does washing and ironing for the rebbe's family and the rich goyim. I think she had to take in laundry when I was away and Frima was working in Minsk, but I'm not sure . . ."

Vey iz mir! *What my sister and mother have to put up with. Mama, with a bad hip, taking care of the girls and slaving over other people's laundry. How could you have been so stupid? Why were you hanging around with a bunch of goniffs? Didn't you, a married man with responsibilities, know they were up to no good? Were you really tricked or did you know about the horse-stealing plan?*

"How long were you away?"

"I was supposed to be in Siberia for eighteen months, but I was very lucky. The Cossack in charge of the Guard took a liking to me . . . he had a horse that he kept in a stable. Like a baby he treated that horse . . . a beautiful Arabian steed. When he found out I was a blacksmith, he picked me to groom, shoe, and exercise it. I did such a good job that he let me train someone else to take charge of that beauty when my time would be up. I asked him to speak to the head commissioner and my term was reduced to twelve months."

"Was Frima working in Minsk the whole twelve months you were gone? What kind of a family did she work for? Did they treat her well?"

"I suppose so; I never heard her complain about them. She was hired by the family of a rich, old couple to take care of them. She once mentioned they were *kvetchy* but not unkind. I'm not sure how long Frima worked for them; I was having my own troubles."

"Did they have children or grandchildren? Did anybody else live in the house?"

"I think they had a daughter who lived nearby, but I'm not sure. I'll tell you, it was a good thing Mama was with the girls. I understand Gelde got diphtheria when Frima was gone. Mama ran with her to the town doctor, who made a hole in her throat so she could breathe . . ."

"I can't believe they never wrote me about Gelde! How is she now? Can she breathe okay? Did Chaje catch it from her?"

"Everything is fine now."

"But what about Gelde? Does she have a big scar where they closed up the hole?"

"To tell the truth, it's not so big. A chasan doesn't look for those things when it's time for a girl to marry. Besides, the girls always wear high collars, even in the summer."

"Tell me about you and Frima. How did you meet? Was the marriage arranged by a matchmaker or did the two sets of parents make the arrangements?"

"I guess you didn't hear. My parents, of blessed memory, passed away before I met Frima. One day I was walking through the fields, leading a horse to be shoed, when I saw her. What a change! She was a skinny little nothing when I was attending yeshiva. I didn't see her for a long time until that day when she was working in the fields. Not such a pretty face, mind you, but nice and buxom, with a full bosom—a real *shtarke!* I started calling on her, and I asked your Mama and Papa if we could be married. I was a good catch—after all, I had a trade."

Did you and Frima have to get married? Mama and Papa had no dowry to give, so why did you choose a penniless girl who wasn't such a beauty? Did you take advantage of her when Mama and Papa were working in the fields? I wouldn't be surprised. How do you treat her and Mama now? Are you respectful? I hope you don't yell or G-d forbid hit Frima or the girls!

"I'm sorry to hear about your parents," Minnie said aloud. "I remember that they were nice people."

Yaakov nodded abruptly. Minnie could see that Yaakov was getting tense and restless under her barrage of questions and talking about his dead parents.

"I have to use the toilet," he told her. "I'll be right back."

When he reentered the kitchen, he said, "Don't we have a lot to do? Shouldn't we be getting out of the apartment soon?"

"We still have some time, and I have to finish the wash. Have another cup of tea. I saved a piece of babke from our last Shabbos dinner. Would you like it?"

"I wouldn't mind."

Minnie waited until he finished the coffee cake and tea and turned to him, smiling.

"Tell me about the girls. What are they like? I only have that old picture of them when they were practically babies. Were they very upset when you left?"

Yaakov's face lit up.

"Chaje is like a little mother to Gelde except once in awhile she gets jealous and pinches her when she thinks nobody is looking. Gelde is dark like me, with big, round eyes. She's very affectionate and loves to cuddle in my lap. I call her my little princess. Chaje is the image of Frima when she was a child; at least that's what Mama says. In fact, she could be your daughter—slight with fair hair and hazel eyes."

Minnie's eyes welled with tears.

When I felt so frightened and miserable, it was Frima who would lie in bed next to me, her skinny little arms clutching me, whispering loving words in my ear . . .

"You won't recognize Frima now. She put on more weight after the girls were born. She looks like a real Polack. Anyhow, that's the way I like my woman, with a little meat on her bones . . ."

Minnie glanced down at her own thin, compact frame, then turned back to the huge kettle and stirred the clothing.

"The children are a joy, but I'm hoping that the next one is a boy . . ."

"What, Frima is expecting again? I didn't know that! How far along is she? Why didn't anyone write me?"

"We were too busy trying to get me out of Russia!"

"So when is she expecting the baby?"

"I'm not sure—I was so busy running around, trying to get everything ready for leaving—maybe in the spring . . ."

What an idiot! I'm surprised he even knows that Frima is having another baby, let alone when she's expecting. It's like trying to squeeze a drop out of a dried-up lemon to get him to say anything important. What did they talk about in that house? I could just see him bolting down his food at the dinner table and then rushing out with his cronies for some schnapps.

"It is getting late. I'll need your help to carry the clothes bucket and the wringer downstairs. I just hope there are enough lines in the basement to hang up all these things."

He gestured to the ridiculous outfit he was wearing.

"Here, put on Mr. Pinchek's clothing. You'll at least be able to button them."

When Yaakov came out of the bedroom in his borrowed finery, he looked only slightly less silly. He could button the clothing, but the pants and sleeves were much too short, and his hairy wrists, forearms, and shins stuck out.

"Maybe the coat will cover you up."

* * *

The first thing they did was go to the barbershop, which was on the way to Markowitz's Used Clothing. Yaakov refused to take off Mr. Pinchek's coat as the barber clipped away at his mustache, beard, and long hair.

"You have to pay ten cents for that? At home, we don't have a barber—Frima or Mama always cut my hair and beard."

Minnie didn't respond but carted him to the next stop. She bought him two pairs of overalls, work shirts, underwear, and a pair of dress boots that almost fit. They were about to leave when she saw a Shabbos suit that looked about the right size.

"How much?"

"A dollar fifty. It's practically new."

"*How much?* After we bought so much from you? Is that your best price?"

"All right, I could take off a little. Believe me; I'm giving it away at a dollar and a quarter. A deal like that you won't get anywhere else."

"One dollar; not a penny more!"

They finally settled on one dollar and ten cents for the suit, with a dress shirt, bowtie, and a broad-brimmed hat thrown in for another fifty cents.

When Yaakov came out of the makeshift dressing room, he looked positively transformed. Minnie could see what had attracted her sister to Yaakov now that he looked presentable. With his well-trimmed hair, beard, and mustache and the new Shabbos suit, Yaakov was very handsome. His dark eyes sparkled as he admired himself in the new clothing, turning this way and that in front of the chipped, full-length mirror.

He refused to take off the suit when they got back to the apartment at dusk. Minnie made him wear her apron so that he wouldn't soil the suit when they ate supper that night. When Zelig came home for dinner, he was amazed at the transformation as well.

Look at that shnorer. He looks like the crown prince on our money. His table manners haven't improved any; he still eats like a pig. He'd better get his tokhes moving and get a job.

After dinner, Yaakov gave a resounding belch and, without a word, made his way to the lavatory in the hall.

Minnie and Zelig looked at one another. Teaching him to be halfway civilized would be quite an endeavor.

* * *

Yaakov had been with them for a month but still had no steady work.

"Don't give him any more money for the baths, Minnie. Maybe that will give him a reason to get a job. He thinks he's on a vacation! All he wants to do is hang around the shvits and schmooze with his new friends. You'd think he'd at least make an attempt to look for something . . . and the way he eats! Forget about the revolting manners, even though it's hard to get through a meal sitting across from him. He eats enough for an army."

"He was looking for blacksmith work, and he did help out in the store when you needed someone to schlep all those heavy materials. I know he's no good with customers, but what can you expect from a greena just off the boat? A bargain my sister didn't get! I don't know why he keeps dragging his feet when he should be out looking."

"Why should he look when we take care of his every need? A mensh would want to get his family over as quickly as possible . . . and I don't want him in the shop! Did you see how he leers at every woman under the age of eighty? Even a greena should have more sense. He's *your* brother-in-law. You tell him he'd better start looking for something, or he'll find himself out in the street."

"So what's he suited for? Blacksmiths aren't exactly in demand these days with everyone using trolleys to travel. Soon people will be riding around in those motor machines . . . what are they called again? Even if he could get a blacksmith job, his tools are rusted beyond repair."

"Automobiles . . . look, he doesn't have brains but he has a strong back. There has to be something that shmendrik can do where he can make a living."

They hung up a big sign in the front window of the furniture store.

POSITION WANTED

STRONG, CAPABLE YOUNG MAN

JUST ARRIVED

LOOKING FOR EMPLOYMENT

SKILLED BLACKSMITH, IRONWORKER

WILLING TO WORK IN ANOTHER FIELD

INQUIRE WITHIN

Times were hard, and work was scarce. There were illiterate, unskilled workmen spilling off the boats and flooding all the immigrant neighborhoods. The sign sat prominently in the window, but there were no inquiries.

As it turned out, Yaakov's bathhouse schmoozing paid off. He met a landsman from the Nolopina area who was looking for a coal delivery man. By now he was tired of Minnie's nagging and Zelig's contemptuous looks over the dinner table . . . and he just might have felt a twinge of guilt about being a shnorer. He missed Frima and especially the girls. Yaakov was hoping for a son this time . . . not that he didn't love his girls . . . but imagine if they had a boy; someone to carry on the family name. Besides, it was humiliating to go to Minnie for every cent and risk an inquisition and a lecture on frugality. He'd pay them for room and board and save for passage, but maybe there would be a little extra to spare for some fun.

* * *

"Now that he has a job, he can move over to the rooming house and leave us in peace. I feel like the apartment is just full of him. Everywhere I go for a little privacy, he's there. Even when I go to the privy, he always seems to get there first, stinking up the place."

"That's ridiculous. First of all, we share that privy with three other families on the floor. You're hardly ever home. If you're not in the shop, you're in Crown Heights or at the Socialist center."

"Maybe I'd be home more if it wasn't so unpleasant with him around."

"Zelig, think of the money we could save by having Yaakov here. Mama, Frima, and the children could come over that much sooner. It's not safe for two women and the children to live by themselves in Chalupanich. There's always the threat of a pogrom or some drunken Cossack coming into the house. Who knows what could happen to them?"

"I keep telling you they should move in with the relatives in Nolopina until we're ready to send for them. Believe me, your family could use all the help they can get to work the farm and look after Raisa's children.

Besides, we're sending Mama and Frima money. It's not as if they're going to the relatives as paupers, to be an extra burden."

"I want them here as soon as possible. With all three of us working and saving toward their passage, we could probably do it in less than two years. How would you feel if your parents, of blessed memory, were alone and in danger? If your sister Gittel wanted to come, we'd be saving for her too."

"Now who's exaggerating? If Mama and Frima go to Nolopina, they'll be safe. I just can't stand the idea of living with that lump for nearly two more years. Don't we count for something? Do you enjoy cooking for him, cleaning up his shmuts, all the time treating him like some special guest? He's in *my room*! I want it back!" The argument went on for several months with Yaakov still living in the apartment. Minnie made sure she got Yaakov's pay envelope every Friday, doling out just enough for carfare and necessities. She kept the money in a box inside her bedroom dresser, hidden between her corsets and undergarments.

Of course, Yaakov found her hiding place and helped himself to a few dollars. There was an enormous row when he got home, since Minnie accounted for every cent she took from Yaakov.

"How dare you go in my bedroom and look in my drawers? That money is for your wife and children! Don't you have any shame? How can you be so selfish?"

"It's my money, damn it! Stop yelling at me!"

A furious Zelig grabbed him by the throat, wrenching his collar open. "That's enough! How dare you talk that way to my wife? After all we've done, you go sneaking around, pawing through Minnie's underwear? Get the hell out of my house before I kill you!"

Yaakov grabbed Zelig's offending hand, thought better of it, and let go. He ran out of the apartment, seeking refuge in the bathhouse where he could tell all his friends how ill-treated he was by his in-laws.

"That's it, Minnie. Either he leaves or I do. Tell Mrs. Epstein she has another boarder right now. I won't spend another night with him under our roof."

He stalked into Yaakov's bedroom, flung open the drawers, and began throwing all of his belongings into the parlor.

"Stop it! I never saw you act like such a maniac . . . you'll give yourself a heart attack! I'll pack his things and we'll take them to the boardinghouse. I promise he'll be out of here tonight. Just calm down."

"It's bad enough he's a shnorer, but a thief too? I never want him in this house again!"

Yaakov didn't come back until the next morning. Zelig had already gone to work, but Minnie was at the door, waiting for the black sheep to arrive.

"Your belongings are at the boardinghouse. You can get breakfast over there."

Yaakov couldn't understand why they made such a big *tsimes* out of a few dollars.

It was my money; it's not like I was stealing from them. I couldn't stand it there anyhow, always being treated like a bad child. Don't put your feet on the covers! Eat with the fork, not with your hands! Wipe your face, it's all greasy! *It may take longer to get Frima and the children over, but at least I'll be free of them. Good riddance!*

After a few weeks, Minnie relented and asked Yaakov over for supper on a night Zelig wouldn't be there. He was still family, and how would it be if they weren't speaking when Mama and Frima came? She wasn't able to ask him over for Shabbos because Zelig refused to sit at the same table with him. Hopefully he'd change his mind once the whole family was reunited.

28

Enterpreneurs

Greenberg arrived unexpectedly in the shop early one evening. "What's going on here? I've been getting complaints from customers about their orders."

"You know, Mr. Greenberg, I was sick for awhile. I'm just starting to get back on my feet. Please explain to the customers; I'm trying to catch up."

"So why is the Shmolowitz table done and the Kantor bureau, which came in three weeks before, not even started?"

"I needed to get my strength back before I could manage such a huge piece of furniture. Please apologize for me to the Kantors; I'll do their order next."

Greenberg looked around the shop and examined the sample ketubas artfully arranged on the wall.

"What is this? You can't get my work done that I pay you an honest wage for, but you can do these on my time, using my workshop and my materials? I should call the police—you've been stealing from me!"

Zelig turned deep red at the accusation.

"Excuse me, Boss. I haven't touched the ketubas since before I got sick. I always did your work first. I made the ketubas on my own time."

"Still, you're using *my* wood, *my* workspace and *my* oil for the lamps!"

"But Mr. G., I only used scrap wood, never the good stuff. You told me it didn't pay to cart the scraps out to a pulp mill. Before the ketubas, I always threw scrap wood in the trash."

"So you're making a nice business off my back. I won't allow this! Once you're up to date on every order, you can start making the ketubas and frames, but I want half of everything you make on them. If I wasn't so generous, I'd make you pay for all the ones you made in the past . . . no, don't make excuses; things are going to be different around here!"

"Boss, do you know how many hours I spent in the shop making your furniture when there was a rush period? Sometimes I'd have to sleep here; I wouldn't get through until maybe three in the morning. You promised me when I started that you'd raise my salary when business started to improve. I'm still making almost the same salary as the day I started. Now you call me a thief because I need to make a living wage on my own time with wood you said to throw away?"

"Zelig, catch up on those orders. You'd better do them on time, the way they come in. I don't need aggravation with customers kvetching that nothing is done on time. Don't think I won't be checking up on those ketubas—I want fifty percent of the price."

Zelig was beside himself. There wouldn't be any intervention from Mrs. Greenberg, now that she had her new pet artist to sponsor. Zelig heard that she'd set up a private show for that no-talent pisher at her friend's gallery on the Lower East Side. It gnawed at Zelig, but he was curious to see the new Fauvre craze. He just didn't have the time or energy to visit the gallery. He'd do it maybe early one Saturday, when the gallery opened. Then he'd be sure not to run into either Mrs. Greenberg or her artistic discovery.

Zelig went home and told Minnie about the entire encounter with Greenberg. She listened quietly at first but became furious when he told her about being called a thief and that they'd have to split the ketuba and framing money with Greenberg.

"That cheap mamser has been cheating us for years. We can't put up with his ridiculous demands. Besides, you may not be able to go back to working on large pieces like before. Let me think about this and we'll talk in the morning. Don't worry, Zelig. He won't get away with this."

They opened the shop early the next morning but kept the CLOSED sign up for an additional hour. Sitting in the back room, Minnie hatched her plan.

"We have to start our own business, Zelig. If we can get a cheap enough rent, we can do it."

"We can't make a living from just frames and ketubas. Even if we include small furniture and my paintings, it won't be enough. Now we'll have to pay for rent and materials. We'll have to advertise to get our old customers back. You know how long it takes to get a new business off the ground?"

"Remember we talked about getting a camera? Why can't we set up a photography studio in the front and have sample frames for the customers to pick from? We can buy scrap wood from Greenberg's competitor near Pitkin Avenue—you can be sure he'll give us a good price if he has a chance to put Greenberg out of business."

"Minnie, you're dreaming! What do I know about photography? I'd need a good camera, a darkroom, and chemicals—where am I going to learn all that? Where will we get the money to buy all those things?"

"That's why we have to bide our time. Finish up that mamser's work. Greenberg doesn't have to know if you get any ketuba orders . . . do them at home. You can get Yaakov to schlep around the heavy stuff for you. It's the least he can do . . . he can help you after work instead of running off to the baths to *trumbanik* with his cronies. I had a little talk with Yaakov and told him if he didn't give me three dollars every week from his pay, I would go back to Ellis Island and talk to them about revoking his visa. He's so scared about being sent back that he's been giving me the money every week without excuses."

Zelig smiled in spite of himself.

"You really know what works with that no-goodnik. I tip my hat to you."

Then he got back to Minnie's meshugena plan.

"Even if I find someone to teach me, how am I going to find time to learn about photography? I never even held one of those newfangled camera gadgets in my hands."

"How hard could it be? All you have to do is point the camera, put in one of those glass plates, and squeeze a bulb. You're so good with your hands; you'll learn in no time, with just a few lessons. We'll find a photographer to teach you . . . instead of spending your time playing chess on Wednesday nights, you could learn."

Zelig should have given Minnie a firm "no"; it was a crazy scheme. At the same time, he knew they would never get ahead working for Greenberg. He went home that night with a monumental headache and self-medicated with a few shots of schnapps. He lit the gas lamp and looked at the stunning impressionist landscapes by Monet and Van Gogh in his art books.

* * *

A few weeks later, Minnie ran to the back of the furniture store, her wig askew and her coat open.

"Zelig, guess what? You remember Geller, the photographer further down on Pitkin Avenue? I hear he's going out of business and selling all the things in his shop."

"How do you know?"

"I just went out for a few minutes to buy things for supper and I passed the shop. I saw a big sign in his window. It said, GOING OUT OF BUSINESS: INQUIRE WITHIN. So I did. I spoke to Geller and he says he's willing to sell his equipment. Zelig, it's perfect! The front would make a wonderful studio—he even has a whole mural of a fancy house. You know how people like to send pictures back to the old country, making it look like they live in a palace. He says he's taking one of the cameras, but he has a very good one that he'll give us at a fair price—he'll even throw in the mural."

"Why is he going out of business?"

"He said he's getting too old; he wants to move near his children."

"Probably the business is going down the drain."

"We could at least find out. Geller said he'd show us the accounts. He said he's making a living just with the photography. I bet we could do three times as much business with the frames, ketubas, your pictures, and other knickknacks we come up with. It's our opportunity to get out from under Greenberg."

"Let me think about it."

"I told him we were coming over tonight, after we closed the shop. He'll be waiting for us at six."

"Why did you tell him that, Minnie? Why do you want to rush into this? He could be a cheat. He could be changing the figures in the ledgers. He could have lousy equipment. And what do we know about him anyhow? I never heard that he had a good reputation."

"Did you ever hear that he had a bad reputation? I never did, and I'm in the community more than you are. Look, let's just go and talk to him—no harm in that."

* * *

Geller showed Zelig the camera that was for sale and how to operate it. It looked like a huge wooden box on a stand with a Cyclops eye in the center.

"It's practically new; just two years old. All the commercial photographers are using the matte collodian technique. You'll always need to put it on this pedestal. It's called a tripod. If you hold the camera in your hands, the picture will be blurry or on a slant. Also, you have to be very careful of the glass when you slip it in the back. Believe me, it can crack very easily, so slip it in like this . . . no, you have to make sure it's straight when you slide it in. I'll show you again."

Geller showed Zelig the darkroom and all the chemicals needed to develop the pictures. Even with the windows wide open, the chemical smell was overpowering. The fumes gave Zelig a headache and he wondered if

Geller was getting out of the business because the chemicals were making him sick . . . not that he would ever admit it to a potential buyer.

"First, you put the paper in this tray for no more than two minutes; then you take it out with these tongs and put it in the second tray. You have to be very careful of the timing; otherwise the pictures will be either too light or too dark. You want to get it right the first time; the paper is very expensive."

After some haggling, Zelig was allowed to take the camera home to practice.

"Remember, if anything happens to the glass plate or the lens, you'll be responsible."

Zelig appeared stricken, and Minnie gave him a warning look.

Geller showed him how to set up a small darkroom in the apartment so he could practice developing the pictures. The fumes permeated the whole place; at first Minnie and Zelig would gag from the acrid odor. The windows were wide open, even when the wind was blowing fiercely, but they couldn't get rid of that smell. Minnie hesitated to turn on the stove for fear she would blow up the place. They waited until Zelig was finished in the darkroom before doing any cooking. Sometimes the fumes were so pungent Zelig would sleep in the shop. Minnie seemed to mind the disruption less and was more tolerant of the noxious odor.

"This is going to free us from that miserable man. I can stand bad smells if I know that we'll have our own place."

At first Zelig took pictures of everything for practice—the furniture, Minnie, a few self-portraits, even Yaakov. Now that the shmendrik was contributing regularly toward his family's passage, Zelig reluctantly let him in the house. He caught Yaakov telling them a joke that he'd heard at the bathhouse. The photo was blurred, but the irrepressible Yaakov was laughing uproariously, capturing a moment of complete enjoyment and merriment. Most of the pictures were terrible. Some were streaked and blurred, some were too dark or light due to developing errors. There were even a few where he either cut off the person's head or feet. He found out just how expensive it was for the chemicals and paper, so he became a little more judicious about the photographs he took. Zelig was nervous that he would mishandle the borrowed camera and have to pay for the damages. Sure enough, he scratched the glass plate, which cost half their week's salary to replace.

Minnie, usually so careful with money, said, "Well, it's an investment in our future. We have to expect that something might go wrong."

At last he presented Minnie with a photograph that he took of her face, which was in focus, centered, and a delicate shade of sepia. Minnie peered at the photo for a long time. There she was, frozen in time, with the beginnings of lines around her mouth, furrows on her forehead, and two vertical lines between her eyebrows that she never noticed before. She took the photograph to her bedroom, lit the gaslight and stared at her face in the glass. Minnie looked at her down-turned mouth and gave a mirthless smile at her image in the mirror. She puffed out her cheeks and lowered her eyebrows to erase the newly etched lines in her face.

When was the last time I laughed? I can't remember!

An image flashed through her mind of running after Frima in the fields when she was little, catching her and the two of them tumbling in the grass, laughing uproariously. It was the last time she remembered feeling truly joyful. She stared once more at the photo and her image in the glass.

Is this what I look like? When did I get so old?

She went back in the parlor, and Zelig took the photo from her hand.

"This is the best picture I've taken. We have to put it in the window to advertise."

Minnie snatched the picture back.

"You will not! I don't want everybody looking at me. I don't even have my nice wig on. Do you want everyone in the neighborhood laughing at me?"

She tore the photograph in tiny pieces and threw it in the garbage pail.

* * *

When Zelig and Minnie told Greenberg that they were leaving, he was livid.

"We have a contract! You can't just leave—we have new orders."

"Show me a written contract!"

"It doesn't have to be written. We shook hands on it! If you had an ounce of integrity, you wouldn't be leaving with all these orders coming in. If it's more money you want, we can talk about it . . . you think you'll be able to make a living on those farshtunkena ketubas and frames? Be sensible!"

In the end, Greenberg offered to double their salaries and only take five percent of the profits from the framed ketubas. Zelig recalled his last encounter with Monaghan at the farm. Now he was even more wary of what they were doing, but Minnie was adamant. When they refused his offer, Greenberg began to threaten them, just like Monaghan had done.

"You know, I have a lot of influence in this neighborhood. I can tell the community not to buy from you, that you're a thief and a goniff who doesn't honor a contract! We'll see how much business you get."

Zelig was upset by Greenberg's threats, but Minnie wasn't the least bit perturbed.

Why didn't Minnie feel the same kind of doubts that he did? When it came to business, she was always ready to forge ahead, no matter what the consequences might be. Zelig wished he had her confident, single-minded purpose.

* * *

Four months after Greenberg delivered his ultimatum, Minnie and Zelig opened the business. Minnie wanted to name it "Frumkin's Framing and Photography Shop" but Zelig insisted on calling it "The Phoenix," after the mythical bird that rose from the ashes. She argued that nobody would be able to figure out what kind of business it was from the name; it sounded like some fancy Crown Heights dress shop. They compromised on "The Phoenix Framing and Photo Shop." Minnie wanted Zelig to get joy out of owning his own business. Maybe it would help him forget the whore.

The first month they only made four sales of ketubas. Nobody seemed interested in being photographed. Zelig became very discouraged and fervently wished that they hadn't been so hasty about leaving Greenberg.

Why did I listen to her? Greenberg offered to double our salaries and take only five percent out of the ketuba business. I should have taken it. Minnie gets a meshuge idea and I follow along like a sheep. What's the matter with me?

"I told you it wouldn't be any good. Now we have less than nothing, thanks to you. You just plunge right ahead and I, like a shmuck, get dragged along."

"You have to have a little patience. Of course, it will be slow at first; you said so yourself. Fortunately we have a little money set aside. As long as we can pay for rent and food, we'll be able to make do until business picks up. You know it takes awhile to get a new business started. We'll just have to do more advertising . . . yes, I know we can't afford to advertise in a magazine or *The Daily Forward*, but we can hand out leaflets around the neighborhood. There's a bulletin board in the hallway of the shul. We can put an advertisement there; I'm sure the rebbe will let me."

Minnie spent part of her time placing leaflets in tenement hallways and asking local businesses if she could be allowed to put an ad on their walls. While they waited for customers, Zelig taught Minnie how to make simple frames and she even began to learn the rudiments of taking photographs. At first Zelig was afraid to allow her to touch the photography equipment, but he recognized the need for both of them to be able to run the business. What would happen if he got sick again? He still hadn't fully recovered his strength, and sometimes he felt as if his heart skipped beats or was racing like a horse in full gallop.

Over a month passed before they got their first photography job. Sura Leah and Binyamin from the shul were celebrating their first son's Bar Mitzvah. They wanted photographs of the Bar Mitzvah boy and the whole family to send back to the old country, and at least three large photos to display on the parlor walls of their apartment. Minnie figured out a simkhe rate, charging them ten percent less if they bought more than six photographs, and threw in an extra photo of the boy. By now Zelig was adept at taking studio portraits and made frames that were beautifully carved, stained, and finished. Everyone was happy with the results. It gave Zelig and Minnie some financial breathing room, and Sura Leah and Binyamin were so pleased they showed off the photographs to the entire neighborhood and congregation. They invited the family and all their friends to the house for a viewing. They showed the Teppers, who were having a wedding for their daughter. The Teppers took an expanded simkhe package and were so pleased they showed the Ginsbergs, who just had a new baby. All of a sudden, Zelig and Minnie began to get steady photography business, especially for weddings and Bar Mitzvahs. They took photos, supplied the frames, and Minnie came up with the idea of a shipping service to the old country as well.

"Don't worry, Mrs. Cohen. You have so much on your head planning the simkhe. Just let the bride and groom come in before the wedding all dressed up. You'll have the pictures even before they get married, and the family in the old country will feel like they were at the simkhe. How much more? Don't worry; I'll set a good price for you. Of course there'll be shipping and handling, but you save yourself the nuisance of having to schlep the pictures to the post office and wait on those lines. We have a new type of fancy matting for the photographs. Do you want to see it? If you buy, I'll throw in a couple of free ones for the bride and groom's parlor photographs."

Soon they had neighborhood and congregation business for births and engagements too. Zelig hardly had time for the ketubas.

"Minnie, you were so right. If only I had your determination and faith."

"You have the golden hands, Zelig. Between us, we make a good team."

Walking home one night, they passed Greenberg's Furniture Store and saw a FOR RENT sign in the window. They looked at each other, smiled, and Minnie took Zelig's hand.

"You see, Hashem punishes evil," said Minnie.

29

Letters From Home

9 May 1906
Dearest Mama,

Finally! We saved enough money to get you boat passage. All we need to do is get the proper documents. Now that you're all in Nolopina with the cousins, maybe Dina can take you to the Immigration Bureau right away. We must get started working on the papers you'll need to come to America. Then we can book passage for you in good weather. I'm so excited at the thought of hugging and kissing my beloved Mama! As soon as Yaakov and I save some more, we can get Frima and the children to come, maybe by next year.

Zelig and I hope that you're well. We send our loving thoughts to you, Frima and the children. Give fondest wishes to the relatives.

Your loving daughter, Michla

------

31 May 1906
Darling Michla,

You should send for Frima first. She should be with Yaakov. A father has a right to see his children. He's never seen the baby, his first son. Then we'll decide if I'm coming or not.

Lovingly, Mama

------

21 June 1906
Mama Dearest,

What do you mean by "we'll decide if I'm coming or not?" Of course you have to come. All of your children and grandchildren will be in America . . . how can you even think of staying in the old country? Maybe we can arrange it so that all of you come together. That way, you can help Frima; how will she manage with all the children? Now that Zelig and I are doing well in the shop, we can do it together with Yaakov's help. Please, Mama, have Dina or Raisa help you and Frima get the papers you'll need. We don't have time to lose. Kiss Frima and the children for us. We all send our love.

Michla

------

12 July 1906
Dearest;

    I don't know how to tell you what I must. Please just send passage for Frima and the grandchildren. I can't come. I'm not the Mama you remember. I was such a shtarke *before you left, and now I'm a weak old lady. I could never survive the passage. I'm too old to learn a new language and new ways. How can I live in a strange city? Papa and I were always farm people. I can't leave Papa in the cemetery alone. We must be buried together; that was always our wish. Please understand, dearest girl. We'll always be in touch by letters and pictures.*

Your Mama

------

30 July 1906
Mama,

    I beg you to change your mind. You'll be without your family. I know the relatives have been very good to you, but they aren't your close family. We will always love and care for you.

    You say you need to be buried with Papa, but only his bones are in the cemetery. His soul is in heaven and you'll join him there, Baruch Hashem, not for many years. If you're worried about learning English, I promise that you'll never have to know a word of it in this neighborhood. Everyone talks Yiddish here.

*I know you're worried about coming over on the boat . . .
When I came, I saw so many women your age by themselves.
You were just 54. Is that so old? And you would be coming
with Frima.*

*Mama, I said the grandchildren need you, but I need
you even more. It kills me to think that I will never see my
beloved Mama again. Here I am, a grown married woman,
crying like a baby for you. You say we'll be in touch by
letters and pictures. That's not really talking, counting the
scribe's words so it won't cost too much. You were always the
one in the family with the most common sense. I need your
guidance now.*

> *Please tell me you'll come.*
> *Your Heartsick Michla*

----

21 August 1906
Michla,

*I just can't. Please understand. You have your husband
and Frima has her family. I would just be a burden, and I'd
never adjust to a place that's so foreign to me. Don't think
that I don't long to see you, my dearest daughter. I'll always
carry the guilt that Papa and I didn't protect you when we
sent you to Minsk, but that's done. We can't go back and
change what happened. We're all in Hashem's hands. I carry
you in my heart and think of you every day.*

> *Your loving Mama*

* * *

Zelig heard the whine of the siren signaling the beginning of Shabbos. He was late again and didn't want to see Minnie's annoyed look. He bounded up the stairs, opened the door, and was met by darkness. The parlor was always dark, even at midday, due to the lack of windows, but Minnie always lit the Sabbath candles on the heavy wooden hutch, which gave a welcoming glow to the room. There was no smell of the Shabbat meal, no mixture of the flavorful scents of kugel, roast chicken, and freshly baked challah.

"Minnie, are you home?"

He found her sitting at the table with a piece of paper in her hand.

"What's wrong? Is it your Mama or Frima?"

Zelig sat across the table and awkwardly reached for her hand. The paper fell to the floor. He scooped it up and lit the gas lamp.

Zelig read through the contents of Mama's letter and covered Minnie's trembling fingers with his own.

"I'll never see her again."

Zelig remained silent.

Minnie sat and wept.

Zelig knew he should go over to Minnie and take her in his arms. He walked over and patted her shoulder.

"Minnie, why don't you light the Shabbos candles?"

* * *

Yaakov wasn't quite ready to be a married man with children again. Although he had moments of missing his family and couldn't wait to see his new son, he reveled in his freedom from constraints. Now that Minnie and Zelig were so busy in the shop, they didn't have time to oversee his activities, except for calling on him occasionally for their shipping orders. He usually was invited for Shabbos, but he preferred to go out to a tavern with his friends, getting a little shikker and occasionally visiting one of the whores in a rented room nearby, if he had an extra dollar or two. Now that Frima's voyage was paid for, Minnie didn't hound him for money the way she used to.

Minnie had a terrible sense of foreboding. She knew when the *Bohemia* was due to arrive. How had Frima fared on the journey to Hamburg? She wouldn't be any safer on the boat. Minnie couldn't imagine a woman alone in steerage with an infant and two young daughters. She remembered the story Zelig told her about his trip over and how a baby died from rat bites. Little Szol was never so strong. He was born early, and the midwife wasn't sure he would live. And what about Gelde? She'd had diphtheria when Frima was working in Minsk. She'd recovered, but who knew how healthy she was? Chaje would be a help to her mother, but she was still a child. Minnie recalled the dreck that traveled on those boats. How could Frima nurse and take care of an infant while keeping an eye on the girls?

The day finally arrived. Zelig couldn't take the day off, but by now Minnie had more confidence in her ability to read signs in English and ask directions to Ellis Island. Also, Yaakov would be with her. He didn't speak English, but he was a real shtarke; she knew that nobody would approach with his looming presence behind her. Still, she felt uneasy. Suppose they wouldn't let Frima and the children off the ship, or, once in the building, they were chalked and whisked off to the medical authorities? They might want to send Frima and the children back. She kept her fears to herself, knowing that Zelig would scoff at her, telling her what a worrier she was, and there was no sense in mentioning anything to Yaakov. He didn't have the imagination to worry; he had a head like a plate full of *kishke*.

My poor sister will have her hands full with him; it's like having another child and a bad one at that! Maybe I'm worrying for nothing; Zelig always says I worry ahead of time. I suppose he's right, but things are going so well in the shop. It just seems too good.

Minnie insisted that Yaakov come an hour early so they could make sure to be there when the boat arrived. She knew that it took hours to unload each ship, and they would be waiting half the day before Frima and the children set foot on land, but she wanted to be certain that they would have familiar, loving faces to greet them, just on the chance that the ship might arrive and unload early.

"Make sure to wear your Shabbos suit, Yaakov. Let me see your hands—here's a scissor. Cut your fingernails, and wash that dirt from your hands."

After Minnie inspected Yaakov's hands and made sure there were no further signs of him being unkempt, they were ready to catch the first of the three trolleys to Manhattan. When they finally arrived at Ellis Island, it took Minnie awhile to find the right building where the *Bohemia* passengers would disembark. She was right about the half-day wait, but finally, after the arrival of many other ships, she saw a sign that said ss *BOHEMIA*. Bedraggled passengers carrying babies, suitcases, trunks, and bedding folded up in worn sheets wearily made their way toward the waiting area to see the doctors and immigration officials. Minnie and Yaakov craned their necks, trying to spy the family. Finally, Yaakov cried out "Frimala!" and barreled his way toward Frima, who was clutching Szol to her breast with one hand and dragging a trunk with the other. The two girls, similarly laden with suitcases and packages, attempted to stay close to their mother and each other. Minnie hung back for a moment, trying to reconcile the image of her little sister with the large, squat woman just yards from her. The girls caught up to Frima and hid behind her skirts. By now Yaakov had reached his family and embraced Frima and the baby together, sweeping her off her feet. Then he turned his attention to the two little girls. Minnie was amazed to see tears streaming down his cheeks.

"Give your Tati a hug—I've waited so long to see you."

Minnie approached her sister. Yaakov had taken the baby and was making cooing sounds to the frightened little boy. The two women stared at each other for a moment and then fell into each other's arms.

"Darling sister, I never thought this day would come," said Minnie. "Hashem, of blessed name, brought you over safely."

Gelde and Chaje were shy with Minnie until she took two rag dolls from a large bag and presented them to the girls. Their eyes widened with joy.

"Thank you, Minnie. My girls never had a real doll before. I usually make dolls out of onions or potatoes stuck on sticks. Now they know they're really in the Golden Medina. Girls, give your Tante a big hug and thank her."

The girls curtsied and dutifully gave her a hug. She peered at the fretful baby being held by an awkward Yaakov.

"Can I hold him? I want to take a look at my nephew."

She took Szol and found an available bench. At first he screamed, but he calmed down as Minnie started to sing to him and shake a brightly colored rattle she had made for the child out of beans and painted cardboard.

"It's time to feed him, Michla. He's been too upset to nurse."

Minnie reluctantly vacated her bench seat and handed the squirming, sodden bundle back to Frima. She sat down, placed a cloth over her breast, and fumbled with the fastenings of her blouse. Little Szol nursed lustily at first, but after a few minutes he fell asleep. Frima reached down and tapped on the sole of his foot, poking out through the bundling. He opened one eye and his little mouth and tongue moved rhythmically until he connected with the breast again. After the feeding, Minnie stretched out her arms.

"I'd like to burp him. Is that all right?"

Frima placed Szol in Minnie's arms, putting the cloth over Minnie's shoulder. Minnie held the baby upright against her chest and rubbed his back until she heard a resounding *grepts*. She stood him up on her lap and rubbed noses with the little one, who smelled of breast milk, urine, and dirty cloth. He stepped from one foot to the other on her lap and smiled at her. Minnie pulled him close and kissed his round baby cheek.

* * *

It was fortunate that Minnie brought enough challah and chicken for all of them. The girls were ravenous, Yaakov could always eat, and Minnie wanted Frima to have enough nourishment so she could nurse the baby. They waited for hours on the benches to be called by the medical examiners. Finally it was their turn. Minnie and Yaakov minded the girls while Frima and the baby were examined. She came out with a relieved smile on her face; they had passed the examination and were given medical clearance. Minnie held the sleeping baby while Frima escorted the girls into the medical area. She watched the large clock on the wall, but Frima and the girls didn't come out of the office. Minnie gave Yaakov the baby to hold and timidly knocked at the door of the examination room.

"Nobody allowed in here!" she heard in Yiddish.

Finally, Frima came out with tears streaming down her face.

"They want to send Gelde back! What am I going to do?"

"Why? Is she sick?"

"Everything was going well until they looked at her scalp. She has sores on her head. They want to deport her, and I'll have to go back with her. How can I leave the baby?"

This time Minnie refused to be kept outside. She followed her sister through the door and confronted the official.

"Chaje, go outside to your Tati." She turned to the official and said, "What's wrong with my niece?"

"Lice. Her scalp is infected with sores. Her hair is infested with them."

"You send a child and her mother back for lice? Isn't there a treatment to get rid of them?"

"I don't know. Ask the doctor."

He gestured toward the desk. A burly, blond man in a dirty white coat sat there, filling out forms.

Frima approached him, speaking in Yiddish.

"Please doctor, don't send my child back."

He said abruptly, "I don't speak your language," and turned back to his papers. Minnie stepped forward, speaking to the doctor in broken English.

"Doctor, she not *krank* except the *kop*, no? I pay for medicine. She get better."

"We have rules to follow."

Minnie glanced frantically around. At the next desk she saw a dark, tired-looking man in a white coat speaking Yiddish to the immigrant couple in front of his desk. He got up and said to them, "Stay there, I'll be right back."

Minnie caught up with him.

"Doktor, du bist a Yid?"

He turned to her and nodded.

"Please don't send my niece back. My sister will have to go with her and take the baby. He's healthy now, but I don't know how he'd survive another ten days in steerage. Please, take pity on us."

The doctor looked at her, a mixed expression of exasperation and compassion on his face.

He answered her in Yiddish.

"Who are you?"

"I'm the tante. Please sir, you can cure her. What has to be done to get rid of the lice? I'll gladly pay."

"It's not my case."

"Please, Doctor, just talk to the other doctor for one minute. My husband and I are sponsoring them. Whatever my niece needs, we'll pay for. Please, just a minute of your time."

He reluctantly went over to the desk and conferred with the stocky doctor who kept shaking his head. Finally he walked back to Minnie and Frima.

"It's not just lice. She has infected sores all over her scalp. We'd have to shave off all her hair, disinfect her scalp and make sure those sores heal. They could make her very sick. It's Dr. Morrissey's case, anyhow."

"I'll take responsibility for everything. Any medication, I'll pay for. Please, Doctor, if you let her come home, I'll make sure she puts on the medication right. Just tell me what to do and where I can get the medicine."

He started walking to his desk without a response, but then turned back to the stocky doctor. They spoke quietly for a couple of moments. Finally Dr. Morrissey stood up and handed him the file.

"Katz, if you want to take responsibility, it's on your head. Here's the file; be my guest. Remember, if anything happens I have nothing to do with it." He muttered under his breath, "Those Yids all stick together." Then he gestured to the next group to come forward.

Dr. Katz took the offered papers and said curtly to Minnie and Frima, "Just wait behind the line near my desk. I have other people to take care of first."

When Dr. Katz finally finished with his patients, he reluctantly agreed to let Gelde go home with her aunt if she followed the medication regimen to the letter.

"Doctor, we kiss your hands. You've done such a mitzvah for our family!"

"Just make sure to take her to the barber and follow all the directions they give you at the infirmary. It's down the hall; turn to your right when you leave. We have to disinfect her scalp and shave her hair off. It will be very painful because of the sores. I'm shocked the rest of the family didn't catch them. It's a good thing your sister wears a *sheytl* and the older girl has her head covered. After her hair is shaved, the barber will direct you to the infirmary for the medicine. Good luck."

"Thank you, Doctor, thank you."

Gelde pressed herself against the wall, too scared to move or even cry.

Frima knelt down in front of the child.

"Gelde, you heard what the doctor said. It has to be done."

Gelde squeezed her eyes shut and vehemently gestured "no."

"Please, Mamala, they'll send us back. I can't leave Szol."

"It's going to hurt, Mama. I heard what he said. They'll cut off all my hair."

"Hair grows back. It will only sting for a moment, and I'll be with you. You can sit in my lap. Please don't make a fuss; we have no other choice. The doctor is being very kind to us."

The barber tried to be gentle with the child, but it was impossible to shave off her hair without scraping the already-inflamed sores. Little Gelde, sitting on her mother's knee, shrieked when he put the disinfectant on her scalp. Frima and Minnie led the sobbing child out of the hair-cutting area and they went to the infirmary for the medication. It took another hour waiting in line to buy more disinfectant and salve before they got back to Yaakov and the two children. Chaje looked at her sister in horror.

"Gut in Himmel, what did they do to my little girl?"

"They shaved her hair, Yaakov," Frima replied. "She has lice. It will grow back."

"What's that brown stuff all over her head?"

Minnie answered Yaakov.

"It's disinfectant. We have to put it on every day and use this salve to heal the sores. We're lucky we found a Jewish doctor. They were ready to send her back."

Frima rummaged through her trunk and found a babushka for the child, placing it gingerly over Gelde's bald head, pocked with sores and stained a reddish-brown color. She scooped the child onto her lap, rocked her, and placed the rag doll in her hands. Minnie took a piece of cake from her bag and offered it to Gelde, who refused it with a shake of her head.

The rest of the immigration process was a long, tedious ordeal made more difficult by a screaming baby, a sobbing little girl, and a sullen big sister irritable from the long wait. They had to wait two hours more in another office before Gelde could get her medical clearance card.

Yaakov tried to placate the girls, without much success, by telling them about the magic tram they were about to ride on. When they finally boarded the streetcar heading through lower Manhattan, Szol and Gelde fell asleep from exhaustion. Chaje ran from one side to the other on the moving tram, much to the annoyance of the other passengers, gazing in amazement at the tall buildings and multitudes of strange people on the streets.

Finally Minnie had a chance for a word with Frima.

"Tell me about Mama."

The trolley and street noises made it almost impossible to hear.

"Michla, let's talk when we get to the house. I'm too tired to scream and we have so much to talk about."

"I'm being thoughtless. You need a good rest after what you've gone through. When we get home, I prepared my room for you and the girls to sleep overnight. Yaakov will sleep at the rooming house. I can hold Szol, and you put your head on my shoulder and rest awhile. I can't tell you the joy it gives me to see my family!"

30

Bad News

Minnie wasn't giving up.

10 October 1907
Mama Dearest;

Your whole family is here and waiting for you. Frima misses you, I miss you, and the children ask about you all the time. I know that you can't travel alone, but suppose you come with Dina? I'm sure she still wants to come to America, and she would take care of you throughout the journey. What's there for you in Nolopina? Everyone you love is here. I can arrange everything if you just say you'll come.

We kiss your hands.
Michla and Frima

------

10 October 1907
Dear Dina,

    I haven't forgotten my promise to you. Please let me know if you still want to come to America. If you come, I think Mama will come too. Zelig and I will sponsor you and help you get started in America. If you can save toward your passage we can get you and Mama over sooner. Please let me know. We send our best regards to you and all the family.

                                    Michla (Minnie)

-----

11 November 1907
Dear Family,

    I would be more than happy to accompany your mother to the New World. I wouldn't be able to pay my entire passage until next year, but if you can lend me some money, I would pay you back and come in the spring with your Mama. I wait expectantly to hear from you.

                                      Fondly,
                                      Dina

------

12 November 1907
Dearest Family,

    Don't you think I miss my children and grandchildren? Why would you want your old, sick Mama living with you,

*like a stone around your neck? I'll never survive the journey.
Please understand.*

With love and blessings,
Mama

------

30 November 1907
Mama Darling,

*How can you call yourself a stone around our necks?
There's nothing that would make us happier than to have
the whole family together. We worry about you all the time.
Please reconsider; we need you here. We just received a letter
from Dina saying that she wants to join you on the trip to
America. Now there's no reason for you not to come. With
greatest affection,*

Michla and Frima

Minnie waited for a response from Mama. Each day she went to the
post office hoping to find a letter; each day she was disappointed. As the
weeks passed, she became very worried.

"Why hasn't she written back, Zelig? It isn't like Mama not to write.
Maybe she's sick."

"You know how the post office is, especially in these small towns.
You'll probably get three letters from her at once. If I had a kopek for
every worry you have, I'd be a rich man."

"It's been nearly three months. I never went this long without hearing from Mama. You think it's silly, but who knows what could happen?
Maybe the Cossacks destroyed the farm in Nolopina. Maybe the police
took the relatives away; you know how they treat Jews."

She picked at her cuticles and began to chew on her thumbnail.

"Wait a few more days. If you don't hear from her, write to Dina again."

Finally a letter arrived.

27 February 1908
Dear Michla and Frima,

> *I'm sorry to write bad news, but your Mama is sick. She was complaining of chest pains and shortness of breath. We took her to the goyische doctor in Nolopina and he thinks there's something wrong with her heart. Don't worry, she's resting in bed, and I'm sure she'll get better. We can forget about traveling to America this spring. Maybe in the summer or early fall we can think about it. Please send money for her doctor bills; the doctor made us pay before he would even look at her. Don't worry. We're looking after her. With fondest regards,*

> *Dina*

Minnie left work and ran to the rooming house to show the letter to Frima. They both sat on Frima's bed in the dank bedroom and cried.

"I told Zelig there was something wrong," Minnie said. "I can feel these things." She wiped the tears and honked into a large handkerchief she unpinned from her bodice.

"How can we help her?"

"I'll send money to Cousin Dina for her care and to pay the doctor. I wish there was someone else for her to see. Maybe Dina will take her into Minsk to a real doctor, someone who knows what he's doing. That's it . . . I'll send Dina money for a good doctor in Minsk."

She wired money to Dina with instructions for Mama's care. A few days later, she received a letter from Aunt Malka. Minnie tried to open the letter, but her hands were trembling too much. When she returned to the shop from the post office, Minnie propped up the letter on the counter with the back facing her. It haunted her for the rest of the afternoon, but she waited to bring it directly to Frima after work.

"Frima, please open it. I can't do it."

Frima turned the envelope several times before placing it back in Minnie's hand.

"I can't read, Minnie."

"I know. Just open it, darling. I'll read it to you."

3 March 1908
Dearest Michla and Frima,

We're so sorry to be the bearers of bad news, but your mother went to Hashem and your father yesterday. Dina would have written, but she's been crying all day. You know, she was very attached to your mother. Just like a second mother she was to Dina and Raisa. We will all miss her terribly, but she went very quickly and is in the Other World with your Tati where she wanted to be. She was getting weaker and weaker by the day. We got in a young girl from the village to mind the children and look after your mother. Don't be too sad. She never wanted to be a burden to anyone and talked all the time about joining your father. We got the money for her care and are using it for her burial. She'll be in the ground next to your Tati; we'll look after everything and visit their graves. Don't worry about saying Kaddish for her. My husband will make sure her soul is remembered at shul every morning and evening. We know how much you wanted her to come to America. She was wise enough to realize she would die during the journey and leave the space next to your Tati empty. We send our deepest sympathy to you.

With love and condolences,
Aunt Malka, Uncle Yosef, Dina and Raisa

Minnie and Frima sat shiva for a week in Minnie's apartment. All the friends from synagogue paid their respects, and the neighbors brought in food so the grieving family wouldn't have to worry about their earthly needs. They covered all the mirrors, sat on hard benches, and alternately cried and told tales of how strong and capable Mama was. Even Yaakov sat with them and mourned, though he was able to sit on the sofa instead of the hard benches. Frima had one photograph of Mama, taken when she and Yaakov were married, and they placed it on the mantle for all to see.

"After the mourning period is over," Zelig told Minnie, "I'll make two portraits from the photo for you and Frima to hang up. I never knew your Mama, but I feel like I did."

"Thank you, Zelig. You would have loved her almost as much as Frima and I did. See how Yaakov cried for her? Chaje and Gelde miss her so much. You'll be doing a mitzvah for Frima and me with the portraits."

After the memorial candle burned down, the two sisters got their coats, held hands, and walked around the block to signify that the mourning period was over.

20 March 1908
Dearest Cousins,

Sorry I didn't write sooner, but I really didn't feel up to it. I wanted to let you know that everything will be taken care of. We thought of your Mama like one of ours, and my Papa prays for her in shul every day. When it comes time, we'll have the unveiling for her, if you will send money to purchase and engrave the stone.

Maybe this isn't the right time to ask, but if I can make enough money for half the passage, are you still willing to sponsor me? I was thinking of working in Minsk for a few months so that I could get the money together for next fall's crossing. Please respond as soon as you can. With great fondness, Dina

31

A Long Winter

21 June 1908
Dear Cousins,

It's been three months since I heard from you. Is every-one well? It isn't like you not to write back. I just wanted you to know that everything is being taken care of for your Mama, but we will need money for her gravestone. The un-veiling should be before the winter, otherwise the snow and ice would make it impossible to put up her stone.

I asked if you were still willing to sponsor me. I got a job as a chambermaid in Minsk and have been saving money toward the passage. You know I'm a hard worker, and I wouldn't have to stay with the family for very long. I don't want to be a burden. Please answer, because I'm very anxious to come to America.

We all send our love,
Dina

------

18 July 1908
Dear Dina,

I'm sorry that we haven't answered you sooner, but things have been very hectic here. Frima and Yaakov had to get out of the rooming house. It was only one tiny room for five people, and they didn't have a place to turn around. There's the parents, two girls, and Szol. We found an apartment for them with two bedrooms, which they can't afford without our help. The landlord said he would take a little off the rent if Frima would be a janitor for the building, and Frima and Yaakov are renting out the extra bedroom. The girls are sleeping in the kitchen on chairs; it's near the stove, so they'll be warmer when winter comes.

Zelig and I are still trying to build up a new business, so we have extra expenses and don't have a steady income to rely on. Yaakov has a job delivering coal, but it doesn't pay much and some of his customers don't have the money to pay him right away. I know how anxious you are to come to America, and I haven't forgotten all the things you've done for me and my family. I especially appreciate how kind you and the family were to Mama, and how you took care of things when she got sick. I wish I had the money right now to send to you; unfortunately, times are hard. I hope our situation will change next year. I haven't forgotten my promise.

Thank you again for all your help with Mama. I'm sending money for the stone and inscription. If it's not enough, please let me know. We send our love to all the relatives,

Michla (Minnie)

* * *

Chaje and Gelde were enrolled in public school. Each day they returned from classes speaking more English. After a few months, they chattered in English to each other and even began to answer their parents in English when they felt like being fresh. Chaje and Gelde gave up their immigrant names. They were now known as "Ida" and "Anne" in school. Even Frima changed her name to "Fannie," stating that she had always hated her given name. Minnie paid for Hebrew school three afternoons a week so they would learn their aleph, bais and be around Jewish children for at least part of the day.

It was a quiet time in the shop, and Zelig was grumbling about sending the girls to Hebrew school.

"You know, Minnie, it's too much. We're helping to pay their rent. Business isn't so terrific during the winter. Besides, they're children. They need time to play and get some fresh air. Look how pale Chaje looks. They need to be outside, playing with kinder their own age."

"Outside? Playing with those ruffians? They go to school with goyische children all day, and they're going to school with boys! They'll forget who they are. As it is, they don't want to answer to their real names and when I talk to them, they answer only in English. At least in Hebrew school they'll be around nice, respectable children and teachers and rebbes that will instill a sense of *Yiddishkeit* in them. They're getting fresh, like these American stinkers, telling Fannie they have too much homework when they should be helping her clean the hallways. Oy, imagine if I tried to get away with that; Mama would have beaten me with the broom!"

"It's a long day for them; they have to get up before six o'clock to help their mother before they go to school. It's different here, Minnie. Learning for girls is the same as for boys. Don't you want them to have opportunities they wouldn't have in the old country? They're not going to be farmer's wives. They need an education to get a good job. Maybe they'll even be able to go to high school and get a nice, respectable job in an office. Do you want them to be maids, cleaning up other people's dirt? Don't you want them to have an education they couldn't get in the old country?"

"Not if it means they forget they're Jews!"

* * *

Zelig was very fond of the two little girls. He would make up stories for them on Shabbos and loved when they cuddled with him in the large armchair as he read to them. Minnie always had a pocket of treats for them. They loved to come on Shabbos to help Minnie bake challah, mixing ingredients and braiding the dough under her guidance. Zelig taught Gelde how to play checkers and would purposely give up his king to see the expression of excitement and glee when she won. Chaje had a sly sense of humor and would tease him by calling him silly names. He made dolls for them out of spare pieces of wood with joints that moved, and Minnie made clothing for the dolls from colorful pieces of rag. However, the joy of his life was Szol, who toddled after Zelig whenever he had the chance. Zelig sat on the floor with him, playing roll the ball. One of his first words was a variant of "uncle," which thrilled Zelig beyond belief. He became more tolerant of Yaakov those Shabbos evenings and even tried to strike up conversations with him.

"So, Yaakov, how is the coal business?"

"A lot of schlepping, but at least it's steady. People always need coal. I just wish there was more money in it."

There was an awkward silence.

"What's happening with the photography? Are you getting new customers?"

"It depends on how many simkhes there are in the neighborhood. Some days customers come, and some days there's nobody. It isn't steady, like coal."

"Oh."

* * *

In December a huge snowstorm blanketed the houses, sidewalks, and streets. When Zelig tried to get out of the tenement, he attempted to push the snow away but couldn't get the door open.

"Well, Minnie, there won't be any business today. Help me push the door open, so we can at least get out of the house."

They struggled with the outer door, pressing their bodies against it, until they were finally able to push away the great mound of snow and ice that had accumulated on the landing near the steps. They stood outside for a few moments, bundled up in their heavy coats, scarves, and gloves, looking at the deserted street until they were forced inside by the stinging snow and ice pellets propelled by a strong wind.

"Let's go upstairs, Zelig. I'll make a nice cup of hot tea for us. We can relax a little today. I wonder if the schools are closed. I can't imagine that any of the teachers or children can get there in this weather."

The wind died down, and the snow and ice abated. By late morning people came out of their houses with shovels, babbling in many languages, their breath visible in cloudy puffs. You could hear the high-pitched shrieks of children's voices as they pelted each other with snowballs or tried to put snow down the back of their friends' necks. Minnie and Zelig were out, helping their neighbors shovel the steps and walks when they saw Yaakov's wagon inching its way up the street. The old horse kept slipping on the unusually wet, glassy surface but managed to stop in front of Zelig and Minnie's tenement house. The girls piled out of the cart, and Chaje lifted little Szol out of the back of the wagon. Minnie ran up to them and addressed Yaakov.

"Don't tell me you're going to work in this weather! You won't be able to get through the streets with that old horse pulling such a load in the ice and snow."

"Listen, people need coal, particularly in this weather. Can I leave the children here with you and pick them up after I make my deliveries? There's no school, and Fannie will be cleaning up *shmuts* and snow all day that everybody tracks into the hallways."

"Uncle Zelig, please . . . can we make a snowman like they're doing on our block?" Chaje and Gelde took Zelig's hands and pulled him down the steps onto the sidewalk. Little Szol was bending down and putting mounds of snow in his mouth from the street. Zelig scooped him up in his arms.

"Come, Tatala, don't eat that; it's dirty from the street. We're going to make a big snowman. Can you help me?"

They took some lumps of loose coal from the wagon before Yaakov lumbered off. Minnie went upstairs and got a carrot and old cap from the house.

"Now we make three balls," Zelig directed. "One is very big for his legs, then a medium-sized one for his belly and chest, and a smaller one for the face. Come, Szol, you help me make the big one. Girls, make the other two snowballs . . . that's right, pack it firm and make it as round as you can."

Minnie watched as Zelig and the children assembled the snowman, making eyes and a smiling mouth with the coal, the carrot his protruding orange nose. Szol's mittens were soaked and caked with ice, but he shrieked in delight as he tried to pack the snow on the huge ball, just like Uncle Zelig was doing. When they were through putting the snowman together, Zelig lifted up the little boy and let him put the cap on the snowman's head.

"Tatala, put the hat on top. That's snow, Szol. Can you say it?"

"So, so," yelled the child.

"That's right, little boy. Come, let me warm up your *henties* in mine."

He peeled off the frozen mittens and rubbed the child's red, cold hands between his own, lifting them to his mouth to blow warm air on the tiny, icy fingers.

"Zelig, the children are freezing," said Minnie. "Let's take them upstairs and give them a hot drink."

"Not before we name the snowman. Well, girls, what will it be?"

"Uncle Zelig!" Gelde screamed.

As they went into the hallway, Szol started to cry and pull back toward the door.

"So, more so," he sobbed.

Zelig picked him up again and put him on his shoulders.

"Don't worry, sweet boy, we'll do it again the next time it snows."

Szol was having such a good time perched on his uncle's shoulders, he soon forgot about the snowman.

* * *

Yaakov trudged up the stairs of the dismal tenement, lugging a heavy sack of coal, the cold and wet slush seeping through his boots.

"Why is it that all my deliveries have to be on the fourth floor? They can't be on the ground floor?" He muttered to himself as he lugged up the coal.

Yaakov had become more of a family man. Now that they were expecting their fourth child, he stopped going to bars with his bathhouse friends and devoted more time to making a living. It was hard schlepping a hundred-pound sack of coal up four flights, only to find out that the tenant either couldn't or wouldn't pay. When he got upstairs, panting from the heavy load, he rapped at the door of a bedraggled-looking woman with a skeletal face, three ragged children clutching at her skirts.

"Mistah, my man left us. I have no money for milk or bread for the kinder."

"Coal isn't free, Missus. I have to make a living. Don't you have family that can help you?"

"My family is on the other side. I was a picture bride."

Without a word, Yaakov put the bag of coal in front of the door. As he turned to leave, she said, "I'll do anything for a few dollars. My children need milk."

He hesitated and took a quarter out of his pocket.

"I can't give you anymore. I have to take you off my delivery route; I'm sorry."

"If you keep bringing me coal, I could be nice to you."

He shrugged his shoulders and shook his head *no*.

She took the quarter, nodded her thanks, and closed the door.

It's a good thing she wasn't better looking. I might have accepted the offer.

When Yaakov got home, he told Fannie the story of the deserted woman (leaving out her offer, of course).

"Baruch Hashem we have a family, not like that poor woman. Where would we be without them? They're so good to us and the children, always giving us whatever they can spare. We're so lucky."

* * *

Minnie became more involved with her shul when she wasn't at work or helping Fannie with the children. She joined the Chevra Kadisha Society, the burial society that cleaned and dressed dead bodies in preparation for their heavenly journey. This was considered the highest charity since the dead could not come back to earth to thank the giver of this favor. While the grieving family was at the cemetery, women from Chevra Kadisha would arrange and cook a nourishing lunch for the mourners, setting the pitcher of water and towels outside the apartment door for ritual cleansing. They made sure there was enough food during the week of shiva and cleaned the dishes and glasses when the visitors left. In the evening, Zelig often would stay to work in the shop or do his artwork. On Wednesdays, he continued to play chess with a group of men he met at the shvits who argued endlessly about politics between moves. If he had any time between jobs, he visited Fannie's apartment to play with little Szol, always bringing him a treat or a small toy.

"You and Minnie spoil the children," Fannie told him. "Minnie is always baking their favorite cookies and buying them clothing and toys. Never a week goes by when she's not surprising them with a Shabbos gift. If Szol falls down and scrapes his knee, does he come to his Mama? No, he runs to his Tante, who gives him twice as much sympathy and always has a little something for him in her apron pocket. Whenever Szol sees you, he expects a toy. He's going to drive me meshuge with that toy drum you brought for him. He sleeps with it, schleps it around with him all day, and cries if he can't find it. He even tries to take it into the sink when I give him a bath."

"The boy loves music. Look how he dances around when we sing songs on Shabbos. They have no grandparents; let Minnie and me play that role."

Fannie sat down across from Zelig and passed him a plate of cookies.

"I know you both went through a lot. Sometimes I see the look on Minnie's face when she holds Szol. I know she loves him, but she looks so sad."

"Having the children here is a great joy for us. I know Minnie feels the same way. She always tells me how wonderful it is to have her family with her. Imagine how much worse it would have been for her when she found out that Mama went to the Next World. You and the children are a great comfort to her."

Fannie decided to let it go.

* * *

During that long winter, Minnie and Zelig spent many solitary hours in the shop. He taught her to play chess. Zelig marveled at how quickly she learned the pieces and moves. Before long, she became rather adept at it. Every once in awhile Minnie saw a chance to take Zelig's king, if his full attention wasn't on the game. She never did. Zelig had taught her to play, and she didn't want him to feel that she surpassed the teacher.

They spent long hours reminiscing about their childhoods, their indentured servitude on the farm, and their experiences in Greenberg's Furniture Store. Now that Zelig could look back on his experience with Monaghan, he grudgingly conceded that maybe he wasn't as terrible a boss as he'd thought when they left Suffolk County. Zelig reminisced about how his interest in art started in yeshiva when he began to draw rather than listen to the droning of a particular rabbi. Minnie described how she learned to cook and bake by watching Mama. She talked about running through the fields with Fannie and the feeling of freedom it gave her. They laughed about their experiences with Yaakov and difficult customers from Greenberg's shop. Zelig acknowledged his disappointment in being dismissed by Mrs. Greenberg and how appreciative he'd been when Minnie supported his artwork. Minnie talked about her feelings of losing Rivka's friendship. She conceded that the Irish girls, particularly Maureen, were generous and kind in their own way, and she should not have judged them as harshly as she had done.

Occasionally a passerby would look in the store window. They waited expectantly, but the potential customer would be gone with the next gust of wind.

Business picked up after the snow melted, and Minnie and Zelig got very busy with photographs, framing, and ketubas. Minnie hardly had a chance to go to the post office for a few weeks, but slipped away for a half hour one day and walked briskly to collect the mail. The sun was out, and she enjoyed the warm glow on her face. She arrived at the post office, picked up the mail, and quickly sorted through the envelopes. There was another letter from Dina. Minnie started to open it but changed her mind and put all the correspondence into her large purse. When she got back to the office, she dumped the mail on the desk and went into the studio to help Zelig. At the end of the day, she finally picked up the letter.

12 March 1909
Dear Cousins,

We had the unveiling for your Mama just before the first snowfall. Some of the neighbors from Chalupanich came, and of course our whole family was there. Thank you for the money. The engraver did a good job matching the letters to those on your Tati's headstone. We said a prayer for your Mama just the way we knew you would want it said, and placed stones on their headstones for you and Frima. My Papa continues to say prayers for her soul in shul.

I nearly have the money for passage, and by August or September I'll definitely have enough. I'll even have a little extra for living expenses. I know you aren't in a position to send me money. I'm not asking you. I need a sponsor, and I'm hoping that you'll do it. I don't want to be a burden, but if I don't book passage by September, the latest, I'll have to wait another year.

I've waited a long time and I'm not getting any younger. Please write back.

Love, Dina

Minnie gave an exasperated sigh, got pen and ink out of the desk drawer, and began to compose a letter.

32

A Promise Kept

"Minnie, for goodness' sake! Stop pacing. You haven't sat down all evening. What's the matter?"

Minnie began clearing the table of Shabbos plates, glasses, and cutlery. The girls ran through the kitchen playing tag, nearly crashing into Minnie and their mother.

Fannie sat down heavily on the kitchen chair. Her legs ached, and her burgeoning belly met her thighs.

"Sit for a moment, Minnie. The dishes can wait."

Minnie finally sat across from Fannie, shifting in the chair and tapping her foot.

"You're upset. Are you nervous about Dina coming?"

"A little, I suppose. It was different when you came with the children. I couldn't wait until you got off the boat. Dina has always been . . . well, difficult. She was always bossy and wanted to know everybody's business. I feel a little guilty about not being there all those years for Mama. Dina took every opportunity to remind me that *she* was the one who acted like the daughter and looked after her. Every time I got a letter from her, she put in every detail about what she did for Mama, even though it must have cost a fortune for the scribe."

"I don't think she wanted you to feel badly. I think she was trying to tell you that Mama was taken care of. Mama was good to them too, like a bubbe to Raisa's children. She was a great comfort to me, especially when Yaakov left for America. I don't know how I could have managed without Mama, being pregnant with Szol and having to work."

"Zelig and I are private people. It will be like having a stranger in the house, and I'll have to share the bedroom with Dina until we're able to make other arrangements. I can just hear her . . . 'Minnie, why are you using those dishes? You're making pot roast instead of roast chicken for Shabbos? How come?' No matter how you did things, she always knew better."

"You remember her from years ago. How do you know she hasn't changed? Besides, I told you that our boarder is leaving at the end of the month. She can take the bedroom, especially if she gets a job and can pay something toward room and board. Minnie, she'll be a stranger in a new world. She'll be looking to you for help and guidance. She won't be the one who knows everything."

Minnie hesitated for a moment.

"Fannie, I never asked you this before. What did Mama say about me leaving Russia to go to America? You must have asked her."

"When you left, I cried for weeks. I was still a child, but I knew how miserable you were about leaving the family. I kept pestering Mama to tell me. All she said at first was that you got a very good opportunity in America and would send us money. When I got a little older, Mama finally told me why you had to go. I knew by then what had happened in Minsk, and I knew about the baby, but Mama never wanted to talk about those days. She only said that you would never have left us if you'd had a choice."

"Did you ever discuss it with Yaakov?"

"Mama made me promise never to talk about you to anyone, even my own husband. Besides, you know that Yaakov doesn't have a curious bone in his body if it doesn't apply directly to him. Minnie, I always wanted to tell you how badly I feel—two babies born dead and a miscarriage. It's been terrible for you."

Minnie walked behind Fannie's chair, put her arms around her neck, kissed the top of her head, and leaned her cheek against Fannie's sheytl.

"Please darling, never talk about it to anyone, especially Yaakov and Zelig. Nobody here knows anything about me. I told Zelig as little as I could. Maybe that's why I'm nervous about Dina coming here. She's always had a big mouth."

"You worry too much, Minnie. Everything will be fine. Dina is family."

* * *

The ship finally arrived. It seemed like the two women had been waiting in the Immigration Hall for an eternity. Fannie spotted Dina first, leapt to her feet, and ran toward her.

"Dina, here!"

Dina put down her bundles and trunk, opening her arms for an excited Fannie. She hugged her, then took her by the shoulders to give her an appraising look.

"Well, Yaakov didn't waste any time! Look at you, pregnant again. Mazel tov!"

Then Minnie approached her. The two women peered at one another intently before clasping hands.

Minnie stepped back and surveyed the tall, stocky woman in front of her. Dina had never been a beauty, but she had a fresh-faced, rosy complexion and a ready, wide-mouthed laugh. Now her face had deep crow's feet sprouting around the corners of her small, narrowly spaced eyes. Two severely etched lines on either side of her long nose ran down to her chin. They seemed to pull her mouth down in perpetual disappointment. She wore a floral babushka over her black, wiry hair that was now flecked with gray. Over a faded dress of indecipherable color, she wore a shabby brown coat, which was torn near the armpit, cloth strings hanging from the jagged tear.

"Welcome to America. I hope the trip wasn't too difficult," Minnie murmured.

Dina had already passed a medical screening of sorts when she was let off the ship at Ellis Island: There were officials at the stairways watching the newly arrived immigrants, searching for obvious disabilities, such as limping, infected eyes, missing limbs. Although she would never admit it, Minnie would have been relieved if Dina had failed the health exam and had been sent back to Europe.

When they heard Dina's name called, they picked up her belongings and headed for the interviewing area. Unlike Fannie and Yaakov, Dina had smooth sailing when it came to approval from the authorities. Minnie showed the sponsorship papers to the official in charge of Dina's case, who hardly looked up before stamping the documents. He pointed them toward the medical area, where Dina, with no incriminating chalk marks, was given a cursory medical examination by a disinterested doctor.

Dina, proclaimed healthy, was given medical clearance, and the three women began the long trolley ride back home.

* * *

Dina sat heavily on Minnie's bed and looked around the room. There were starched white curtains on the window, a large mahogany dresser with crisp doilies under the family pictures, and an imposing wardrobe in the corner of the room. The wallpaper had a vertical pattern of tiny blue flowers that was repeated in the coverlet on Minnie's narrow bed. A small table with an oil lamp and a leather-bound book stood alongside the bed. On the other side of the room was a fold-up bed prepared ahead of time for Dina. She walked over to the wardrobe and opened it. She poked through dresses, skirts, blouses, and a black coat hanging from the wooden pole. Under the clothes were two sensible pairs of women's shoes and snow boots. Several ladies' hats were nesting on a shelf above the clothing. She rummaged further and found some lacy handkerchiefs, several babushkas, and a small change purse. Dina closed the doors of the wardrobe, went back to the end table, picked up the book and flipped through the pages. It looked like Hebrew writing, but it was indecipherable to her.

Huh, just like an American lady. She even has an American name.

"Dina, come and wash up. Supper is ready."

The smell of pot roast and turnips wafted to the bedroom and Dina's stomach churned in anticipation. At the table, Zelig questioned her about the voyage while the girls peeked shyly at her. They needed to get reacquainted with their cousin Dina as their memories of the old country were fading. An exhausted Minnie served the meat and vegetables. Yaakov wolfed down everything on his plate and mopped up the last of the gravy with his bread.

Fannie juggled her dinner with one hand as she held Szol in her lap. When dinner was over, Minnie quickly got up from her chair and addressed Dina.

"I hope you don't mind if we retire early. It's been a very long day, and Zelig and I have to open the shop at seven o'clock tomorrow. If you feel up to it, you can come and see the shop or you can rest tomorrow, but please don't unpack. We have to look over the contents of your trunk to make sure there are no lice. I can do that with you tomorrow night; I borrowed a chest of drawers from the rooming house, and you can store your personal things there for the time being. It's right outside the bedroom in the foyer."

Fannie got up and helped Minnie clear the table.

"We have to get up early too. Come, children. You have school tomorrow. Give Tante and Uncle Zelig a kiss and thank Tante for a wonderful supper. Yaakov, get our wraps and take the children downstairs. I'll be along in a moment."

She kissed Minnie and Dina as she prepared to leave.

"If there's anything I can do, please let me know. I can help Dina look over everything in the trunk tomorrow."

After they left, Zelig excused himself and went to his room. Minnie washed the dishes, handing them to Dina to dry. She put on a kettle of water to boil.

"Let's have some tea, Dina. It's been a long time since we've seen each other. Tell me about the family; is everyone well in Nolopina?"

They talked of this and that for a while until Dina blurted out, "I see you don't share the bedroom with Zelig."

"How do you know that? You didn't look through my things, did you?"

"Of course not. It's just that the bed is so narrow, only enough room for one person. Zelig doesn't sleep on the fold-up bed, does he? How come you don't rent out the second bedroom? It would be a nice, steady income for you."

Once a yenta, always a yenta. I knew I made a mistake bringing her here. While I was preparing dinner, she was probably looking over my room with a magnifying glass.

"Zelig needs his own room. He stays up late reading and sometimes does artwork in the spare room. Besides, he snores so loudly, he wakes me up."

Why am I making excuses to her? It's none of her business.

"You know, Dina, sometimes things are said that shouldn't be. I know you mean only the best, but it's very important that you promise me never to talk about what happened in the old country. Can you do that?"

"Oh, Minnie, it happened so many years ago. It feels like another life. Of course you can rely on me; I would never betray your trust."

"We'll do anything we can to help you. You know, Zelig wasn't so crazy about the idea of bringing over a cousin when we have so many other responsibilities. I really had to convince him. Promise me you won't tell anyone about Minsk. You know how word gets around and how gossip starts."

"I'll be very discreet."

"Promise me, on the soul of my Mama. I know she was very dear to you."

"Okay, I promise. Minnie, stop it. Why would I want to get you in trouble? You know I only want what's best for you and Frima . . . uh Fannie. I appreciate what you've done for me, and I'll try to pay you back."

"I'm not interested in being paid back. This isn't about money. I just need to know you'll keep your lips sealed."

"I told you already. I promise. It's enough. Where's the toilet? I have to pish."

"When you go out to the foyer, make a right turn. It's down the hallway on the left-hand side; you can't miss it. By this time of night you just have to follow your nose."

Minnie waited for Dina to return before turning out the oil lamp. While she waited, she tried to chant psalms from her hymnbook, but the words stuck in her throat. When Dina returned, they wished each other a peaceful night's sleep and Minnie turned off the gaslight.

. . .

The Cossacks came to Nolopina and broke down the door to the farmhouse. Seven-year-old Minnie tried to hide under the bed, but they were everywhere, shouting curses and poking under the bed with their swords. She could smell sweat and alcohol as they bent down to look under the bed. She squeezed herself into the furthest corner, trying to roll herself into a ball. They finally left the room, leaving the door open. She could see them beating Zelig with the handles of their swords, and then one of them turned the sword, piercing Zelig's throat and laughing. She was too scared to come out from under the bed, but cried out "Papa!" Suddenly, she was out in the forest in just her nightdress, walking in the snow with no shoes. She spotted two wolves foraging around a clearing. They looked up at the same time, staring at her with their yellow eyes gleaming as they advanced toward her.

. . .

Minnie could swear she screamed herself awake, but Dina slept peacefully across the room, breathing heavily through her mouth. She tried to compose herself for sleep again, but it was no use. Her heart was still pounding wildly with a secondary beat in her temples. She got up, put on her robe and slippers, and took her psalm book into the kitchen, where she spent the rest of the night. The dream would recur many nights, with yellow wolves' eyes threatening her.

33

Marriage of Convenience

Minnie was delighted when Dina finally moved to the spare room in Fannie and Yaakov's apartment. What a relief not to hear the constant chatter, the unrelenting questions, and suggestions on how to run her own household.

At least Zelig could retreat to his workshop or the bathhouse, but what was Minnie to do? She had started volunteering even more time at the shul but found it too exhausting after a full day's work and household duties.

Even after Dina moved to Fannie's apartment, Minnie still saw her every Friday. The family's tradition was for Fannie, Yaakov, and the children to come for the Shabbos meal; how could Minnie not invite her?

Minnie was always on her guard, expecting Dina to blurt out something that needed to be left unsaid in front of the family.

In the meantime Dina set about looking for work.

"Maybe she should work in the shop? We could use some extra help, especially when we get rush jobs," suggested Zelig.

Minnie quickly squelched that suggestion.

"You know, she's no good with customers, she knows nothing about photography or framing, and it would take forever to teach her the business. She's not so clever."

Eventually Dina found a job in one of the tenement sweatshops, as she was a decent seamstress, but it didn't last because she got into arguments with the owner, his wife, and the other worker. Finally she landed a job making women's blouses in a large factory on the Lower East Side. At first she didn't know how to travel alone, so Minnie made several trips with Dina to the new workplace.

In the beginning, Dina was exhilarated. She found several friends who worked alongside her machine. There were Katya and Feigie, but Dina was particularly fond of a girl named Fania, who reminded her of her sister, Raisa. They ate lunch and whispered together when the supervisor wasn't looking. However, after a few weeks, Dina started complaining about the endless trolley ride, the long hours, and terrible working conditions.

"Could you imagine? It's hot as blazes in that place now, and it isn't even the summer. At least the managers have windows in their offices, but we have nothing. They lock all the doors and won't even let us outside during our lunch break. Fania and I have to eat at our sewing machines. They start blowing the whistle even before we finish eating. God forbid we should cheat them out of a minute's work if we have to use the toilet."

There was only one logical solution. They would have to find Dina a husband. Minnie put out the word to the local matchmaker and inquired at the shul, extolling Dina's virtues.

She's such a hard worker! She would keep a nice home and make all the clothing for the family. Such a balabusta; she's an exceptional homemaker!

Dina was probably too old to conceive and hold a pregnancy, so she would be a good match for a widower with children of his own.

The matchmaker found several possibilities, but they didn't work out.

"She's no beauty, and she never shuts up. She constantly complains about her job and America. When I matched her with Mr. Feingold, he couldn't wait for the evening to be over."

The matchmaker nearly threw her hands up in disgust until Heschel, the butcher, became available. His wife of twenty years suddenly died of a massive stroke, and he was left with seven children, ranging in age from six to nineteen years old.

Miraculously they liked each other. Heschel's wife had been a quiet, mousy, scrawny woman. He considered Dina lively and attractively buxom. Besides, he needed to marry soon so his children would be taken care of. They set a wedding date immediately after the required mourning period.

Dina quit her odious job immediately, now that she would be taken care of financially.

A week after Dina left the job, Zelig ran over to Fannie's house, waving *The Daily Forward* frantically.

"Look at the headlines!" He had forgotten that Fannie and Dina couldn't read. "Never mind, I'll read you the important parts."

TRIANGLE SHIRTWAIST DISASTER

March 25, 1911

Most of the workers were locked in the factory when the fire started. The fire trucks made a valiant effort to save the women, but their fire ladders couldn't reach beyond the sixth floor. Many young women jumped from windows on the eighth, ninth and tenth floors to their deaths to escape the fire.

The owner and managers have been prosecuted for Fire Ordinance Violations. All doors were locked, except for the front entrance, to prevent the workers from leaving early. There were no escape routes for the workers.

One hundred forty-six employees, mainly young women, died inside the factory from smoke inhalation, the fire itself, and from attempts to escape the fire.

Dina collapsed in a chair, her whole body shaking.

"Do they have names? Read me the names of the girls."

Zelig read the list of names of bodies they were able to identify. When he got to Fania's name, Dina burst into tears. Katya and Feigie were also on the list of the dead.

"Dear God, taken in the prime of their lives. It seems like just the other day we were giggling and whispering together. That could have been me."

Minnie sat across from Dina and held her trembling hands.

"Hashem works in strange ways. Maybe He wants you to live a long life."

That Saturday when the congregation recited *Yizker,* the prayer for the dead, Dina and Fannie stood in memory of Fania, Katya, and Feigie, those poor young souls whose lives were taken much too early. Then the entire congregation rose to honor the victims of the Triangle Shirtwaist Fire.

* * *

Minnie and Fannie were only too happy to arrange and host the simkhe at Minnie and Zelig's apartment. Since Heschel had lost his wife recently, they weren't expected to make a lavish wedding. Dina and Heschel were married in Minnie's parlor, surrounded by Heschel's children and Dina's small family.

"My wife, of blessed memory, must be looking down from heaven with relief, knowing her family will be taken care of.

Such romantic words for a new bride.

Anyone with half an eye could see that Heschel's children would be trouble, especially the older ones. As Mendel stepped on the glass, the four teenagers clustered together, scowling and muttering to each other. Dina was exchanging one unpleasant job for another.

Now that Dina had a family of nine people, that meant no more Shabbos meals with her cousins. Dina would be living on the fringes of Brownsville, on top of Heschel's butcher shop. Minnie and Fannie dutifully visited her most Saturday afternoons after Sabbath services.

On one of those Saturday afternoons, Minnie went to Dina's house alone. Dina served tea and fresh-baked mandelbrot as she regaled Minnie about her new trials with Heschel and the children.

"They're so fresh to me. The older ones are the worst; they show me no respect, and the three younger ones copy their nasty ways. Heschel pretends not to notice. He never says a word to them, no matter how disrespectful they act toward me. When I speak to him about it, he always has excuses for them."

Dina did a good job imitating Heschel's high-pitched, nasal voice. "They just lost their Mama. Give them some time to get to know you."

"This would never happen in the old country," she continued. "Any self-respecting man would take a strap to all of them. In America, it seems like the children run the house."

Minnie comforted and placated her as best she could while attempting to change the topic. They started to talk about how much they missed living on a farm, with wonderful fresh fruits and vegetables, clean air, and lots of open space.

There was finally a lull in the conversation. Minnie plucked on Dina's sleeve and blurted out, "I have to ask, Dina . . . What was it?"

"What was what?"

"The baby. Was it a boy or a girl?"

"Minnie, why do you torture yourself after so many years? What does it matter? What's done is done."

"Please tell me. It was a boy, wasn't it?"

Dina hesitated a few seconds.

"No, Minnie, it was a girl."

A girl . . . maybe she looked like . . . I thought it would look like him.

Minnie wept silently, large tears rolling down her cheeks. Dina got up from her chair and awkwardly placed her large, chapped hands on Minnie's shoulders.

"You must forget. Leave the past in the old country."

When Minnie stopped crying, she reached for her coat and stood up. She thanked Dina for her hospitality and started the walk home, taking a rambling, circuitous route.

34

Zelig's Demise

Zelig was stricken with a heart attack one morning when he tried to get out of bed. It was as if a stone was crushing his chest; he could barely breathe. Nausea overcame him, but his chest hurt so much that he couldn't even turn on his side and practically choked on his own vomit. The pain eased a bit and Zelig called out feebly to Minnie, who at first didn't hear him from her room.

When she entered, his face was ashen and he couldn't answer her frantic questions. She ran out into the hallway, banging on their neighbor's door.

Mrs. Shmolowitz peeked out at a hysterical Minnie.

"Get Dr. Shapiro right away. I think Zelig is dying!" Then she ran back into his bedroom, clutching his hands in terror.

"Mamala, I feel a little better. I'll be all right."

It's been years since he called me Mamala.

Dr. Shapiro arrived in about ten minutes, panting heavily from the climb up the stairs. He immediately took out a stethoscope, put the tubular plugs in his ears, and listened to Zelig's heart as he searched for his pulse.

The doctor listened for what seemed an interminable amount of time before he carefully placed his stethoscope back in his black bag and sighed.

"What's the matter, Doctor? Is he going to live? What can be done for him?" Questions tumbled out of Minnie's mouth like discordant, frenetic musical passages.

"Let's go into the parlor and let Zelig rest."

Once in the parlor, Minnie paced the room from end to end.

"Please sit. I'm going to give you a bromide to calm you down."

"No, Doctor, I can't be sleepy if I have to take care of Zelig. Just tell me what's happening."

"He's a very sick man, Minnie. He had a bad heart attack. The good thing is that he survived this one. With the right care he could live years. I'm giving him heart medicine, and he should have complete bed rest for at least three weeks. He needs lots of meat and eggs to build him up; he's much too thin. He shouldn't even get up to go to the bathroom; you'll have to get him a commode."

Dr. Shapiro wrote out instructions for Minnie to follow. When she tried to pay him, he wouldn't hear of it.

"When Zelig recovers, he can take a picture of my family. That would be more than enough payment."

Zelig was sleeping when the doctor left. Minnie asked Mrs. Schmolowitz to look in on Zelig while she hastily penned a note that the shop would be closed until further notice.

She would need Fannie's help until Zelig recovered. Minnie had to keep the store open at least part of the time so the customers wouldn't forget about them and find other sources for their artistic and photographic needs. Amidst all the worry and confusion, she felt a sense of relief that she learned so much of the business. Zelig would have to curtail his activities even if he recovered fully.

Fannie came to the apartment, schlepping baby Joey and Szol up the stairs, to keep an eye on Zelig. She made sure to give him his medication on time, bring him the heavy meals Minnie left, and even empty his bedpan when needed. Between coaxing Zelig to eat and ministering to him, she breastfed little Joey, all the while trying to keep a very disappointed Szol occupied so he wouldn't disturb his Uncle Zelig. Szol didn't understand why Uncle Zelig didn't play with him the way he used to.

"Tatala, you know when your tummy hurts or you have a boo boo, you don't feel like playing either. When Uncle Zelig feels better, he'll want to play with you again. No, you can't beat your drum now; go to the parlor and look at your picture book."

* * *

After the requisite three weeks flat on his back, Zelig was allowed to sit up in a chair and even walk to the table for lunch and dinner. His books were piled up on the bed stand, but he didn't have the energy or focus to read them. Zelig began to talk about going back to work.

"Only when the doctor says okay," Minnie said, "and you'll have to work on a very light schedule for awhile . . . No, don't argue with me. Do you want to have another heart attack? Yes, the customers are still coming; they all ask for you. If I need extra help with heavy work, I'll ask Yaakov. Stop worrying so much."

After six weeks, Dr. Shapiro finally declared Zelig fit enough to go back to work on a reduced schedule the following week. They all breathed a sigh of relief. Both Fannie and Minnie were worn out, and Zelig couldn't bear the interminable hours of doing nothing.

Minnie waited for Fannie to come after she dropped the older girls off at school. When Fannie arrived, Minnie hugged and kissed her as never before.

"What would I do without my darling *shvesta*? I don't know how I could have managed. I feel so bad that you had to care for Zelig on top of everything else you have to do. Soon that will be over, thanks to Hashem."

"Where would our whole family be if you weren't for you and Zelig? You helped even more than the midwife when I gave birth to Joey. You and Zelig were always giving to us. I'm only too happy to be able to repay you in a small way for saving us."

* * *

Minnie was in the midst of hammering together a large frame for the Kirschner family's wedding picture when a distraught Fannie rushed into the workroom.

"Minnie, leave that! Come right away!"

Minnie raced out into the cold without her coat, ran the three blocks to her apartment, dashed up the stairs, all the time praying that Zelig would be alive when she got home. She all but crashed down the door in an effort to get to his bedroom. Mrs. Schmolowitz and several other neighbors from the building were in the room. Minnie pushed them aside as she kneeled by the bed, staring at Zelig. There was no need for the doctor; she knew he was gone.

She clasped his inert hand and lifted it to her lips. Tears and mucus dripped on the coverlet as she began to wail.

Decades

35

April 1926

This year Passover was being held at Fannie's apartment. The family congregated around the table with Yaakov holding court as the Seder leader. But Gelde was missing, and Fannie worried that she wouldn't arrive on time.

"I told her she had to leave work earlier today. She gets involved in who-knows-what and forgets the time."

"So we'll start the Seder a little later," Yaakov responded.

"Sure, the food will dry out and we'll be here until after midnight. You have to read every word in the Haggadah while everyone is dying of hunger."

At that moment Gelde burst in the door, juggling her pocketbook, a large parcel, and a bottle of Peysekh wine. Everyone stared at her. Her long tresses, usually done up in a bun, were no more. Her straight, lustrous hair was bobbed with marceled waves throughout.

"How do you like it?"

Minnie answered in a combination of Yiddish and English.

"Gelde, you look like one of those floppers who spend the night drinking bootfoot poison and dancing that silly dance with any bum that asks."

Gelde's eyes twinkled with mirth.

"You mean the Charleston, Tante, and it's 'flappers' and 'bootleg.' Please call me Anne. That's my name now."

"I don't care what you're called. A respectable young woman doesn't chop off all her hair and keep the family waiting on a special holiday."

Anne looked chagrined.

"You're right, Tante. I should have been more aware of the time, but I still need some things for my California trip."

The family was shocked when Anne announced her engagement to a man ten years her senior who lived in California. They were even more upset when she told them she was going to Lake Arrowhead to meet his family.

Yesterday, when Fannie and Minnie were making gefilte fish for the holiday, Minnie wiped her hands, placed them on her hips and chided Fannie.

"How can you let her go, Fannie? A young girl taking a train alone for five nights, to meet some man you hardly know. What do you know about him? She should be marrying a man from Brownsville, with a respectable family. Why you didn't arrange for a match years ago is beyond me. Now we'll never see her. She'll be living so far away, and you not being well. She should think of her mother!"

"She's a grown woman of twenty-six; I can't stop her. It's true I don't know the family, but he's an educated man, a lawyer yet. She wouldn't be happy with some local yeshiva boy."

"So who's to blame for that? I told you she shouldn't go to that fancy high school and get all kinds of ideas in her head. If she went out to work like Chaje, she would be married by now and having her third child. Who knows if she'll even be able to have a baby? She's waiting too long."

"The school principal told us she was the smartest in the class, and it would be a crime not to allow her to go to Hebrew Tech. Gelde graduated with honors in just eighteen months. She was president of her class. I was very proud of her. I can't read, but I have a daughter who's educated and is marrying a professional man."

"Will she be here to help if you or Yaakov get sick? It will all fall on Chaje. Thanks to Hashem, you have a sensible daughter who married a local boy. You'll have the joy of seeing your grandchildren from Chaje, but not from Gelde."

"Minnie, please. Let's stop this bickering. There's nothing I can do. And call them Ida and Anne like they asked you to."

"You always let them get away with murder. Now the boys are starting to be *Americana shtinkers*. Szol only wants to play his drums instead of helping his father. He said he wants to play in a jazz band. What's a jazz band? Is it like klezmer?"

"I don't know. He's always klopping away at that drum. It gives me a headache, but at least I know where he is. It was Zelig's fault; he gave him his first drum."

Fannie gave Minnie a coy smile.

Minnie ignored Fannie's attempt at humor and continued to chide her.

"What about Yussel? You and Yaakov, always so proud that he was the first American child. Now all he wants to do is fool around with cars."

"Joey will become a mechanic. It's a good trade. Cars are here to stay. It's the horse and buggy that we'll never see again. Come, let's start cooking the fish before it spoils."

* * *

As expected, the Seder lasted until well after midnight, with Yaakov indulging in every ritual. When it was finally over, a jubilant Yaakov walked an exhausted Minnie to her house. Since Zelig died, he was the only man around who could conduct the Seder.

Ida left with her husband, carrying a sound-asleep baby in her arms. Anne helped clear the table and wash the multitude of dishes.

"Mama, she's impossible. Can't you at least teach her our English names? Nobody but Tante calls me Gelde anymore. Why is she so stubborn and old-fashioned? Maybe I should start calling Tante 'Michla,' her original name."

"Don't talk that way about your Tante. She has our best interests at heart. Remember what we owe her."

"I've been hearing what an angel she is for years, but she can be a pain in the neck. She's so . . . well . . . harsh."

Fannie gave Anne a wounded look. There was silence until they finished cleaning up. Anne put her arms around Fannie's waist and kissed her on the forehead.

"I'm sorry. I know what she did for our family, and it's not that I don't appreciate it." Anne took Fannie's face in her hands.

"Don't worry, Mama. I'll come back twice a year to see you and the family. The trains are getting faster all the time. I want you, Papa, and the boys to come visit me when I get settled. . . And of course I'm coming back for the wedding. Do you think I would get married without my Mama and Papa by my side?"

Anne sighed and yawned.

"I really am tired, Mama; I have to go to work early. I'll see you in the morning. I love you."

Anne took the large parcel into the tiny bedroom she shared with the boys. Her bed and dresser were partitioned off with a long curtain. She took out a silver shimmy dress with tassels and held it next to her body.

It's a good thing Tante didn't see my party dress. Then she'd really be sure I was up to no good!

36

September 1934

The 1929 crash hadn't affected Minnie right away. Brownsville was a world apart from Manhattan. The only person in the family initially affected by the crash was Anne. She had bought stock on margin, which meant that she not only lost the money she put in but now owed what she had borrowed on the stock. Anne broke her engagement to her California beau. Her mother was ill, Anne's nest egg was gone, and she needed to continue working to pay off her debt and help the family.

Minnie had done rather well with the shop during the twenties. Now that Zelig was gone, she had to rethink how to turn a profit in the business. She scoured the neighborhood to find a helper and came across an artistic yeshiva student named Dovi to help out with framing. He could even replicate Zelig's style in the making of ketubas, but he didn't have Zelig's flair and spontaneity. Minnie was finally accepted as a good photographer who could be bargained with. Although the profit margin from the actual photographs was slim, she was able to make it up in the framing.

The matchmaker kept pestering Minnie about marrying again. A number of potential suitors had shown interest in her since she had a good business and was unencumbered by children. She was an exemplary homemaker and pious to boot. Minnie turned down every offer; she had no intention of ever remarrying.

Minnie's personal needs were small. She needed rent money for the shop and her apartment, money for food, fuel, and a pittance for personal expenses such as clothing. If she bought a new dress once a year, it was a lot. The clothes she did buy were sensible, durable, and replaced an item of apparel that had finally worn out. Her only extravagances were helping Fannie, buying the children gifts, and giving *seduka* to her shul. Minnie was proud of her charitable contributions to the synagogue, as well as her service. She was able to accumulate a nest egg for emergencies, which was desperately needed in the 1930s.

When the effects of the crash finally reached Brownsville, Minnie was no longer able to keep Dovi. She regretfully let him go, knowing how much he relied on his part-time job so that he could keep learning in the yeshiva.

As her business diminished, she found that she was unable to pay her store's rent on time. Minnie and Zelig had always prided themselves on keeping up with their obligations, so it was an extremely embarrassed Minnie who had to ask for a reduction in her rent. The landlord complied; a reduced rent was better than none.

Residents of Brownsville were tightening their belts. Her downstairs neighbor went out of the soda business, since everyone was now drinking water. In good times, Minnie's business was considered a necessity to preserve special memories and keep contact with relatives on the other side. It was now a luxury to be able to put food on the table.

Minnie needed a new source of income to keep the shop open. She finally had to advertise in the shul for a family to board with her. The Bermans were a couple with three children who had fallen on hard times and could no longer afford their home. Minnie was a private person and had difficulty adjusting to the Bermans inhabiting her apartment. She rented out the two bedrooms to them—one for the parents and the other for the children—and now slept in the parlor on a cot that was folded and hidden behind the sofa every morning. Two meals were included in the arrangement, so she had to get up very early to prepare breakfast for the Bermans. She closed the shop early each day to shop and prepare dinner for a household of six, while worrying that perhaps late customers had come when she wasn't there to give them service.

Minnie could no longer provide Shabbat and holiday meals for the family. She generally spent Friday evenings at Fannie's apartment, her one night off from cooking for the Bermans. Not that they weren't nice. The children were well behaved, and the Bermans tried to be considerate boarders, but she felt like a servant in someone else's home.

At first Minnie wasn't pleased when the whole family was invited to Dina's house for the first night of Rosh Hashanah. Her husband Heschel was doing reasonably well despite the Depression. People still had to eat, though they now chose the inexpensive cuts of meat. When times were good, he had expanded his business, taken in his sons as partners, and bought a house to accommodate his overflowing family when they came for the holidays. Minnie said to Fannie, "At least we'll eat well. You can be sure that Dina will outdo herself, trying to show how she married such a successful man."

The oldest boy had become a dedicated communist and married an Irish shiksa in the bargain.

His wife reminds me of that Irish girl, Bridget, at the potato farm. At least she shows some respect when she visits the family and dresses conservatively. Still, I can't believe what they let him get away with. Did they sit shiva when he married the Irish girl? Did the son try to convince the girl to convert, so they'd have Jewish children? Did he ever show respect for his father by going to shul with him on the High Holy Days? Never! He even changed his name from Baruch to Brian and they still treat him like a king. He'll inherit the business when his father retires; I wouldn't put it past him to sell bacon and ham.

When they arrived, Dina had her best linen on the table. An expensive set of hand-painted, imported china and sterling silverware adorned the massive mahogany table. She even hired someone to help her with the serving. When the family arrived, she looked pointedly at Minnie's clean but obviously worn dress with the white collar turned inside out to hide the frayed material of the garment. Dina, always corpulent, was dressed in a new floral print and a frilly hostess apron, which emphasized her girth. Quite a change from the time Minnie and Fannie met her at Ellis Island.

* * *

The *forshpayz* was served, rich chicken soup with noodles, a large platter of chopped liver and gefilte fish garnished with lettuce, tomato, and carrots. Apple slices with honey were passed around to ensure a sweet New Year. There was a selection of brisket, roast chicken, and stuffed breast of veal of the best quality from the butcher shop, accompanied by platters of mashed potatoes and vegetables. The hired maid placed the feast on an enormous table. The children sat at a separate, small table adjoining the main event and were shushed and admonished when they became too boisterous during the meal. Brian (nee Baruch) sauntered in late with his Irish shiksa, carrying an infant in her arms. The child was uncircumcised, much to the sorrow of his grandparents, but at least he wasn't baptized, which his Catholic grandparents had urged their daughter to do.

What does it matter that he's not circumcised? Minnie thought. *The mother never converted, so he's not Jewish anyhow.*

After a few shots of schnapps, Brian began haranguing his captive audience about his belief in communist principles. As a new convert, he passionately proclaimed his independence from organized religion.

"Karl Marx and Engels were Jews, and they turned their back on all the dogma and restrictions that go with organized religion. They saw how it oppresses the masses and rewards only the rich. Only stupid people believe that they'll be rewarded in heaven while they suffer on earth for their whole lives!"

The family and guests were silent, except for an embarrassed scuffling of feet. After a few more monologues extolling communism, Minnie had had enough.

"How can you dishonor your parents on such a sacred holiday and at their table? You should be ashamed."

"Parents? I only have a father. My mother is dead. Don't act so outraged when your precious Zelig was an atheist and a socialist! I heard all about how Zelig attended every socialist meeting at the Brownsville community center, and I heard other things about him too. If he were alive now, he'd be agreeing with me."

Minnie could almost smell Maya's lilac perfume. She was livid.

"Are you accusing my Zelig of being a communist? He was an honorable, hardworking businessman, not somebody who browbeats his whole family with nonsense and is so disrespectful to my cousin."

Much to Minnie's shock, Dina rose to Brian's defense.

"You're always so high and mighty; you know more than everyone else. How can you come to my house and insult my husband's son. What gives you the right when you're a guest at my table? Now you've ruined our whole holiday!"

She stormed into the kitchen, leaving an astonished Minnie in her wake. Minnie began to follow her, then changed her mind and ran out of the house, leaving behind her jacket and purse. Fannie collected her sister's belongings, and all the Scholichs followed Minnie, mumbling their regrets and goodbyes.

* * *

Before Yom Kippur, Minnie went to Dina's house to apologize, although she couldn't understand how Dina could stay silent after being insulted by that bully. Minnie was upset that she'd spoiled Rosh Hashanah for the whole family. She knew she had to make amends to start the New Year with a clean slate.

Dina accepted the apology coldly. It took years and the aftermath of World War II for them to come to terms with each other. In the back of Minnie's mind was always the fear that Dina would be vindictive and tell stories.

* * *

The Brownie Camera had been in existence since 1900, but the newer point-and-shoot models became very popular in the late 1930s. Stylized family portraits fell out of vogue. People wanted more casual, spontaneous pictures instead of stiff, formal studio portraits. As film and cameras became smaller and more affordable, everyone was becoming an amateur photographer. Professional portraits at weddings and Bar Mitzvahs were now shot on site. Minnie's career as an early female photographer came to an end; she couldn't afford to change her outmoded equipment or keep up with changing photo trends.

She was now selling ready-made frames, photo albums, and knick-knacks in the shop, with a few calls for passport photos. When she had an occasional request for a handmade frame, her now-arthritic fingers and ebbing strength prevented her from taking the order. Business fell off precipitously. Some days she would open the shop and see no paying customers. Occasionally a congregant or neighbor would stop by for a chat, but her customers were going elsewhere.

She held off until she was offered a sum of money to vacate the frame shop far in excess of what she ever could have gotten for her outmoded inventory and "good will."

Mr. Stein, the grocer next door, wanting to enlarge his store, cast his eye on the space that Minnie occupied. He was a kind man and a good neighbor. Instead of going around Minnie to the landlord, he offered her five thousand dollars to vacate the shop in three months.

What should I do? Aside from a few dollars, I don't have anything except for the business. I can't be a burden to my nieces and nephews. If I take the money, how long will it last? Will I outlive every penny that I have? My sister has children to take care of her; who will look after me?

At first she didn't mention the offer to her family, knowing full well that they would hound her to take the money. Instead, she went to the rabbi for counsel.

He gave her sound advice.

"I know how you feel about the shop, but there comes a time when we all have to make unpleasant choices. Do you want to depend on your relatives for a place to stay and your daily bread? Think about your future."

Minnie asked for a meeting with Mr. Stein. There were no legal papers to sign, so she had a check for $5,000 in hand by the next day. She immediately set up funeral arrangements with the rabbi.

On Saturday morning, the day before she closed the shop, Minnie hosted a kiddush at her synagogue, inviting family, congregants, and friends to join her. During the rabbi's sermon that morning, he talked about the important role the Phoenix Frame and Photography Shop had played in the Brownsville community and praised Minnie for her service and devotion to the neighborhood and shul.

Minnie felt as if another cherished family member had died.

37

Fannie

Fannie hadn't felt well for years, but she continued cooking, shopping, and running the house. Anne and Chaje, who was now known as Ida, tried to convince Fannie and Yaakov to move to a first-floor apartment in a better neighborhood that would be closer to them.

"Mama, please don't be so stubborn. It's getting too hard for you to climb all those stairs. I see how you have to stop at each landing, and we don't like it that you're always out of breath."

Anne and Ida took turns trying to convince Mama to move, but she would fold her arms, give them a stern look and say, "This is my home!"

"Well, at least we got her to give up the janitor job," Ida told Anne. "Maybe we can convince her to get some help in the house; of course, we'll pay for it." Ida turned back to the stove and her pressure cooker. She was the one who became the balabusta, an excellent cook and household manager. She and her husband Joe had recently moved to a large house in East Flatbush where the family would gather every Sunday. Ida made sure that either Joey or Irving, as Yussel and Szol were now known, would pick up Mama and Papa, so they could enjoy visiting with the grandchildren.

Anne snorted derisively.

"Can you imagine Mama allowing anyone near her kitchen stove? When I wanted to send a cleaning lady over, she nearly had a fit! I know she feels a lot worse than she's telling us."

In all her years in America, Fannie had learned only a smidgen of English. She'd never needed it in Brownsville, but if she moved, she would have to rely on her children for the household chores and routines that required knowledge of English. Minnie, Dina, and her friends were in Brownsville, so she would have to turn to her daughters for all her shopping, social interactions, and doctor's appointments. Minnie joined her occasionally at Ida's house, but most of the time she was busy helping out in shul.

Yaakov hadn't assimilated much better. He spoke a combination of Yiddish and English that was hilarious and made the grandchildren roar with laughter. They would tease Yaakov, telling him that Aunt Ida was serving *ham*burgers for lunch. He feigned anger, scowling fiercely and pretending to chase the children. They all enjoyed the game.

One Sunday when they were visiting Ida, Fannie walked to the corner candy shop to get a newspaper for Yaakov. She asked repeatedly for "the *tug*," meaning *The Daily Forward*, but just got a shrug of incomprehension from the store's owner. Beet-red with humiliation, she sent one of the grandchildren to get the paper. It was hard communicating even with the grandchildren. They only heard Yiddish from Fannie, Yaakov, and Minnie, and they usually answered in English.

One morning as she was schlepping groceries up the stairs, Fannie collapsed on the stairwell. A few of the neighbors helped her into the apartment and assisted her onto the sofa. Mrs. Kantor ran for the doctor, who was on another call. The doctor finally got there about two hours later.

"She should be in the hospital," he said. "Her heart is failing." The family offered to pay for the best hospital care, but Fannie refused.

"You see what happened to Mrs. Offenbach when she went to the hospital? I'm not going!" At least she took medicine the doctor gave her to ease the pain in her chest.

Now Anne and Ida were faced with the decision of where Fannie and Yaakov should live. At the height of the Depression, Anne had married a lawyer named Harry and had two little girls. They lived in a small, one-bedroom apartment with barely enough room for their family of four, let alone Anne's parents.

Ida, who owned a home, brought Fannie and Yaakov to live with her. Poor Ida. Already caring for her eldest son, who was ill with rheumatic heart disease, she had two other children, and her husband was hardly ever home. Now she also was caregiver for a sickly mother and a cranky father. Anne tried to help Ida as much as possible, but she couldn't get there very often. With two young children, a sick husband—he was diabetic—and a demanding mother-in-law living nearby, Anne had a full plate as well.

"Now you're acting like Mama!" Anne chided her sister. "For goodness' sake, Ida, get in household help. You can afford it, and I'll contribute too!"

Ida's husband had become wealthy making airplane parts for the war effort, but she was her mother's daughter and insisted on doing everything herself.

Fannie lingered for months, barely able to breathe. She was tethered to a bulky oxygen tank and remained in bed all the time. Minnie came often to be with her beloved sister, taking two buses to sit by her bedside and hold her hand. Several nights a week, she slept on a cot next to Fannie, jumping up whenever her breathing became even more labored than usual.

It happened on a night when Minnie was at her own apartment. Shmul, the next-door neighbor with a telephone, knocked loudly at the door.

"Minnie, come! Call your nephew!"

* * *

Irving picked up Aunt Minnie, and they drove wordlessly to Ida's house. The children were sent to a neighbor, and the rest of the family clustered around Fannie's bedside. The oxygen mask had been removed, and she looked more peaceful than she had in months. Yaakov kneeled beside her bed, his chest heaving with sobs. Minnie went to the other side of the bed, clutched Fannie's cold hand, and lay her cheek down on the coverlet, closing her eyes.

We were running through the fields. My baby sister was just ahead of me, giggling and pretending to scream in horror. "I'm going to catch you! I'm going to tickle you!"

I could see her long blond hair flying in the wind as I caught up with her, and we both tumbled into the dewy wet grass, smelling of earth and early spring flowers. I tickled the creamy skin under her neck and the taut skin covering her ribs. We rolled in the grass, legs entwined, laughing so hard that we finally collapsed, barely able to breathe. When we were able to catch our breath, I took her little hand in mine, planting loud, wet kisses on her palm.

* * *

Minnie scrupulously observed the mourning period, sitting shiva for a week at Ida's house. When she returned home, she could barely get out of bed each morning, but she forced herself to dress, eat, and pray for Fannie's soul. She insisted that Yaakov go to synagogue every morning to say Yizker, the prayer for the dead, for Fannie.

I never thought I would outlive my baby sister.

38

The Holocaust

Minnie's financial needs were small, and she subsisted on her meager savings from the sale of the photography shop. She rented a single room in the neighborhood in the home of a religious couple; Minnie could no longer afford the luxury of a two-bedroom apartment. She grudgingly accepted money placed by her nieces in a savings account, although she was adamant about being independent until the last of her savings ran out. Minnie was still very involved in synagogue and community activities.

She was in the process of tacking up a sign in Mr. Stein's shop window. On Thursday night there would be a presentation at the local community center by one of the neighborhood boys, Marvin Silverstein, who joined the army right after the Pearl Harbor attack. Minnie remembered him: when he was about to have a Bar Mitzvah, his mother and father had brought him into the shop for photographs. Marvin was a plump, apple-cheeked, mischievous boy who took every opportunity to stick out his tongue or make faces just when Minnie clicked the shutter. He finally behaved and sat for formal pictures when Mr. Silverstein gave him a *potch* on his generous behind.

When victory was declared, there were countless block parties throughout the neighborhood and reveling in the streets of Brownsville. The joy that the war was over, however, was short-lived; the Jews of

Brownsville knew that the Nazis had targeted Jews for extermination. Nobody realized the extent of the killings as the slaughter began to be publicized. There were stories coming out of foreign newspapers and accounts of roundups from Jews who had managed to escape, but six million Jews dead? How was that possible?

On Thursday evening, Minnie and the whole family squeezed into seats at the community center. Fortunately they came early, because many people were standing in the back and even in the aisles to hear Marvin Silverstein's testimony. He had been a Master Sergeant in the 3rd Army Battalion, under General George S. Patton, that liberated Buchenwald on April 11, 1945. He consented to speak at all the synagogues, churches, and community houses in Brooklyn, telling the people about his experiences when his battalion entered the camp.

After he was introduced, Minnie couldn't believe her eyes. Every vestige of the rambunctious youngster was gone. In his place stood a tall, ramrod thin and imposing soldier in uniform, with medals and decorations attached to his shirt. His face was almost gaunt, and his mouth turned down as his dark eyes swept over the audience. The audience started to applaud but he held up his hand and waited for silence.

"It was a cloudless, sunny day in April when I walked into the camp with Rabbi Schachter, the chaplain. Buchenwald was a Class II camp, which meant that it was a place for dangerous, hard-core political prisoners. They were Soviet communists mostly but included anyone who opposed the Nazis. Jews were sent to Buchenwald toward the end of the war from other extermination camps, like Auschwitz and Dachau, to be quarantined. The conditions were horrible, but even worse for the Jews. They were confined to the *Kleine Lager,* or small camp, at the bottom of the hill, away from the main barracks. The communists were the Kapos, or captains, who gave out work assignments and distributed rations to the prisoners. The only way a Jew could get extra food or a better assignment was to bribe the communists. All the Jewish prisoners came from other camps; needless to say, they had nothing to give the Kapos as bribes.

"Some of the prisoners who could still walk came out of the

barracks—huge heads, emaciated bodies like matchsticks, with black-and-white striped rags barely covering their limbs. The soldiers in my battalion froze in shock, seeing these human ghosts approaching. Rabbi Schacter held up a bullhorn, shouting in Yiddish, *'Shalom Aleichem Yidden, irh zint frei!'* (Peace be unto you Jews, you're free!)"

The sergeant looked at the audience with a bitter smile.

"What were they free for? Free to die?"

Sergeant Silverstein continued his story.

"When one of the survivors saw the rabbi's yarmulke, he fell to his knees and tried to kiss his boots. An emaciated prisoner, stinking and full of lice, approached us. He said he had been a professor at the University of Prague and would take us around the camp. He could barely hobble on his stick-thin legs, but he seemed intent on showing us the horrors of Buchenwald. Slowly, he led us to the crematoria and morgue.

"He told us, 'When the Nazis knew they were losing, they stepped up the killings. They would go into the small camp and select a tier of prisoners . . . We slept in wooden, tiered bunks. The tiers stretched from floor to ceiling, and in each tier were about sixteen prisoners, including children. The SS Guards forced the Jews to a place near the crematoria, where there was a shaft that led to the morgue. If they were still alive after falling about five meters, the guards inside the morgue would bash them in the head with a huge club and hang them by the throat on meat hooks. They hung there until there was room in the crematoria, and the dead were transported upstairs in an electric elevator to be burned. Some of the Russian prisoners said the Jews were already dead when they got to the morgue, but then why the bloody clubs? The overflow was put in three death wagons, to be buried in a mass grave somewhere . . . I saw the bodies piled in the wagons near the barracks. There were so many; bodies were strewn around the whole compound. We didn't want to bury them until the Americans came, so there would be no doubt about what happened. Many of our Jews died in the small camp from starvation or disease, especially during the typhus epidemic. If you woke up in the morning, the prisoner to the left or right of you was probably dead. I saw one prisoner, #53782, go through the pockets of his dead father, looking for something to eat. He found a filthy sliver of bread, full of lice, and stuffed it in his mouth.'

"I asked the professor how he had the strength to survive . . . he wasn't a young man. The professor told me that one of the Kapos was a former student who gave him extra rations and lighter work details. Then I asked if the other Jews in the small camp resented his better luck. He said he would only eat one-third the ration outside the barracks and give the rest to the younger prisoners with better chances of survival.

"He told me, 'When we first came to Buchenwald, we were fed watery cabbage soup full of cabbageworms and stale bread full of lice. When the Nazis stepped up the killings, we only got a tiny piece of moldy bread. After the SS heard of the American advance, we never got another drop of food.'

"He looked at me with a hideous smile, showing his few black, rotten teeth. The smell coming from his mouth and body was indescribable . . . I turned my head so I wouldn't vomit.

"'Maybe I survived because of the lice and cabbageworms,' he told me. 'That was the only protein we got.'

"We passed the house of the commandant and his wife, which was on the top of the hill. I had to help the professor by practically carrying him up the slope. I tried to breathe through my mouth, so as not to show how revolted I was by his odor. A huge wooden fence surrounded the house. There was a large, grassy area inside the fence that looked like a horses' corral. This walking skin and bones, our guide, said the wife was so cruel that she was known as 'The Bitch of Buchenwald.'

"'She loved riding horses,' the professor said. 'I can't tell you how many prisoners lost their lives clearing that area for her horseback rides. I remember one time The Bitch sashayed in front of a Jewish work detail. They were ordered to show her their tattoos. She went up and down the line, tapping about ten prisoners with her riding crop. They were pulled out of the line and never seen again. I heard from my Kapo friend that the Jews were taken to the medical clinic, where her lover did autopsies and experiments on prisoners. The good doctor had their skulls bashed in and removed the tattoos, leaving enough skin for tanning. Three lamp-shades were found in the house, made of human tattoos. I guess some were from the political prisoners, since the lampshades had pictures as well as numbers.'"

There was a collective gasp from the audience. A few of the women had to be ushered into the main hallway.

Sergeant Silverstein once again put up both hands and waited for silence.

"Another survivor grabbed my arm and began speaking to me in Hungarian, I think. Someone interpreted what he was saying into Yiddish. He told me that he was originally at Auschwitz, where the sign at the main gate said *ARBEIT MACHT FREI*, meaning work brings freedom. The sign inside of Buchenwald's main gate said *JEDEM DAS SEINE*. A loose translation is, everyone gets what he deserves. The Hungarian said that when the Americans were closing in, the SS Guards tried to escape into the surrounding woods. The Soviets, who had taken control of the camp, chased them down and brought back about forty SS guards. The communists beat most to death; a few lucky ones got shot with their own guns. The Americans had just found half-burned bodies in the crematoria and looked the other way when the SS guards were slaughtered. In fact, some of them joined in.

"The Red Cross came, deloused the prisoners, and gave them clean clothing. They tried to feed the emaciated prisoners soup and liquids . . . many were so weak, they had to be fed by hand. Most of them couldn't eat or drink; their stomachs were so shrunken. Because of Rabbi Schacter, the orphans were given extra medical help. As soon as they were strong enough, they were transported to France and Switzerland.

"Shortly after we liberated the camp, General Eisenhower ordered the entire U.S. 4th Armored Division to tour the camps, so nobody could deny what happened there. He made the German villagers, who pretended not to know anything, tour Buchenwald so they could see what their wonderful Führer was capable of. I understand that when the Russians liberated Auschwitz on January 27th, it was even worse, if that was possible. I can't imagine how it could be more horrible than what I saw, but I know that thousands of us died every day in huge gas chambers . . . the SS were very efficient."

At this point the sergeant clutched the podium and reached for a glass of water with a trembling hand. His voice was hoarse and started to crack, but he continued.

"It's my duty, as a Jew and as a human being, to document what happened so that nobody can ever say it wasn't the truth. I want to tell it all over America, in every shul, every church, and every town meeting, because so many people won't believe what really happened. *Never forget!* Tell everyone you know what I experienced."

Silent tears were running down the sergeant's cheeks. The stunned audience sat stock still for at least five minutes before they shuffled out of the auditorium. A few women were crying and wailing, but most participants were silent, their faces gray and crumpled.

Minnie caught sight of Dina and her family. Ever since that explosive Rosh Hashanah scene, they hadn't had much contact with one another, except for a formal greeting card on the New Year. They would occasionally meet in shul on the High Holy Days and exchange greetings with each other. Dina saw Minnie and pushed her way through the crowd to reach her. She held out trembling hands to Minnie and burst into tears.

"Minnie, my whole family—they're gone. My Mama and Tati, Raisa and the children . . . I haven't heard from them since the beginning of the war. I'm so afraid. Can you help me?"

Minnie grasped Dina's hands tightly. She couldn't help wondering why Heschel's well-educated sons didn't help her, but she pushed down that thought.

"Of course, Dina. They're my family too."

* * *

After Zelig died, Minnie had continued the correspondence he'd had with his sister Gittel in Leningrad. Then the letters had stopped abruptly. She'd read in the *Forward* about the siege of Leningrad, how for nearly three years the Germans had blockaded the city, not allowing any food or medical supplies to reach the population. There were stories about people eating rats, mice, and vermin to stay alive. Had his family survived the siege? In a way, Minnie was glad that Zelig didn't have to hear that his flesh-and-blood family was missing. She would leave no stone unturned looking for them, but she doubted that she would ever get a response. Minnie only prayed that if they hadn't survived, they died quickly.

Minnie, with the help of Anne, contacted agency after agency, the State Department, displaced persons organizations . . . anyplace that might have some word of Zelig's and Dina's families. They wrote scores of letters and went to many of the displaced persons agencies in person, hoping to find someone from Nolopina or Leningrad who might know something about either family.

After a year of frantic searching, Minnie and Dina had to face the inevitable. Only a miracle could have saved anyone in either family, and it would take an even bigger miracle to contact a family member who might have survived.

The next Shabbos morning, the two cousins attended services together, stood when it was time to say Yizker, the prayer for the dead, and recited the age-old litany holding each other's hand.

After the service, Dina said to Minnie, "How could a just and righteous G-d ever allow six million of His people to die in such hideous ways? I never was a believer like you, Minnie, but I always thought Hashem looked after his children."

Minnie said, "I still believe. Hashem's ways are unknowable to us. Maybe we'll understand better when we get to the other side."

39

Minnie's Secret

M oira O'Shea had just received her credentials as a registered nurse and was assigned to a private overnight shift at Beth David Hospital to care for an elderly lady with heart failure and pneumonia. For the first week the patient was too ill to talk, so Moira just monitored her intravenous fluids and breathing apparatus. Occasionally the night nurse would come in to take her vital signs, usually when the patient had just fallen asleep.

"Can't you do that later?" Moira asked. "She just dozed off."

"We have a time schedule to follow. Do you know how many patients I have to care for on this ward?"

After the first week, Minnie had rallied a bit but wasn't allowed to have anything by mouth. Moira hummed an Irish folk tune as she watched over Minnie and was startled when Minnie spoke to her.

"Such ah pretty tune. When I work the farm, I hear it. Also, my husband, of blessed memory, sing songs from the old country. Where you from?"

"County Cork. I came from Ireland years ago for my education. I just completed my nursing studies."

"What's your name, dear?"

"Moira O'Shea. Let me fix your covers and plump up the pillows. How are you feeling?"

Minnie just grimaced and shrugged.

"Once I know a Irish girl when I was on the farm. Maureen was her name. She was good to me; then I didn't appreciate."

At the end of Moira's shift, she spoke to the morning nurse about her brief conversation with Minnie.

"That's strange," the morning nurse said. "She never says a word during the day. I thought she was senile."

"She sounded perfectly lucid to me. Does she have visitors during the day?"

"I see her nieces and occasionally her nephews. Sometimes an old man comes with them; I think it's her brother-in-law. I never heard her talk to them; she just stares blankly or closes her eyes. They speak at her bedside as if she isn't there."

"Well, she sounded perfectly clear to me. I'll let you know how she's doing during the night."

The following night, Moira brought an English-language paper and asked Minnie if she wanted to be read to.

"No, dear. The cares of the world I don't need; troubles of my own I have. But it is kind of you to buy the paper. Better you should sing to me—such a lovely voice you have. It make me feel better."

They struck up an odd friendship, with Moira holding Minnie's hand as she softly sang "Danny Boy," "Fiddler's Green," "Heather on the Moor," and other Irish folk tunes. One morning, after a different nurse had come the night before, Minnie startled Ida and Anne.

"I want the Irish girl. She should come at night."

The nieces immediately got in touch with the nursing office to request Moira every night, even on weekends. They were overjoyed that Minnie was talking and conveyed the news to the rest of the family and friends. The nursing office reluctantly gave Anne and Ida Moira's phone number after securing Moira's permission for the family to call her.

Dina, who also visited Minnie, said, "I'm not surprised she can talk. She's so stubborn and moody. It's strange that she's talking to a goy instead of her own family."

Anne responded, "I don't care who she's talking to, just as long as she starts getting better."

Minnie's road to recovery was brief. Her heart rate was spiking erratically when she was checked with Moira's stethoscope, and her blood pressure fluctuated between dangerously high and low. She was moved to an intensive care unit where the nurses and doctors were constantly bustling around, but the family kept Moira on even though there was no medical need.

After three nights in intensive care, Moira felt Minnie's hands and feet. They were ice cold; not a good sign. Tears rolled down Moira's cheeks, and she reached for her handkerchief. Minnie stirred.

In a labored voice, she said, "Do you believe G-d forgives sins?"

"Yes, Minnie. He's a just and forgiving God. He died for our sins . . . I mean, He loves and forgives all His creatures as long as they truly repent."

"I'm dying. I want to, but I'm afraid. One of His Holy Commandments I break. Never His face I'll see, or join the souls of my family . . ."

Moira interjected, "You, Minnie? I've been speaking to your nieces and they tell me what a wonderful person you are. You saved them from possible death by bringing them here. You were a devoted wife and a credit to your community and chur— uh, synagogue. You did only good deeds."

"They don't know. Dina, she know, but she never cared."

At this point Minnie's blood pressure became alarmingly high. When Moira checked her heart, it was pounding wildly.

"I'm calling the nurse. You need something to calm you down."

"No, please, let me tell . . ."

Moira sat down and stroked Minnie's hand for a while. Her breathing and pulse rate slowed down.

"A good wife I was? Our whole marriage I lie to Zelig. I push him to the arms of another woman. Religious I am. I do good deeds to make up for what I did."

"Minnie. You're getting overexcited again. Let me call the nurse . . ."

"Please! Listen!"

* * *

Minnie began to tell Moira the story of what happened in Russia and how she became a maid in Minsk. She would run out of breath and start to wheeze. Moira tried to stop her, but Minnie was determined. As soon as she regained her breath, she would start again.

"I am seventeen the year the crops die. Papa sell his cows, but he still don't have enough for seed money. We would starve. The neighbor Mendel, he get me a job in Minsk with his rich cousins. I be a maid. They offer me five rubles a month. Five rubles! So much money Papa don't make in a year. I beg Mama, *let me stay home*, but could Papa and Mama say no?

"I am so scared on the train. We get to Minsk and I stand like a stick, waiting at the station. Sasha, the cook, she come with Boris in a carriage. Never before I see such a big, fancy house. I think, *all houses in my village could fit in that house.*

"Sasha take me to meet the mistress, Madam Ostrovsky. I want to do good job. I bother Sasha all the time. 'How you do this, how you do that?' How does she put up with me?

"The son, Chaim, he come home from yeshiva for Purim and Peysekh. Sasha say bad things about him. I'm surprised. Never before I hear Sasha speak bad about nobody, 'specially a boy studying to be a rebbe.

"Before Passover start, I am cleaning in the library. On my back and behind I feel a tickle. Chaim make believe he is looking at a book. I don't say nothin'.

"I help serve the Seder meal. They all *kvel* over Chaim like a prince.

"After the Seder, I fall in bed with my clothes on and go to sleep. I wake up; something heavy hold me down. Chaim is on top of me, pressing me down. He stink from wine and sweat. He put a hand over my mouth. He tell me if I scream, he tell his parents I ask him to my bed. I can't breathe. I can't push him off. He rip my underpants. The bed is rocking. I feel terrible pain down there, like knives. When he's done, he slap my face. 'Don't say nothing,' he says.

"My whole supper I throw up. I'm so dizzy, my head is buzzing. I try to wash the gooey stuff and blood coming out down there, but I can't stand up and fall back in bed. Should I tell Sasha? If I get sent back, how can my family live without the five rubles? He was drunk. Maybe he don't bother me no more. Soon he go back to yeshiva.

"The next night I push the dressing table against the door. Chaim laugh. He push the door open and he does it again. Next day, Sasha ask me, 'Minnie, are you sick?' I tell. She say I'm not the first one. Five times it happen until he go back to school.

"I miss my monthly bleeding. I can't hold nothin' in my stomach. I lose weight, but my belly start getting big. The other servants talk behind my back, and the mistress, she find out. She scream at me; tell me I sleep with Boris, the coachman, but she don't look me in the eyes. She knows!

"The Madam, she send me home. I hide in the house until I'm ready. The neighbors can't know. We tell them I get diphtheria in Minsk so nobody should visit. We try to bring on my bleeding with mustard baths. I jump off chairs. Mama make me tansy tea to bring on my bleeding. I just throw it up. Nothing work.

"My time is near. Papa go to get my cousins, Dina—you know her, she visit me sometime—and Raisa. The day has come. We leave the house and go far into the woods. The cousins hold me up with my legs apart. The head, it start coming out. I scream and scream. I feel a big push with water coming. Another push and the skinny body follow. I shut my eyes; I don't want to know. But the cord, it's still attached. I lay down on a flat rock full of snow. I hear a weak cry. How is it possible it still alive?"

At this point, Minnie began to cough violently. Moira became alarmed.

"Please Minnie, don't speak anymore. You can tell me later."

The coughing subsided and Minnie raised up her hand.

"Let me finish!"

"Dina and Raisa stand next to me. They yell, 'Minnie, crush it. You have to. It won't live anyhow. Do it!'

"I roll over on it. I push down as hard as I can. There is no more sound.

"The cousins, they cut the cord. When the afterbirth come out, they wrap everything in cloth and take it away. We stuff rags between my legs and the cousins half carry me home. Mama and Papa wait by the door.

"Dina tell them, 'It was born dead.'"

* * *

Minnie was totally depleted after she told her story to Moira.

"You a religious girl. You see why Hashem never will forgive me?"

"Minnie, you did it to save your family and yourself. Think of all the children who wouldn't have been born if you didn't bring the family over."

"I never told. Not even my sister. Only Dina know; she don't care."

"Thank you for trusting me. Rest now, Minnie."

* * *

A few nights later, Minnie died toward the end of Moira's shift. Moira lifted Minnie's withered, leathery hand, full of veins and dark spots, and kissed it. She stood, made a sign of the cross over Minnie, and went to find the nurse.

Dina arrived just as Moira was about to leave.

"They move my cousin? I don't see her in the room."

Moira looked intently at Dina for half a moment.

"I'm so sorry. Your cousin died about an hour ago. Her nieces were notified; they're making funeral arrangements."

Dina took a deep breath and sighed. "Thank you for taking such good care of Minnie. The girls tell me you was so good to her."

"She was a nice lady; I'll miss her."

Dina turned and slowly walked down the long corridor with her head bent, a stooped, white-haired, elderly woman clutching her coat around her. Moira could smell disinfectant wafting up from the floor. As Dina walked slowly down the corridor, a young attendant passed her, walking briskly.

Moira stood watching until Dina made a turn toward the elevator.

May the Lord walk with you.

Epilogue

Ida (Chaje) was the eldest child of Fannie and Yaakov, born approximately in 1898. She emigrated to the United States in 1907 at age nine with her mother and two siblings. Ida married a mechanic who became wealthy in later years as a partner in a factory that sold airplane parts for the World War Two effort. However, Ida and Joe were an incompatible couple with few common interests. They had three children, but lost their oldest son to rheumatic heart disease. When Joe developed diabetes, they moved to Miami Beach. He became a fight promoter and died in a hotel in New York City under mysterious circumstances. To this day, his daughter believes he was murdered by gangsters who owed him money. Ida died in Miami Beach at age seventy, succumbing to heart disease.

* * *

Anne (Gelde) took the birth date of March 7, 1901, since there were no official records of her birth. She came to the United States in September 1907 and passed away in 1998, at the approximate age of ninety-seven. Anne married a Brooklyn lawyer named Harry, who came with lots of baggage, most notably a mother who was vicious and self-serving. Harry, afflicted with diabetes and heart problems, passed away in 1948 at age forty-seven. Anne became an insurance broker, living frugally while bringing up two young daughters. She remarried six years later, and lived in her own home until shortly before her death. Her two daughters married and remained in the New York Metropolitan area. Her eldest daughter passed away in April 2016.

* * *

Joey (Yussel) was the youngest sibling and the only child born in the United States. He was born in 1908 and died at age thirty-nine of a massive heart attack, precipitated by shoveling snow after a heavy downfall. Joey, always interested in cars, owned a car parts shop in East New York. He was survived by a wife and three daughters. The wife never remarried; her brother moved in with the family and took care of them. The daughters married, and live in Florida, New Jersey, and Long Island.

* * *

Irving (Szol) was eleven months old when he came with his mother and two sisters to the United States in 1907. He became an electrician and married a woman with deep emotional problems and an explosive temper. Irving developed bipolar disorder and died at age fifty-two in a mental hospital. He and his wife had two daughters who married and remained in the New York Metropolitan area. Both girls died very young.

* * *

Jacob (Yaakov) was born in the Pale of Russia in approximately 1874 and passed away in 1957. He emigrated to the United States in 1906, a year before his wife and children, in order to avoid the czar's draft. After Fannie's death, Yaakov would spend half a year in Brooklyn with Anne and half a year in Florida and the Catskills with Ida. He unsuccessfully pursued women, but became religious in his later years. Yaakov lived until age eighty-three, succumbing to a heart attack.

* * *

Fannie (Frima) was born in approximately 1880, emigrating to the United States with her three children in 1907. She was uneducated and never learned more than a smattering of English, but was an extremely devoted wife and mother. Fannie kept an immaculate household and was a consummate cook and baker. Although illiterate, she was intelligent and creative, fashioning toys for her children and grandchildren out of the most humble materials. She died in 1940 at age sixty, succumbing to heart disease.

* * *

Dina was born in 1868, emigrated to the United States at age forty-one, and passed away in 1957 at age eighty-nine. She continued to live on the outskirts of Brownsville with her husband until he died. He didn't leave a will, and his children inherited everything. They gave Dina a minimal stipend and sold the house. She moved to a two-room apartment in Brownsville. Dina survived Minnie by five years.

* * *

Moira, born in 1932, emigrated to the States as a child of twelve. She became a registered nurse and worked at Beth-David Hospital in East New York for many years, becoming Head Nurse of Geriatrics. She never married. When she retired, she moved back to Ireland and died there in 2002. Moira left her money to her local church and a home for the aged.

* * *

Maya was born in Paris in 1874, emigrating to the United States at the age of thirty. She was passionate about women's rights and socialism, writing columns and essays for a variety of feminist and socialist journals. After ending her affair with Zelig, she spent a year in Paris with Max, her preferred lover. They broke off their relationship, this time for good. She traveled across Europe and England, writing for a feminist periodical, *Women Awake!* She had many lovers, both men and women. Maya died in Paris at age sixty-two.

* * *

Michael Monaghan was born in 1855 to poor tenant farmers in Ireland. He emigrated to America, saving enough money to buy a small farm in Suffolk County. A good businessman, Monaghan soon enlarged his farm, employing immigrant workers as laborers. He continued running the Suffolk County potato farm until several seasons of bad weather devastated his crops. He returned to County Kerry, Ireland, and opened a bar and inn, which prospered. Monaghan never married. After his death at age sixty in 1915, his property was divided up among his six nephews and nieces.

* * *

Rivka, born in 1875 in the Pale of Russia, was orphaned as a young child. She lived with cousins before emigrating to Suffolk County in 1892, at age seventeen, as an indentured laborer. Rivka married another orphan; she and her husband completed their indenture in Suffolk County, had seven children, and moved to the Lower East Side of Manhattan. She never resumed correspondence with Minnie after giving birth to her first child. She died in 1950 at age seventy-five, surrounded by her children and grandchildren.

* * *

Zelig, born in 1860 near St. Petersburg, emigrated to Suffolk County in 1889 as an immigrant laborer. He died in 1912 of heart disease at the age of fifty-two.

Zelig is being treated as a fictional character since nothing is known of his life or marriage to Minnie, except for his first name. I came across a picture in the family archives of Minnie, formally posing with a man, who I assume was Zelig. He was younger and handsomer than I depict Zelig in the novel.

* * *

Minnie (Michla) was born in 1872, in the small village of Chalupanich near Minsk, Russia. Forced to flee to the United States in 1891 at the age of nineteen, she subsequently met and married Zelig, another Jewish immigrant who worked as an indentured laborer on a large potato farm in Suffolk County, New York. When Minnie moved to Brownsville, New York, she became very religious and was active in her synagogue and community. She was responsible for bringing my family to America. Minnie lived to an old age, passing away in 1952.

* * *

Minnie and Zelig were buried next to one another in Mount Moriah Cemetery in Queens, with a single headstone. Their graves became overgrown with weeds and vines. The stone inscriptions are completely obscured.

Glossary

OF WORDS, TERMS AND PHRASES

aguna	no longer marriageable
aleph, bais	first letters of Hebrew alphabet
Americana shtinker	lazy, irreverent American children
babke	a coffee cake
babushka	head scarf
balabusta	excellent homemaker
Bar Mitzvah	ceremony for a Jewish boy at age 13, entrance as a full member of the Jewish faith
Baruch Hashem	Thank the Lord
besom	a broom used for scrubbing in a steam bath
beytsem	testicles
boweron	Celtic drum
bris	ceremonial circumcision of a Jewish boy
Bubbala	term of endearment
bubbe	grandmother
bubbe meiser	old wives' tale
bucha	a yeshiva scholar, referred to as "yeshiva bucha"
ceili	a tumultuous Irish celebration
challah	traditional braided bread made for the Sabbath
Chalupanich	a tiny village in the Pale of Russia, spelled phonetically
chasan	bridegroom

chazarai	"junk food," unappetizing food
cheder	Yiddish school for boys
chupah	canopy for wedding ceremony
chutzpa	nerve
colleen	an Irish girl
Cossack	a corps of the Russian military who performed police services during time of the czars
daven	recite Jewish prayers
fahkokta	crappy
farshtunkena	stinking
forshpayz	appetizer
Frimala	nickname for Frima/Fannie
frum	religious
get	religious divorce according to Jewish law
goniff	a huckster, trickster
gotkes	underwear
greena	an immigrant just off the boat
greena bubbe	immigrant grandmother
grepts	belch
Halokhik	according to strict Jewish law
henties	little hands
hooys	Russian for penises
Italyanas	Italians
Kaddish	prayer for the dead
ketuba	a written wedding contract, often decorative
Kiddush	prayers said over wine after services, followed by a small repast
kinder	children
kishke	beef or fowl casing stuffed with meat, flour and spices, then cooked

kop	head
kopek	a small denomination of the ruble
krank	sick
kugel	a baked pudding, such as potato kugel
kurve	whore, prostitute
kvel	pride in someone's accomplishments, particularly family
Lashon Hara	evil tongue, gossip
Mamala	term of endearment, pet name
mamser	bastard
mandelbrot	a biscuit, similar to Italian biscotti
matte collodian	photography technique
mazel tov	congratulations
megile	a fuss, long story
mekhia	a relief from pain or discomfort
mekhitza	curtain or divider used to separate men and women
mensh	an upstanding man
meshuge	crazy
meshugena	crazy person
mikva	ritual bath to cleanse women after menstruation
Minnala	pet name for Minnie
minyan	at least ten Jewish men needed for prayers
mishpokhe	family
mitzvah	a blessed deed
mohl, mohel	person who performs ritual circumcisions
Oneg Shabbat	repast after Friday night services
oy	expression of dismay
peyes	earlocks, sidelocks worn by religious Jewish men

Peysekh	Passover
pish	urinate
plotzed	died, fainted with astonishment
potch	slap, smack
poteen	homemade, illegal Irish whiskey
pupik	navel, "belly button"
Purim	a joyous Spring holiday celebrating the delivery of the Jews
rebbe	rabbi
rugelach	small pastry
Seder	Passover meal
seduka	giving charity
Shabbat, Shabbos	Jewish Sabbath
shande	a shame, disgrace
Shaynem dank	thank you very much
sheytl	wig worn by observant Jewish women
shikker	drunk, a drunkard
shiksa	a non-Jewish woman, generally Christian
Shiva	ritual observance after the death of a close relative
shlekht	weak, ill
shlemiel	a buffoon, a jerk
shlub	an unattractive, stupid man
Shma	a prayer stating the oneness of God
shmate, shmates	rags, old, unattractive garments
shmendrik	a jerk, a foolish, inept person
shmuck	a coarse expression for a stupid man
shmuts	dirt
shnorer	a sponger, a beggar, parasite
shokhet	ritual slayer of kosher animals

shtarke	a strong person
shteble	a small synagogue, often presided over by a Hasidic rabbi
shtetl	a small village
shtup, shtupping	having sexual intercourse
shul	synagogue
shvanger	pregnant
shvesta	sister
shvits	bath and steamroom
Simkhe, simhah	a happy occasion, such as a wedding, Bar Mitzvah
Talmudic/Talmud	interpretation of Jewish laws
Tante	aunt
Tatala	term of endearment, pet name for a boy
Tati	Yiddish for Daddy
The Daily Forward, **the *Forward***	a Yiddish newspaper
tokhes	a person's rear end
treyf	non-kosher
trumbanik	fooling around, wasting time, a person who parties
tsimes	a big deal, taken from a dish of mixed ingredients
tzitzit, tsitses	a fringed garment worn by religious males
yarmulke	skullcap worn by religious Jewish males
yarzheit	lighting candles on special holidays to memorialize the dead
yenta	a gossip
yeshiva	Jewish school for boys
Yiddishkeit	Jewishness
Yizker	a prayer for the dead
zaftik	plump

About the Author

M arilyn Parker is a speech and language pathologist who is involved with several writing groups in Manhattan, Brooklyn, and Roxbury, New York. Tante Minnie originally began as a short story that was published in an upstate New York journal. Parker resides in Brooklyn, New York, with her husband. Tante Minnie is her debut novel.

Made in United States
North Haven, CT
20 November 2021

11327464R10176